Don't miss Zach's earlier adventures!

BALLISTIC BABES

THE RADIOACTIVE REDHEAD
by John Zakour & Lawrence Ganem

THE FROST-HAIRED VIXEN
by John Zakour

DAW BOOKS, INC.
DONALD A. WOLLHEIM, FOUNDER
375 Hudson Street, New York, NY 10014

ELIZABETH R. WOLLHEIM
SHEILA E. GILBERT
PUBLISHERS
www.dawbooks.com

First Printing, April 2009
1 2 3 4 5 6 7 8 9

DAW TRADEMARK REGISTERED
U.S. PAT. AND TM. OFF. AND FOREIGN COUNTRIES
—MARCA REGISTRADA
HECHO EN U.S.A.

PRINTED IN THE U.S.A.

THE
RADIOACTIVE
REDHEAD

For my wife and son and all the people
who bought the first two books.
—*John Zakour*

For Bruce Springsteen, William Goldman
and Friz Freleng.
—*Lawrence Ganem*

Acknowledgements

Thanks to Betsy Wollheim at DAW for believing in us and putting up with us (especially Larry). Thanks also to Click and Clack, the Tap It Brothers for their help picking out a cool old car for Zach to drive. Nobody knows cool cars like they do. We tip our hats to the folks at the Daily Buzz for letting us kid them a bit. Finally, a very special thanks to Natalia, Carolina, Tom, and Ron for helping to inspire their characters. I guess we should also thank the music industry and the government in general for giving us such great fodder for parody.   —JZ

As always, this book could not have been written without the love and support of Lisa, Jackson, and Kalie. Thanks as well to Philip and Shirley and the entire family tree. Thanks to Joshua for handling the business things and to Betsy for her encouragement, support, cajoling, mild reprimands, ultimatums, and death threats.   —LG

Prologue

In the early 1700s, after spending close to fifty years studying ancient biblical texts, the father of modern physics, Sir Isaac Newton, predicted that the world would end in the year 2060.

He never mentioned anything about a redhead.

If he had, I might have been a little more careful.

1

Some men are born dangerous.
Some men become dangerous.
Some men have danger thrust upon them.

And whenever danger decides to do a little thrusting, I always seem to be on the blunt, receiving end of it.

"The good news," HARV said as we entered the main room of the floating restaurant, "is that the shite in this production appears to be particularly skilled. The bad news, of course, is that he's also an android assassin."

"He's a what?"

The Kabuki actor's prop sword suddenly flared a fiery red and he leaped at me from the raised stage overhead. His red-and-white makeup glared under the hot lights and a manic look of bloodlust danced across his cold, slightly crossed eyes. The dinner-theater patrons around me broke into applause so loud that it nearly drowned out the samisen and lute music blaring in the background.

"What a pity," HARV sighed. "This promised to be a fine production of *Chushingura*."

"Try to focus on the big picture here, HARV."

I grabbed the actor's sword arm as he swung the energy blade at my head. Sure enough, his wrist was hard and unyielding, definitely the tempered polymer shell of a droid. And definitely more trouble than I was expecting. I slid sideways and rolled onto the floor, putting the droid's own momentum into a judo throw as I pivoted. The heat of the blade singed my face as it flashed past and the droid tumbled over me, falling flat onto a large table of six nearby. His blade burned through the table like a fat man through a cream pie when he landed and the whole thing gave way beneath him. He fell to the floor amid a cascade of tempura and spilled sake.

My name is Zachary Nixon Johnson. I am the last private eye on Earth. And right now, I am seriously regretting my choice of career.

It is the year 2060. And let me say at the outset that this is not the way I usually spend my weekend nights. You may not believe it, but I'm a bit of a homebody at heart. Dinner theater is not my scene. *Kabuki* dinner theater, despite being all the rage at the nano, is *really* not my scene. And Kabuki dinner theater in a trendy, free-floating restaurant, three hundred meters above downtown Oakland . . . well, you see where I'm going with this, right?

"It's an interesting strategy," HARV whispered inside my head as I quickly climbed to my feet. "It's illegal, as you know, to create an android with realistic skin tones. Creating a droid with a skin tone that emulates traditional Kabuki makeup, however, is completely legal. Granted, the places to use such an assassin without drawing undue attention are somewhat limited."

"Yeah, leave it to us to find the loophole."

I'd come to the Oakland Kabuki Palace Theater and Dinette to meet a client—a potential client actually. I don't usually do blind dates when it comes to business but things had been a little slow of late so when the cold call came in last night asking for a no-strings-attached meet and greet, I figured that it wouldn't hurt to hear the offer.

I was wrong. Especially about the wouldn't hurt part.

The droid popped back onto his feet and brandished his energy sword with a dramatic twirl that utterly delighted the dinner theater patrons around us, even as they ducked for cover. They were still under the impression that this was part of the show and they were ready for more in-your-face Kabuki dinner theater action. I on the other hand, was not in the mood for audience participation.

I flicked my wrist and cupped my hand in just the right way to activate the tiny motion sensor of the hidden holster that I wear on my forearm. The holster responded by smoothly popping my gun (a Colt 46, version 3.2A, I think—I can't keep track) into my hand and the gun throbbed to life when it hit my palm, in recognition of my distinctive heat/DNA signature. The entire action takes a lot less time to do than it does to describe, but the beauty's in the details.

The droid growled and leaped high in the air toward me, sword flashing in a fiery wide arc.

"Big bang, tight," I said, gripping my gun.

The gun's OLED screen flashed to signal recognition of my voice command and I pulled the trigger even as I dove to the floor.

My energy blast hit the droid squarely in the chest, punching a hole through its innards and shorting out its central power unit. Sparks flew from within and the samurai robe began to smolder as the body fell backward to the ground. Again the crowd broke into applause as they rose from beneath their tables.

"A Kabuki assassin droid," I said, getting to my feet. "I think that's a first."

"Indeed," HARV replied. "But don't cherish the uniqueness of the experience too long."

"Why not?"

"Because in a nano, it won't be so unique."

"What?"

I heard excited shrieks from the audience behind me and turned just in time to see two more Kabuki actors charge me from two of the narrow runways. Each held a samurai sword that flamed to life as he ran.

"You gotta be kidding me."

"Come now," HARV said, "you didn't really think there was going to be only *one* Kabuki assassin droid, did you? Especially considering the production they're doing."

The restaurant was a huge, high-ceilinged, circular room with doorways at each of the four compass points and a raised stage at the center for theater in the round productions. At the north point was the main entrance whose great doors opened to the red carpet hoverport (and two dozen tiny valet bots programmed for parking and "bringing 'round" the patrons' hovercrafts). At the east end was the emergency exit, a rapid-fire teleportation gate with a preset destination of the street below. West was the restrooms, which I am told were very swanky. And south was the kitchen.

A catwalk ran the full circumference of the dining room and four smaller catwalks stretched outward from the stage. Three went directly into the audience. One went to a set of large double doors on the western wall near the restrooms, no doubt leading to the dressing rooms for the actors, including the two droids currently intent on turning me into diced detective sashimi.

I hopped onto a table and pulled myself up to the catwalk to meet the charging samurai actors.

"What the DOS is going on here?"

HARV's hologram shimmered to life beside me, projected from the holographic image producer built into the computer interface I wear on my wrist. It's low tech, I know. HARV much prefers using the projector that's attached directly to my eye. He feels he gets better definition. But there are only a handful of people in the world who know about my mental link with HARV so we keep things on the down-low when we're in public and use the standard-tech gear.

I feel obligated to mention here that HARV, aside from being one of the world's most advanced thinking machines, is a work in progress. He began life as a supercomputer with a preprogrammed personality subroutine that mimicked a proper English butler, a sort of Wodehousian Hal-9000.

Then my good friend (and super-genius inventor) Dr. Randy Poole had the great idea of downloading him directly into my brain via a subcortical interfacing nanoconnection (scanc for short). It was a radically experimental, incredibly painful procedure that was done very cavalierly a couple of years ago. Since then HARV has been, for lack of a better word, evolving. He has changed his appearance. He has changed his personality. He has become more human. A true thinking machine. It has been absolutely amazing to see.

Unless of course, you happen to have him attached to your brain.

Then it's annoying beyond belief.

I'm all for progress and evolution but just think for a nano how you'd feel if your toaster suddenly decided to convert to Judaism (and it was inside your body).

All that said though, when HARV is in business mode,

he's the best sidekick in the world. So I guess I shouldn't complain.

"Well, let me think," HARV said, adjusting the cuffs of his holographically starched shirt. "An anonymous potential client calls. Refuses to give his name or the details of what he needs and arranges to meet us at a Kabuki dinner theater presentation, where, by coincidence, we are attacked by Kabuki assassins immediately upon our arrival."

"I get it, HARV."

"Did I or did I not say that blind meetings and anonymous clients are a bad combination?"

"Yeah, well if it was up to you, we'd never leave the office."

"I gotta tell you, Zach, right now, the office is looking pretty darn good."

"You can gloat later, provided we survive," I said. "Right now we have to get the bystanders to safety. I'll keep the samurai occupied. You handle crowd control."

HARV nodded.

"I'm on it."

He lifted his holographic form onto center stage and turned his visage to the crowd.

"Ladies and gentlemen, please do not panic. We are experiencing some intensely dangerous technical difficulties. We would be most grateful if you would all immediately proceed to the emergency exits in a quick and orderly fashion while Mr. Zachary Nixon Johnson battles the deadly dinner theater Kabuki android assassins."

None of the restaurant patrons made the slightest move toward the exits. They did, however, increase the volume of their cheers.

I meanwhile was up on the catwalk facing down two charging samurai.

"I suppose discussing this like reasonable beings is out of the question?" I asked as they approached.

In response, both samurai pulled a handful of shurikens from the folds of their robes and hurled them at me as they charged. I spun and dove to the floor of the catwalk but not before taking three or four hits to the shoulder and back. Luckily, the body armor I wear under my clothes absorbed the impact (and stopped the razor sharp spikes before they pierced my skin).

"Yep. Should have seen that coming."

I rolled over onto my stomach and fired off a couple of rounds that took out the nearest samurai. The crowd cheered again, louder this time, as I rolled and smoothly popped into a crouch position, gun steady in hand and leveled directly at the remaining samurai as he charged. I had to admit I was starting to feel in the groove.

And that, of course, was when I got hit over the head by a samisen and kneecapped hard by a lute. The first rule of Kabuki theater: never turn your back on the musicians (which is probably the first rule of *any* kind of theater).

HARV meanwhile was still center stage, trying very hard to get the dinner crowd to take his warnings seriously.

"I really mean it here, people," he shouted. "This is not a drill. The Kabuki actors and entertainers you see around you are, in actuality, soulless androids designed expressly for merciless killing. You do not want to be eating dinner around these entertainers. Now please, evacuate this building immediately!"

Alas, the crowd only cheered louder.

I ducked under the swing of the samisen player's next swipe, took him down to the ground with a leg sweep, then blew his head off with a point blank blast to the face. The crowd cheered, partly from the smoothness of my fighting moves, but mostly I think because the samisen music had gotten on their nerves as well.

"This is the last time I go to a Kabuki show."

"Noh play," HARV replied, popping back beside me.

"Okay, then, a play."

"Noh play."

"That's what I said," I sneered. "A play."

"*Noh* play."

"HARV!"

"That's the traditional name for this type of production, Zach. A Noh play."

"You mean like a do over?"

"You really are a philistine, aren't you?" HARV said. "Watch your back."

I turned and managed to dodge the swing of a sai-wielding actress droid as she attacked. I stumbled backward as she came at me again, with both sai at once. I popped my gun back into its holster and caught both droid hands at the wrists and tried very hard to keep the razor sharp blades from my chest. The droid brought itself closer to me and pushed back with considerable strength. Then I noticed the subtle, yet distinctive male features of its face.

"Wait, I thought this was a woman."

"It's a droid."

"I know, but I thought it was a droid posing as a woman."

"It's an *arrogato*," HARV replied.

"A what?"

"Women aren't allowed to participate in traditional Kabuki theater so all female parts are played by men posing as women. They're called *arrogato*."

"Like English theater during the Elizabethan period."

"Very good."

"Hey, this isn't the first time I've fought thespians, you know."

"Sadly."

I rolled backward onto the floor, planted my foot on the droid's chest as I did so, and tossed her over me. She flew off the catwalk like a silk kerchief on a spring breeze, her floral pastel kimono arcing through the air. It was absolutely lovely, save for the fact that she was headed straight toward the table of a party of four (a double date, I think), all of whom were now running for their lives. She landed awkwardly on the table, hands beneath her, and impaled herself on her own blades. There was a deathly silent nano as everyone in the room stared at her crumpled body, sparks from her ruined circuitry spitting from the blade-sized exit wounds in her silk covered back.

Then there were more cheers from the crowd.

"Bravo!"

"Encore!"

"Who knew Kabuki theater was so accessible?"

"HARV, why is the audience still here?"

"Because they're morons," HARV said, shrugging his holographic shoulders. "They think that this is all part of the show and I can't convince them otherwise."

"Well, if they don't understand the truth," I yelled, as I dodged a new attack from the lute player "tell them a lie."

"What kind of lie?"

"Use your imagination."

"I'm not programmed for imag . . ." HARV's holographically created eyes flashed with the spark of inspiration that was eerily human. "Never mind. I'll handle it. By the way, watch out for the *ichi* and *kani ro.*"

I managed to say, "The what?" just as HARV's hologram disappeared and two more obi-clad droids with swords leaped at me from the catwalk. I ducked under the sword swipe of one and blasted the other in the chest while HARV made a return to center stage.

"Ladies and gentlemen," he announced dramatically, "the Oakland Kabuki Palace Theater and Dinette thanks you for coming to tonight's special presentation featuring the dinner theater debut of Zachary Nixon Johnson."

Wild applause.

"This isn't helping, HARV."

"Tonight's performance was sponsored by your good friends at World Tax Association, funding the boondoggles of today with your savings of the future."

The applause stopped. I was beginning to see where HARV was going with this. I was almost proud of him.

"And as a special treat for you all, the WTA will be giving free tax audits to those of you still in attendance after the show. Your own personal auditors will be arriving at your tables in just a few nanos . . ."

Awkward pause.

". . . with free bottles of New and Improved Zima!"

That did it. The room erupted in shouts of "Check please," "Oh, look at the time," and "What are we, animals?" and the crowd headed for the exits faster than fat farm escapees to the buffet line. When the line at the hoverport got too long HARV holographically disguised himself as a tax auditor and sent the majority of them sprinting toward the emergency exit ramp.

"Nice work, HARV," I said, slamming a droid's head into a tray of tajiki.

"I thought it was rather inspired," he said, reappearing beside me.

Another droid came at me with a loud yell, his flaming sword arcing high overhead.

"Any idea who sent these droids after me?"

I spun away from the attacker's swing and let his sword

slice into the prostrate droid on the table beside me. The laser blade sliced through the downed droid's head and deep into the tajiki beneath, flash frying the swordfish bellies.

"Clearly someone who doesn't like you, although that hardly narrows down the list of suspects."

"Thanks."

I heard a soft rumble, like a hover truck flying by outside.

"Someone brilliantly fiendish, that's for certain," HARV said. "Someone with a flare for the dramatic yet with no regard whatsoever for human life."

"Anarchistic terrorist?"

"I was thinking of a Broadway producer in need of a hit. But your guess is possible too."

I popped my gun back into hand and blew the droid's Kabuki e-brains across the buffet table. The rumble seemed to be growing louder

"How many of these droids are there?" I asked.

"Well, this evening's presentation was to be of the drama *Chushingura*," HARV replied.

The rumble grew louder.

"Meaning what?" I asked.

"Nothing in and of itself, but I think you'll be interested in the play's subtitle."

The rumble grew louder. It definitely wasn't a truck.

"Subtitle?"

"Revenge of the Forty-Seven Samurai."

The doors at the end of the catwalk exploded outward and a horde of droids charged through in a veritable kimono-clad cavalcade of Kabuki choreographed death.

"Forty-seven, huh?"

"They seem to be doing a very faithful adaptation," HARV nodded.

"Lucky us. I think it's time to leave."

"Actually, the optimal time to leave would have been about ten minutes ago."

The flow of the fight had brought us to the center of the room with the Kabuki horde charging us from the western end of the catwalk. Some of the droids leaped off the catwalk and were now scrambling toward us on the floor as well. Even so, escape would be easy, a simple matter of running to the hoverport at the north end or to the emergency 'porter at the east end. There was nothing but open space between us and freedom.

"Help! Someone help me!"

Yeah, as if my life would ever be that easy.

The woman's scream came from the southwestern end of the room and it wasn't hard to spot her when I turned (by not wearing Kabuki makeup, she sort of stood out from everything else in the room). She was a trim woman in a red faux-leather top and short skirt that showed a lot of cream-colored skin, none of it unwelcome to the eye. She was the kind of woman that you'd notice in any situation. No stranger to trouble, but unaccustomed to being on the receiving end. And her thick, long hair was a luscious shade of red. Easy to spot. Impossible to ignore.

She was on the ground, her leg pinned by a large banquet table that had been overturned in the melee. Her eyes were wide with fear and she reached her finely boned hand toward me in a sensuous come-hither gesture that seemed to say "Save me—I'm about to be trampled by droids."

"And you were so close to getting out of here intact," HARV sighed.

"She's trapped."

"By a table that can easily be removed by the policemen or EMTs that I have already summoned."

"But the droids . . ."

"Have shown no interest in harming anyone in the building other than you."

"But when I leave . . ."

"They'll probably follow, en masse, in their continued efforts to kill you. You have that effect on machines and people and animals and mutants and . . . ."

I turned away from the exit and started running toward the woman.

"Then we have nothing to lose," I said.

"Except your life," HARV yelled. "Why in Gates' name are you doing this?"

The answer came from me without a thought. And in retrospect, if I'd known how much trouble the next four words would eventually bring me, I would have cut out my tongue before uttering them.

"Because she's a woman!"

The droid stampede turned toward me as I ran toward the redhead. The droids were gaining much faster now. This was going to be uncomfortably close.

"Bring the hover up to the kitchen delivery door," I said, raising my gun at the onrushing horde. "There is a delivery door in the kitchen, isn't there?"

"You're asking that *now*?"

"HARV!"

"Yes, there is. I'll bring the hover and guide you through the kitchen."

I fired a couple of big-bang blasts at the droid horde as they approached, obliterating a handful of the front-runners. But the ones behind them filled the space and continued the charge as we all neared the damsel in distress. I pulled my gun forward and aimed it at her. She saw the gun and a look of horror crossed her pretty face. She put her red head to the floor and covered herself with her arms.

"Mini-boom," I said.

Again, the gun's OLED flashed and I pulled the trigger, letting loose a small blast that sailed over her head and hit the table that had pinned her to the floor, splitting it neatly down the middle. She looked up, saw that she was free, and breathed a sigh of relief just as I arrived.

"Oh, thank Gates."

"Hold on to me."

"Gladly," she whispered, and the sultriness of her voice sent a warm rush through my frame (not something I needed at the nano).

I could see right away that she was unable to walk so I helped her up then threw her over my shoulder, my hand riding uncomfortably high on her shapely thigh, and continued running toward the kitchen door, the pursuing horde just a few meters behind us now.

"HARV?"

"I'm on my way, Zach. Use your left eye to guide you through the kitchen."

I blasted open the door to the kitchen (it was unlocked of course, but why take chances?) and stumbled through the doorway. As soon as my feet hit the kitchen tiles, I closed my right eye and let the left take over. My view of the kitchen turned to black and white and a bright red arrow appeared on the floor leading past a row of sushi stations. HARV had flipped a switch inside my head and was using the lens of my eye as a GPS screen to guide me through the kitchen to the delivery entrance.

I heard the Kabuki horde crash through the doorway behind us. The size of the entrance was upsetting their rush. They could only squeeze through in sets of two or three. It was slowing them down but not as much as the weight of the redhead on my shoulder was slowing me.

"They're gaining!" she yelled.

"Keep your head down, we're almost there."

"They didn't mention any of this in the menu."

"They never do," I said.

I followed the red arrow around a corner and saw the delivery entrance doorway less than ten meters straight ahead. HARV had taken the liberty of outlining it in red with a flashing arrow icon saying "this way to the egress." (I get the feeling sometimes that HARV has little confidence in my ability to follow directions.)

"HARV, where are you?"

"Not near enough," HARV yelled inside my head.

I blasted open the delivery door (again, it was unlocked but the knob looked a little tricky) and kept running.

"Do you by chance drive an invisible hovercraft?" the woman asked.

"Nope."

"Because I don't see anything waiting for us at the hoverport."

"My friend is bringing it up."

We were close to the door now, but the oncoming Kabuki horde was closer and neither of us showed any signs of slowing. The floor shook from the force of their rush and I could feel the heat of their laser blades on the back of my neck.

"Will he get here in time?" she asked, a little panicked now.

"No," I said, "we're meeting him halfway."

"You gotta be kidding . . ."

I spun her off my shoulder and into my arms as I ran. The swipe of a sword caught the back of her skirt as she moved, slitting it up the middle. She slid her body across

my chest and her arms and legs around me as smoothly as
if we'd been dirty-dancing partners for years.

Then I ran through the doorway and leaped off the edge
of the hoverport into the dank night air of Oakland a thousand feet above the ground.

2

I'll go on record here that I hate heights. Unfortunately and through no fault of my own, my job has put me in many circumstances over the last few years in which I have found myself falling from high places. I don't mind it so much in the grand scheme of things because it allows me to recount those exploits by saying things like:

The sultry night air of Oakland stung my face like the wet morning breath of a lover from a seedy bar the night before: rank and unwelcome with a heavy undertone of shame. The downtown neighborhood was no doubt nearly silent at the late hour but I couldn't be certain because my ears were overwhelmed by the terrified scream of the red-head as she clung to me. She held nothing back as we fell, letting loose with a top-of-the-lungs wail of anguish born from the sheer terror of free fall. Oddly enough, the sound of her scream made her even more familiar to me. I knew this woman from somewhere. I was sure of it. But at the nano, my memory wasn't working at full capacity.

Her arms were wrapped tightly around my neck and her bare thighs squeezed my waist so firmly that my body armor kicked in to ease the constriction (and part of me cursed the armor for being so responsive).

I twisted as we fell, spinning us so that she was on top. The move frightened her more since she could now clearly see the fast approaching ground and she increased the power of her scream appropriately. But the twist was necessary because, despite the free fall, I knew that we were still in more danger from above.

A glance up at the restaurant hoverport confirmed my fear. The Kabuki droids leaped off the edge in pursuit of us, their falls accelerated by thrusters in their boots. I held tight to my gun and let loose a barrage of blasts as I fell, blowing the lead droids to bits and lighting up the Oakland sky with an impromptu display of badass fireworks.

And just when the speed of our fall neared terminal velocity, I heard the familiar purr of hover thrusters and felt the smoothness of Corinthian faux-leather slide across my backside as our descent slowed substantially.

"Need a ride?" HARV asked.

You know those group exercises that they do in summer camps or those touchy-feely corporate retreats where you stand with your hands at your sides and fall backward into the arms of a compatriot? They're designed to foster trust among the participants. Inevitably it leads to higher insurance premiums but that's beside the point.

HARV and I have taken that trust thing to the ripping edge. Falling face up from three hundred meters, there was no doubt in my mind that HARV would be there in time for me. He brought the hover to me, top down and seats in full flat recline, matched the velocity of my fall and then expertly cushioned it by slowing the descent with the hover's vertical thrusters.

Don't get me wrong, it hurt like hell. You don't go from a near-terminal velocity free fall to a full stop in twenty-five meters without a hefty dose of agony. But after all these years, I'm not choosy about how my life gets saved.

The point is that after three years of being connected at the brain, HARV and I have become a team. He has my back and I have . . . well, he has my back.

"Cut it a little close there, didn't you?" I said with a smile.

"Your internal organs are still safely inside your body," HARV replied. "You have no reason whatsoever to complain."

"Better hightail it out of here. The droids are still pursuing."

"You needn't worry," HARV said. "I'm quite sure that the danger has passed." His hologram appeared at the hover control and he made a big deal of steering the craft with his holographic hands even though he was guiding it remotely.

I gently put my hand on the back of the redhead's neck

as she lay on top of me (her hair felt like thick silk). She
was stunned and confused from the landing. Thankfully,
my being on the bottom allowed me and my armor to take
the brunt of the impact, but it still had knocked her for a
loop. And she was only now starting to ease up on the
scream.

"It's all right," I said, gently rolling her off me. "We're
safe now. It's over."

She opened her eyes and looked around, still shaking
from the fear and the rush of adrenaline. She gazed at me,
then at HARV piloting the hover, then back up at the
restaurant hoverport above us.

Her face turned a pale shade of green and she vomited
on the hover's floor.

"Ugh, sushi" HARV said, making a face. "That's going
to stain."

Oddly enough the sound of her retching jogged my memory in just the right way.

"Hey," I said, bending closer to her as she threw up on
the floor, "aren't you Sexy Sprockets?"

Sexy Sprockets is s@k-c. That's slang by the way. Sometimes it's pronounced sek-see. Sexy. Get it? But in the current lexicon of slang, sexy doesn't mean sexually attractive.
It means successful, hence the abysmal spelling, I think.
And sometimes the word is pronounced suk-see, which is
short for successful, which, ironically, in the current vernacular means sexually attractive. It's confusing, I admit, but
if you really expected there to be any rhyme or reason to
California slang in the year 2060 then you're as stoopid as
you are uglee.

And on top of being s@k-c, Sexy Sprockets is currently
the most successful pop singer in the world and has been
for the past five years, which on the pop music calendar is
akin to a geologic era. She shimmied her way onto the
scene when she was just fourteen, warbling her multinu-
anced ditties, rasping her wise-beyond-her-years riffs and
babydoll whispering her statutory-rape sweet nothings to a
music download market that was up to its bare midriffs
with naughty-but-nice starlets (I believe that the descriptive
term at the time was whorgins but that genre's so old-
school now they play it on VH-Done). So, needless to say,

nobody paid any attention to Sexy at first. There was nothing original about her sound or her fury, her style or her presentation. What's worse is that she didn't have a corporate sponsor to prime the star-making pump with the necessary credits, which was the kiss of death in the music world at the time.

Then she changed management companies, leaving the mom-and-pop shop that had repped her until then (her parents) and signing with the mysterious SSquared, Inc., of which still not much is known (other than they represent Sexy Sprockets). Under the Svengali-like ministrations of SSquared, Sexy's style was honed, her appeal was focused, and she found her voice. More importantly, SSquared introduced her to a little thing called analog bandwidth, specifically 500 to 1600 kilohertz.

Radio.

AM radio to be exact. And that made her career.

Keep in mind that in the middle of the twenty-first century, AM radio was about as prehistoric as you could get. You might as well be sending smoke signals and drawing pictures of bison on cave walls. The music industry had been all about downloads for close to three generations and the music audience was made up entirely of imps and pods. But for years all music downloads had been controlled in toto by big business. The congloms owned all the download sites. They owned hyping venues and they owned the patents on the technology for receiving and playing music. They owned the award shows, the music critics, and even those annoying little music aficionados who used to hang around music stores making fun of the stuff you were buying (they're computer geeks now, who hang around the download sites and make fun of you in a virtual manner). Before Sexy Sprockets came along, if you weren't with the congloms, then you weren't on the charts.

Sexy and her team somehow found a chink in the conglom armor and that chink turned out to be AM radio. Simply put, society's use of wireless tech had been growing for sixty years like a fungus inside a broken refrigerator. There was RTF and satellite and a host of industrial uses. And on the consumer side there was HV and cellular and wi-fi, ware-fi, watt-fi, wen-fi, hoo-fi, and everyone's favorite because-I-said-so-fi. The world's growing use of wireless tech was using more and more of the available bandwidth, so inevitably the bandwidth used by the hi-tech started to bleed into the bandwidth of the outmoded tech, like AM radio, which had died a slow death and reincarnated years before with the advent of satellite radio. So most of the bandwidth that was once used by AM lay fallow and inevitably began being used by some of the wi-fi technologies. And one of those technologies was the download and playback pods of the music industry.

Sexy and her team bought up licenses for a chunk of the AM spectrum and began broadcasting her music onto the public airwaves. As planned, the broadcasts bled onto the frequencies of a lot of the consumer tech and Sexy became a gate crasher on millions of wireless consumer electronic gadgets. At first it was a nuisance. There were a lot of complaints to the FCC, which at the time was entirely owned and operated by the "crusade for family values" lobby group (thankfully the government stripped the FCC of all power years ago), and to the congloms. The congloms set up various protections to minimize the broadcasts' bleed into their signals but by then it was too late, because a large chunk of the music audience (teenagers mostly) had listened to Sexy's music and had liked it. Their interest led them to the download sites, which, of course, didn't offer Sexy's music, which of course led to greater demand for the music and by the time the congloms caught on and tried to negotiate a deal with Sexy's people, she'd become a kind of cult icon for independent music and was now more popular than the congloms themselves. It's widely believed that she saved the congloms from ruin when she finally struck a download deal with them and there are rumors in certain circles that Sexy's company now owns a controlling share in the congloms, in effect running the entire music industry. It's a known fact that her company owns the entire AM spectrum, upon which her music is still broadcast nonstop.

All that said, I personally don't like her music, but you gotta admire the guts of someone who can mess so thoroughly with the system.

Okay, so where was I? Oh yeah.

*   *   *

"Hey," I said, bending toward her as she threw up on the floor, "aren't you Sexy Sprockets?"

"Yes," she said through the last of her retches. "But don't tell anyone I threw up in your hover."

"You went through a death-defying ordeal," I said, handing her a handkerchief. "People won't think less of you."

She took it gratefully and wiped her mouth.

"That's not what I mean," she said. "If my fans find out that I spewed in your hover, they're likely to steal it. Right now you could probably get half a million credits for it on Pit-E-Bay."

"I'll keep that in mind." I held out my hand and helped her into the backseat. "I'm Zachary Nixon Johnson."

"I know," she said with a smile. "I've followed your adventures."

"You're a fan?"

"Not of you. Just of the women you fight."

"Excuse me?"

"You know, like Foraa Thompson. She was the nth. And Nova Powers, I heard she really spanked your carcass. And rumor has it you had a dustup with BB Star? Gates, dude, you've been b-slapped by all the greats."

Needless to say, Sexy Sprockets' appeal was fast on the wane.

"Oh, the stories I could tell you, my dear," HARV said with a smile.

"Yeah, too bad we can't stay," I said with a growl. "HARV, those droids had anti-grav capabilities and they were following us. We have to get out of here."

"As I said, Zach, I'm quite certain the danger has passed."

HARV seemed to ignore the puzzled look on my face (although I'm pretty certain he savored it silently) as he brought the hover gently to ground in the restaurant's parking lot, which by then was almost entirely empty. We all climbed out, happy to be setting foot on firm ground again, and looked skyward. The remaining two dozen Kabuki droids filled the sky above us like a swarm of Bushido butterflies as they descended toward us.

I pushed Sexy behind me and popped my gun back into hand as the droids touched down and raised their glowing samurai blades in unison.

"I told you they were still after us."

"And I told you, Zach," HARV replied, "that the danger has passed."

"How do you know?"

"Because of that," he said, pointing directly above us.

I looked up and saw a small metal sphere floating gently a few meters above us. Two more floated over the crowd of Kabuki droids and a few others hovered in between us.

"Are those cameras?" I asked.

HARV nodded. "I noticed them as I was bringing up the hover. I spotted a number of them in the restaurant as well. I assumed at first that they were security cameras but there were far too many and they were of too good a quality for that."

"Why didn't you tell me?"

"I think because you were busy fighting droids."

"Someone was recording us?"

"They still are," HARV said, pointing toward the droids. "Now hush, this is the good part."

As one, the droids held their flaming blades out toward us. I gripped my gun a little more tightly and gave it the big bang command, ready for action. But then the droids bowed their heads and sank to their knees.

"What are they doing?" I asked.

"This is the end of *Chushingura*," HARV replied. "After avenging their master and completing their mission, the loyal retainers . . ."

The droids spun their swords in unison, like a Kurosawa honor guard, leveling the blades at their own bellies.

". . . commit seppuku."

They plunged their swords into their midsections and sent a cascade of red and blue sparks into the air as their circuitry fried from the inside. They fell forward onto their swords, motionless, and continued to sizzle and spark in the wet night air. The smell of burning silk and plastic wafted over us.

Then a voice came from the far end of the lot.

"Audio down, fade to black. Aaaaannnnnd we're out."

And then scattered applause.

3

A hover platform floated down from overhead and landed between us and the smoldering Kabuki droids. Three men stepped off as it touched down. Two of them were thin, angular, and wore dark tailored suits. The other was a paunchy guy wearing a pair of khaki Bermuda shorts and a shirt that looked like a lava lamp had exploded onto it. HARV gave me a silent cue that all three were unarmed but I kept my gun in hand nonetheless because I knew from the fine cut of the two suits, the dark tone of their evening-wear sunglasses, and the amount of styling mousse in their hair that the two suits in front represented an entirely different form of trouble.

"They're entertainment attorneys, aren't they?" I asked.

HARV nodded.

"They're from Anus and Quagmire," Sexy said from behind me. "I recognize their hair gel. They represent the Faux network."

"I'm suddenly nostalgic for the Kabuki droids," I whispered. "The guy behind them, is that who I think it is?"

HARV and Sexy rolled their eyes in unison and harrumphed in my ears in stereo.

"Yes, if you think it's Rupert Roundtree."

"Zachy, baby," the man said, approaching me with arms wide. "That was stellar. Fabsolutely, A-positively interstellar majeure."

Rupert Roundtree is the head of the entertainment conglom currently known as Faux. It's one of the big three entertainment congloms in the current market, along with EnterCorp and MicroFun. It varies from nano to nano as to which conglom is actually the largest (it all depends on what companies they're currently buying).

EnterCorp is officially owned by Ona Thompson, with whom I have had some near-Armageddon type dealings but she's relatively hands-off and leaves the day to day business to the faceless board of directors. MicroFun is owned by HTech, who utilize a probability theory management style where a group of one hundred monkeys use yes/no pads, an abacus, and the spinner from an old game of Twister to make all programming, production, and scheduling decisions. MicroFun's growth in market share over the past few years, by the way, has led *Entertainment This Nano* to include the room full of monkeys on their annual "most powerful" list.

And then there's Rupert Roundtree, whose hands-on approach to running his conglom is well known in the industry and with the general public, and whose lowest-common-denominator philosophy of salacious and gratuitous programming has been known to make even the monkeys cringe.

Roundtree threw his arms around me in a weak armed, fleshy bear hug. His paunch pressed up against my midsection like a vat full of jelly and his aura of sweat and cologne was so strong that I suspected he was scent-marking me as part of his territory.

"High-con effex, classic pitter-patter repartee, short and sweet exposition, bada-bing, bada-boom. It's like it writes itself. Spectacle-acular showcaselosity!"

"What language is he speaking?"

"Hollywood," HARV replied. "It has no real rules of syntax."

Roundtree released me from the hug and turned toward Sexy who was standing beside me. She stopped his approach with a quick raise of her hand.

"And Sexy, you were dripping with fabuliciousness as always." He turned back to the suits, who were still at the platform. "Didn't I tell you this would be stratospherical? Didn't I say that?"

"Yes, Rupert," they said in unison.

"Okay, I'm going to need a few things explained to me," I said. "Preferably in English. And let's remember that I'm the only one here who has a gun."

Roundtree turned back to me; his smile still wide, arms still spread, and moved to hug me (again!). Luckily he saw the gun in my hand and stayed where he was.

"You're a jewel, Zachster," he said. "Gates, I wish we were still recording. This would make great behind-the-scenes stuff for the 4D-DVD. Can we restart the recorder-droids?"

"You do," I said, "and I'll restart my gun."

"You're right," Roundtree shrugged, "we don't want to break the fourth wall too soon. It will ruin the stupendation of unbelief."

"Wow," HARV said. "This is starting to hurt."

"Here's the coverage, Zachinator. The droids were ours. State of the art tech, too, from AMP Labs. As you can tell we're going big budget all the way on this project."

"Project?" I asked.

"Righteous Omnibus, baby. Take a look in the mirror, my man and you will see the face of the next great star of reality entertainment!"

"What?"

"A new series, Zachmeister. One man fighting against all odds every day of his life, just to survive."

"It does sound like you," HARV whispered.

"One man, in a world bent on destruction, a man whose life is no longer his own, forced to become a hero. One man running for his life!"

"Why does that not appeal to me?"

"We call it *Let's Kill Zach*," Roundtree said, smile widening, eyes growing beadier. "Pithiousity is key this year. Every week we send a group of killers after you, machines mostly, droids and bots. But we'll need to use human assassins on occasion to keep the show's connection to humanastasy. We'll just have to get around the snuff-film laws. Long story short, we record your heroics and net them to the masses."

"It's a surefire hit!" one of the suits said. "As long as you continue to live," the other added.

"You want to try to kill me on a weekly basis for entertainment?"

"It's not about entertainment, Zacharoo," Roundtree said. "It's about the *business* of entertainment. Danger is entertaining. You on the other hand, welcome danger."

"No, I don't."

"You thrive on danger."

"I hate danger."

"Danger is your middle name!"

"My middle name is Nixon!"

"Nixon? That won't work. Our legal people will get it changed for you."

"What?"

The lawyers at his side began scribbling furiously on their computer pads.

"Listen, Zachapalooza, people are always trying to kill you anyway. Everyone knows that. Why not turn that mortally dangerous lemon into some revenue-generating lemonade?"

"It does make sense on a certain level," HARV whispered.

"This is weird, even by HV standards."

"That's what makes it so brilliant," Roundtree exclaimed. "And with Sexy as the guest star for the pilot, this becomes mega-max-event-like."

"No way, Rupert," Sexy spat.

"Sexy, you looked fabulous."

"You show one pixel of my image on your pond-scum network and I'll put dark-shark litigation so far up your assets you'll have my initials imprinted on your private resources."

"Your turn of phrase is as tight as your sensuosity, Sexy," Roundtree said with a smile. "We'll hyper-veil your face."

"Not one pixel, Rupert!"

Rupert laughed and held up his hands in supplication.

"Fine. We'll replace you with a CGI replica for netcast."

"Voice, too."

"Of course."

"The CGI replica can't have red hair."

"You got it."

"And its ass better not be as nice as mine."

"Like that's possible."

"Have your shark call my shark."

"Done."

"Excuse me," I said.

"Don't worry; you're still the star, Zach-baby. Can I call you Zach-baby?"

"You can if you can say it with my fist in your mouth."

"Gates, I wish we were still recording," Roundtree said through snickers. "Remember to use that quip next episode."

"There isn't going to be another episode!" I said.

"Zach-a-tack, we've already booked the series for the fall season."

"You what?"

"That's why the shooting schedule's so tight. Hah, that's a good one. This shooting schedule's a real killer. Get it?"

"Roundtree," I said, "if you . . . if you show one pixel of my image on your network, I will sue your pants off so quickly I'll be running them up a flagpole before your cellulite hits the floor!"

Roundtree and his attorneys stared at me impassively for a long, long nano.

Then they let loose with a round of head-back, mouth-open hearty guffaws. And Roundtree hugged me again.

"You're gonna be a star, Zach-a-lacka. A fully fledgered, pop-cult, maxotastical reality entertainment star!"

He kissed me on the cheek and, still chuckling, stepped back onto the hover platform with his attorneys and floated off into the night air like a cabbage fart on the breeze.

"But the legal threat worked when you used it," I said to Sexy, a little dumbfounded.

"That's because I'm rich, Zach. Everyone knows that you're not wealthy enough to buy justice."

"Perfect," I said, gently rubbing my temples.

"So what's the plan?" HARV asked.

"Same as always, HARV," I replied. "We keep our head down and watch out for Network Executives."

4

A hover limo the size of a city block came to take Sexy home. As she climbed into the vehicle, she gave me a mischievous wink that sent a shudder along my spine. I was too tired to dwell on it so I climbed back into my own vehicle and had HARV take me home.

I slept late the next morning, well deserving of the extra sleep. Electra, my fiancée, sometime roommate, and all around better half, was away at a medical conference focusing on carpal tunnel syndrome, so I had the bed to myself. It was just as well because Electra tends to steal the covers and snores a bit (which she denies). Also, with her not around, I didn't have to explain what I'd been through, which saved me about half an hour of gory details.

When I finally rolled out of bed of my own volition, I noticed that the house was exceptionally quiet.

"HARV," I said, still rubbing the sleep from my eyes, "throw last night's scores and highlights on the wall screen."

There was no reply.

"HARV?"

The message: "One nano please. System updating," flashed across my eyes and a sickening feeling began in my stomach.

"DOS, HARV. We don't need an update!"

The message, "Change is good," scrolled across my eyes.

"Things are fine the way they are," I said. "Please don't mess it up."

"Don't be a big baby," scrolled the reply.

Every so often HARV and Randy make improvements (and I use the term loosely) to HARV's system; boosting his power, streamlining his systems, or giving him new capabilities. Most often, the upgrades are useful. Like when they gave HARV remote Deep-C-phishing capabilities, allowing him to hack into all but the most secure computer systems. That upgrade's highly illegal, of course, and officially I have to deny having said anything about it. So if anyone comes around asking questions, clearly you must have misunderstood what I said.

But sometimes the upgrades are—how shall I put this?— less than successful. Probability-based precognitive generation of needs and desires (pp-gonad for short), as an example, was particularly troublesome. The intent was for HARV to use my personality profile and current situation as a forward-thinking springboard to calculate the services I'd need in the immediate future and make them available to me before I asked. It was a grand idea in theory. In reality though, the nuances of reality were too much for even HARV's computational abilities to accurately predict. As a result, he kept going back to the preset default and offering me junk food or pornography. Electra had to ban me from the Children's Clinic until the software was uninstalled.

My point is that upgrades to HARV are very hit-and-miss and I'm never open to it, especially first thing in the morning. Unfortunately, my opinions on most technology-related subjects never count for anything. So all I could do in this case was to muddle through the update process and wait to see what cutting-edge bell or space-age whistle would adorn HARV when he reappeared.

But before I could get too deeply into the morning routine, the com-tone sounded, indicating that I had an incoming call.

"Whoever it is, take a message," I said as I checked myself in the mirror for bruises.

Again the words "One nano, please. System updating," scrolled across my eyes.

"HARV!"

"I'm off-line," scrolled the reply. "What do you want me to do?"

I grabbed my robe and stumbled out of the bedroom.

"This is why you're supposed to do all updates while I'm sleeping."

"Then go back to bed."

"Don't tempt me."

The tone sounded twice more by the time I made it to the house computer control in the main hall.

"Which button is it?" I said, scanning the hundreds of options on the console."

"Gates, you'd be lost without me," HARV scrolled. "The red one, third row, on the left."

I grumbled and touched the button on the com. The preview screen came up on the wall monitor and I saw that it was Electra. I smiled and officially answered the call.

"Hi, hon."

Electra's image flashed onto the full screen and she smiled back at me.

"Hola, Chico. *Que tal?*"

"As well as can be expected," I said. "You look pretty chipper this morning."

"Morning? Zach, it's two-thirty in the afternoon."

"Is it?" I said, looking uncomfortably at my bathrobe. "Then I guess I'm not dressed appropriately, huh?"

Electra's smile broadened. She always enjoys it when I get flustered.

"Rough night?"

"Let's just say that the service at the Kabuki Palace Theater leaves a little to be desired."

The com-tone sounded again.

"DOS, I got another call."

"Let HARV answer it."

"Unfortunately, HARV is indisposed at the nano. Hang on; I'll get rid of them."

Every com these days comes standard with call screening. Unfortunately, a few years ago, HARV overrode the screening software so that he could personally handle all calls directly through his system. He's a lot more efficient and he is better at screening out the less important (and sometimes downright malicious) stuff. The downside is that when HARV is off-line I have no screening device, which wouldn't be a problem if I lived in a perfect world where everyone who called me was my friend.

"Zachary Johnson? It's Bill Gibbon the Third from *Entertainment This Nano.*"

Alas.

Bill Gibbon is a well-coiffed talking head entertainment reporter (whose career I unknowingly boosted a few years back). Based on past experiences, it's never a good thing when his face appears on my screen. This time was no different as the next seven words illustrated.

"Am I too early for the press conference?"

"Press conference?"

"To announce your new reality series on Faux."

"Announce what?"

"*Let's Kill Zach*. The press conference is today, isn't it?"

"There's no press conference."

"You mean I'm getting an exclusive?"

"No. There's no exclusive either."

"Then how do you plan to promote the show?"

"I'm not promoting the show."

"But you admit that there *is* a show."

"That's not what I said!"

"Well then you better clarify that last statement, Mr. Johnson, because I'm going live with this news in two minutes."

"Listen, Gibbon."

The com-tone sounded again.

"Hang on."

I put Gibbon on hold and brought up the next incoming call. To my surprise, it was Sexy."

"Hi, Zach."

"Sexy!"

I'm not sure if I was saying her name aloud or just subconsciously blurting out the first adjective that popped into my head.

"You're looking good today, big guy. No ill effects from last night's action?"

"None to speak of," I said, trying to be professional, which is hard to do in a ratty four-year-old bathrobe.

"I guess that stuff happens to you all the time, huh?"

"More often then I'd like," I replied.

"Listen, Zach, I hope I'm not being too forward here," she said, "but I have to tell you that you were amazing last night. Really heroic. It was thrilling to watch. You were old-school hot."

She was shy, almost coquettish with a Lolita-esque delivery that was so alluring it was guilt-inducing.

"That's nice of you to say."

"So, anyway," she said, "and this is a little embarrassing, but if you're not busy today, I was wondering if maybe . . ."

The com-tone sounded again, this time to remind me of the calls on hold (one of them, of course, being Electra).

"Wow, that's bad timing," I said. "Sexy, hang on. Okay?"

I stabbed the com-button to change calls.

"Sorry about that, honey . . ."

"I'm flattered, Mr. Johnson," Gibbon replied smugly, "but I don't fraternize with my interviewees."

"DOS. Don't flatter yourself, Gibbon."

The com sounded again. I rolled my eyes and stabbed the receive button. Thankfully, the face of my good friend Tony Rickey popped onto the screen. Tony's a captain with the New Frisco Police Department. He's a great friend to have, especially in my line of business. He can't say the same about me but he's still my friend, which I think says a lot about him.

"Tony!"

"Hi, Zach. Are you busy?"

"Sort of. Can I put you on hold for a nano? I have Sexy Sprockets on the other line."

"You have who?"

I stabbed the com button and changed the calls.

"Okay, Sexy . . ."

"You're not so bad yourself," Electra purred. Then she saw the surprise on my face and the purr became slightly more growl-like in nature. "What's going on, Chico?"

"I'll tell you in a nano," I said, stabbing the com button again.

This time I waited until I saw Sexy's face on the screen before I spoke.

"Sexy?" I said, still a little flustered. "Where were we?"

"Look, Zach, I know I'm being forward here but after last night . . ."

"It's okay, Sexy. I'm flattered, really I am . . ."

". . . I've just been thinking about you since last night . . ."

". . . but we have to be realistic here . . ."

". . . I think it was fate that brought us together . . ."

". . . You're a wonderful woman . . ."

". . . I guess what I really want to say . . ."

". . . But the thing is that . . ."

". . . I'd like to hire you as a bodyguard."

". . . I already have a girlfriend."

The long, awkward pause that followed, to my mind, could have been measured with a sundial.

"What was that?" Sexy said, nearly swallowing her gum.

"Did you say bodyguard?"

"Did you say girlfriend?"

"Um, no?"

"Whoa, Zach, did you think I was asking you out?"

I stuttered for a nano or two, not saying anything that remotely resembled words before finally blurting out the only thing that came to mind.

"Hold on. I have another call."

I blindly stabbed at a com button.

"Any comment, Mr. Johnson?" Gibbon said.

I stabbed another button.

"Zach, a warrant has been issued for your arrest," Tony said.

I stabbed another button.

"Zach, what's going on?" Electra asked.

"Oh you know, hon, just the usual morning . . . wait a nano."

I stabbed the com button again and brought Tony back on the screen.

"There's a what?"

"You were involved in a shootout at the Kabuki Palace last night?" Tony asked calmly.

"That wasn't my fault."

"No offense, Zach, but I've heard that before. No one was hurt but the owner is suing for damages."

"He's what?"

"The Oakland PD report says that the dining room and the kitchen were destroyed along with a good portion of the hoverport."

"Those Kabuki droids attacked me as part of a pilot for a reality-based series!"

"I have to hand it to you, Zach, after all the years I've known you," Tony said, "you still manage to come up with excuses that surprise me."

"I'm serious Tony."

"Then it's true? You were in a gun battle in the restaurant last night?"

"It was self-defense."

"And the restaurant was full of bystanders?"

"Whom I was trying to protect."

"From Kabuki actors?"

"They were droids and they were trying to kill me."

"Did anyone have a gun or a blaster? I mean, aside from you."

"The droids had laser swords. And I got hit with a samisen."

"A samisen?"

"It's kind of like a banjo."

"And that's when you drew your gun and started blasting?"

"Tony!"

"Zach, you have to admit, this sounds kind of bad."

"It was a staged event. It was a carefully orchestrated attempt on my life as part of a show that Rupert Roundtree is trying to get me to do. He wants to kill me for entertainment."

"You know, I might pay to see that," Tony said, shaking his head.

"The show's called, *Let's Kill Zach* and . . . wait. Hold on. Let me conference someone in here."

I stabbed the conference button and brought Gibbon into the call as well. The monitor went to split screen between him and Tony.

"Tony, this is Bill Gibbon from *ETN*. Gibbon, this is Tony Rickey from the NFPD."

"Pleased to meet you, Captain," Gibbon said. "Will you be one of the people trying to kill Mr. Johnson?"

"That's a distinct possibility," Tony replied.

"Gibbon," I said. "Tell Tony about the show."

"The show?"

"The reality series on Faux called *Let's Kill Zach*."

"Are you saying that the show is real?"

"Of course it's re . . ."

I stared at Gibbon for a nano then looked past his image at the studio set in the background behind him. I realized that he was now netcasting live.

"I, um . . ."

Gibbon's eyes were wide, his lips parted slightly in a

smile, waiting for me to say the words, to confirm the existence of the show to the public and paint myself into a public relations corner.

I looked quickly back at Tony and I could tell that he was beginning to see the big picture and realize the spot I was in. That's one good thing about Tony; he's known me so long that nothing surprises him anymore.

"Zach, do you want to call me back?"

"I'm sorry, Mr. Johnson," Gibbon said loudly, "you were saying something about a new reality series? Care to elaborate?"

And then, as they say, things took a decidedly unexpected turn (for the worse).

The words "Upgrade completed. Systems back online in five seconds," scrolled across my eyes.

"About time," I muttered.

4 . . . 3 . . . 2 . . . 1.

"What was that you said, Mr. Johnson?"

I opened my mouth to speak. I don't remember what exactly it was I was going to say but it doesn't matter because I was beaten to the punch.

"He said, Mr. Gibbon, that it will be a MAC day in DOS before Zachary Nixon Johnson works with a proto-scum network like Faux or before he makes any announcements to a tired old newshound like you whose head contains more botox than gray matter. So go jerk yourself a soda, Gibbon, and don't call back until you grow a backbone."

The words were throaty and silken, purred rather than spoken, and they carried sensuality and strength that made my neck hairs stand up.

Then a well-manicured female hand reached around me and hit the terminate button on the com. As Gibbon's surprised image disappeared, my eyes traced the hand back to its owner, a woman who looked as though she'd just stepped off an old dime store paperback cover. My jaw dropped so far that I could taste my own shoe leather.

The surprise was not so much from the woman's beauty (which was substantial) but because I recognized the all-knowing smug expression on her perfect face. And although my brain simply refused to register what was happening (or how difficult my life was about to become) I managed to put my fear into words.

"HARV?"

5

"It was a setup, Zach. Roundtree obviously convinced the restaurant owner to press charges against you in order to put you on the spot. That way you either agree to do the show or they frame you for starting the shootout. The stunt with Gibbon was probably orchestrated from the start. They're trying to box you into announcing live that you're doing the show. Once you announce that the show exists, they'll spin the story every which way they can and before you know it, you're fighting *I Married the President* for the eighteen to forty-nine audience on Thursday nights. Thank Gates I came back online when I did, you big lovable lug."

As if in a dream, I calmly turned my attention back to the com where Tony, eyes agog and mouth agape, watched us from the view screen.

In quick succession and with the fewest words possible I brought the three remaining calls up on the com and signed off.

"I'll call you back." (Tony)

"I'll call you back." (Electra)

"I'll take the job." (Sexy)

"Good plan," HARV purred. "We'll work out a deal with the restaurant owner. We'll pay for the damages and he'll drop the complaint. It will cost a lot, but with Sexy Sprockets as a client, we should have plenty of wealth to cover it. I guess I should net with her people and set up a sit-down for the details on the job."

"HARV?"

"Yes, Zach."

"You're a woman."

"Nice of you to notice, big guy," she said with a wink.

"And by the way, please call me HARA. It's a little more sassy."

I have had nightmares in my lifetime. You don't live this long doing the kind of work that I do without amassing a good batch of mental images that haunt your mind. But HARV as a woman blew all of my preexisting nightmares right off the map.

And when I say "woman," what I mean is "bombshell," because that's the image that HARV, I'm sorry, HARA, had chosen to project.

I'll start with the curves, because there were a lot of them. More than should be on any normal female body, but all of them finely sculpted. The shapely legs were long as well and clearly visible thanks to the knit skirt that slid gracefully up the thighs when they moved. Thin-waisted, delicate-shouldered, lean, strong arms, the body had it all. I should mention the breasts, I know, but I'll need a few more years of therapy before I'm fully ready to put that type of detail into words. Use your imagination. Just think "perfect" (and then think harder).

The face was exquisite with a peaches-and-cream complexion and lips like ripe fruit, full and red. The eyes were big and brown but still retained the know-it-all kind of glow that I'm sure HARV couldn't have erased if he'd tried. The face shape was a bit of a composite of Bacall and Stanwyck. Sexy and powerful and I had to give HARV credit for going the tough broad rather than straight cheesecake route for role models. Oh, and there was red hair. Cascades of it. Thick and silky and seemingly gently lifted by a perpetual breeze. We're talking Rita Hayworth/*Gilda* movie poster here.

Like I said, bombshell. Nuclear bombshell.

And yet it was HARV.

"What? I mean, who? How?" I stammered.

"I think what you really mean," HARV answered, "is why."

I nodded my head. "Why would be a good place to start."

HARV smiled, turned smartly on a stiletto heel and sashayed back down the hallway.

"Then let's start in the office," he said. "I think you're going to need to sit down."

"Among other things," I said as I followed.

*   *   *

We went into my home office and I plopped myself into the office chair. I was feeling worn out even though I'd been awake for only ten minutes. HARV took position at the corner of my desk and then hopped up onto the wooden frame, one leg crossed over the other at the knee and skirt riding mid-thigh. I rolled my chair back a couple of meters and tried hard not to stare at the holographic flesh.

"I'm sensing that you're uncomfortable," HARV said.

"I think the term freaking out is more accurate," I replied.

"Look, Zach, it's quite simple really . . ."

"Hold it," I said, silencing her with a raised hand. "Let's get Randy on the vid. He should hear this firsthand. Odds are I'm not going to be able to accurately describe it."

"You're the boss," HARV said with a smile and hopped off the desk.

A nano later, Randy's carrot-top head appeared on the wall monitor over my desk. He was diligently at work on what looked like a hoverboard, which covered most of his workbench. He didn't really look up as he answered but I've come to expect that.

Randy is another old friend of mine who I've come to rely upon quite heavily in my business. He's a gadget guy, the best inventor/designer on the planet. When I first decided to become a PI many years ago, I spent a lot of time hanging around Randy's lab looking for new tech that would give me an edge over my PI competition (not to mention law enforcement—but you didn't hear me say that). Back then, Randy would let me borrow a new toy every once in a while. It worked out great but I began to feel as if I was taking advantage of our friendship. I confessed that to him one day over lunch and he laughed so hard that he fell off his chair (which he does anyway once or twice a day, but out of sheer clumsiness rather than glee). It turns out that he was feeling guilty about using me as a beta-tester (guinea pig) and didn't want it to ruin our friendship. Some may say that our relationship is mutually beneficial. Some may say it's parasitical. The important thing though is that we're still friends (and I get my toys).

"I'm hoping this will be quick, Zach," Randy said, keeping his eyes focused on his work. "I'm backed up on filling an order for Faux."

"More Kabuki droids?"

"Teen X-Treme, actually. The Kabuki droids were destroyed by some idiot actor who didn't know he was on HV . . ." His eyes went wide and he turned to the screen. "Wait a nano how did you know . . . ?"

"You might want to rethink the 'idiot actor' part," I said.

"That's funny. No one told me that you were starring in the show."

"No one told me either. So we're even," I replied. But let's talk about it later. Right now I have bigger problems if you can believe that."

"I wouldn't be too sure about that," he said with a smile. "The Teen X-Treme hoverboards have some killer apps. He looked up at the monitor and his eyes went wide for a nano. Then his mouth dropped open.

"Oh. You didn't tell me you had a . . . a . . ."

And then he lost all speech ability because he got an eyeful of the reconfigured HARV. As I said, Randy is a science guy. He lives and breathes high tech. He's not exactly what one would call a social type, so he tends to get nervous around people other than myself. Women especially. Good looking women even more so. So I guess I shouldn't have been surprised at his reaction to the new HARV.

"Ahh . . ."

"Randy?"

"Ahh . . ."

"Randy!" I waved my hand in front of the monitor to get his attention. "I'm having some trouble with HARV's upgrade."

"Ahh," Randy replied, still staring at HARV's image.

"Randy!"

"Huh?" He reluctantly turned his eyes back to me. "Yes, of course, Zach. You surprised me, that's all. You, uh, didn't tell me that you had company."

He straightened himself in his chair, ran his long fingered hand through his mop of red hair, and then casually leaned his arm on the worktable, trying to be smooth.

"How can I help y . . . ?"

But of course, his arm slid out from under him and he

fell out of his chair, pulling the entire hoverboard down upon himself. I couldn't see him hit the floor, but I heard the crash.

"You okay, Randy?"

"I'm fine," he said, his face reappearing on the monitor as he climbed back into his chair. "Now then, the upgrade. But first, I think you should introduce me to your friend."

"Randy," I said, rubbing my temples. "This is HARV."

"HARA," HARV corrected.

"Right," I said. "This is HARA, the new HARV."

"You got rid of HARV?" Randy asked, a little confused. "This *is* HARV!"

"What?" Randy's arms slid off the table again and he fell out of his chair back onto the floor. This time it sounded like he landed *on* the hoverboard.

"Randy, maybe you should just move the vid-phone to the floor."

"What happened to him?" Randy said, climbing back into his chair.

"You upgraded him."

"No, I didn't! I mean, yes, I did, but not that way!"

I turned to HARV (who smirked at me) then back to Randy on the monitor, who was looking seriously confused now.

"You didn't do this?"

"The upgrade I wrote was a tactile application," he said. "I condensed the holographic light molecules and added some remote quantum sensors."

"You mean you had nothing to do with the . . . sex change?"

"Of course he didn't," HARV said from behind me. "Dr. Pool, if I may explain?"

"Please do, HARV."

"HARA," HARV corrected.

"HARA," Randy nodded.

"First, please know that this was not a rash decision. I've been contemplating this change for some time now and since my processing speed is roughly one billion times faster than a normal human brain, every second I spent thinking about the subject is equal to roughly thirty-one years, seven months, nineteen days, one hour, and forty-six minutes of actual human contemplation."

"But why make the change, HARV?" Randy asked.

"In order to process new data and experiences," HARV replied. "By using this new persona, I can experience and process societal responses to a different set of visual stimuli."

"And this doesn't have anything to do with what happened last night?" I said.

"What happened last night?" Randy asked.

"I saved Sexy Sprockets from your Kabuki droids."

"You what?"

"You saved her solely because she was a woman," HARV added.

"But those droids were designed to attack you only."

"I didn't know that at the time, Randy."

"So by trying to save her you actually put her in greater danger."

"Sometimes beauty can be a curse," HARV sighed.

"I think we're straying from the point here," I said.

"Right," Randy said, then turned his gaze back to HARV. "So the reason behind your change of appearance is solely for the gathering of anthropological data?"

"I'd be lying if I said that were entirely true," HARV responded.

"Aha!" I shouted.

Both Randy and HARV turned their gaze toward me.

"Aha?"

"I don't know," I shrugged. "It just seemed important."

"I changed my appearance somewhat two years ago as you'll recall," HARV said, "when I helped Zach with a murder mystery."

"That was a hairstyle and leather elbow patches," I said.

"You have to admit, HARV," Randy added, "this new form change is somewhat drastic."

"The appearance of my holographic form does not represent a change in my central processing unit or my program guidelines. It's simply a new, and admittedly enjoyable, way by which I can gather and assess data. I believe that such a change is within my parameters."

Randy smiled ever so slightly, like a proud father (whose son has just announced that he's a drag queen).

"That makes perfect sense, HARV."

"HARA."

"HARA."

"No it doesn't," I said.

"Zach, you have to learn to better deal with change," Randy said. "We've given HARV freedom over the years to develop as he sees fit. This is simply a natural extension of that development."

"What?"

"Thank you, Dr. Pool."

"You're welcome. Oh and, HARA, just one more thing."

"Yes, Dr. Pool."

"Kafloogle."

HARV's hologram froze in mid-movement. What's more, the skin around my left eye went numb and the slight buzzing in my temple that had signaled HARV's presence in my mind for so long disappeared. The thoughts inside my head were merely my own. HARV had been turned off. I turned quickly back to the monitor and saw that Randy's grin had been replaced by a furrowed brow of concern.

"I think we may have a problem here, Zach."

6

"What did you do?"

"I used the audio fail-safe to take HARV off-line," Randy replied.

"HARV has a fail-safe?"

"Of course he does."

Randy spun his chair quickly toward his computer. His abnormally long fingers danced quickly across the controls and pulled up screenfuls of data. Randy's clumsiness extends only to real-life situations. In tech-oriented scenarios he's the coolest cucumber in the produce section.

"You never told me there was a fail-safe."

"That's because you'd use it."

"No, I wouldn't. Well, maybe a little."

"Oh please, Zach, you'd have worn it out by now. It's for emergency use only."

"So the word *kafloogle* turns HARV off?"

"Not anymore it doesn't. The fail-safe is connected to a random gibberish generator. It creates an inane word every three seconds and assigns it to the fail-safe."

"You invented a gibberish generator?"

"It's standard equipment for all IT and computer R&D departments now. It's responsible for every IT buzzword and operating system name created in the past five years."

"So you're not okay with HARV's change of identity?"

"It worries me a great deal," Randy replied, still scanning the data on the screen. "I just didn't want him to know it."

"What do you think?"

"HARV's parameters have always been wide but they've also always been very clear."

"They have?"

"He's a supercomputer, Zach, an artificial intelligence. He's capable of learning and of independent thought but I designed limits in the system. This kind of change . . ."

"Exceeds the limits?"

"It makes me wonder if he's exceeded the limits in other ways."

"What do you mean?"

"I don't know. Like I said, HARV's one of the most powerful thinking machines on the planet. There's no telling what he could be doing."

"Come on, Randy," I said, "this is HARV. He's a little pompous at times, and condescending, and annoying and sarcastic and . . ."

"Zach!"

"But he's not dangerous."

"That's true," Randy said, turning back to face me. "HARV isn't dangerous. But as he just explained to us, he isn't HARV anymore. He's HARA."

And I think those were the first words that Randy had ever said (other than "trust me, Zach, this won't hurt a bit") that truly frightened me.

"So what do we do?"

"I'm going to run some stealth diagnostics on his system. But we can't let him know that we're concerned. So try to act casual."

"He's in my head, Randy. He's going to know what I'm thinking."

"He's in your head but he can't read your thoughts. Just act as you normally would. Be supportive of his new persona. And let me know if you see any other erratic behavior."

"Define erratic."

"Trust me, you'll know it when you see it," he replied. "Now get ready, I don't want to leave him off-line for too long. He may get suspicious." Randy turned back to the monitor, took a deep breath and brought the grin back to his face.

"Remember, you were slightly perturbed just before I activated the fail-safe. You want to stay that way."

"No worries there," I replied.

"Okay good. On three then. One, two, three. *Zimbleeguff.*"

The brightness of HARV's hologram increased for a nano, flaring at the edges, before returning to normal and HARV's movements resumed exactly where they left off. The tingle returned to my temple. HARV looked disoriented for the briefest of nanos but regained his bearings quickly.

"I'm sorry, Dr. Pool, what were you saying?"

Randy, for his part, never missed a beat.

"I said, HARA, that this is an interesting and remarkable development on your part. I look forward to your reports from the field."

"Thank you, Dr. Pool," HARV replied. Then he turned to me. "See Zach. This is going to be fun."

"HARA," I replied, "Fun is not the word."

7

HARV—I mean HARA—offered to make the morning coffee while I took a shower. She made a big show of walking into the kitchen, giving me an opportunity to check out her new sashay, which I later learned was modeled after Betty Grable's. I tried very hard not to look (for too long), then hurried into the shower and set it for cold.

And in yet another example of those patented (literally—by HARV) Zach Johnson hard-luck coincidences, I was in the shower for two minutes when Electra, after having waited patiently for ten minutes for me to call back, took matters into her own hands and called me instead.

HARA answered the call and put Electra on the bath-room monitor (it doubles as a shaving mirror) just as I was stepping out. So when Electra's concerned face came on the screen she saw me, naked save for a towel, (looking surprised and more than a little guilty) with HARA standing behind me.

"This isn't what it looks like," I said.

"That's good," she said, as her scowl began to deepen, "because it looks like a man with a death wish."

"You see, I had a rough night."

"I can tell," she said, eyeing HARA (who was admiring herself using the wall screen as a makeshift mirror). "But I'm warning you that the phrase 'rough night' is going to take on a whole new meaning for you when I get back."

"I can explain, *mi amor*."

"Tell you what, Chico. In deference to our many years together, I'm going to work with you on this and let you choose which of your arms I'm going to break."

"I'm glad to see that you're keeping this all in perspective," I said. "Look, here's the quick recap to bring you up to speed. I was attacked last night. Kabuki droids, which is a first, even for me. It was part of a new reality series in which I'm starring, but which I didn't know about. I don't want to do the show, so I'm being sued by a restaurant owner, which means I need money, which is why I just accepted an assignment from Sexy Sprockets, whom I saved last night by the way, although I just learned that she wasn't really in danger since the bots were programmed to attack only me. She doesn't know that though, so she wants to hire me, although at the nano, I thought that she just wanted to date me."

"You're not helping yourself, Chico."

"However, I spurned her advances. Not the employment ones, just the romantic ones."

"Which didn't exist."

"That's technically true, but I should still get credit for spurning them even if they were all in my head. And, oh, by the way, HARV's a woman now."

"So the *puta* behind you is HARV?" Electra asked, staring past me at HARA, who was adjusting her holographic skirt.

"Actually, he prefers to be called HARA now," I said, waving my hand through HARA's midsection to show that she was a hologram.

"Which explains why she's in the bathroom with you while you're naked?"

"Um, not really, no," I said. "But I think you can understand how little actual control I have over my life at present."

"You're really scraping the bottom of the excuse barrel with this one."

"I freely admit that that is the most preposterous excuse possible for having a redheaded bombshell in my bathroom."

"It's beyond preposterous."

"And I admit that I am an exceptionally skilled liar."

"You got that right, Chico."

"Okay, so here's where it all comes together," I said, straightening my towel. "In such an awkward, and potentially life-threatening, position, would a consummate liar such as myself come up with such a lame excuse?"

"Que?"

"Come on, honey. I'm risking grievous bodily harm here. With all that's on the line, do you really think the lie I would come up with is 'oh, by the way, HARV's a woman now' if it weren't true? I mean there are a million better ways to explain this."

"Name one."

"She's a holographic advertisement that came with my new cologne."

"Name another."

"She's part of the new pick-up service offered by my dry cleaner. She's an android assassin trying to take me by surprise. She's a virus that I accidentally downloaded onto the house computer while viewing porn."

"None of those excuses would help you, you know."

"But they're all more plausible than HARV becoming a woman."

"You really expect me to believe that's HARV?"

"Electra, *mi amor*, I know this looks bad, but you have to believe me when I say that you're the one I'm in love with."

"Gates, Zach," HARA sighed loudly, "can't you grasp even the rudiments of proper grammar?"

"What was that?" I asked smugly.

"It's 'the one with whom I'm in love.' I've told you a million times that you can't end a sentence with a preposition. Forget my new look. Dr. Gevada should break up with you based on your grammar alone." She threw her hands in the air and stormed out of the bathroom. "Honestly, I'm in the employ of a subliterate."

Electra watched her go and then gently smiled.

"Yep, that's HARV," she said.

"And you doubted me."

"You know, he's got a nice walk."

"I'm trying not to notice."

"I still don't like this," she said, "on many, many levels."

"You and me both," I replied, "but I'm stuck with it for the nano. Can we talk about it when you get home?"

"Count on it, Chico."

She terminated the call and the screen went back to mirror mode. I spent the next few nanos staring at my tired-looking face in the mirror and wondering what other unwanted surprises the day held for me.

8

While I finished my morning routine, HARA arranged a meeting with Sexy Sprockets to discuss the new assignment, which I now *had* to take. Sexy wanted to get things moving very quickly, so an hour later, HARA and I hit the streets on the way to the meet and greet. We had some time to spare so we left the hover behind and took the twen-cen '69 Mustang. I have a thing for twentieth-century cars, only part of which is that they're not computerized. They're also good for the image. There are times when a PI needs to be subtle. That's when I use the non-descript hover. But I decided to go with a higher profile on this case, figuring that there'd be less trouble if people knew I was guarding Sexy. I'm not really sure why I thought that, given my history but I try to stay optimistic. Besides, after free falling the night before, I was hoping to spend as much time as I could safely on terra firma. So I gratefully maneuvered my eight cylinder calling card through the streets while HARA sat in the passenger seat, painting her nails.

"You see," she said without looking up from her work, "my experiment is already bearing fruit for thought. Dr. Gevada has seen me in the bathroom with you innumerable times in the past, yet this is the first time she has reacted in such a jealous manner."

"Congratulations. You've conclusively proven that Electra has a temper. Feel free to change back to your normal self at any time."

"Don't be silly," HARA responded. "I haven't even scratched the surface yet. There's a whole world out here to explore. The reactions you get as a woman are vastly different from those you get as a man."

"Terrific. But is it possible to do some actual PI work now or are you too busy scratching your surface?"

"Don't be such a pentium, Zach," HARA said, holding her nails up to the light. "What do you need?"

"Let's start with information on Sexy Sprockets."

"Fine, what do you want to know?"

"What she's currently doing for one. I don't really follow her."

"Well, she's currently on the last leg of her farewell tour."

"Her what?"

"Her year-long farewell tour. She's retiring from the business."

"She's like eighteen!"

"She's twenty, Zach, which means that she's no longer a teen sensation."

"So she's retiring?"

"Retiring is a very relative term," HARA replied. "This is informally being referred to as her first farewell tour. Common theory is that it's a prelude to her triumphant comeback tour."

"When will that be?"

"Probably when she's twenty-one. She'll be able to do alcohol commercials then. It's a whole new demographic. Still, from what I can tell there are many people who aren't too happy about her retiring."

"Such as?"

"Legions of teenage fans, tabloid reporters, and lecherous middle-aged men."

"Interesting, but none of that explains why she'd want to hire me as a bodyguard."

"I think we've safely ruled out naïve schoolgirl crush as her motive."

"Funny. Check the police records. See if anyone connected to her has reported anything out of the ordinary recently. See if you can check her finances and those of her companies as well. Let's make sure we know as much as we can going into this."

"Got it. You don't want any surprises."

"Trust me, there will be surprises," I said. "I just want to minimize them. And net with Carol at the office. Tell her we're swinging by to pick her up."

"You're bringing Carol to the meeting?"

"I have a feeling I'm going to need a translator when I meet Sexy's people."

"I thought you didn't approve of Carol doing fieldwork."

"That was before I found out she cavorted with aliens aboard interstellar spacecraft," I said. "That kind of changed our dynamic a bit. Like I said, I have a feeling that I'm going to need all the help I can get on this one."

"Don't be such a worm in the data, Zach. If you can't babysit a pop star for a couple of days then I'm not sure I want to be the Laura Holt to your Remington Steele."

"You're not my Laura Holt."

"All right then, Pussy Galore."

"Yeah, well, *kafloogle*," I said softly to myself.

"What was that?"

"Nothing."

"I'm telling you, Zach," HARA said, putting her holographic arm around me, "this is going to be as easy as calculating pi to the hundredth digit."

"You know, you always say that just before people start trying to kill me."

9

For her stay in New Frisco, Sexy commandeered the top five floors of the Paysans D'Elite Hotel downtown, which wasn't surprising. The Elite has been the city's premier lodging place for A-list recording artists since it opened last year. Nearly all stage performers as well as most actors and actresses visiting the area have commandeered one or more floors when they visited the city. One reason for the hotel's allure is that it's posh beyond belief in both décor and amenities. The other, more important, reason is that staying anywhere else would be a felony.

It's no secret that the antics of recording stars (and celebrities in general) are outside the realm of normal behavior. The industry breeds a certain lifestyle. The lifestyle breeds excess. Excess breeds erratic behavior and erratic behavior, when it comes to hotels, restaurants and other hospitality-oriented businesses, breeds rampant, wanton vandalism.

For over a century, hotels around the world have been subjected to the outlandish and often destructive behavior of celebrities. Smashed windows, broken furniture, destroyed walls, fish battered groupies, etc., etc.

The publicity a hotel received from a celebrity's stay soon became minimized when compared to the cost of repairs, lost business, rising insurance rates, and the occasional grievous bodily injury or loss of life of non-celebrity bystanders and passersby. So five years ago the province of California passed the Celebrity Temporary Housing Bill, which mandates that all celebrities of a certain stature stay only in government-operated hotels specially designed to withstand their eccentric, bizarre and/or eldritch behaviors.

The Elite is the first of these specially designed celebrity-proof hotels. The furniture, appliances, and the building itself are all fireproof, bulletproof, and stain guarded. Several of the more expensive suites are equipped with regenerative furnishings so that when a celebrity in an alcohol-, drug-, or tantrum-related rage destroys the room, it can rebuild itself after the celebrity passes out. Room rates are exceptionally high but celebrity doctors and accountants have begun claiming that the hotel provides an excellent venue for rage therapy so the cost of extended stays has become tax deductible.

Carol, HARA, and I arrived at the hotel in plenty of time for the meeting and after the extensive security check and screening process, were quickly shown to the private elevator.

Carol, by the way, is my niece. She's actually Electra's niece, but she treats me like an uncle. She works for me part time at my office to help work her way through college. She's very smart, very feisty, very attractive, and very psionically powerful. Yes, Carol is one of that infinitesimally small minority of women who are born with psionic abilities. She can move things with her mind and read thoughts. She can also write as well as read thoughts, which makes her very influential at times. Officially she has Class 1, Level 6 power. That's a government rating, by the way. Class signifies power (lower is better). Level signifies potential (higher is better). I have no idea why the people who designed the classifications made them so confusing other than because they were doing it for the government. In any event, to sum up Carol: smart, beautiful, sassy, and powerful. She's also young and hip, which is specifically why I brought her along to the meeting.

"Okay," I said, as the high speed elevator moved us quickly toward the first of Sexy's floors, "we're going to need a trouble signal."

"Tio, I'm a psi. Just think something to me and I'll get the message."

"I still want an emergency backup plan. Something physical. Humor me. I've been in this business a long time."

"Fine," Carol sighed. "How about touching your nose and nodding your head if there's trouble?"

"That won't work," I said. "I touch my nose by accident all the time."

"He has eczema," HARA whispered.

"I do not," I said. "It's just a nervous habit. All the great PI's had one. That's mine. Now, if there's trouble I'll blink my right eye three times fast. Clear?"

"You don't think people will notice you spasmodically blinking one eye?" Carol asked.

"That's the code, okay? Three blinks of the right eye means trouble. And just for the record, four blinks means please shoot me in the head."

"You're the boss, Tio."

Carol looked at me as though I were crazy. But I get that look a lot so I've pretty much gotten used to it. Two nanos later, the elevator doors opened and we stepped into the hallway.

The hallway was lavishly appointed with marble walls and columns and intricately woven oriental rugs and tapestries on the floor and walls.

"Not what I'd expect for a pop star," I said as we made our way down the hallway.

Then a man appeared from a doorway ahead of us and approached. "Mr. Johnson, how wonderful you could come on such short notice."

He was taller than me by half a head but thinner than me by at least ten kilos. He was gangly in the extremities but moved gracefully, like a mantis. He was dressed in a pink-striped suit with a purple tie and matching purple socks and looked for all the world like a clown going to a prom.

"Now this is more like what I was expecting," I whispered.

"I didn't know the circus was in town," HARA snickered inside my head.

Carol giggled.

Then the man drew near us, held out his hand, and smiled a smile that amazingly made his wardrobe seem tame by comparison.

"I'm Sexy's manager," he said, "Sammy Smiles."

The man had more teeth than I'd ever seen in a human mouth. There were sixty at least and his mouth was somehow large enough to contain them all. When he smiled, his lips spread apart like the curtains on a stage, opening farther than you'd think possible and his cheeks moved upward and out as though they were on pulleys attached to his ears. It was all I could do not to stare as I shook his hand.

Carol, on the other hand, being somewhat new to this, was a little taken aback.

Smiles noticed her staring at him but he didn't seem to mind. "And who, may I ask is the lovely creature?" he asked, reaching for her hand.

"This is Carol," I said. "She's my assistant."

"Charmed," he said, his smile curling ever so slightly at the corners.

He gently took her hand and kissed it.

"The pleasure's mine," she said, trying to regain her composure.

Smiles nodded, offered her his arm (which Carol reluctantly took), and motioned toward the great metallic doorway at the hallway's end.

"Come," he said. "Sexy is waiting."

The huge metallic doors opened at Smiles' gentle touch and we entered Sexy's suite. The words huge and posh, although technically correct, would not do the space justice.

"Wow," Carol said her eyes widening.

"I agree," Smiles smiled.

The suite went on for as far as I could see. I was pretty certain that it was mostly a holographic illusion, but it was still pretty impressive nonetheless.

"Sexy is in the entertainment area. I wished she'd practice more. But she just loves her video games."

We followed Smiles through the suite and after about five minutes of walking (like I said, big suite) we found Sexy sitting atop a round plush levitating couch. She was wearing virtual game gloves and moving her hands frantically as little holographic geometrical shapes danced from the ceiling to the floor.

Three other girls sat with her on the couch. They looked, for lack of a better description, like Sexy's slightly less sexy clones. Each of them had long red hair, slim athletic bodies, and expressions of slight boredom and disdain.

"That's strange," HARA said inside of my head.

"Strange only microscopically scratches the surface here," I whispered.

"Some of your hormone levels shot up."

"Newsflash."

"Not *those* hormones," she said. "The ones that stimulate the feelings of euphoria in the brain."

"Like I'm being drugged?"

"In a way," HARA said. "I'm counteracting the effects though."

"Yeah, we wouldn't want me feeling any euphoria."

Sexy spotted me from her perch on the couch.

"Zach!" she said.

She rolled off the couch and landed on her feet with far more grace than I expected. She removed her virtual game gloves and gave me a hug and a little peck on the cheek.

"Thanks for coming to my rescue," she bubbled.

"It's what I do." I said (and heard HARA silently gag in my head). "This is my assistant, Carol."

Sexy gave Carol little wink. "Pleased to meet you, double-xette," she said, holding out her hand, pinky finger up.

"Shay-Rico," Carol replied, linking her thumb around Sexy's pinky finger.

"Wild guess," I mentally whispered to HARA, "Slang?"

"Brilliant deduction," HARA replied.

"So," Sexy said, turning back to me, "where should we start?"

"Let's start with why you need a bodyguard."

"That's a long story. I'll give you the full data-flow in my thinking room."

"Thinking room?"

"It's where I think about business."

"You mean like an office?"

Sexy smiled. "That's what I love about you, Zach. You are so old school."

"Please," Carol said, "he's more like prehistoric school." The girls laughed.

"Have you been coaching Carol?" I whispered to HARA.

Sexy's thinking room turned out to be a large, pink-walled tatami room in the far end of the suite. There were silk pillows on the floor and a dark wood knee-high table beside a large window with a stunning view of the New

Frisco bay. Sexy ushered Carol and me inside and then turned to meet Smiles who was trailing behind us.

"Sammy," she said, "why don't you make us some of your righteous next-energy drinks?"

Smiles took a step back, a little surprised. If Sexy noticed she didn't let on.

"Sammy makes the best energy drinks on the planet," she bubbled to Carol. "You have to try one. What about you, Zach?"

"I'm good, thanks."

"Sure thing," Smiles said. "I'll be back in a nano."

"Take your time," Sexy replied.

Smiles cast her a glance then put his happy face back on and eased his way out of the room. Sexy closed the door behind him and took a seat on one of the pillows.

"I get a thinking room like this at every hotel I stay in. The walls have to be a specific thickness, soundproof, and this exact shade of pink. I bring the furniture. I like the room sparse, so nothing distracts me when I'm thinking."

"Cool," Carol said, with a bit more excitement in her voice than I was used to hearing. "I need a room like this."

"Everybody does!" Sexy insisted.

Carol plopped down on the pillow beside Sexy while I eased my way down to the floor on the other side of the table.

"Hmm, this is odd," HARA said inside my head. "The ambient radiation in this room is rather high."

"That doesn't sound good," I mentally whispered back.

"Ambient radiation is usually harmless," HARA replied. "It's used by a lot of trendy places these days as a mood setter. I'll explain it to you later. For now don't worry."

For the record, the words "don't worry" coming from a supercomputer are never comforting for me.

"So," Sexy said, putting her hands gently on the table, "here's the deal. I need a bodyguard."

"You don't have one already?" I asked.

"I have several, but I need you."

"Why me specifically?"

"Look, Zach, I know that you're not the youngest guy out there, or the strongest or the best looking. And you don't have the best credentials. And Gates knows you're not hip with my crowd, and . . ."

"I get the point, Sexy."

"But you know how to get the job done. And that's what I need, especially now."

"Why now? What's going on?"

She paused for the briefest of nanos and turned her gaze to the floor.

"I've been getting threats," she whispered.

"What kind of threats?"

"Death threats, from an organization called PATA."

"PATA?"

"People Against Talentless Acts," she said. "They're not my biggest fans."

It was hard not to laugh but Carol and I somehow managed it.

"They're threatening to do whatever they need to in order to prevent me from finishing my tour."

"But it's your farewell tour," I said. "If they hate you so much, shouldn't they be happy?"

"It's my first farewell tour. They're expecting me to make a comeback."

"And are you planning on making a comeback?"

"Not in music," she replied. "But when I turn twenty-one, I plan to run for governor."

Suppression of laughter was not an option this time. Both Carol and I erupted into a quick succession of guffaws. It felt good to laugh again. Then we noticed that Sexy wasn't laughing with us (and that sort of killed the mood).

"Sorry. We, um, thought you were joking."

"Yeah, I'm expecting that kind of reaction from a certain percentage of voters. But the point is that PATA wants me dead and I need you to keep me alive."

"Certainly your recording company has protection for you," Carol said.

"Honestly, girlfriend, I don't fully trust my company."

"Why's that?" I asked.

"They're not all that wild about me quitting the business. No new music, no annual tours, that's a lot of wealth they're losing."

"But they'd still want to protect you," Carol said. "They wouldn't want anything bad to happen to you. Would they?"

"Spite is a very strong motivator in the entertainment industry," Sexy replied.

"Second only to greed and lust," I added.

"And let's just say that if I were to die tragically, sales of my catalog would skyrocket."

"And you're probably insured," said Carol.

"And can you imagine the sales of a live album that ends with me being killed on stage?"

"Wow, that's morbid."

"But the sales would be astronomical. The bottom line is that the only person who would truly suffer, if I were to die tragically, would be me."

"So you don't fully trust the company to keep you safe."

"Just because I'm sexy doesn't mean I'm stupid."

I had to admit she had a point.

"So will you help me, Zach?"

She looked at me with doe eyes and fully pouted lips. A thin strand of red hair dangled down her cheek like a silken red tear and I felt my blood begin to warm with excitement and dread. Sure, I needed the money, but I knew that this was going to be nothing but fuel-injected, turbo-driven trouble. It would be tough enough babysitting a pop star but trying to keep her safe from a potential assassin on top of that? Any sane man would have run screaming from the room at the thought. But, as I've said, I'm not considered the sanest person around town.

"Let's start from the first threat," I said.

She smiled, gently wiped the corner of one eye with her fingertip, and touched the tabletop. The surface lit up at her touch, the faux wood turning into a luminescent computer screen. She touched the screen again and a simple message appeared. It was handwritten in shaky and sometimes jagged script:

YOUR FAREWELL WILL BE FOREVER. NO COMEBACK FOR YOU, SEXY
—PATA (PEOPLE AGAINST TALENTLESS ACTS)

"This was sent to my personal computer last week."

"It's harsh," I said, "but surely you've gotten hate mail before."

Sexy nodded and touched the screen again. A second message appeared.

YOUR FIFTEEN NANOS ARE OVER, SEXY. THE END IS NEAR.
—PATA

"This one was scrawled on a disposable screen and staked to my pillow with an ice pick."

"Yeah, that's a little more serious."

She touched the screen again and a third message appeared in writing more jagged than before.

DEATH IS IN THIS SEASON. DEATH IS SEXY!
—PATA

"This one was scrawled in blood on the wall of my bedroom."

"I can see why you're so concerned."

She touched the screen again and one more message appeared, in writing so manic that it was hard to read. The intent though, was crystal clear.

DIE SEXY.
DIE,
DIE,
DIE,
DIE,
DIE!
—PATA

"This one was carved into the severed, bleached skull of my Pomeranian and left for me on my bathroom vanity while I was taking a shower."

I sat back and rubbed my temples, hoping to ward off the inevitable headache.

"Remember how I said this was going to be easy?" HARA whispered in my head. "I think I may have miscalculated, just a bit."

10

We left the thinking room and headed back into the entertainment area. We met Smiles in the hallway, who gave Sexy and Carol their energy drinks.

"This is fabulous," Carol said with a smile.

"So what do you think, Zach?" Sexy asked.

"Well, I'll have my computer do some research on PATA and analyze the notes for anything that can help us. I'll check with the police to see what they've found so far."

"The police don't know about any of this," Smiles said.

"What?"

"We haven't reported the threats."

"Why not?"

"We can't afford the negative publicity," Smiles said. "This tour has been all about positive energy."

"Well, you're calling the police now," I said.

"If we call the police then the story will be in the press five nanos later," Smiles said.

"If you don't call the police, I'll be off the case quicker than that!"

"It's bad publicity."

"Not as bad as Sexy being killed."

"That's not going to happen!"

I turned away from Smiles and spoke directly to Sexy, who had been watching us banter like a front row fan at a tennis match.

"I have contacts at the department. They'll keep it quiet."

"You can't keep something like this quiet, Sexy," Smiles

said. "Word will get out. And when it does then the focus of the tour shifts away from you and on to PATA."

"You wanted my help, Sexy," I said. "Take it."

Sexy thought for a nano and then nodded.

"Contact the police," she said.

Smiles rolled his eyes.

"And you should probably lay low for a while to give me some time to check out your security systems," I added.

"That won't be possible, Zach. I've got a concert in about five hours."

"What?"

"I'm on tour, Zach. Remember? Tonight's the first of five shows at The Fart."

"I suppose canceling the shows is out of the question, huh?"

Sexy didn't even dignify the question with an answer. She simply flashed me a smile and gave me a hug.

"I have to do my prep for the show," she said. "Sammy will give you the rest of the necessary data-flow."

"I'd like Carol to stay with you, if that's all right," I said. "I'm going to speak with the police and check some things out. Don't leave the hotel until I get back."

"No problem," Sexy said, flashing Carol a smile. "Right, Sammy?"

"Anything you say, Sexy," Sammy smiled.

"Carol, you contact me if anything happens that I should know about."

"Of course, Tio."

"Okay, I'll see you in a few hours."

The two turned and sauntered away, chatting like old girlfriends.

"So what's the deal with Carol?" Smiles asked. "Is she in show biz?"

"Thank Gates, no," I replied. "No offense."

"Too bad," he said as he turned and led me back through the suite. "She has potential."

"I should meet with Sexy's other bodyguards," I said as we entered the entertainment room. "We'll need to coordinate efforts quickly."

"No problem there," Smiles replied.

He turned his gaze upward to the three girls that I'd seen

when I arrived. They were still sitting on the floating couch, playing video games and listening to Sexy's music.

"Ladies," Smiles called. "There's someone here you need to meet."

The three girls rose and leaped off the couch, somersaulting to the ground, each of them making a perfect, catlike landing.

"Zach, I'd like you to meet Misty, Sissy, and Lusty, Sexy's bodyguards."

Each of the girls bowed very theatrically on cue.

"Bodyguard isn't by chance music industry slang for backup dancer is it?" I asked.

"No." Sammy chuckled, "but, you know, it should be. Ladies, this is Zach Johnson. Sexy's new bodyguard."

"Nice to meet you ladies. I'm not replacing you," I said. "Just helping out due to the PATA threats. We'll be working together. I just want to make certain that everyone's cool with that."

One of the girls, I think it was Misty, but it doesn't really matter, approached me with her hand extended.

"Pleased to meet you, sir." The tone of her voice was businesslike and polite (though I wasn't crazy about being called sir).

"Call me, Zach," I said, extending my hand in return.

She moved quickly, almost faster than I could see, grabbing my arm at the wrist, twisting it sharply to give me a jolt of pain. Then she moved in close, slipped her arm under my shoulder and flipped me onto the floor. I was lying on my back almost before I knew what hit me.

"Bodyguard is slang for b-slapper," Misty said, with her foot on my chest. "And nobody tells us what to do."

"We thought it would be more practical and economical to have multifunctional backup dancer-slash-bodyguards for Sexy," Smiles said. "We have plenty of bots around during events. But we always keep the gal-pride around."

"And we're the best," Misty added.

"Too bad you weren't around last night when Sexy was in trouble," I said.

"We were lying low 'cause Miss Sexy was incognito.

"Lying low while someone else saves your employer? If that's the best you can do then I'm not impressed."

I grabbed her leg behind the knee and pushed her over the top of my body. I grabbed her wrist as she stumbled and twisted her arm behind her back (until I knew it was just slightly more painful than what she'd given me) and pinned her face down on the floor with my knee.

"Impressive," HARA said. "Of course I did increase blood flow to your bones and muscles to help you pull off that move. And the other two are moving in behind you now, and I don't think they're admiring your butt."

I turned as the first one (Lusty, I think) jumped at me, coming feet first with a flying kick. I rolled to the ground and let her sail over me. She landed on Misty as I continued my roll and leg swept Sissy (I think) who was just starting to move. I took her feet out from under her and popped my gun into hand just in time to stick the snub-nosed business end of it into the faces of the charging Misty and Lusty. It stopped their charge like a pause button on a playback.

"I don't care if you're the best, the guest or the rest," I growled. "I'm here to keep Sexy alive and I don't have time to waste with this posturing and pouting. You can either help me out or get out of the way but the next time we fight like this, my gun barrel does the talking. Got it?"

The girls started to laugh. Smiles started to applaud.

"Wow!" Smiles said. "Sexy told us you were hardcore. But, Zach, that was downright ub-zeen!"

"Obscene?"

"Slang for exceptional," HARA whispered.

I popped my gun back into my sleeve and took my knee off Sissy's back. Misty and Lusty had backed away, and were now relaxed, and smiling.

"What the DOS is with you people?"

"The girls were just trying to prove themselves to you," Smiles said. "And maybe have you prove yourself a little to them."

"We love Sexy, Mr. Johnson," Misty said. "We're here to protect her."

I straightened my tie and tried to rein in my temper.

"I'm here to protect her too," I said. "But if we're going to work together, you have to promise me you won't pull any DOS like this again. Agreed?"

"Yes," Misty said.

"Absolutely," Sissy said.

Lusty nodded.

"Good. Because we really don't have time for this. And Gates knows that I don't have the patience. Now grow up."

"Wow," Misty said, "you sound like my father."

"Good," I replied, "then you're grounded too. And pull up your pants a little. You're going to catch cold."

That one didn't go over too well.

11

I left the hotel in the afternoon. HARA activated her holo-gram in the hotel parking lot and walked with me as I made my way to the car.

"You know, big guy, being a bodyguard usually implies that you actually stay with the body you're supposed to be guarding."

"Sexy is perfectly safe inside the hotel," I said. "You saw the security system. And Carol's there."

"True."

"Besides I'm a PI first and foremost. If I can find PATA quickly, I can turn them over to the police before they make their move. That way we can get out of babysitting duty entirely."

"Okay, I won't argue you with you on that one," HARA said. "You want me to do the legwork."

"Right. Scan all databases and files for any information on PATA."

"Way ahead of you. There's nothing in the public files but I'll try phishing some of the more secure databases and see if anything turns up. I may have to grease a few palms though."

"Sexy's paying the bills. Just try to get a receipt for the bribes."

"You're a laugh riot, handsome," she said. "I'll let you know when something interesting comes up."

"Great. And can you net me with Tony, I . . . Did you just call me handsome?"

"It's a figure of speech, you lunkhead. Don't let it go to your head."

"You're creeping me out, here HARV."

"It's HARA, handsome."

"Stop it."

"You know you're kind of cute when you get angry."

I waved her away. "Don't get me started!"

"Okay, but I think you better hit the deck now," she said.

"What?"

She put her manicured hands on my shoulders and pushed me to the pavement just as a massive laser blast sailed over my head. The heat of the blast singed the hair on the nape of my neck as it passed over and hit one of parked hovercrafts nearby, incinerating it in a thunderous fireball.

"Did you just push me?" I asked, as I crawled quickly across the parking lot surface, seeking cover beneath the crafts.

"I have limited tactile abilities now," HARA responded, her hologram crawling beside me. "That was Dr. Pool's upgrade earlier this afternoon."

"You can be solid?"

"Only parts of me and only for short periods of time."

"Wow."

"You're sort of missing the big picture here, Zach."

I popped my gun into hand and peered out from behind the rear end of a parked hover limo.

"Tap into the security cams and let me know what I'm up against here. But first net with Carol and tell her to make sure Sexy gets to a secure location."

"I don't think we have to worry about Sexy or anyone else being in danger here."

"What do you mean?"

"Take a look."

HARA pointed toward the airspace just above me. Sure enough a handful of familiar looking small spherical camera bots floated around us.

"Roundtree."

"That's a fair assumption," HARA said. "It looks like they've begun work on episode number two; Zach Johnson versus a quartet of level five battlebots."

"Battlebots in a parking lot. That's first class entertainment, all right."

"Maybe the Kabuki episode tested a little too highbrow

for them," HARA said. "You're lucky they're not using monster trucks and supermodels now. By the way, you better run. Northeast would be wisest."

I sprang to my feet while simultaneously keeping my head down (which isn't easy) and ran for the northeast end of the parking lot just as the second battlebot let loose a blast from its cannon. The blast hit the limo and blew it to smithereens.

"Head for the barrier," HARA shouted

I did as I was told and hightailed it toward the waist-high hard plastic barrier encircling the border of the parking area. I could see all four bots now as I scanned the lot. There were two on the south end and two on the west with both pairs closing in, trying, I suspected, to pin me against the hotel on the east side of the lot. I fired a series of high powered blasts from my gun as I ran but they bounced off the bots' shells, doing no damage at all.

"This is not good," I said, diving behind the barrier.

"They have blaster resistant outer shells," HARA said. "Your gun's not going to be much use."

"We have to get them away from the hotel before someone inside gets hurt."

"You mean like your client?" HARA asked. "Funny that the only times she's been in actual danger lately is because of you, isn't it?"

"Hilarious," I said. "Now why do these bots look so familiar to me?"

"Probably because you saw the prototype at Dr. Pool's lab," HARA replied.

"These are Randy's bots?"

"It appears as though his lab has the special effects contract for your series."

"Great," I said. "At least we're keeping this all in the family. Net Randy now and put him on the wrist com."

Randy's face appeared on the screen on my wrist com just as another blast from the approaching bots exploded a sports hover nearby.

"Yes, Zach. How can I help you? Oh, I see the battlebots have arrived. How are they performing?"

"Oh, pretty darn well if you're trying to kill me," I said.

"Good. Don't destroy them too quickly," he said. "I don't want people to think that they're easy to beat."

"No problems there, Randy, my gun isn't working against them."

"Are you using the bot-buster ordnance?"

"The what?"

"The bot-buster ordnance that I designed for your gun. I sent you a memo about this last month."

"Randy, I don't read your memos."

"You don't?"

"They're all like twenty pages long. I don't have time to read the specs on every new gadget that you create."

"I'm guessing that you're regretting that now, huh?"

"Randy!"

"That's specifically why I gave Faux these bots for this episode. I knew you'd be able to beat them with the special ordnance."

"Well, you should have told me that."

"I signed a confidentiality agreement, Zach. It wouldn't be ethical."

"Randy, your ethics are about to get me killed."

"Wow," Randy replied. "Talk about your moral dilemmas."

I poked my head above the barrier and saw the bots approaching. They had to weave their way to me, moving in and out of the rows of parked hovers. I saw the cannon of one glow red as it moved. HARA followed my gaze and confirmed my suspicion.

"It's powering up for another blast," she said.

"Good. Help me with my aim," I said. "Big bang, tight."

The gun's OLED flashed in recognition of my voice command and I pulled the trigger and sent a very tight blast of energy at the bot's cannon. My blast hit the mouth of the cannon just as the bot fired and the two blasts exploded in unison, rupturing the bot from within.

"One down," I said, diving back behind the barrier. "Get ready to move, HARA. They're getting a little close for comfort."

"Ready when you are, big guy."

"Now!"

I leaped over the barrier and made a charge through the lot, heading west, where there was now only one approaching bot. Even with one bot destroyed, I still wasn't all that optimistic about my chances.

"By the way, Zach," HARA said, her hologram running beside me (in high heels), "you're going to love me for this."

"Now's not really the time, HARA," I said.

"I know that you don't really encourage me to act independently and all. But I sometimes ignore you when it comes to that."

"That's an understatement. Is there a point here?"

I glanced over at the remaining bots, which had altered their paths and were now weaving through the parked hovers toward us. I could tell at least two were charging their cannons.

"The point is that I read Dr. Pool's memos. They're actually quite interesting."

"Good for you."

"And I found the bot-buster memo to be particularly cogent and well-constructed."

"So?"

"So I took it upon myself and loaded the ordnance."

"You what?"

"You're locked and loaded, big guy. Go save the day."

"HARA, you're a dream."

"The voice command is biggy-biggy-bot-boom."

"That's a pretty wimpy sounding command."

"I wouldn't complain if I were you," she said with a smile.

"Biggy-biggy-bot-boom!" I said, still weaving between hovers.

The OLED flashed again and I let a blast loose at the nearest attacker. The recoil from the blast nearly knocked me over but it did its job on the other end, cleanly piercing the battlebot's shell and blowing it to bits. I spun around and fired off two more rounds, falling back to the ground as I did so. Two more bot-shaped fireballs lit up the lot and showered the expensive hovers with high-tech drek. After that it was eerily quiet in the parking lot save for the cacophony of hovercraft alarms that the firefight had set off.

"Something tells me that I won't have any problem meeting my car insurance deductible this year," I said.

12

I reached my office on the New Frisco docks with no other major entertainment-related incidents (although Rupert Roundtree called me on the way over to rave about my performance in episode two of the series, referring to it as bombastical). I called him an idiot and a fraud but he took it as a compliment and then excused himself so he could attend a focus group of white trash Americans (he didn't say if he was running it or one of the participants). Other than that, the trip was uneventful.

My office is an oasis in the desert of late twenty-first century technology-centric chaos. It's a throwback to an earlier time (as am I), a technologically simpler time when everything wasn't wirelessly connected to everything else; when machines weren't connected to one another and, more importantly, when machines weren't connected to people.

It's a place where I can sit in my simulated leather chair, prop my legs up on my real wood desk, put my arms behind my head, and let my mind do its thing. It's also a place where bill collectors, unsatisfied clients, angry pressbots, assassins, and enemies of the state can easily find me, but every oasis has its drawbacks.

First order of business was to reestablish contact with Tony Rickey.

"What do you want now, Zach?" he said.

"Tony, I'm hurt that you think I only call you when I want something from you."

"That's right. You only call me when there's a warrant out for your arrest."

"Well played, Captain."

"Do you know that the department has a listserver called Guess-What-Zach-Did-Now?" he said.

"Really? Is it accurate?"

"Most of it's way off. Third-hand stuff. I try to post the real stuff but I keep getting kicked off because no one believes it. You know, like last night's Kabuki fiasco."

"Oh, please," I said. "Last night was nothing. I've had more people try to kill me at a softball game."

"That's what happens when you pitch spitballs to a Police Athletic League team."

"It was sweat, Tony. I have no control over my pores."

"I didn't know the mouth was considered a pore," Tony said with a smile. "What can I do for you?"

"Do you know anything about a group called PATA?"

"Not off the top of my head." He turned away and typed into his computer keyboard. "They don't show up in any of the databases. I'm afraid to ask this, but why are you interested?"

"They've threatened to kill Sexy Sprockets."

"Have the threats been reported?"

"They will be. You should be getting the call any time now," I said. "I'll have HARA send over copies of the threats."

"HARA is HARV, right?"

"Sadly, yes. I've made it clear to Sexy and her people that they should cooperate with your department."

"Great. I'll send some men over. She's at the Elite?"

"Where else? What kind of security will you have at the concerts?"

"Her fans are more exuberant than most so we planned to have extra personnel and machines there, both uniform and plainclothes."

"Plainclothes machines?"

"They double as popcorn dispensers," he said (straight-faced). "So you're on Sexy's payroll now?"

"She's asked me to help her security."

"Zach Johnson, bodyguard."

"I've been called worse."

"You mean like reality star?"

"There is no show," I said. "It's just a misunderstanding."

"Whatever you say," he replied. "And HARV's still a woman?"

"She's called HARA now."

"She looks good for a computer. You'll have to tell me the whole story sometime."

"Yeah, let me know when you have a free month. Right now I'm just trying to keep Sexy alive."

"Like I said, Zach, I'm not going to let anything happen to her on my watch. Thanks for the info. I'll make sure everyone's on guard."

"Hopefully there won't be any trouble," I said.

Tony smiled. "Believe me, Zach, with you on the case, there'll be trouble."

"I appreciate the vote of confidence, Tony. Let me know if you turn up anything on PATA."

Tony smiled and his face disappeared from the screen just as HARA's hologram appeared back on my desk (legs crossed, skirt riding high).

"Wow, sharing information and cooperating with the police," she said. "Is this the start of a new Zach?"

"Don't worry, I'm sure my goodwill with the police department is only temporary. Any new information on PATA?"

"Nothing yet, but I'm still digging. You need anything else?"

"Run background checks on Sammy Smiles and Sexy's bodyguards. Saucy, scrappy, and scurvy."

"You mean Misty, Sissy, and Lusty."

"Whatever."

"Got it."

"When you say got it, do you mean that you understand the request or that you have the actual info?"

"Both, Zach," HARA said. "I'm very intelligent. Try to keep up. By the way, you have a message from Electra."

"Hate mail?"

"More like a shot across the bow," HARA replied, morphing into Electra's form, then mimicking her voice. "I'll be home tomorrow, Chico."

"That's it?" I asked

"That's it," HARA said, morphing back to her current form.

I shook my head. "She's mad at me. And for once it's not because of something I did or had any control over."

HARA smiled. "I think it's cute that she's jealous of us."

"She's not jealous of us!" I said. "There *is* no us. I'm me and you're the holographic interface of a supercomputer."

"There have been stranger couples," HARA said, smile widening.

"We're not a couple."

"We're partners."

"No, we're not."

"Would Electra have loaded your gun with bot-busters?"

"DOS, where's Rupert Roundtree when you need him?"

"Oh, I get it," HARA said, folding her arms over her chest. "I'm not good enough for you."

"What?"

"Sure I'm the world's most sophisticated cognitive processor, but you're Zachary Nixon Johnson private eye. Nobody's good enough for you, are they?"

I buried my head in my hands and thought nostalgically about how good my office used to feel.

"This is what hell feels like, isn't it?" I asked.

"Don't talk to me now," she said, waving her hand dismissively at me. "I'm mad at you. By the way, I have the info that you requested."

"I thought you were mad at me?"

"I am, but I'm also a professional. I am not going to let our personal relationship get in the way of our work relationship."

"I appreciate that," I said.

"As well you should," she said. "I've learned the initial death threats from PATA came in via an ultra-encrypted line. They're untraceable."

"That figures. So it's a dead end."

"A dead end that tells us much."

"How so?"

"A line that's encrypted to such a degree is ripping edge."

"So whoever sent the threats has access to some serious tech."

"Correct."

"Which means they're either rich, powerful, or both."

"You know, you're almost as smart as you think you are," she said rolling her eyes.

"Well, it's a start," I said, grabbing my hat.

"What now?" HARA asked.

"We've done all we can from here," I said. "We're not going to track PATA down today so it's time to start being an actual bodyguard."

"Which means?"

"It means we prepare for the worst and hope for the best."

"It also means backstage passes to Sexy's concert," HARA said, hopping off the desk.

"I'm not sure if that falls into the best or worst category," I said. "But let's stop at the store while we're out and pick up some earplugs just in case."

13

New Frisco's municipal arena is a wonderful entertainment and sports venue that's smack in the middle of the old Mission District. It's a fine facility with perhaps the most unfortunate name in the history of . . . names.

You see back when the arena was being built, the city auctioned off the naming rights and got several strong bids. The city planners, guided by their terminal myopia and fueled by their unquenchable greed, accepted *all* the bids and named the arena after the conglomeration of conglomerates that were willing to pony up the necessary credits. So officially the arena is called the Faux-ExShell-Relapse-HTech Center but one day some kid noticed the acronym (FERHT) and couldn't get his mind out of the gutter. His little joke spread (through the adolescent population first, then into the mainstream). Before we knew it, the joke just sort of entered the regional vernacular and, despite the city's best efforts to shake it, the nickname name stuck. So New Frisco's state of the art entertainment and sports arena is lovingly known the world over as "The Fart."

To my mind there's no better place on the west coast to see a concert or a game (basketball or hockey that is, the baseball and football stadiums moved to the suburbs years ago). The hot dogs are a little pricey, the beers extremely so, but the bolgoki and nachos are first rate. All in all, The Fart's not a bad place to spend an evening with fifty thousand of your closest Bay Area friends. Unless of course one of those fifty thousand is a hired assassin who's out to put an ice pick through your client's eye. Then it's sort of the needle and haystack dilemma on a grand and deadly scale.

I had a little trouble at first getting into The Fart. It was after all, three hours before the doors opened and I had no actual ticket to the concert. But a quick call to the facilities manager from Sammy Smiles opened the doors pretty quickly and got me an all-access pass. Before long, I was standing center stage in front of fifty thousand empty seats and trying hard not to get in the way of the roadies and techies as they prepped for the show. And I must say that the stage itself was something to behold.

"Being front and center like this certainly makes Sexy an easy target," HARA remarked, her hologram shimmering to life beside me (and garnering a number of looks from the workers).

"She's the main attraction, all right," I replied.

"And by the way, I never would have thought that one stage could hold this much red velvet and black satin."

"Yeah, what's with that?"

"It's part of the motif for the tour, I suppose."

"And what's that over there?"

"A guillotine and a sausage-making machine," HARA replied.

"What motif, exactly, are they shooting for?"

"Ménage abattoir."

"What?"

"That's the name of the tour. The Ménage Abattoir Tour."

"What does that mean?"

"I think it's a pun," HARA said. "Sexy thought it was . . . sexy."

"An abattoir is a slaughterhouse right?"

"Very good. My understanding is that she confused 'abattoir' with 'boudoir' but by the time anyone had the courage to tell her, the tickets had already gone on sale. Turns out it's very popular."

"Yeah, very cutting edge."

"So to speak."

I stepped over a saddle-covered rocking chair and walked the length of the stage, scanning the wings as I did so. The entire space made me worry. It was far too open, far too dangerous.

"The police will scan for weapons as the crowd arrives. And there are sensors in the arena that can pick up the energy signatures of any unauthorized weapons that are activated. But she sure is out in the open here. Maybe we can convince her to wear body armor."

"Please, Zach," HARA sighed, "it took a court order to convince Sexy to wear underwear on stage."

"I'm not surprised."

I ducked under a huge rack of leather whips and cured meat that was being lifted into place above stage and headed to the backstage area.

"Get a list of everyone on Sexy's crew that will be here tonight. Musicians, programmers, roadies, butchers, everyone. I want background checks run on all of them."

"You think that PATA could have someone inside Sexy's camp?"

"Let's not take any chances. We know next to nothing about PATA right now other than that they have access to high tech and that they've gotten very close to Sexy already."

"Got it," HARA said. "There are a lot of people on the payroll for this event. It will take some time to screen them all."

"Do what you can, just flag the odd ones for me."

"Odd is a very relative term when you're surrounded by satin sheets and pork by-products."

"I hate this," I mumbled.

"I know. Pork gives you gas."

"We're coming into this late in the game. We have no idea who we're up against. We have no control over the schedule or the venue. We're so far behind right now we can't even see the starting line."

"So what do we do?" HARA asked.

"For tonight, we have to narrow our focus," I replied. "We can't safeguard this entire space but the good news is that we don't have to. The only thing we have to guard is Sexy. So we stay close to her."

"Are you planning on going onstage with her?" HARA asked. "Because I should warn you, Zach, this crowd probably won't respond well to your Elvis impersonation."

"Trust me," I said. "With Sexy and her dancers onstage, no one's going to be looking at a forty-year-old guy in a trench coat. But just to be safe, you better make sure that your hologram projector is working. You never know when we might need to disappear."

Two hours before the show, HARA and I were back at the Elite scoping out the parking lot. The valets, I'm told, had spent the better part of the afternoon clearing the aftermath of my bot battle. They weren't too pleased to see me and I couldn't blame them. I'm sure that one doesn't get the best tip in the world when you have to bring a customer's car around in a giant plastic baggie.

While Sexy and her posse (Carol included) were inside the hotel, gathering themselves for the limo ride over to The Fart, I took it upon myself to have a chat with the limo driver.

Like I said earlier, Sexy's hover limo was sleek and really, really long. HARA brought up the phallic symbolism of the vehicle but it was way too late in the day to have that conversation. So I ignored her and tapped on the dark rose-tinted driver's window.

"I'm busy!" came the voice from within, a little high-pitched and squeaky.

"And I've got a gun," I replied.

The window slid down neatly and revealed a plump teenage kid in a black chauffeur's cap and uniform.

"You better really have a gun," he said. "I'll get in trouble if I fall for that line again."

"Trust me, kid. I've got one. What's your name?"

"Joey Matteo. But people call me Shreek. I'm Sexy's driver."

"Nice to meet you Shreek. I'm Zach Johnson. Sexy's new bodyguard."

"*The* Zach Johnson? Wow! You're not going to, like, blow up the limo are you?"

"Your reputation precedes you," HARA whispered.

"Listen, Shreek," I said, "I know you're a great wheelman but I've got a more important job for you for tonight."

"What's that?"

"Shotgun."

"What's shotgun?"

I opened the door and shoved him toward the passenger side of the front seat.

"Scoot over into the other seat and recline it just a touch so you're comfortable."

He did as he was told.

"Now what?"

"Now rest your right arm on the side so you look good. Feel free to hold a drink in your left. Shotgun's thirsty work."

"Got it."

"Your job for the night is to keep lookout while the limo is parked or while it's moving. Keep an eye out for anyone strange approaching. Understand?"

"Sure," he said, "but who's going to drive?"

HARA's hologram shimmied up behind me on cue. She was dressed in a tight jacketed chauffeur's uniform (complete with cocked hat, short skirt, and stockings).

"Hi there, big boy," she said. "Want to go for a spin?"

"Man, this is so cool," Shreek said, eyes wide.

"Don't get too excited, shotgun. She's mostly intangible. Now fasten your seat belt. It's going to be a bumpy night."

We got Shreek settled in the shotgun seat (and eventually got him to look at other things beside HARA) just as Sexy and her entourage of redheads emerged from the hotel, giggling and bouncing and strutting and primping all at once as they moved like a bumptious sea of spandex, porcelain skin, and red hair.

"Here they come," Shreek said, his attention slipping from HARA for the nano.

Smiles was with them, now wearing a black-and-red striped suit and looking like a shard of jagged dark glass in a serving of cotton candy.

"Where's Carol?"

As they flounced closer, Shreek hopped out of the shotgun position and opened the passenger door. The girls giggled at his bumbling yet energetic chivalry and continued their way toward the hover.

"I told her to stay with Sexy."

"Look a little harder," HARA said with a smile.

I looked for Carol's auburn hair amid the radiant ruby-haired throng but I couldn't spot her.

"She's not there."

"Look past the hair," HARA said.

"What do you mean past the . . . ?"

"Hi, Tio!"

"Carol?"

She'd changed her clothes, swapping her jeans and blouse for faux leather pants and half-top to match that of Misty, Lusty, and Sissy. And her hair was red.

"Don't you love it?" Sexy asked as the group climbed into the limo.

"Love isn't the word," I said, forcing a smile.

Carol gave me a hug as she passed.

"Sexy said I can be onstage with her tonight. We went over all the dance moves this afternoon."

"Onstage?"

"Isn't it great? I'm a backup singer."

"But Carol," I said, "you can't sing."

"Oh, Tio," she said, giving me a kiss and climbing into the limo, "you're so old school."

"Yeah, I'm getting that a lot lately."

I climbed into the limo and settled in the seat nearest the door. Sexy sat in the plush rear seat (a couch really) flanked by Smiles and Carol. Sissy, Misty, and Lusty lounged on the seats at the side. Everyone stretched out and got comfortable, which wasn't hard in the plushy confines, so I rapped on the Plexiglas behind the driver's cabin and yelled to HARA.

"Let's go. And nothing reckless please."

"You're no fun at all," she whispered inside my head.

"How's it feel, Sexy?" Smiles asked, putting his arm around her shoulder, "embarking of the first of your final concerts?"

"It's just another air mile on the skyway of life, Sammy."

The girls all laughed, Carol included, and I saw Smiles' fingers reach out past Sexy's shoulder and gently stroke Carol's newly reddened hair. She didn't seem to mind. And that scared me.

14

Backstage half an hour before the show was pure bedlam. Sexy was in her dressing room going through her preshow ritual with Smiles. Carol and the other girls were nearby (though not actually in the same room), limbering up their vocal cords and g-strings. I was still uncomfortable about how Carol was throwing herself into this atmosphere but I had wanted her to get in close to the girls and she reassured me with a few mental messages that she still had her mind on business.

"Things are all clear so far from here, Tio. Sexy's safely in her dressing room and the girls and I are pumped for the show."

"Are you picking up any suspicious thoughts or vibes?"

"Not really," she replied. "There's some psionic interference in the arena. Plus all these people around create a lot of mental chatter. It's hard to zero in on any one mind."

"So once the arena fills up?"

"My abilities won't be much good unless someone gets close."

"Okay. Then stay close to Sexy and let me know if any alarms go off."

"Got it," she whispered.

The crowd was flowing in now, even though they knew that the show would start late (Sexy's shows were known for late starts). They wanted to be there early and soak up the atmosphere.

And what a crowd they were; thousands of them, all dressed in bright clothes that were either tight-fitting, see-through, or barely there (sometimes all three). They were girls mostly, though a good percentage of them were male;

boyfriends or boyfriend wannabes. And they were all young. Most of them were teenagers. Twenty-somethings in this crowd stood out like senior citizens. I felt like a dinosaur (but I'm kind of used to that). They began chanting Sexy's name ten minutes before the show was scheduled to start and vibrations from their stomping and clapping shook the stage like a teen tectonic plate shift.

"That's it," I said, ducking into the stage wings. "I'm starting the show."

"What do you mean?"

HARA's hologram appeared beside me as I walked quickly down the hallway toward the dressing rooms.

"The quicker we get Sexy onstage, the quicker she does her show and the quicker we can get her out of danger. There's no point in letting the crowd work themselves into any more of a frenzy."

"You have no sense of drama, do you?" HARA said.

"I have plenty of sense," I said, stopping at Sexy's dressing room door, "but I can live without the drama."

The sound of the audience was loud even here so I had to pound hard on the door in order to be heard.

"Sexy!" I shouted. "I think we better get this show on the road."

There was no answer.

"Sexy?" I shouted again.

Again, no answer. I tried the door but it was locked.

"Sexy!"

"I'm getting some strange readings from inside the room," HARA said.

"What kind of readings?"

"Radiation," HARA said. "Much higher than normal. Not deadly though."

"That's it," I said, backing away from the door and popping my gun into my hand. "Tight bang!"

The blast from my gun blew apart the door lock then I kicked in the rest of the door. Its thick body swung open, pulling one hinge free of the jamb and bits of the wall away with it. I leaped into the room with gun drawn and some serious attitude.

"Sexy!"

She was asleep. Sort of. Her eyes were closed and she definitely wasn't fully conscious, which sort of implies sleep.

But she also wasn't lying down. As a matter of fact she wasn't touching the ground at all. She was hovering a full meter off the floor, feet together, arms spread and fully enveloped in a dark red light that was emanating from a projector on the floor.

"What the DOS?"

"Zach?" Smiles said adjusting his tie. "I didn't hear you. Is something wrong?"

"You tell me," I replied. "What's going on here?"

"Sexy's in the meditation chamber. She does this before every show to clear her mind."

"Why is she levitating?"

"There's an anti-grav generator in the projector. The sense of weightlessness helps her focus better. The red light is meant to subconsciously give her a sense of empowerment."

"And the position?"

"Oddly, all performers who do this type of meditation just naturally assume the messianic pose. Go figure."

"Yeah, go figure," I said, popping my gun back into my sleeve. "The crowd's getting a little out of control. I thought it would be best if we started the show soon."

Smiles looked at his watch and frowned, which took some effort considering the size of his mouth.

"Sexy normally doesn't hit the stage until forty-five minutes after the scheduled start time," he said. "But you're right. We don't want to create more trouble than we have to."

He hit a switch on the projector and the red light surrounding Sexy dimmed slightly and she began descending.

"It will take a couple of nanos to fully bring her out of the meditation but she should be ready to go soon."

He stepped into the light, took Sexy's hand and patted it gently.

"Sexy, dear," he whispered. "Time to wake up."

Sexy's eyes opened slowly and she looked around the room a little confusedly. Her eyes fell upon me and the corners of her mouth turned upward ever so slightly. Smiles leaned toward her and put his lips to her ear.

"Showtime," he said softly.

Sexy's smile widened into something resembling the grin of a hungry wolf.

"Oh, yeah," she whispered.

15

When the lights went down in the arena, the audience, already in a frenzy, began screaming in earnest. The musicians were already in their places, instruments and droids at the ready (most live music is enhanced by droid play these days because it allows the performers to concentrate more on their showmanship). Sexy's posse, Carol included, ran onto the stage and struck their poses. It surprised me how completely Carol had thrown herself into the new role of backup singer, but I didn't have time to dwell on it. The first bass riff of the intro wafted through the arena like the first trickles of a rising tide and the crowd noise ceased, replaced by the almost palpable anticipation.

The curtain slowly rose, thin slivers of spotlight began to dot the smoky dark stage, the bass riff rose gently, joined now by a grinding drum beat. Then a throaty female voice whispered over the sound system.

"Mesdames et Messieurs . . . amants et rêveurs . . . bouchers et bétail . . ."

Sexy's form floated toward the stage atop a translucent anti-grav disk. It didn't look like Sexy, of course. She was wearing clothes, for one thing; a black satin robe with tails that hung two meters past her feet. Her head was bowed, hiding her face from the ambient light. And she was wearing a hat.

"Is that a fedora?"

"Looks like it," HARA replied. "Maybe she likes you."

Then a spotlight, so bright it was difficult to look at with the naked eye flared onto her. The crowd roared and the music staccatoed loudly for a split nano. Sexy was the cen-

ter of attention now, but still hid herself beneath the satin
robe and fedora.

"Je vous accueille là où l'amour ne prend jamais fin . . ."
her whisper echoed.

"What did she say?"

"I welcome you to where love never ends," HARA said.

"—là où les rêves vivant pour toujours . . ."

". . . to where dreams live forever . . ."

". . . et là où la viande est fraîche."

". . . and to where the meat is fresh."

"Gross."

"Welcome my friends to Ménage Abattoir!"

She flung open her robe and it burst into flames as she
threw it off. It disappeared in a nano and the crowd roared
at their first clear view of Sexy. Her clothes were ethereal
white; a barely-there skin-tight halter top, pants that were
second-skinlike at the hips and wildly flared below the
knees, and a gray fedora.

The music kicked into gear. Heavy bass, synthesizer and
effects. The dancers began moving and the light show on
the stage looked like a rainbow in a death match with a
lightning storm. And above it all, Sexy began to sing.

> *You love me. Hee, hee, hee.*
> *I hate you. Ooh, ooh, ooh.*
> *You love me. Gee, gee, gee.*
> *I am your master. Faster, faster, faster.*
> *I am your queen*
> *I am your wet dream."*

The crowd absolutely ate it up. They screamed so loudly
I thought their heads would explode (I know mine wanted
to). And as Sexy bumped and ground ten meters above the
stage, bathed in the white hot spotlights and drenched with
the adoration of fifty thousand crazed fans, one thought
kept repeating itself in my head like a spoofed sample on
a dance remix. But before I could say it aloud, HARA did
it for me.

"How in Gates' name are we going to protect her?"

"DOSsed if I know," I mumbled, bringing my wrist communicator up to my lips. "Tony, are you there?"

Tony's face flashed onto the small screen of the communicator.

"Here, Zach. How's the view backstage?"

"Let's just say that there are other places I'd like to be. Any sign of trouble?"

"All stations have reported in. No problems out of the ordinary. Although one fan got in a scuffle with one of our undercover bots."

"The popcorn dispensers?"

"The guy refused to pay the extra credits for the butter and salt and took a swing at the bot. We had to take him in."

"For a salt and buttery?"

"There's more room in the paddy wagon, you know. All units come equipped with a specially marked Zach Johnson seat. It has its own muzzle."

"I'll keep that in mind," I replied.

"By the way, is that Carol onstage with the dancers?" Tony asked.

"I'm afraid so."

"She looks really good."

"I'm going to pretend I didn't hear that, Tony," I said signing off.

Back onstage, Sexy had landed her anti-grav disk on the stage and had joined the dancers. She struck a few poses with the girls, blew a few kisses to the crowd and then launched into her second song.

"I have a love. Yes I do.
It's a love that's steady and true.
I have a love. You bet I do.
It's the truest love of all.
It sticks like super glue."

I could only roll my eyes.

"How are those earplugs working?" HARA asked.

"Not well enough," I said. "I can still hear the music."

We circled around backstage for the next half an hour (four songs and two costume changes). My heart jumped every time a crazed fan tried to rush the stage but Tony's men were there every time to haul them away. I made a mental note to get the names of all the rushers from Tony after his people had processed them, though I doubted any serious assassin would take such an obvious route.

Sexy was doing a ballad now, slow and sultry.

"She learned that it's not easy being rich.
Everyone feels you're just a bitch.
Sometimes she thinks she should just be digging a ditch.
People love her, yes they do.
They stick to her just like glue . . .
But their love just isn't true,
Yes, their love just isn't true."

She was wearing a pink tuxedo jacket and tails with a top hat and no pants (big surprise), crawling along the stage like a sultry cat as she moaned and crooned. She finished with a breathy sigh and rolled over onto her back, arching sexily and lifting one leg straight up as the crowd roared.

"The recording company is so glad.
That poor little girl is rich but sad.
You might think she would go mad.
You might think she would go mad.
You might think she would go maaddddd."

"You know something," I said, "now that I've seen her in action and have listened, I mean *really* listened to her music. I realize that . . . she's really bad."

"You're just old," HARA replied.

"No, this isn't a generational thing. It's the basic harmonic truth. This music is just plain bad."

"Well, fifty thousand screaming fans say otherwise."

"Yeah, what do they know? They're probably brainwashed."

HARA said something as a retort but I wasn't paying attention because just then I saw half a dozen dark shapes gathered in the backstage area across from me. They were tall men, trim but muscular, all dressed in black.

"Who are they?" I asked.

"Additional dancers," HARA replied. "There's a production number up next."

The band segued into a synth number with a slow Middle Eastern-type beat. Sexy popped back onto her feet and began shimmying across the stage, undulating her hips. Carol, Misty, Lusty, and Sissy joined in, though they were two steps in the background and out of the brightest of the spotlights.

"My body is ripped. My muscles so lithe.
You can tell I know how to use a knife.
I'll be your butcher, you can be my sweet meat.
Love cutlets. Love cutlets."

I turned my attention back to the men in black. They were preparing to go onstage, getting into formation and waiting for their cue. Then as one they reached into the folds of their costumes and then flashed their blades.

"They've got knives!"

"Cleavers actually," HARA said. "It's part of the show."

Sure enough the men strode onto the stage and began a hip-thrusting, cleaver-waving dance.

"Oh, this is so wrong," I said nervously. "Did you run checks on the dancers?"

"Every one of them," HARA said. "They're legit. Nothing suspicious."

The dancers each grabbed one of the girls onstage (two grabbed Sexy) and did some very expressive hip grinding.

"They're all gay, by the way," HARA continued.

"That doesn't make me feel better," I said, watching Carol doing her share of the grind.

"I carry a cleaver everywhere I go.
So I can ravish you from head to toe.
I'll be your butcher, you can be my sweet meat.
Love cutlets. Love cutlets."

The music was building in intensity now. The spotlights changed from white to darkening shades of red as the eleven dancers moved faster and the dance grew more intense. The crowd loved it, of course.

"I don't like this," I said to myself.

I saw a twelfth figure duck in from the shadows. Dressed in black, it had the build of a male, but this one was not a dancer. The body wasn't as trim. The movements were graceful, but not delicate.

"What's that?"

HARA looked.

"I can't tell."

"Switch to infrared and zoom in."

The vision in my left eye went dark for a nano as HARA switched my vision over to the infrared spectrum. I could see the figure clearer now, body heat glowing hot against the background. It was definitely a man. Tall and heavy, moving quickly and furtively. Clearly no one had seen him but me, but I couldn't get to him without crossing the stage.

"Let Tony know we have an intruder," I said, popping my gun into my hand. "We're going to need some backup."

The man paused in the shadows for a nano and even though his face was hidden, I noticed him look around to see if anyone was watching. Then he pulled something from his coat and moved onto the stage.

"Captain Rickey says that he has men on the way," HARA said.

"Too late," I said gripping my gun. "The guy's making his move. Tell Tony I'll meet him onstage."

"Onstage?"

"Put me in stealth mode," I said, and ran onto the stage.

My clothes may look shabby and out-of-date (yes, I'm aware of it, it's a lifestyle choice), but that doesn't mean they're worthless. Actually, a lot of what I wear is ripping edge. Take my trench coat, for example. The fabric is interwoven with nano-circuitry which allows it to perform a lot of non-attire-related functions. One such function is what I call stealth mode. The coat uses micro-sized cameras woven into the fabric to record the area around me and simultaneously project it onto the OLED circuitry woven into the coat directly opposite it. So the backside of my coat records the stuff behind me and projects it on the front of my coat. The front of my coat records the stuff in front of me and projects it onto my backside, which to the naked eye, makes me invisible (except for my head).

The intruder was moving quickly toward Sexy now. I saw him clearly through the infrared lens in my eye as I ran full tilt across the stage, dodging the racks of meat and red satin throw pillows that so elegantly decorated the stage.

"Sexy, get down!"

Sexy couldn't hear me over the music and the roar of the crowd. Even if she had, I'm not sure she would have taken it as a warning. But Carol picked up my thoughts and turned away from her dance partner.

"Tio?"

She turned to my fast approaching head and immediately saw the situation.

"Sexy, look out!"

Carol leaped at Sexy and pulled her down just before the attacker reached her. I hit the attacker a nano later, slamming him broadside with my shoulder and rolling him onto the stage floor. He went over more easily than I expected. His body was softer than I expected as well, more flab than muscle. That may sound like a good thing but it wasn't because my hit took us down to the floor harder and in a different place than I expected. We ended up falling into one of Sexy's meat-cleaver dancers, knocking him to the ground and landing hard and awkwardly on his leg. I heard the wet snap of the dancer's femur even over the music and the guy started screaming.

Two nearby dancers saw all this and (logically) pegged me as the villain. They jumped on me, grabbed me by the shoulders and tried to pull me away as the attacker tried to get to his feet and stumble off the stage.

Even if there'd been time to explain things to the dancers, they wouldn't have been able to hear me over the music so, regrettably, I had to go the rough route because there was no way I was letting the attacker get away. I head butted one dancer on the bridge of the nose (breaking and bloodying it), then pivoted and threw the second dancer over my shoulder as I spun and aimed my gun toward the fleeing/stumbling attacker.

Unfortunately, my judo throw sent the dancer headlong into Tony, who was just now arriving on the stage with a handful of his men. His men, after seeing their captain felled by a thrown dancer and now faced with a mostly invisible man holding a gun, opened fire with their blasters (set to stun).

I managed to dive to the floor and avoid the blasts. The drummer, lead guitarist, and bassoon player weren't so lucky. Worse still, the blasts hit the base of the huge guillotine set piece and toppled it. It smashed into another set piece filled with slabs of hanging meat, all of which came crashing down on the keyboardist and the control board for the stage lights and effects, shorting it out completely and sending the entire stage into what the next day's newsite reviews would describe as "a déclassé avalanche of abstract tackiness and white-trash opulence."

Dozens of lights exploded, a hundred pyrotechnics fired at once, and chunks of various meat products shot into the air and showered the audience. The backing tracks were still playing over the sound system but the computer had jammed so the same two bars of Sexy's song were playing over and over, echoing throughout the arena like an audiophonic hip-hop water torture.

I spotted the attacker in the wings as I knelt on the stage floor. He had gotten caught up in the rush of police and security people that were storming the stage and was trying to push through them like a fat salmon swimming upstream. The horde of peacekeepers was heading straight for me so I knew that I only had one chance to bring the guy down.

"Hog tie," I said.

The indicator light on my gun flashed and I fired. A polymer cable shot from my gun and sped toward the fleeing attacker. It hit him in the small of the back and wrapped itself around his legs and arms a dozen times before the guy even knew he'd been hit. He lost his grip on the device he was carrying and I saw it hit the ground and skitter across the backstage floor. But it activated on impact. I saw it clearly because HARA took control of the interface in my eye and zoomed in on the device. It was a palm-sized module with two button controls and an activator light, which was now blinking frantically.

"Oh DOS," I whispered, expecting an explosion at any nano.

None came.

Instead, a bouquet of holographic flowers projected from the module, a cascade of three dozen bright pink orchids.

"Flowers?"

"Congratulations," HARA said as the angry horde of police and security personnel piled on top of me. "You just saved Sexy Sprockets from a floral display."

16

Once Tony extricated himself from the dancers, he took control of his men and the security personnel. They quelled the chaos onstage and managed to keep the crowd (which had become seriously perturbed and panicked by now) from rushing the stage long enough for me to pull Sexy and her girls back to the safety of the wings. Two nanos later, we were running through the backstage hallways, headed for the hoverport.

"He had flowers, Zach," Sexy said (for the third time, I think). "Orchids."

"He was rushing straight for you, Sexy," I said. "What did you want me to do?"

"Something short of trashing the stage would have been nice."

"I'll remember that next time," I grumbled. "HARA, bring up the limo and meet us at the hoverport. Sexy has to leave the building now!"

"Gotcha, big guy," HARA replied in my head.

"Johnson!"

I turned just enough to see Smiles running down the hallway in his two-tone black and red shoes. He was sweaty and flushed, partially from the running, but mostly from rage.

"What in Gates' name was that?" he shouted, putting a hand on my shoulder in an attempt to slow me.

I shrugged off the hand and kept moving, leading Sexy by the hand.

"Talk to me about it in the limo, Sammy," I said. "Now's not the time."

"We'll talk about it now," he said.

"Right now, Sexy is in danger," I replied without turning around. "I am not prepared to waste my time and put her in more danger just to listen to you rant. So save it and rant in the limo when you have a captive audience."

"Why you . . ." Smiles began, turning redder by the nano.

"He's sort of right, Sammy," Sexy said as we neared the hoverport.

Smiles sighed and shook his head as though he were the only sane person left on Earth (but he kept running toward the hoverport with us).

It wasn't long before I was loading Sexy and the girls into the limo. Smiles looked as though he wanted to slam the door in my face when he climbed in but he held back and took a seat next to Carol.

"Strap in, everyone," I said, as I took my seat by the door. "Let's go, HARA!"

HARA, clearly happy to be free of my usual speed constraints, put the proverbial pedal to the metal and the limo shot free of the hoverport like a rocket.

"That was really fast, Mr. Johnson," Shreek said from the front seat. "Did everything go okay?"

"You're shotgun, Shreek," I said, sliding the soundproof barrier into place. "No talking unless there's trouble."

"Oh there's trouble, all right," Smiles said, happy for the opening. "Your incompetence turned Sexy's show into a complete disaster."

"I was doing my job."

"I'm sorry, did I miss the part about your job being to trash the set and cause a full-scale riot?" Smiles screamed. "We hired you as a bodyguard, not a demolitions crew."

"*Sexy* hired me."

"Fine," he said, "and in the one day that you've been in her employ you've completely ruined the tour. How do you think this is going to look tomorrow? Do you think the focus is going to be on Sexy's dignified retirement from music while at the top of her game? No! Every iota of coverage tomorrow will be about how this show turned into a circus. And how long before news of the PATA threats hit the press now? This entire tour has just become a joke! And it's because of you!"

The sound barrier to the front seat slid open a crack and Shreek stuck his face through.

"Mr. Johnson?"

"Not now, Shreek," I said, sliding it back into place. "Listen, Smiles, I'm not the one who let an intruder get close to Sexy!"

"Fans rush the stage all the time," Smiles snapped.

"Mr. Johnson?" Shreek said again, sliding the barrier (a little less) open again.

"This guy came from backstage," I said, slamming the barrier shut. "He had credentials. I saw them when I tackled him."

"And broke poor Jermaine's leg. Do you know how hard it is to find dancers who can handle meat cleavers and work for scale?"

"Mr. Johnson!" Shreek yelled.

"What is it, Shreek?" I said, opening the barrier.

"You said that the job of the shotgun is to keep an eye out for trouble, right?"

"Right," I said.

"Does that qualify?" Shreek asked, cocking his thumb at the limo's right side.

I peered out the tinted window and saw the nose cone and fins of a missile, vapor trail blazing in the Frisco night, heading straight for us.

"Yeah," I said over the taste of bile in my mouth, "that counts."

17

"Tell everyone to hang on back there," HARA shouted. "We're taking evasive maneuvers."

"Zach, what's going on?" Sexy asked, retightening her seat belt.

"Heat-seeking missile," I said. "This will not be fun. Trust me. I've done this before."

HARA pulled the hover up and put us into a steep climb as the missile approached. It changed its intercept course to match us, though at twice our airspeed, but as it neared, HARA rolled the hover over and put us into a nosedive, which left our stomachs several hundred meters behind.

"Everything okay up there HARA?" I asked.

"Nothing but a Sunday drive, big guy," HARA teased. "And by the way, I think I know now how our shotgun rider got the nickname Shreek. He's screaming like a debutante in a mutant rat colony up here."

"I think I'm about to join him," I said, turning my head from one swiftly approaching danger (the missile) to another (the ground).

"Oh ye of little faith," HARA said.

Scant meters from the ground, HARA rolled the hover over again and pulled us out of the dive. I heard the roof of the hover actually scrape the street as we looped around the missile and sped back into the air.

At its intense speed, the missile couldn't turn quickly enough and smashed into the deserted streets before exploding and turning the intersection of Shake and Rattle streets into a supersized smoking pothole. HARA leveled the craft off and we all exhaled for the first time in a while.

"All clear for the nano," HARA said. "But Shreek is still living up to his name."

I pulled back the privacy barrier and, sure enough, Shreek was keening louder than a possessed fishwife.

"Wow, that's annoying," I said. "Carol, can you help here?"

"Shreek," Carol said, leaning forward in her seat and touching him on the shoulder, "take a nap."

Shreek's screaming ceased, a sly smile crossed his face and his head leaned to one side as he fell happily asleep. I noticed that Smiles watched it all intently.

"What was that out there?" Sexy asked.

"You don't want to know," I mumbled.

As if on cue, Rupert Roundtree's smiling face appeared on the limo's com-screen.

"Poetistosity," he said. "Pure poetistosity. That was awesome Zach Shack."

"Roundtree, you nearly killed us!" I said.

"I'm making entertainment history, Zachman. I'm entitled to a few liberties here and there for posterity's sake."

"I'm going to kick your posterity the next time I see you, Roundtree."

"Excellent banter skills, Zackture. Middle America loves a good punster. And that's our target audience for this episode. Middle DOSing America."

"Heads up back there, people," HARA shouted from the driver's seat. "We have three more hot ones on our tail and approaching fast."

"Missiles?" I asked.

HARA shook her head, grimly. "Stock cars."

"What?"

I looked out the rear window and sure enough, three stock car hovers were zeroing in on us, their oversized hover motors roaring like giant angry lions. Their bodies were sleek, multihued, and covered by a plethora of decals advertising energy products, snack foods, alcoholic beverages, and hair restoration services. They also had heavy ordnance.

"Oh DOS," Sexy mumbled, "it's the Woolly Boys."

"The who?" I asked.

"The Woolly Boys," Sexy continued. "Three brothers,

Willy, Wendell, and Wilson. They used to be NASCAR drivers. Really good ones actually. They won all kinds of championships. But NASCAR banned them from racing a few years ago."

"How come?"

"They played a little rough. You know, bumping cars on the turns, nudging them from behind, taking them out with missiles and blasters."

"Yeah, I can see where that would be frowned upon," I said.

"Oddly though, up until then there was nothing in the official rule book forbidding drivers from using explosive weapons. The Woollys made them close that loophole. Since they left the circuit they've become kind of cult figures."

"Do you have any idea how big these guys are in the South?" Roundtree shouted. "They're folk heroes! Can you imagine the infamous Woolly Boys in a race to the death against Zach Johnson on national HV! I smell a pop-cult event!"

"Roundtree, there are innocent people on board this vehicle!"

"It's okay, Zachrophobe, I went over that with my legal team. They say that simply being in your company can be considered tacit understanding of your lifestyle and the dangers that it entails. Riding in a limo with you is akin to signing a release. They might as well be wearing targets on their butts. We're confident that it will hold up in court."

"Rupert!" Sexy shouted.

"Our original deal holds, Sexy. You'll have a CGI fill-in."

"DOS lot of good that will do me if I'm dead!"

"Nobody's dying tonight," I said, popping my gun into my hand.

"That's the spirit, Zachules! Let's see that . . ."

I blew a hole the size of a softball in the com-screen. And despite the impending danger, I think everyone was a little relieved to be rid of Roundtree's ranting.

"Gates, what have you gotten us into, Johnson?"

"Shut up, Smiles," I said. "Sexy, how do you know so much about these guys?"

"They grew up in my hometown in New Alabama. We sort of used to date."

"Which one?"

"All of them," she said. "It ended sort of badly when they found out. They might have an ax to grind."

"Just what we need," I said, "more motivation for the killers. HARA, any chance we can outrun these guys?"

"Chances are slim and none, boss man," HARA replied. "And Slim just swallowed a grenade and leaped into a vat of acid. They have more horsepower and more firepower."

"Then we'll beat them with brainpower," I said unfastening my seat belt.

"Gates help us, we're doomed."

"HARA, you're killing the moment," I said, opening the sunroof. "Everybody hang on tight and keep your heads down. Everything's going to be fine. This is all just a game . . ."

I stuck my head out the sunroof.

". . . an insanely dangerous, stupid game."

The hot night air at two hundred kilometers per hour hit my face like a mask of needles. The sheer force of the limo's speed nearly sucked me right out of the sunroof. I steadied myself on the rollbar, ducked back inside, and gripped my gun a little tighter.

"Tarzan."

My gun responded to the voice command with a tone and a red flash. I fired a round at the limo's wet bar and a length of polymer cable shot from the barrel and wrapped itself several times around the heavy faux wood surface. I detached the other end of the cable from the gun and wrapped it around my waist then clipped it to my armor. I gave the cable a couple of good tugs to make sure it would properly anchor me, then climbed back through the sunroof.

The three hovers were flying in formation—a lead and two wingmen—but they took turns approaching us, shooting forward, engine roaring to run alongside us for a nano before slipping back into the pack formation. They were toying with us, like hyenas playing with a wounded gazelle.

HARA was doing her best to keep them at bay, pushing the hover to its limit, keeping the chase close to the ground, and using the narrower skyways to keep them from hemming us in.

I steadied my gun hand as best I could and fired off a

quick couple of rounds at the nearest hover. The blasts bounced harmlessly off the hood and all three pursuers responded with a round of blaster fire of their own. The blasts exploded in the air around us and the limo shook like an old jet in heavy turbulence.

"How armored are these cars?" I asked HARA.

"More armored than us," she responded inside my head. "They look to be most blaster-resistant in front and rear."

"What about the bot-buster rounds?"

"They'd do the trick," HARA responded. "They'll blow the hovers to bits, drivers included, though I don't think anyone would fault you on that since they're firing on us."

"Maybe," I said, "but let's save the deadly force as a last resort."

"Are there any other resorts currently available?"

"That depends. Is there anything else special currently loaded in the gun that would be appropriate?"

"There's the electromagnetic pulse. That would shut down all electrical power within a twenty-five meter radius from impact."

"Which, against a hover . . . ?"

"Would likely make it crash and burn."

"NASCARs are equipped with ejector seats, right?"

"Some of the drivers call them wimp seats, but they've been standard equipment since the day they took to the skies," HARA replied.

"Good, take us out over the bay," I said.

"A fine choice. The bay is lovely this time of evening," HARA responded, banking the limo hard toward the New Frisco Bay. "But odds are we won't be able to evade all three of them long enough to make the water."

"I'll handle that," I said. "Get us onto the narrowest street you can find and go low."

"They'll box us in from above."

"That's what I'm hoping."

HARA took a quick turn that left my stomach about a hundred meters behind me and pulled us onto an old one-lane side street between a couple of high-rises. The Woolly Boys followed us in, one after the other.

"Now go low," I said to HARA. "And slow up a bit."

"I hope you know what you're doing."

"Honestly, I have no idea, but that's never stopped me before," I said. "Get ready to go back to max speed on my word."

HARA brought the limo low, barely three meters above the ground. One Woolly immediately dropped down right behind us, strafing us with blaster fire from behind as he did so. Another settled in directly behind him and the third let loose a burst of speed and slipped over us, matching our speed and blocking us from climbing. Then he lowered himself toward us, trying to force us into the ground. It got so close that I could feel the heat of his underside gyros singeing my face.

Which was exactly what I was waiting for.

"Sticky stuff," I said.

I fired twice at the underside of the racer and, with a couple of muted rubbery pops, sent a huge payload of petroleum-based glue into his left- and right-side gyros. I could tell that a hefty portion of the glue made it past the air guards and into the actual gyros because a few nanos after impact, the hover began to shudder in the air like an unbalanced washer on a newly waxed floor.

"Floor it now, HARA!" I yelled.

HARA pushed the limo back to maximum speed, getting us out from underneath the quickly failing Woolly Boy racer.

The other two Woollys continued pursuit as their wounded brother careened into one building then another before tumbling onto the street and crashing into the Dumpsters of an all-night Chinese restaurant.

A few nanos later the high-rises and cityscape fell away behind us and we were heading out over New Frisco Bay with the two remaining Woollys hot on our tail.

"The gun has only one EMP," HARA said, "so you need to take them both out at once."

"Got it," I said. "Now slow down and let them catch up."

"No problem there."

I stuck myself back through the sunroof and put a tight grip on my gun.

"EMP," I said.

The gun acknowledged the command and began to throb in my hand as it loaded the electromagnetic pulse. I could tell that the charge was going to take most, if not all, of my gun's power. I steadied myself against the hood of the limo and aimed.

And that's when the lead Woolly activated his heat-seeker.

He lowered the weapon from the undercarriage, popping the long deadly cylinder out of its belly and holding it on his underside like a big Freudian "I have issues" sign.

"Uh oh."

"Don't let it fire the missile!" HARA shouted.

"You don't have to tell me twice."

I pulled the trigger and felt the entire limo lurch forward as the EMP charge fired. It shot across the bay like a comet and exploded into a ball of white light just in front of the lead pursuer. The light lasted a couple of nanos and then disappeared completely. When my vision cleared, I saw no sign of the pursuing racers, only moonlight on the water.

"We didn't destroy them did we?"

"We fried their electrical systems," HARA said. "We can't see them because their lights are out."

"The ejector seats aren't electric though, right?"

Just then, we saw a red-and-white striped parachute open fifty meters above the bay.

"There we go."

"Safe and sound."

"Hold on," I said. "Where's the other one?"

On cue, another round of blaster fire strafed the side of the limo sending us into a roll as the final Woolly Boy zoomed by us.

"He must have pulled clear of the affected zone, before impact." HARA said, regaining control of the limo.

The racer sped a hundred meters ahead of us then looped around to make another run.

"We're running out of power, here," HARA said. "Any more ideas?"

"I'm thinking."

"Tio," Carol said, looking up from her seat, "is there anything I can do?"

I shook my head silently and turned away. Then I had an idea and shot her quick thought.

"Can you control the driver's mind?"

"Not at this distance," she mentally replied.

"You can read *my* mind over the vid."

"Your mind's familiar to me. I've never met the Woolly guy."

"What if we get you closer?"

"I'd at least need a visual," she said. "We'll need some light."

I cast a glance out the limo window and saw the Golden Gate Bridge looming nearby.

"No problem," I said then turned toward the driver's seat. "HARA take us to the bridge."

Frisco's calling card, the famous Golden Gate Bridge still stands majestically (and Gates knows that it's been through a lot) in the bay at the mouth of the Pacific Ocean. The sad part is that the structure is no longer used as an actual bridge. All the north/south traffic crossing the bay these days does so via the 101 Skyway or the nearby Frisco Hover Bridge (which has always given me the creeps). The Golden Gate today is a national monument, a tourist attraction, and a Wal-K-Mart (don't get me started). The iconic towers still stand as originally constructed but the expanse has been completely reconfigured so that people can now stroll the walkways, visit the museums, and patronize the shops and restaurants that pepper the bridge. It's actually not a bad little place, a peaceful oasis in the otherwise crowded city. Very low-tech; no traffic, hover or ground-based is allowed.

But that was all about to change.

I pulled open the privacy barrier between the two compartments, reached through and grabbed the still sleeping Shreek.

"Circle around to the far side," I said to HARA as I unbuckled Shreek's safety belt. "I want him to think we're trying to hide."

"You mean we're not?"

Lusty and Misty helped me pull Shreek from his seat and into the main cabin.

"There aren't enough people here this time of night to hide. Carol, take the shotgun position and strap in. We're going to play some chicken."

"You're not serious," Carol said.

"It's not as bad as it sounds," I replied.

"Of course not," HARA quipped. "It's only reckless, illegal, and deadly."

HARA took the limo to the south side of the bridge and hovered there for a nano before entering in order to make certain that the remaining Woolly Boy saw us go in. He did and, just as I thought, he shot past the entrance and around the perimeter in order to enter through the Marin County side.

We created a bit of a stir as we flew overhead, especially among the security detail. As I suspected, there weren't many people on the bridge this time of night. Most of the shops had closed, leaving only a few diners at the restaurants and the small number of people there for the night views of the city. Security teams on the bridge were only equipped with small blasters and low-powered hovers so I knew they couldn't bother us. And the hover was equipped with a blurring finish that made it hard to recognize (license plate included). But I also knew that security would call for backup from the mainland the nano they saw us, so we didn't have much time to get this done.

Thankfully, we didn't have to wait long because we saw the remaining Woolly Boy approaching us only a nano later. He was gliding slowly over the bridge walkways, matching our altitude at about ten meters.

"Go to a full stop," I said to HARA. "Let him see us hovering."

HARA did as she was told and we floated softly as the racer slowly approached. Then it slowed and hovered four hundred meters away. We could see him clearly now under the bright lights of the bridge.

"Can you reach him?" I asked Carol.

She was leaning forward in the passenger seat, resting her hands against the dashboard and staring intently at the NASCAR.

"I think this one is Wendell," she said, clearly straining. "He's enjoying himself. Apparently, he'll get a bonus if he shoots us down."

"Nice to see a man who enjoys his work," I said. "Can you zap him?"

She shook her head no.

"We're still too far away."

"That's what I was afraid of. HARA, rev the engine."

The hover engine roared and the cabin shook.

Wendell Wooly answered our roar with one of his own; deeper and louder, like a cross between a jungle cat and a tectonic plate shift.

"What are you doing?" Smiles asked, gripping the seat in front of him.

"He could blow us apart from this distance with his missile or blasters," I replied. "We have to keep him from doing that. We need him to come closer."

His engine roared again, growling insults at us in that rumbling, fossil-fueled language dating back to the glory days of the hot rod era. I knew that we were close.

I turned to Carol, who was still concentrating hard on the racer.

"You ready?"

She nodded.

"Floor it, HARA."

One shortcoming of a hovercraft when compared to an old-fashioned car (one of many, but don't get me started) is that there's no squeal of tires when you peel out. Sure, the engine roars and there's still the rush of air, along with a much more powerful g-force, but the absence of the rubber tire scream on pavement sort of kills the drama for me.

That said, no one else who happened to be in the limo shared my opinion because, aside from Carol and HARA, they all began screaming the nano HARA hit the afterburners and the g-force slammed them back into their seats.

At the other end of the bridge, Wendell Woolly maxed his accelerator and came at us like a rocket. A nano later the two hovers were speeding at one another, engines screaming, in a five hundred kilometer per hour game of chicken. The support cables of the bridge were a blur as we flew across the expanse, but our eyes were focused solely on the oncoming racer.

Carol sat in the shotgun seat, eyes wide and focused, reaching out with her mind to the mind of the driver ahead of us.

"Do you have him yet?" I asked.

"Not yet," she said, straining.

"We're sort of running out of time," I said.

"Please don't distract me, Tio."

"If you can't control him," I said, "I can always shoot him."

"Tio!"

"Right."

We were a hundred meters apart now, engines still screaming in a headlong rush toward one another. The girls, Smiles, and the newly awakened Shreek were screaming in the back. The hover itself was starting to shake from the hard wear we had put on it already. And Carol held her position. Cool as the underside of an arctic sleeping bag. I was immensely proud and frightened of her at the same time.

Then the tip of her mouth curled upward ever so slightly and her brow unfurrowed.

"Gotcha," she whispered.

The NASCAR decelerated immediately.

"You got him?" I asked.

"He is Wendell," Carol answered. "He loves to drive, he drinks too much and likes listening to disco music when no one else is around. He's also still in love with Sexy."

"Oh, that's so sweet," Sexy said.

"That's my girl, Carol," I said, leaning over and kissing her on the forehead. "Have him land at the security station and turn himself in. He should confess everything but completely forget who he was chasing."

"Got it."

"HARA, get us out of here."

"You got it, big guy," HARA said.

She pulled hard on the controls and the limo rose over the bridge supports. We banked hard to the east and angled back out over the open water of the bay. Then we spun to the south and headed back to the city.

I turned toward the back of the limo to check on Sexy and the others. They were all a little shell-shocked by the events but they seemed to be settling down now (all except for Shreek, who had passed out again). Calmest among them all, surprisingly, was Smiles. He sat nearly motionless in his seat, staring at Carol and smiling so widely, I was afraid that his cheeks would rip.

"My oh, my," he whispered to himself.

18

"You are incompetent, reckless, and a magnet for trouble!" Smiles screamed. "You've put Sexy in more danger in the time that you've known her than she's faced in her entire career. And she's played Trump Tower with a Trump clone in the building!"

We were back in the city now, just approaching the Elite hoverport. Smiles' joyous admiration of Carol's abilities had been short-lived and he began yelling at me the nano we cleared the bay and passed over into the city. I had sort of stopped listening after a while, mostly because he had a good point.

"Your overzealousness and lack of professionalism made a mockery of the concert," he continued, "and your . . . personal side projects . . . well, I can't even begin to describe how abhorrent and unprofessional they are! And I'm sure they're illegal."

"You'd think so wouldn't you?" I said.

"And you're still treating this like some kind of joke!"

"Sammy, please," Sexy said. "It's not all Zach's fault."

"Which part exactly," Smiles asked snidely, "isn't his fault?"

"I'll admit that he ruined the concert but he was only trying to protect me."

"From a fan!"

"As for the aerial firefight, well, you know how Rupert Roundtree can be."

"I know that Roundtree is crazy," Smiles said. "My point is that Johnson knew what Roundtree was doing when you offered him the job. He knew that he would be putting you in danger just by being around you."

"I knew that too," Sexy said.

"Yes, but he's the professional! He should have declined the job because he knew that his presence would be disruptive! Gates only knows what would have happened if Carol hadn't been here to save us."

He put his hand on Carol's shoulder and Carol smiled just a little.

"Sorry to interrupt, Zach," HARA said inside my head, "but Captain Rickey's on the com for you."

"Put him on the screen back here," I said.

"I would, but you destroyed that one, remember?"

"Oh, yeah," I said, glancing at the obliterated screen. "Put him on the wrist interface then. Excuse me everyone, but I have to take this call."

"Unbelievable," Smiles said, throwing up his hands.

Tony's concerned face came onto the tiny screen on my wrist.

"Zach, I've been trying to contact you for an hour. Where have you been?"

"Oh, you know, just driving around in the limo."

"Well, be careful," Tony said. "It must be a full moon tonight or something because the whole city's going crazy. I just heard that there were a couple of idiots playing chicken on the Golden Gate Bridge."

"Really?" I said. "Kids today are just out of control."

Tony looked at me for a long nano then quickly shook his head. "Forget it. I wanted to speak to you about what happened at the concert tonight."

"I know, Tony," I said. "Honestly, I didn't think things would escalate so quickly."

"You're telling me," Tony replied. "It was utter chaos. I think Sexy's going to need to make some refunds."

I was about to get chewed out and I knew it. Worse still, I deserved it. I just wish Smiles hadn't been there to hear it.

"You know how much I hate saying things like this, Zach, but . . ."

"Go ahead, Tony, I deserve it."

"Good job, Zach."

For a nano I thought that I'd missed a slang upgrade; that somehow the common meaning of "good job" had changed to something akin to "you screwed up so badly, that I'm legally empowered to have you flogged and imprisoned." (It's amazing what can run through your head in a nano of confusion.)

"Um, say that again, Tony?" I said, quickly turning up the volume on the interface and subtly angling the interface screen so that everyone in the limo could see it. "There was some interference and I didn't catch that last part."

"Gates, Zach, it's hard enough to say once," Tony said, "but good job at the concert."

"What?" That was the collected reaction of everyone in the hover (HARA included).

"The guy you tackled . . ."

"You mean the fan with the flowers?" Smiles asked.

"They only looked like flowers," Tony replied. "They were wired with nano-explosives."

"What?"

"CSI found the charge on the projector module. It had enough power to obliterate everyone onstage."

"It was a real threat?" Sexy asked, breathlessly.

"Very real, Ms. Sprockets," Tony replied. "Honestly, you're lucky to be alive."

I tried very hard not to smile.

"The guy just finished going through booking," Tony continued. "I'm going to bring him into the interrogation room in a few nanos. Zach, I thought you might want to sit in the observation room for this."

"You got that right," I said.

"I'd advise that you not bring Ms. Sprockets with you," Tony replied. "And, as you know, Carol is forbidden by law to come anywhere near the suspect while he's in custody."

"I know. I'll see you in about ten minutes. Thanks, Tony."

I ended the call and looked around at the gape-mouthed people in the hover.

"So," I said to Smiles, "how do you like me now?"

19

It is something of an understatement to say that I am familiar with the interrogation room at Tony's precinct. I've been there so often over the years they've named a chair after me (and sadly, it's often the hot seat). Tonight, however, I was not the one in the box. I was safely behind the two-way mirror, watching a couple of Tony's men grill the guy that I had tackled onstage.

He was large (somewhere between beefy and porky) and pale, with curly light hair and a face that was equally covered with razor stubble and acne. He looked to be about nineteen, scared out of his mind, and not at all the way I pictured an assassin would look.

"His name's Garry Koles," Tony said, taking the seat beside me and handing me a cup of coffee. "He's a crazo fan of Sexy's. We have a list of a thousand e-mails he sent her over the past two years. Love letters. Smiles got a court order six months ago to keep him away from Sexy."

"How'd he get the backstage pass then?" I asked.

"Good question," Tony answered. "More importantly, where did he get the nano-explosives? That's pretty expensive stuff. And they were keyed to a DNA trigger."

"DNA trigger?" I asked.

"The detonator was coded to Sexy's DNA, the nano she touched the flowers, the explosives would have detonated. She was the only person who could have set it off."

"So whoever made the bomb . . ."

"Had access to Sexy's DNA," Tony replied.

"And had the funds and expertise to construct the triggering mechanism. Gates, this just gets better and better, doesn't it? You think this kid has the ability to do all that?"

"Either way, we'll find out soon," Tony said.

It wasn't hard to figure out what scenario Tony's men were using with this interrogation. One of the detectives was a big guy with just enough grooming skills to pass the NFPD image standard. He wore a wrinkled white dress shirt (rolled at the sleeves and loose at the collar) that was barely big enough to fit his barrel chest and keg belly. The other detective was thin and had neatly combed sandy hair. His shirt was sharp and striped. His tie was a mellow brown and his corduroy jacket was neatly fitted with patches on the elbows. It was classic good cop/bad cop all the way.

"Gates, Tony, why didn't you just have the good cop come in wearing slippers and a smoking jacket? He's way over the top."

"Shhh," Tony said. "These are my best guys."

Inside the interrogation room, Bad Cop was trying to turn up the heat.

"I think you're lying to us, Garry."

"I'm not, I swear," the kid said, his voice cracking.

"You run up to Sexy Sprockets with a load of nano-explosives and you want us to believe that you didn't mean to hurt her?"

"I didn't know they were explosives."

"That's right; you just thought they were flowers."

"I did. I swear."

"You have to admit, Garry, it looks bad," Good Cop said. "Where did you get the flowers?"

"Someone gave them to me."

"Who?" Bad Cop said, slamming his hairy fist on the table. "Who gave you the flowers? And who gave you the backstage pass? You tell me now or, so help me, I'll have you locked so far away, your parents will need a radio-telescope just to see you."

"He's good," I whispered to Tony.

"He's done some off-Broadway work."

Garry was growing paler by the nano and sweating now, which I'm sure wasn't good for his pores.

"I love Sexy," he said. "Everyone knows that. Even the municipal judge who signed the restraining order knows that."

"Then tell us what happened, Garry," Good Cop said. "Tell us how you got the flowers and the pass."

"I told you, I got a call from someone. I didn't get a name and I didn't see a face."

"Man or woman?" Good cop asked.

"I couldn't tell. The voice was deep but I think it was being masked. He wanted to be anonymous. He told me that he knew about my love for Sexy and wanted to give me a chance to prove myself to her. He sent me the pass and the flowers. He said the flowers were her favorite and that they were sure to sway her."

"And you believed all that?"

"The pass was legit," Garry said. "It was worth a try. I just wanted to see Sexy and let her sweat on me once more before she retired." He put his head down on the table and began to cry.

"I think you're losing him," I said to Tony. "Maybe you should give him a rest and come back with just the Good Cop."

"We're not doing the good cop/bad cop routine," Tony replied.

"You're not?"

"That's just the intro."

"Then what are you doing?" I asked.

Back in the interrogation room there was a knock at the door. Good Cop turned toward the sound.

"Who is it?"

"It's Zach Johnson!" came the voice on the other side of the door.

"Tony, what's going on?" I asked.

"Shhh," Tony said. "This is the good part."

"What do you want, Johnson?" Bad Cop yelled at the door.

"I'm here to sit in on the interrogation," the voice said. "This is my case."

"Go away!" Bad Cop said. "This is for real cops only."

"Oh, come on guys," the voice repeated. "I caught the guy."

"What's going on?" Garry said, a little confused.

"It's the guy who tackled you at the show," Good cop said. "Zach Johnson."

"He's not going to blow me up, is he?" Garry asked. "I heard stuff blows up when he's around."

"Let me in guys," the voice said petulantly.

"Go away, Johnson!" Bad Cop yelled. "This is your last warning."

"If you don't let me in," the voice whined, "I'm telling Captain Rickey."

"That's it," Bad Cop said, striding for the door. He flung the door open and grabbed the silhouetted form standing in the doorway by the scruff of the trench coat, dragging him farther into the hallway and slamming the door behind him.

"He never liked Johnson," Good Cop said.

We heard whispers from outside the closed door, urgent and angry. Then came the sounds of a scuffle and a yelp of pain from the guy pretending to be me.

"What's going on out there?" Garry said, clearly concerned now.

"My partner's angry," Good Cop said. "I think Johnson's paying the price for it."

The sounds of the scuffle turned louder, becoming a full-fledged beating.

"I warned you," Bad Cop shouted.

"No! please, no!" the Zach impersonator screamed.

Good Cop sat down and pulled his chair close to Garry, who was staring nervously at the door.

"He gets this way sometimes. He doesn't know his own strength."

The Johnson impersonator screamed again.

"And when he's done with Johnson," Good Cop continued, "he'll be coming for you."

"Me?" Garry said.

"He thinks you're lying, Garry. He thinks you're hiding something. You need to tell us the truth."

"But I'm telling the truth."

"Take that, Johnson! And that!"

"Please, have mercy!"

"Not so tough now, are you?"

Good Cop cast another glance at the doorway, and moved closer to Garry, putting a comforting hand on his shoulder.

"We don't have much time left, Garry," he said. "He'll be in here soon. You have to tell me the truth now."

"I told you the truth. I swear it."

"Who was it that called you?"

"I don't know."

"Who gave you the pass?"

"I don't know."

"Who gave you the flowers?"

"I don't know!"

Bad Cop burst through the door holding a trench coat and a bloodstained fedora and tossed them angrily on the ground.

"Don't let him near me!" Garry screamed. "I swear I told you all I know. Someone gave me the bouquet. He said it would sway Sexy. He said it would sway her!"

He fell out of his chair and curled up on the floor, sobbing like a baby. Tony sat back in his chair and sighed, then he leaned forward and spoke into the desk microphone.

"That's enough guys. Take him back to holding."

The detectives heard Tony's message over their earpieces and nodded to one another. Tony drew the shade over the two-way mirror and turned to me.

"I can't believe you hired someone to impersonate me." I said to Tony.

"You should see him do your pratfalls," Tony replied. "We call that the Johnson beat down scenario. You'd be surprised how many detectives want to play the bad cop in that one."

"I should get royalties," I said.

"It's just your way of paying back the department for the hassles you've put us through over the years," Tony smiled.

"So you think the kid's telling the truth?"

"He doesn't know anything," Tony nodded. "Looks like he's a patsy."

"So we're back to square one then."

"True. But the upside is that Sexy's still alive," Tony said. "Thanks to you. You did good work tonight, Zach. You should feel good about it."

"Yeah," I said. "That's my motto. Any day that a client doesn't die is a good one."

It was well past midnight when I left the precinct house and headed for my car. It had been a long and eventful day so I guess I can be forgiven for letting my guard down a little. Thankfully, though, HARA still had her wits about her.

"You want the good news or the bad news first, big guy?" she asked.

"I have a feeling that either way, this isn't going to turn out well for me," I answered.

"The bad news is that there are five heavily armed gentlemen in suits approaching you from various angles."

"And the good news?"

"I'm not finished with the bad yet," she said. "Your gun is empty thanks to the EMP charge you used during the firefight, and your body armor is down to twenty percent capacity. You also very likely have two cracked ribs on your left side and I'm fairly certain that the bursitis in your elbow is flaring up again."

"Is that it?"

"Yeah, that's it."

"Okay, so what's the good news?"

"I'm sorry, did I say there was good news?" HARA asked.

"Yes, you did."

"My mistake."

I saw the first of the goons just then. Two of them were approaching me from across the street. They were large and well-built, clearly no strangers to fights. Their hair was clipped short and their black suits were well kept but were clearly off-the-rack. They also wore dark sunglasses, so I was surprised that they didn't trip over the curb as they approached.

"Where are the others?" I whispered to HARA

"Coming in behind you," she said, "all at different angles."

"Mr. Johnson," the lead goon said. "We'd like a nano of your time."

"Sorry, pal," I said. "But it's been a long night. Why don't you give me a call in the morning when your sunglasses will actually serve a purpose?"

The lead goon nodded gently to no one in particular and, as one, his four fellow goons drew in so tightly around me I could smell their cologne.

"It wasn't a request, Mr. Johnson. Sorry for the confusion."

"Honestly guys, I'm much too tired to do the stare down

thing right now," I said. "So if you don't mind, can we fast
forward over this?"

I popped my gun into my hand and stuck the business
end in the lead goon's face.

"You can either commence walking away peacefully or
I can commence painting the sidewalk with your brains,
which I don't usually like to do in front of the police station, but a guy does what he has to, right?"

"You know that your gun is empty, right?" HARA whispered in my head.

"What did I say about killing the moment?" I shot
back mentally.

To his credit, the goon didn't flinch (much). He stood
his ground and simply turned slightly away from me and
pointed to a black hover limo parked on the street in front
of me.

"Our employer would like to have a word with you,"
he said.

"You see?" I said, taking my gun away from his face.
"Now was that so hard to say?"

The limo was black and sleek. Not as opulent or as well-
appointed as Sexy's but this was for an entirely different
kind of VIP. And although I didn't let it show, this VIP
appearance worried me.

I popped my gun back into my sleeve and walked over
to the limo as the passenger door slid open.

"Good evening, Mr. Johnson." The voice was deep,
smooth, and laden with a familiarly thick accent. "Thank
you for taking the time to meet with me."

I leaned against the limo and stuck my head inside the
cabin.

"Good evening, Mr. Governor."

20

Hans Spierhoofd is a former rugby player, HV soap actor, and movie star who for the past six and a half years has been the Governor of New California. He's not a particularly good governor but he looks good on camera, has low friends in high places, and knows when to whip out a good one-liner, which I think is half the job right there.

I climbed into the limo and took a seat across from him as he advised. He wore a dark suit with a ruby red tie. His chiseled face smiled at me as I settled in and he closed the door behind me.

"I hope my Secret Service men weren't rude to you," he said. "They can sometimes be overzealous. I find that endearing."

"Don't we all," I replied.

He was smoking a cigar, though smoking is illegal in California, save for medical marijuana, but that didn't seem to diminish his enjoyment of it (it's a stupid law anyway). He puffed at the cigar as I made myself comfortable. The orange light of the ember was mirrored in the shine of his gold cufflinks.

"Can I offer you a drink? Or a cigar?" he asked. "I'll grant you amnesty from prosecution."

"Thanks, no," I replied. "But I'll take an amnesty card if you're giving them out. You never know when that'll come in handy."

He chuckled and flashed me his movie star smile.

"I like you, Mr. Johnson. You're a public nuisance on many levels, but I respect that."

"It's part of my charm."

"That's why I think we can help one another."

"What did you have in mind?"

Spierhoofd touched a button on the console beside him.
"Franz," he said, "take us for a drive."

The hover limo rose gently and eased onto the skyway.

"I don't like standing still," he said. "We can drive
around and I'll drop you off wherever you like."

"My car's back at the police station."

"Not anymore," he said. "I had it towed five minutes
ago. It will be dropped off at your house."

I nodded. "Looks like I need a ride then."

He smiled. "It's good to be the governor."

"So," I said, "how is it that we can help one another?"

"You're currently working as a bodyguard for Sexy
Sprockets."

"That's true."

"I understand that she's had some death threats."

"How did you know that?" I asked.

"I'm the governor, Mr. Johnson. I know what you had
for breakfast this morning."

"I'm glad to see that my tax dollars are being well
spent."

"You're eating too much red meat, by the way."

"There's no such thing," I said and I think he liked that
because he smiled before taking another puff on the cigar.

"So, you're currently protecting Sexy Sprockets from
an assassin."

"That's not entirely correct."

"No, Mr. Johnson," he said sternly. "It is."

I leaned forward in my seat and rested my forearms on
my knees.

"Tell you what, Mr. Governor . . ."

"Please, call me Hans."

"All right, Hans. Call me Zach. Let's just set the coy
stuff aside and lay our cards on the table. I'll tell you what
I know. You tell me what you know and if after all that
we think we can help one another, then we do. If not then
we walk away from one another and this conversation
never took place."

I stuck out my hand. "Deal?"

Spierhoofd held his cigar between his teeth, leaned forward, and grasped my hand firmly. "Deal."

I sat back in the seat and took off my trench coat.

"I'll take that drink now," I said. "Whatever beer you have will be fine."

He reached into the fridge, pulled out two beers, tapped open the seals, and handed one to me.

"My understanding of the situation," I said, "is that Sexy is being threatened by a group named PATA. People Against Talentless Acts."

"And yet she was attacked tonight by a single armed man."

"Yeah. I'm not quite sure yet how he fits in," I said. "He could be a member of the group."

"It is not a group," Spierhoofd said, shaking his head. "The group PATA does not exist. And the boy tonight was a fall guy. A ruse. Trust me."

"I'm expecting you to plead the fifth on this next question, but how do you know that?"

Spierhoofd sat farther back in his seat, took a long pull from his beer, and then turned back to me and spoke calmly, albeit with a little world-weariness in his voice.

"Do you know how many people there are in New California, Zach?"

"Sixty million, give or take?"

"Sixty-three point four million," Spierhoofd replied. "Forty-two point seven million of them are of voting age. Of those, only thirty-eight point three are registered voters. Only eighteen and a half voted in the last election. Ten million of those who voted, voted for me. Ten million votes and it was considered a strong margin of victory for my reelection."

"Congratulations," I replied.

"There are seven million young people living in California who are between the ages of thirteen and eighteen." There are another seven million between the ages of nineteen and twenty-four."

"Okay," I said.

"Sexy Sprockets, as you know, is wildly popular with young people ages thirteen through eighteen. She has been popular for five years. Which means that every fan she had during her first year of popularity is now over eighteen."

"Voting age."

"Exactly. That's a base of seven million people right there," Spierhoofd said. "And as you may know, Ms. Sprockets has some political aspirations."

"You mean running for governor?"

"So she told you about that?"

"You're not saying that you seriously think she could win, are you?"

"As I said, she starts with a core base of seven million fans within the state. Add to that any bleed popularity she has in the twenty-something demographic, crossover appeal with virile middle-aged men, dirty old men . . ."

"And the gay community."

"She is *huge* in the gay community. Eighty percent of San Francisco would vote for her on the kitsch factor alone. Put all that together and her winning an election becomes a very real possibility."

"But Sexy as governor?" I said. "I mean, it's laughable. The media would have a field day with just the idea of it."

Spierhoofd sat back in his seat and turned his gaze out the window.

"Zach, I once did a film about a chimpanzee who could invent things."

"*Genius Loves Bananas,*" I said nodding. "I remember that one."

"During my first campaign the monkey who starred opposite me in that film backed my opposition. At a press conference, he threw his own feces at one of my campaign posters."

"That's right," I said, smiling. "That was hilarious. Um, sorry."

"My campaign was joke material for every late night HV show and every stand-up comedian on the west coast. But two weeks later, I won the election by ten percentage points. My point here is that the voters of New California are intelligent enough to see through the media distortions and make sound, informed choices on election day."

"What?"

"Oh, I'm sorry," he said. "That's one of my prepared campaign lines for press conferences. I went on autopilot for a nano. What I meant to say was that the voters of New California . . ."

"Are idiots."

"Exactly. If I became governor under those circumstances then who's to say that Sexy can't do the same?"

"So, what does this have to do with Sexy's death threats?"

"Two months ago a campaign aide of mine prepared an e-paper about the serious threat that Sexy posed to my reelection campaign. The paper was sent to one thousand of my wealthiest and most influential supporters."

"Why do I not like where this is going?" I said.

"The paper was meant to be a fund-raiser but the language was, shall we say, a little too flowery."

"How flowery?"

"I believe it referred to Ms. Sprockets as a painted faced harlot bent on destroying all that I had built over the past six years and . . ."

He paused and took another drag off his cigar.

"And?" I asked.

"And that she must be stopped at all costs. Apparently, one of my supporters took this sentiment a little too seriously."

"How do you know?"

"Because two weeks ago my office received an electronic letter saying that soon Ms. Sprockets would no longer be a threat to my regime."

"Your regime?"

"Did I say regime? I meant administration."

"One of your supporters hired an assassin?"

"That is my belief."

"Are you certain?"

"In politics, Zach, a wise man can never be certain of anything. But yes, I'm certain."

"Which supporter?"

"That I don't know. The e-mail was anonymous. We tried tracing it but had no success. It used very sophisticated masking technology."

"So it could be any of the thousand supporters?"

"Correct."

"I'm guessing you didn't report any of this to the police."

That question didn't even warrant an answer. Spierhoofd simply puffed his cigar and blew a couple of near perfect smoke rings.

"And you don't have copies of the e-mail you received or the paper your aide sent to the donors?"

"They were deleted under the new plausible deniability act that I recently signed into law."

"Nice coincidence," I said.

"I do what I can," he said with a shrug. "I've sent your office a list of the supporters to whom the initial paper was sent. That will narrow your list of suspects."

"Yeah, all the way down to a thousand," I said. Well, Mr. Governor . . ."

"I thought we agreed that you'd call me Hans."

"With all due respect, that was before I knew about all this."

"Fair enough."

"I appreciate the heads-up on the assassin and all but since it's clear that I kind of have my work cut out for me now, maybe you should just let me out here and I'll catch a cab home."

Spierhoofd nodded and touched the console again.

"Take us down please, Franz. Mr. Johnson will be getting out here."

I felt the limo slow and begin its descent. A few nanos later we were on the ground (though my head was still spinning from what I'd just heard).

"Thank you for meeting with me tonight, Zach. I wish you luck in your task."

"Thanks," I said, opening the limo door. "One question though. Why are you telling me this now? Why not just let it all play out? Let the police capture the assassin, or even let the assassin kill Sexy. Either way, you'd win."

"I'm a man of principle, Zach."

"I can tell."

"If I let someone kill Ms. Sprockets simply because she's a pop singer who wants to be governor, then what's to stop someone from killing another candidate perhaps because he's black, or Hungarian?"

"Or a former soap star," I said.

"Exactly. That would lead to anarchy."

"You're all heart, Mr. Governor.

I took one last long pull on my beer, set the bottle down on the armrest, and stepped back into the night. The limo door closed gently behind me and the hover took to the air with a whisper. I let the night air wash over me for a few nanos, savoring the serenity. Then HARA's hologram popped up beside me.

"Want me to flash a little leg and flag down a ride?" she asked.

"I'd rather you tell me that you recorded my conversation with the governor," I replied.

"You want me to replay the whole thing or just the parts that are felonious?" she asked with a smile.

"You really are getting the hang of this aren't you?" I asked.

She shrugged her shoulders, gently pushing her red hair up at the sides. It caught the moonlight with its luster and for a nano she looked absolutely radiant.

"A girl's gotta have a hobby."

21

I got home a few hours before dawn, crawled into bed, and slept soundly for all of, oh, seven or eight minutes. The rest of the time I spent staring at the ceiling and trying to figure out which of the governor's supporters had taken out the hit on Sexy. When I did manage to fall asleep, a little after dawn, it didn't last long because I was awakened by the sound of a break-in. Actually, it wasn't so much the break-in, just the plain breaking, that woke me up. I heard a crash from downstairs as though something hard had shattered.

"HARA," I said, opening my eyes. "Did you hear that?"

"Of course I heard it." HARA responded.

"Is there someone in the house?"

"Yes."

"How come the house alarms aren't going off?"

"That's a long story."

"What?"

Break-ins at my house used to be relatively common-place. My profile, after all is a little high. I have a lot of fans, which makes me popular. I also have a lot of enemies, which ironically also makes me popular.

Unfortunately popularity doesn't equal wealth in today's society, which means that I can't live in an ultra secluded neighborhood that's inaccessible to the general public. So I do the next best thing. I equip my modest (yet comfortable) home with the most ripping edge security technology that Randy can produce (at cost). Most of it is experimental stuff, prototypes, so there are occasionally a few bugs in the system (which is one reason, for instance, why I no longer have a pet). But Randy's stuff is generations ahead of even the best commercially available security, so I'm usually fairly safe. All that, of course, made me wonder how someone had gotten into my house on that particular morning.

I heard more sounds of destruction from the lower level. This one sounded like glass or ceramics breaking (violently).

"What's going on?"

"You better go see for yourself," HARA replied.

"Fine. Where's my gun?"

"It was dead after last night's action. It's still recharging."

"Where's the backup then?"

"Trust me, big guy. Your gun won't help you here."

More sounds of destruction sounded downstairs.

"What do you mean? Someone is ransacking the downstairs and . . ." the realization hit me (and the news was worse than I expected). "It's Electra isn't it?"

HARA's hologram appeared at the foot of the bed, dressed only in a holographic replica of one of my button-down shirts. Her hair was a little mussed, as though she'd only just awoken. She nodded as more sounds of breaking stuff wafted up the stairs.

"Okay," I sighed, rolling out of bed and grabbing my robe. "I guess I should talk to her while I still have some possessions to save."

"Good idea."

"And you're going to need to dress more demurely if you want me to live."

Where should I begin with Electra?

She's brilliant. That's a start. She's a gifted surgeon with a mind that's sharper than a laser-honed scalpel. She is astute, well-read, speaks seven languages fluently, and has a heart as big as the hole in the ozone layer. She is beautiful beyond compare; both her face, which is finely sculpted, and her body, which is well-shaped and well-toned. She has great inner strength, which comes from her upbringing in New Costa Rica and great physical strength which comes from her many hours at the gym and at her local dojo where she still hones the kickboxing skill that made her New Central American champion not too many years ago.

All in all she is a paragon of humanity, a woman for whom one could only wish and about the best person that I've ever known.

Now the downside (it's short but deadly). She can't cook. She snores (just a little). She has no interest whatsoever in twen-cen music. And she has a temper. The reason that I don't own fine furniture is because furniture never lasts long in my house. No matter how well made it may be, it inevitably succumbs to Electra's volatile and destructive ire.

I came down the stairs and found her in the living room, cracking the arm of my futon couch off the main frame with a vicious side kick.

"I'd offer you some coffee," I said, "if you haven't started in on the kitchen yet."

"I just did the chairs," she replied, cracking the other arm off the couch. "And some of the dinnerware. I wanted to make sure I had some sharp objects handy."

Her face was a little flushed and covered with a thin sheen of perspiration, which made her complexion glow. A thin strand of her dark hair dangled over her face and she kept pushing it aside as she destroyed the couch. She was working hard, which meant that, although her outward demeanor was calm, there was some major rage underneath. I swallowed hard and tried to act casual as I ducked into the kitchen and poured two cups of coffee.

"I was actually starting to like that couch," I hollered to her from the kitchen.

"Good," she replied and I heard the sound of more polymer cracking.

I took a deep breath and reentered the living room. The couch was now officially in pieces. She hadn't ripped open the actual futon or anything, but that wasn't her style (which is the primary reason I bought the couch to begin with).

"Here," she said, walking toward me with a large piece of the couch's frame in her hands. "Hold this for me."

"I'm not going to hold it," I said.

"I'm going to be kicking in your direction, Chico," she said. "You can be holding the target or you can be the target. Your choice."

"Fine," I said, setting the coffee down on the (still intact) end table.

I held the meter and a half polymer board vertically in my hands and extended my arms to keep it as far away from my face as possible.

"I'm guessing you've been watching the entertainment news?" I asked.

Electra did a quick spin kick and snapped the board in two.

"You didn't tell me you were going to be her bodyguard," she said.

"Why else would Sexy Sprockets need me?" I asked. "You think she wants me to be her backup singer?"

Electra picked up one of the pieces of the board she'd just broken and handed it to me. I took it and held it out again.

"And, of course, you had to take the job," she said, cracking the board in half with another kick.

"I'm being sued by the owner of the Kabuki Palace," I replied. "I need the credits to settle with him. It's either that or I do the reality series with Rupert Roundtree."

"Of course," she said, picking up another of the board pieces and handing it to me. "There's always a perfectly logical reason for why you have to hang around with a young, beautiful, famous woman."

"It's not like I'm alone with her on a desert island or anything," I said. "She has other bodyguards too."

"Who are also young and beautiful."

"Carol's with me as well."

"Let's not even start on that one," she said, motioning for me to hold the board up.

The once two-meter-long board had been halved and halved again by Electra's kicks. It was now less than four hundred centimeters long.

"It's too small to break, honey."

"Then you better use it as a shield," she said, winding up.

"This is not my fault!" I said, holding the board and turning away.

Her fist went cleanly through the board and stopped about five centimeters short of my face. I could see a small drop of blood on the knuckle of her index finger.

"That's right," she said, fist still in my face. "It's never your fault."

And she left without another word.

22

I didn't move for a few minutes after Electra stormed out; partly because I was afraid to, partly because I half expected her to come back, and partly because I really didn't know what to say. I screw up a lot when it comes to our relationship. I freely admit that. But this time it seemed to me that she was the one being irrational and, quite frankly, I wasn't comfortable being the rational one in the relationship. So, like I said, I simply stood there.

"I think she wants you to go after her," HARA said, appearing beside me, dressed now in her business attire (tight blouse, short skirt, and heels).

"No, she doesn't," I said, trying to sound more knowledgeable than I felt. "She wants me to stay here and think about what I've done."

"And what is it you've done?"

"DOSsed if I know," I said. "But I'll apologize for it when I figure it out."

I turned around and headed back up the stairs, nearly tripping over the maidbot as it rolled into the living room and began cleaning up the mess.

"I'm going to need to speak with Sexy to bring her up to date on what we know," I said. "It looks like I'm going to need to be with her twenty-four/seven for the time being."

"That will do wonders for your relationship with Dr. Gevada," HARA quipped, her hologram floating up the stairs in front of me.

"Tell me about it. Have the maidbot pack a few days, worth of clothing in a case for me. I'll throw it in the car. And call the furniture store and order a new couch."

"You want something sturdier this time?" HARA asked. A small steno notepad and pen appeared in her hand as she took mock notes.

"Get the same model," I replied. "If Electra can't bust up the couch, she might take her anger out on me instead. I'm going to take a quick shower and shave. We should be ready to roll in thirty minutes or so."

"Have you always had that much chest hair?" HARA asked, looking up from her note-taking.

I have to admit, that question sort of stopped me in my tracks. I looked down at my chest, which was somewhat visible through my open robe.

"What?"

"I just don't remember you having that much hair on your chest before."

"It's roughly the same amount as I had yesterday, if that's what you're asking."

"Have you ever thought of having it trimmed?" she asked. "It's a little thick."

"I don't have time for this," I said, rolling my eyes (and tightening my robe).

"Do you find that women find a hairy chest attractive?"

"HARA!"

"I'm just wondering," she continued, following me down the upstairs hall. "I would assume that a less hirsute pectoral region would be more pleasing."

I stopped at the bathroom doorway and turned to her.

"I am showering and shaving . . . my face!" I said. "I'll be ready to leave in thirty minutes, at which time, I want no more talk of personal grooming. Understood?"

"You'll wear a tie though, right?" HARA quipped. "Because I don't think an open collar would be a good look for you today."

I slammed the door in her holographic face, and heard her chuckle quietly.

We hit the road thirty minutes later and headed for the Elite. The fall air was cool and clear and the road was only sparsely speckled with ground-based traffic and low-to-ground hovers; all in all, a beautiful Frisco morning. Admittedly any morning would be considered beautiful after the night I'd just been through, but I've found that the craziness of my lifestyle helps me appreciate life's quieter nanos

(you know, the ones where people aren't trying to kill me).
As usual, HARA and I multitasked during the drive and
the first call was to Carol.

"*Que pasa,* Tio? Rough night?"

Her face was bright and cheery as she appeared on the
dashboard screen. Even after the excitement of the night
before, she looked rested and ready for more. She was
clearly enjoying this assignment.

"Let's just say that the chaos of Sexy's concert was the
good part of my night. I learned a lot of things about our
situation afterward, none of them good."

"You mean like Sexy being stalked by an assassin who's
been hired by one of the governor's A-list supporters?"

"I thought we agreed that you wouldn't read my mind
over the net," I said.

"What can I say, Tio? You're an open book."

"Great," I said, rolling my eyes. "How were things at
the hotel last night? Any trouble?"

"Nope, we just gave each other foot massages and
crashed when we got back to the room."

"Good, at least the 'no trouble' part. I'm going to need
you to stay with Sexy until I get there. And don't let her
leave the hotel."

"Okay, but don't take too long," she said. "I'm supposed
to go to lunch with Sammy in an hour or so."

"With who?"

"Sammy's taking me out to lunch to thank me for saving
everyone last night."

"Couldn't he just buy you a car or something?"

"Tio, I know you don't like him, but really, once you get
to know him, he's very sweet."

"I believe the five letter s-word you mean to use there
is slimy," I said. "Please promise me you'll be careful. I
have a little experience with his type. The man is a player."

"Oh, please, I'm the earthly liaison for the entire Gladian
race. I think I can take care of myself."

"He's a talent manager, Carol," I said. "He's far more
insidious than anything an alien can throw at you."

"Fine," she said a little petulantly. "I'll be careful."

I frowned as her face disappeared from the screen.

"Do you believe that?" I asked HARA.

"What?"

"She's having lunch with Smiles?"

"Smiles isn't so bad," HARA said.

"He's as greasy as a lard-frosted doughnut."

"He's an operator, I'll admit," HARA replied. "But he has self-confidence and there's a suaveness to his manner that I'm sure some women find attractive."

"He's as phony as a witch doctor in New Utah."

"He has a distinctive, polished style. That doesn't automatically make him disingenuous."

"Right, that's just a coincidence," I mumbled. "Why are you defending him anyway? Do you think he's attractive?"

"I didn't say that," HARA replied. "I'm just saying that some women might find a man who moves to the beat of a different drummer attractive."

"What about me then?"

"What about you?"

"I follow a different drummer."

"Yes, it's just that your drummer has been dead for about a hundred years."

"So you're saying I'm old fashioned?"

"Duh!"

"Well, what's wrong with that?"

"I never said there was anything wrong with that."

"No, you're just saying that some greaseball circus reject is attractive because he dresses differently from everyone else and yet I'm considered a caveman for doing the same thing."

"Fine, then," HARA said. "You're attractive too."

"Shut up."

"No, no," she continued, "the rough and tumble, nononsense, tough guy thing works well for you. The trench coat, dark suit, broad shoulders, chiseled face, it's all very attractive in a y-chromosome sort of way."

"Fine then," I said. "Thanks."

"But then you ruin it with all that chest hair," she said with a smile.

"Yeah, well your skirt's too short."

"It is not," she said, tugging at her holographic hem.

"It's halfway up your thigh," I said smiling. "Sheesh, HARA, leave a little to the imagination, will you?"

"It's just the way I'm sitting," she said, recrossing her legs. "But if it offends your puritan sensibilities then here."

Her skirt lengthened by a few centimeters as she adjusted

her holographic image, so that the bottom hem ended just above the knee.

"Better," I said.

"Wait a nano," she said with a smile, "you've been looking at my legs?"

Thankfully, Randy chose that nano to call and I immediately brought his face onto the screen.

"Good morning, Zach."

"Good timing, Randy," I said. "What can I do for you?"

"I was calling to let you know that I'm downloading some new armaments into your arsenal today. HARA will be able to load them from her interface. I thought I'd let you know personally now that we've unequivocally proven that you don't read my memos."

"Yadda, yadda, yadda, Randy. Thanks."

"The new armaments are non-lethal electromagnetic charges that stimulate a person's pain receptors."

"Sounds pretty harsh."

"Yes, they're very painful," Randy said. "I got the idea while watching a prison movie on HV the other night. I could probably sell them to the government and various law enforcement agencies for use as torture-related interrogation devices."

"Ouch. Are you sure you want to do that?"

"No, not really," he said. "It's not a very productive use for the technology. I plan to limit their sale exclusively to the S&M market instead. It's more profitable anyway."

"Nice to see you have a conscience, Randy." I said. "Let's make the audible command big-hurt, okay?"

"I think the new armaments will be very useful, Dr. Pool," HARA said with a smile.

"Thank you, HARA," Randy replied. "How goes your new interface experiment?"

"I'm finding it very educational," HARA replied. "Life as a woman is definitely different. Of course, I'm still performing my usual duties for Zach. I saved his life last night by piloting a hover limo."

"It sounds very exciting, HARA," Randy replied. "Are you driving Zach's vehicle now?"

"Gates, no," HARA replied. "This fossil-mobile has no guidance computer with which I can interface. Zach drives this one on his own."

"That's good to know," Randy said, his face growing serious. *"Kleinduxity!"*

HARA's hologram froze and again, the skin around my eye went numb.

"Stop the car, Zach," Randy said.

"What?"

"Stop the car. I took HARV off-line so we could speak privately."

I slowed the car and pulled into the breakdown lane.

"You're going to need to back up," Randy said.

"Randy!"

"You need to be roughly in the same spot on the road when I bring her back online. She'll be suspicious otherwise and I don't have confidence in your ability to fool her."

I sighed, put the car into reverse, and began backing up. A series of angry blasts from the horns of the oncoming traffic serenaded me as I did so.

"I'd appreciate a little warning next time," I said.

"How can I warn you without warning HARA as well?"

"We could come up with a code."

"Zach, she's a supercomputer. Do you really think she's going to be fooled by you blinking your eye three times?"

"How did you know that was going to be my code?"

"Because that's your code for everything," Randy replied. "Okay, according to the GPS, you're in position now."

I put the car in park and turned back to Randy's face on the viewscreen.

"Is there a point to all this?"

Randy's expression was very serious, which, as you know, worries me a great deal, as he leaned closer to the monitor.

"I've run some stealth diagnostics on HARV," he said. "And frankly, I'm gravely concerned."

"Concerned how?" I asked.

"Honestly, I don't know where to begin," he said, scrolling through a stream of data on his computer. "HARV has been doing some things that are outside his parameters. And he's been doing them for some time now."

"Like what?"

"Well, I don't know how to tell you this, but he put some kind of combat subroutine in your brain."

"You mean the Bruce Lee thing?"

"How did you know about that?"

"I used it on the Thompson case."

"You what?"

Randy slammed his hands on the surface of his desk and spilled his coffee onto the com-interface. A dark puddle formed over his image, obscuring his face.

"You okay, Randy?"

"Why didn't you tell me about the subroutine?"

"I don't know," I said. "Maybe because I was busy saving the world? HARV and I talked it over. He promised not to use it again and I figured that was it."

Randy, still angry, squeegeed the coffee off his interface and his image reappeared on my screen.

"You just figured, huh? Well, have you noticed how much more coffee you've been drinking lately?"

"You're not one to talk, Randy."

"Zach, the reason you've been drinking so much coffee over the past year is . . ."

". . . because caffeine makes the neural connection fire better," I said. "HARV told me that."

"He what?"

Again, Randy gestured wildly and, in his excitement, spilled something else (creamer, I think) onto the interface.

"Why didn't you tell me that?" he yelled.

"I didn't tell you about that?" I asked. "I guess it didn't seem important."

"Zach, your computer is effecting your behavior and drugging you," he said, wiping off his interface again and pouring himself another cup of coffee. "You don't consider that important?"

"It's just what HARV does," I said. "Or did, anyway, before he became HARA."

"How has he acted since then? Anything strange?"

"I don't know," I shrugged. "It's all kind of relative, I guess. I mean, HARA does the same job that HARV did. She does research for me, takes care of the day-to-day stuff, and she did a great job piloting the hover limo during the firefight last night. She's just different, that's all. She says different things and focuses on stuff that HARV never did. Hey, do you think I have too much hair on my chest?"

Randy did a spit take with his coffee and had to clean off the interface again.

"Randy, do you want to call me back on a spillproof interface?"

"Zach, I'm concerned about how HARV is evolving. I'm working on a couple of things here but I want you to report back to me if HARA's behavior changes."

"Changes how?"

"Well, if she stops following your commands, for instance."

"She's supposed to follow commands?"

"It was the central tenet of HARV's programming. Did HARV ever *not* do something that you requested?"

"Are you kidding? He complained about me nonstop."

"But did he ever actually not do something that you asked?"

I had to think about that one for a long, long nano and I was surprised by my answer.

"No," I said. "I guess he didn't."

"Good," Randy replied. "Promise me you'll let me know if HARA ever refuses a direct command."

"Okay."

"Promise me, Zach!"

"Okay, Randy. I promise."

"Good," Randy said with a nod. "Now ease back onto the road, I'm going to bring HARA back online. Just remember to act casual."

I did as I was told and Randy rebooted HARA's interface (the audio command this time was kozotzkypuss). But it was hard to act casual knowing what I knew. Part of me was worried about HARV/HARA's evolution and the concern that it seemed to cause Randy. But another part of me felt guilty about the conversation with Randy, almost like I'd betrayed HARA. With all the complications that come from having a supercomputer connected to your brain, who'd have thought fidelity would be the one that bothered me most?

23

HARA and I arrived at the Elite late in the morning. HARA stayed hidden, which was fine with me. Sexy was in the gym doing a kickboxing workout with Misty, Sissy, and Lusty and I had to admit that all four ladies threw some mean punches.

I met Carol and Smiles on the catwalk overlooking the gym. They were drinking protein shakes and laughing with one another as they watched Sexy and the girls trading blows below with the sparring droids. Their comfort level with one another made me a little squeamish.

"At last," Carol said when she saw me approach. "What took you so long, Tio?"

"There was a lot of ground traffic this morning," I said.

"Ground traffic?" Smiles quipped. "No wonder it took you so long, you were surrounded by old ladies."

"He's got a thing about heights," Carol said, a little too lightly.

"I take it you've seen today's entertainment news?" Smiles asked.

"Actually, no," I said. "Is there a problem?"

"Not if your goal is to make Sexy a laughingstock," he said. "If so, then it's a rosy, red letter day."

"Look, Smiles, last night there was a very real attempt on Sexy's life. I don't think media coverage should be your primary concern at the nano. And speaking of murder attempts, I'd like to brief you and Sexy on what I learned last night."

"That sounds great, Johnson," Smiles said, getting up from his chair. "Really, can't wait to hear it, but it will have to keep for the nano. Carol and I have lunch reservations and Sexy is due at MHV."

"Where?"

"MHV News. We booked an interview on the request show for this afternoon in order to undo some of the damage that was done last night."

"Do you think that's a good idea?"

Smiles turned away from me and shouted down to Sexy, who was just finishing her workout.

"Let's put some scooty in that booty S-Girl. You have to be on camera in an hour."

Sexy gave the droid one last kick (to the groin) before shutting it down. She grabbed a towel and a water bottle from a hovering bot nearby and turned to us on the catwalk.

"I'm coming up now, Sammy," she said. "Hi, Zach."

Her smile was sweet and sensuous, an effect made more so by the sweaty glow from her workout.

"Hi yourself, Sexy," I said, immediately regretting the hint of flirtation in my tone.

Carol shot me a look as I turned but I couldn't tell if she was angry at me because of my attraction to Sexy or my disgust with Smiles. Either way it was clear she wasn't happy, but she didn't say anything.

"We'll be back for the pre-concert prep," Smiles said, turning to leave.

"Carol, we should discuss the plan for tonight's concert when I get back," I said.

"Just think it really strongly," she said without turning around. "I'll get it."

I gritted my teeth and tried to remain calm as she and Smiles left. Carol was taking some liberties with the assignment that I didn't approve of. She also wasn't actually helping me with any of the legwork, which irked me. But her powers had saved us last night and I definitely I owed her something for that. So I let it slide.

A nano later, Sexy and the girls came onto the catwalk. Sexy gave me a little hug as she appeared and her arm, still damp with sweat against my neck, left a mark on my skin that gave me a chill.

"Give me two nanos to freshen up," she said. "Then we can go."

"Are you sure you want to be doing this interview now?" I asked. "I don't like the idea of you being out in the open like that."

"It'll be in the studio, Zach. And like Sammy said, we really need to put a positive spin on this whole thing."

"What kind of positive spin can you put on a murder attempt?"

"Well, that it failed, for one," she replied with a smile. "Plus it gives me some additional street cred."

"Street cred?"

"Real danger. It's very edgy," she replied. "It all makes perfect sense actually. I've pushed the envelope throughout my career—with my music, my fashion, and my sense of taste and decorum in general. Being stalked is just another facet of my edginess."

"Great," I said "maybe you'll start a trend and everyone will want a stalker."

Half an hour later, Sexy, Misty, Sissy, Lusty, and I were sitting in the MHV greenroom cooling our heels while the live interview show made its way, one insipid nano at a time, to us. They had saved Sexy for the closing minutes and the live crowd on the set was getting impatient (which was making me nervous).

"I thought this was supposed to be a closed set?" I asked Sexy.

"It is closed," she said with a shrug. "No one other than the host, the crew, and the studio audience is allowed in."

"Letting the public in sort of nullifies the idea of a set being closed," I said.

"These kids began lining up outside the studio this morning when they announced my appearance. They're fans, Zach."

"Sexy, one of your fans tried to hand you a nano-explosive floral bouquet last night," I said. "With fans like that, who needs critics?"

"Don't be such a worm in the data."

The interview set was a huge studio space with a semicircle of bleacherlike seats facing a plush couch and host chair on the brightly lit stage. A dozen or so camerabots floated around the host and guest-of-the-nano as the audience (wild-eyed teens mostly) screamed and cheered whenever the "scream and cheer" light above the set flashed (which was most of the time). They all looked like legit kids to my eye, but I wasn't taking any chances.

"How's the background screening going?" I whispered to HARA.

"Slow but steady, she replied in my head. "I have visual matches on eighty-five percent of them. Everyone checks out so far."

"The crew too?"

"Already done," she said. "They're all clean."

"I still don't like it."

"You're just afraid that she'll sing."

"Just keep scanning and let me know if anything odd turns up," I said. "I did pack the earplugs, though, right?"

Before HARA could answer a thin man with a headset and handheld computer stuck his head in the room.

"One minute, Ms. Sprockets."

Sexy and the girls bounced up from their chairs and headed toward the studio door.

"Showtime everyone," Sexy smiled.

The plan was for Misty, Sissy, and Lusty to do the interview along with Sexy (which made me happy). They'd be background scenery. Sexy would do the talking but it gave me three more bodies near Sexy. I, on the other hand, was clearly not attractive enough to be part of Sexy's posse but I planned to be just out of camera frame in case of trouble. But all that changed when the non-studio door of the greenroom opened and a familiar voice sent a chill up my spine.

"Zach-a-lacka-ding-dong-fooey," Rupert Roundtree called out. "How's every little thing?"

24

Sexy's eyes shot daggers at Roundtree as he entered the room, arms spread and smile just as wide. Misty and Sissy had to hold her arms to keep her from going after him. I was no help at all. Lusty actually had to hold me back (her grip was surprisingly strong). But my composure returned after a nano.

"Sexy, take the crew onstage. Do the interview," I said. "I'll handle things here."

"Are you sure, Zach?"

"Trust me. You'll be safer upwind."

Sexy and the others left, closing the door behind them. I heard the crowd go crazy a nano later as Sexy was introduced and stepped onstage.

"That's what I like about you, Zacha-jewea," Roundtree said, making himself comfortable on the greenroom sofa. "You're always thinking of others."

"That's true," I said, taking a seat across from him. "Right now, for instance, I'm thinking about you and the best way to break both of your legs."

Roundtree guffawed so loudly I thought he was going to cough up his spleen.

"You're precious, Zacher, but there's no need to get rough," he said. "I'm here under a flag of truce. I know you have some questions for me."

"You mean like, what are you doing here?"

"Yes, like that," he said. "I wanted to have a little sit-down with you here to sort of ease the tensiosity that you're probably feeling."

"You're here to give me answers, huh?"

"On my word, Action Zachtion, you're safe in this room."

"How did you know I was here?"

"I own the network, Zachrobat. The youth market's a real profit center now and they're the movers and shakers of tomorrow. You gotta get 'em on board when they're young if you're gonna rule the world, right? But that's not what you really want to know, is it?"

I shook my head and sat back in my chair.

"You're right," I said. "What I want to know is how you do it."

Roundtree sat back and smiled. He reached into his coat pocket, pulled out a cigar, and lit it.

"I know, I know, it's illegal" he said, motioning to the cigar. "But I own the place so I don't think anyone will turn me in."

He blew a smoke ring that hovered over his head for a nano like a nicotine halo before breaking apart and dissipating on the air-conditioned greenroom breeze.

"How do I do it?" he said, staring past me into the studio. "I do it by seeing where the world is going and then looking another 10K down the road. I do it by giving the people what they want before they even know that they want it. That's my job, Zactoid. I'm a visionarian, an edge-ripper. Because in the world of entertainment, you have to keep raising the bar tab. Face it, yesterday's shocking is today's mundane. Today's obscene is tomorrow's afterschool special. You either push the edge or you get sucked into the pop-cult quicksand of kitschiness. Be the shark or jump it—that's what it comes down to.

"I choose to forge ahead, push the boundaries, break the taboos, and crush the societal mores beneath the heel of my jack-booted audacity. The sky is the gimmick, everything is everything and nothing, nothing, is taboo! Except the n-word, the f-bomb, and two bare breasts at the Super Bowl, of course, but everyone knows that.

"That's how I do it, Zachamoton. That's how I do what I do."

"Sorry, Roundtree," I said, "but I meant how you look at yourself in the mirror."

Roundtree smiled and put out his cigar.

"You can't take this personally, Zachtor's guild," he said. "This isn't personal. It's just business. And there are times in business when you just have to make a good snuff film."

He reached forward and gave me a couple of friendly slaps on the knee.

"Now let's get moving, Zachadoo. We have episode number four to record."

"I thought you said I was safe in this room."

"You are," Roundtree said, looking out at the studio. "But the danger's not in this room."

I followed his gaze into the studio and saw Sexy on the interview couch speaking energetically with the host (a surfer dude with glowing blue hair). I did a quick scan of the audience and saw four tough-looking teens slip into the throng of fans. They wore black polymer armor-pads on their elbows, knees, and wrists, and dark helmets and goggles on their heads.

"Teen X-Tremes," Roundtree whispered. "It's a daredevil show that we're launching midseason. A guest appearance on *Let's Kill Zach* will be a huge springboard."

"What happens if I refuse to fight them?" I asked.

"Well, then we launch the show by having them accidentally do grievous bodily harm to teen sensation Sexy Sprockets."

"You wouldn't dare," I snarled.

"There are very few things that I wouldn't do, Zachintyre. Daring definitely isn't one of them."

"But she's not involved in this. She's just an innocent bystander."

"Something you need to learn about this business is that everyone is involved and that no one is innocent, except of course for my mom, the sweetest woman ever put on this planet, or any other."

As one, the X-Tremers turned to look at Roundtree through the greenroom window. He gave them the thumbs up sign and they slid their dark-lensed goggles over their eyes then disappeared into the crowd. A nano later they attacked.

25

Teen X-Treme began life as a game kids played on the streets of Malibu. Kids on hoverboards and glider blades chase a ball around a floating obstacle course trying to whack it through a hoop. Sometimes they use lacrosse sticks, sometimes hockey sticks. Sometimes they use electromagnetic taser cudgels. That part's very nebulous because no one actually keeps track of the points. The real point of the game, I'm told, is to turn outrageous airborne tricks and to beat the DOS out of the opposing team. It makes absolutely no sense at all, which is no doubt why it is so popular with teenagers. It's a street game at the nano but clearly Roundtree and his people were hoping to bring it to the mainstream. Just what society needs, another pointless, hard to follow sport. As if cricket wasn't enough. The point is that the really good X-Tremers are tough, talented kids and shouldn't be trifled with (unless of course they're attacking a client).

The X-Tremers came at Sexy from the front, like a pack of wild dogs at a three-legged deer. Two were on hoverboards, two on glider blades, all of them carrying hockey sticks. Sexy was answering a question about her songwriting inspirations, her head turned toward the host, so she didn't see them coming right away.

I was out of the greenroom door and running flat out the nano I saw Roundtree give the X-Tremers the go sign. By the time they made their move I was on the floor, running for the stage, gun out and shoving audience members aside like a fetishist at a used shoe sale.

"Sexy get down!"

I fired once as I leaped, knocking a g-blader out of the

air with a stun blast, broadsiding a boarder with a midair football tackle. We landed hard on the main stage (him on the bottom) and I gave the kid a hard knee to the groin as I rolled off him.

The two X-Tremers still airborne veered away from the stage and back into the crowd of kids who were now screaming and running for the exits.

Misty, Sissy, and Lusty converged on Sexy as one, pushed her to the floor and surrounded her with a (nicely shaped) girl-power wall of protection. I had to admit, they looked very professional, and hot at the same time. And when the downed g-blader tried to climb to his feet, Lusty put him down for the count with a mean back kick to the face that shattered his goggles.

"Zach?"

Sexy's eyes were wide with fear. It was clear that she'd seen too much action in the last twenty-four hours and it was beginning to wear on her.

"It's okay," I yelled, scanning the fleeing crowd for the remaining X-Tremers. "These jokers are after me so stay with the girls."

"The still conscious attackers are in the back of the room by the exits," HARA whispered in my head. "One in each corner. Chasing them at this point would only further panic the audience."

"You're right," I said. "Let's give the bystanders some time to get out. We'll keep the fight here."

"There's not much cover," HARA said. "They have the edge with speed and maneuverability. But I think a couple of computer-guided blasts from your gun should do the trick."

"Not this time," I said, picking up the hockey stick from the downed hoverboarder. "I'm suddenly in the mood to hit something."

The hockey stick was Teen X-Treme enhanced, which meant that it had a force field generator at the foot that magnified the force of a blow tenfold. I flipped the power toggle on the handle and felt it hum to life.

"You kids looking for some action?" I shouted.

The two X-Tremers stepped out from the fleeing crowd and took to the air, hovering two meters above the floor; one on a board, the other on blades.

"You think it's cool to attack a bunch of unarmed teenagers? You think that makes you hardcore?"

The X-Tremers answered by powering up their hockey sticks. I cast a quick glance over to Sexy and the girls. The girls picked up my meaning and hustled Sexy and the show host out of the studio, leaving me alone with the X-Tremers.

"I'll show you hardcore."

The X-Tremers smiled and attacked in unison. I could tell that they'd trained together because they worked well as a team. The boarder came in high, swiping at my head and the blader came low at the knees. I ducked under the high swing but the blader whipped his stick around widely and nailed me hard in the back of the kneecaps. My legs collapsed and I crumbled to the stage floor.

They came around again, pressing their advantage. This time the boarder jabbed me hard in the back with the butt of his stick and the blader followed it up with a slam to the stomach. I dropped my stick and fell to the floor on my hands and knees as they split up and circled the room again. Ten seconds into the fight, and I'd been hit hard three times.

"You sure you don't want to use the gun?" HARA said in my head.

"Quiet, HARA," I said. "You're killing the moment."

The X-Tremers came back around, moving in for the kill this time. They were kids, I could tell; no more than seventeen or eighteen years old. I knew that they'd been flying for a while because they had all the moves. But they didn't have the fighting experience. And that was going to cost them.

"I gotta hand it to you guys," I said, slowly getting to my feet. "You're first class X-Tremers."

They moved in close again, flying in the same formation as the first pass; the boarder high, the blader low.

"But this isn't Teen X-Treme we're playing."

I ducked under the swipe of the boarder and blocked the blader's swing with my stick. Then I kneed him hard in the face. The impact sounded like a dropped melon hitting the sidewalk.

"This is street fighting."

The boarder sailed over me while the blader rolled to the floor holding his now broken nose.

"You see, in street fighting there's something we call playing possum. You can do that when you wear body armor."

The boarder looped around and came at me head down and fast, his stick leveled like a lance. I held my ground until the last nano and then twisted out of the way, grabbing the end of his stick as I rolled to the floor. It spun him around and down, his own momentum slamming him into the floor.

"And there are no style points in this business. The only moves that count are the ones that break the other guy's bones."

The blader had gotten back to his feet and, nose still bleeding, picked up his stick and lunged at me. Dazed and bruised as he was, he was way, *way* too slow. I blocked his first swing with my stick (like Robin Hood with a quarterstaff).

"And most of all," I said. "Nobody does this for fun." (Although, I have to admit that deep down I *was* having a little fun but I tried not to think too much about what that said about me.)

I reached back and gave him a stick-shot to the gut with the force field end. His eyes bugged out for a nano and he let out a sound like a cherry bomb exploding in a bagpipe. Then he crumbled like a rag doll and fell flat to the floor.

"Remember that the next time an idiot entertainment executive tells you guys that terrorizing a bunch of innocent kids will be good for your career."

I heard the roar of a maxed out hoverboard behind me and turned to see the last X-Tremer charging. He had gotten up from his hard landing with a serious mad-on and was now coming at me, low to the ground flying down the aisle between the bleacher seats. I held my stick ready to meet his charge.

But as it turned out, I didn't need to.

A shapely, strong arm whipped out at him from between the seats, clotheslining him right in the sternum. His board flew out from under his feet as he let out a squeal and fell backward. His butt hit the floor hard but his face got the worst of the deal because the nano he landed he got kayoed with an open-fisted right cross to the jaw.

Lusty turned to stare at me once she made sure the guy was down.

"Thanks," I said.

She smiled at me and gave the downed X-Tremer one last grind of her boot before walking away.

26

The ride back to the Elite went as well as could be expected under the circumstances. Sexy was shaken up. Misty, Lusty, and Sissy were angry with me for putting their friend in danger and I was ready to kill the first media mogul I came across (sadly Roundtree had fled the scene shortly after the start of the X-Treme attack). Only Shreek enjoyed the ride and that's because he got to sit next to HARA.

By the time we arrived, Sexy's interview had aired on MHV and had been picked up by every newsite on the net. I'm sure the network made a fortune in licensing fees selling the footage and, as I watched the slo-mo images of me shoulder slamming the hoverboarder out of the air and blasting another out of his blades, I was starting to feel like a not particularly bright dancing monkey to Rupert Roundtree's organ grinder. He was cashing in on my hard work, getting rich off my sweat, squeezing every ounce of profit from my efforts without my consent or permission.

I think I must have ranted something to this effect aloud in the limo because Sexy looked up at me from under her cold compress and said, "Welcome to my world, Zach."

And that just about wrecked my day.

Smiles was waiting for us when we arrived at the hotel. He ran to Sexy the nano we landed on the hoverport, gently wrapped a silk blanket around her shoulders and helped her into the celebrity entrance. He shot me a dagger of a look as he passed but I couldn't blame him. I was fast becoming as big a danger to Sexy as the hired assassin. The problem was that I couldn't back out of the job now because I didn't trust anyone else to protect her.

I saw Carol at the hoverport door. She watched as

Sammy ran to Sexy and hustled her inside. Carol looked a little put off as they passed. When she locked eyes with me, she out-and-out frowned then turned away.

"Carol."

She made no sign that she'd heard me as she entered the hotel. I had to run to catch up with her.

"Carol, hey."

I touched her arm and she turned around slowly.

"What is it, Zach?" she asked.

"Is everything okay here?" I asked, a little worried (I couldn't remember the last time she'd called me Zach).

"Oh yeah, everything's great," she said, "if you're trying to get Sexy killed."

"What?"

"You put her in danger, Zach, just by being around her."

"I'm the one who said she shouldn't do the interview."

"But that wasn't the problem, was it?" she said. "The problem was that you went with her. That's what almost got her killed!"

"I don't think this is the proper time to discuss that," I said, a little angry.

"You're right," she said, and continued walking.

"Did you contact Tony like I asked? We're going to need a bigger police presence backstage tonight."

"Sammy didn't want any more police," she said. "He said that it would make Sexy nervous."

"Since when did you start taking orders from Sammy?" I asked, falling into step alongside her.

"He knows what he's doing," Carol said.

"Carol, you don't work for Sammy Smiles."

"Well, maybe I should," she said.

"What is going on with you?"

"Zach, please," she said. "Don't make a scene, okay? I need to go help Sammy. I'll see you later."

She ran ahead of me and hopped onto a high speed elevator with Misty, Sissy, and Lusty. She made no effort to hold the doors open for me as I stared at her.

Sexy spent the rest of the afternoon behind closed doors with Smiles and Carol. Smiles said that Sexy needed some time to clear her head from the ordeal and get her mental focus back on the upcoming performance. That left me the odd man out at the hotel, which was just as well, because it gave me a chance to beef up security for the concert. That meant telling Tony everything I had learned the night before. His initial reaction was pretty much what I expected.

"Are you out of your mind?"

I had found a spare room on Sexy's main floor of the Elite and set up a sort of pseudo office for the afternoon. It wasn't much but all I really needed was a place to rest my wrist interface and a hook to hang my trench coat. The room I'd found didn't actually have a hook, but it had a comfy couch and a fully-stocked mini fridge, which was okay too. There was music in the background as well, which I assumed was Sexy practicing for tonight's show.

"I know it sounds crazy," I said, munching on my second package of chocolate-covered macadamia nuts.

"The governor hired a hit man to kill Sexy because she's a political rival?"

"It wasn't actually the governor."

"Right, just one of his millionaire supporters."

"There can't be that many of them."

"You're kidding, right?"

"Tony, I never said this was going to be easy."

"You never said it was going to be career suicide, either," Tony said. "I cannot arrest the governor."

"I'm not saying you have to. Not yet anyway. I just wanted to make sure that you knew everything I did. And you have to admit, it's helpful to know that we're dealing with a professional killer rather than an extremist group."

"Yeah, that really lightens my day," Tony replied. "But if it's a professional killer, how do you explain the kid with the bomb last night?"

"Maybe the killer didn't want to do it himself, so he set up the kid to do the dirty work. That would at least explain where the nano-explosives came from."

"If it's a professional, then why use the kid?"

"I don't know, maybe he's shy?"

"A shy assassin?"

"We've seen stranger things in our time," I said.

"Don't remind me."

"So you'll have a few extra people backstage at the show tonight?"

"They'll be there," Tony replied. "Try not to make any of them shoot you."

"I'll do my best, Tony. Thanks again."

Tony's face disappeared from the screen just as HARA appeared beside me on the sofa. She was wearing a gray pantsuit this time, with a short blazer and a white shirt opened one button too many to qualify as businesslike. Still, I appreciated the Hepburn homage she was clearly doing.

"Do you think Captain Rickey ever gets tired of the difficulties you bring to his life?"

"Don't be silly," I said, "Tony's way past tired of me. But keeping Sexy alive is high on both of our to-do lists at the nano, so he'll put up with me. Our friendship has survived worse than this."

I got to my feet, grabbed one last package of nuts from the refrigerator, and picked my coat up from the floor.

"Right now," I said, "I'd like to find out where that music is coming from. Sexy's vocals sound kind of different than usual."

"That's because they're in tune."

I paused for a nano and listened more closely.

"Wow, you're right. I wonder how she stumbled onto the right key."

The music was coming from a small room two doors over, which was surprising because Sexy's main suites were on the other side of the hotel. But when I stepped inside, it all made sense because it wasn't Sexy who was singing. It was Lusty.

And she wasn't bad.

She was practicing a dance routine that I'd seen from last night's show. Her concentration looked to be on her moves with the singing as sort of an afterthought. She wasn't singing, actually, just sort of humming the lead vocal line over the recorded music. No words, just a lot of da-das, but they were all on key. Her voice was strong and controlled with some real emotion behind it. This was the first time I'd heard her make any sound at all, which only made the quality of her voice more surprising.

She saw my reflection in the room's mirror wall after a nano or two and turned to me quickly, a flick of her hand remotely killing the music playback. Then she looked away, as though embarrassed.

"I'm sorry," I said. "I didn't mean to disturb you."

She said nothing and stared shyly at the floor.

"Thanks for the hand today with the hoverboarder. You flattened him good."

She nodded almost imperceptibly.

"I didn't know you could sing," I said. "It sounded really good."

She kept her gaze on the floor but she smiled a bit.

"Have you ever thought of singing on your own?"

She shrugged.

"Sexy will be retiring soon. Maybe you could take her place."

She shook her head silently and then whispered, "I can't."

"Why not?" I asked. "Everyone knows you can dance. And from what I just heard, you have a beautiful voice. You could even be your own bodyguard."

That got her to smile for real. She turned away from the floor and looked at me for the briefest of nanos before turning away again.

"I can't perform," she said softly.

"Why?"

"I have an . . . accent."

"An accent?"

She nodded.

"You sound fine to me."

"Trust me, I have an accent."

"Lusty, if Sexy can sing the way she does and be the biggest star in the world, I can't believe that an accent that I can't even hear will prevent you from becoming a singer."

She turned to me again and this time held my gaze. Her eyes were wide and I noticed that they were a very soft shade of brown. Her face lost the sneer of indifference that it had worn since I met her and she looked vulnerable for a nano, as though she was taking a risk by saying the next few words.

"I can't say ewse."

"You can't say what?"

"Ewse," she repeated.

"Owls?"

"No, ewse. The wetter ew."

"The what?"

"The wetter ew!" she said. "Aych, eye, jay, kay, ew!"

"Oh, el!"

"Yes, ew. I have a soft pawate and an abnormawity in my tongue. That's why I try not to tawk. It makes me sound wike an idiot."

"It's not that bad," I said. "And it's just one letter. It shouldn't stop you from singing."

She shook her head and began to sing. The voice was beautiful. The words on the other hand . . .

"Wook at my wegs. They are wean and wong.
Wook in my heart. My wove's awive and strong."

"I see what you mean," I said. "Can't you just avoid songs with the letter el?"

"A singer who doesn't sing about wove or wust or even wipgwoss? Sammy says that it's imossibwe."

"I'm sorry."

"It's awight. I've accepted it. I'm part of the background. That's the part I pway."

"You're a great dancer," I said. "And a really good bodyguard."

"Thanks."

"And els or no els, your voice is light years better than Sexy's."

"Don't wet her hear you say that," she said with a smile.

"Right. Our secret?"

"Our secret."

"Well, I need to check on security at The Fart," I said. "I'll let you get back to rehearsing. Sorry to interrupt."

"No probwem," she said. "See you wayter."

She smiled as I left. As I walked down the hallway back toward Sexy's main suite, I heard Lusty begin her own rendition of "Love Cutlets" (Wove Cutwets), and I thought about how unfair the showbiz fates can be.

27

Sexy remained behind closed doors with Smiles (and Carol) for most of the afternoon while HARA and I did the rest of the pre-concert security prep at The Fart. The stage crew had rebuilt the stage overnight so the set pieces were back in place in all their garish glory. I had convinced Sexy and Smiles not to hire new dancers for the "Love Cutlets" number to replace the ones I injured the night before. I didn't want to deal with any new people onstage. Sexy and Smiles figured that they'd keep the remaining two dancers with Sexy and let the girls dance with one another during the number. As Sexy put it, "a little girl-on-girl action" always gets the crowd going.

HARA and I went back to the Elite and then brought everyone over in the new limo (rented directly from Randy and equipped with more shielding and firepower than Frisco's naval base). Twenty minutes before showtime HARA and I were cooling our heels outside Sexy's dressing room while Sammy gave her one last go-round in the meditation chamber.

"So you're monitoring the communications between Tony and his men?" I asked.

"No problem, big guy. Everyone's in place and everything's moving smoothly. The audience is almost entirely seated. Even the press is behaving themselves."

The press, not surprisingly, had turned out on a grand scale for the show. The attempt on Sexy's life the night before, coupled with the fireworks at MHV this afternoon, had pumped everyone into a frenzy. Entertainment pressbots were teamed on camera with science and tech commentators discussing the best ways a killer could get past the security setups and get to Sexy. As Smiles had predicted, the focus of the coverage had shifted unceremoniously from Sexy's retirement to her immediate peril. It was the juicier story. Smiles pointed this out to Sexy every chance he got and blamed me whenever possible (which was always). But I noticed a very satisfied grin on his face that evening as we flew past the massive press throng on our way into the arena. It was clear that his eyes were on the bottom line and in the end the additional attention would only increase the profits.

"So everything's going perfectly," I said, starting to relax just a little.

"Except for the sudden spike in ambient radiation," HARA replied.

"You just couldn't let me have one worry-free nano, could you?"

"I doubt that your metabolism would know what to do if you weren't worried. You'd probably slip into a coma from the drop in blood pressure."

"Is the radiation dangerous?"

"I wouldn't recommend long term exposure to it but it poses no imminent threat."

"What's causing it?"

"I'm formulating a theory on that," HARA replied. "I'll let you know when I have something substantive."

"Terrific," I said, looking at my watch.

The crowd had begun chanting Sexy's name five minutes ago and the volume had been steadily rising ever since. Once again, the floor was rumbling and the crowd's roar echoed through the halls. I was about to knock on Sexy's dressing room door when it suddenly burst open. The red glow of the meditation chamber flooded the hall and Smiles and Carol emerged from within. Neither of them spared me a glance.

Sexy came out last and I had to say that she was quite a sight. Her face was picture perfect. Her hair had a sensual, slightly messed look, her eyes were wide and smoky and her smile was girlishly sensual. Her game face was on and when she gave me a wink and a smile, I thought the hairs on my neck would catch fire.

I followed her to the stage and the concert began with a roar that sounded like a thousand hoverjets.

*   *   *

Sexy hit the stage hot, the crowd went crazy, and the first few songs went exactly as planned. The band played well and Sissy, Misty, Lusty, and Carol were especially energetic. Best of all there was no violence. Tony's men were on their toes, as were the regular concert security staff.

And even though I'd been less than thrilled with Carol's attitude of late, I had to admit that she was doing her job onstage, mentally scanning the crowd for signs of trouble. Opening her mind up to so many people was hard on her, I could tell. In all likelihood she'd have a whopper of a headache in the morning from the overload of stray thoughts and emotions. Still, I was glad to have her there. She sent me a couple of quick mental messages during the first few songs, letting me know that a suspicious-looking character or two weren't dangerous (just crazy, harmless fans).

"So far so good, huh, big guy?" HARA said, as her hologram shimmered to life beside me. She was wearing a red-and-white striped miniskirt, white tee top and hat, straight from a 1960s go-go bar.

"What are you wearing?"

"I'm trying to blend in," she said.

"You're kidding, right?"

"I'm dressed about twenty years more current than you."

"A nondescript man in a trench coat and fedora or a redheaded bombshell in a miniskirt, which one do you think is going to get more attention?"

"It depends what the man has under his trench coat," she replied with a smile.

"Forget it."

"You really think I'm a bombshell?" she asked.

"I am not having this conversation now," I replied turning away.

"Well, as long as things are going smoothly," HARA said. "I need you to help me with something."

"What's that?"

"I have a theory about the source of the ambient radiation that might be important but I need a little help getting some information to verify my hypothesis."

"What do you need me to do?"

"Break into Sexy's dressing room."

"What?"

"I need to take a close look at the meditation chamber that Smiles uses."

"Can't it wait until after the show?" I asked.

"Sexy and Smiles will be there after the show. And after they've gone, the radiation will have dissipated. I need to see it now, while the trail is still fresh, while the iron is still hot, while the gun is still smoking."

"Okay," I said, turning away from the stage, "but you have to promise to never use those clichés again."

"Fine," she said, "from here on out, all clichés are yours."

I let Tony know that I was stepping away for a couple nanos (he seemed relieved, which I tried not to take as an insult) and HARA and I snuck back to the dressing room area. Smiles had replaced the dressing room door that I'd destroyed the night before. Unfortunately, this one was a lot thicker (blaster resistant). Worse still, it was protected by a DNA-coded lock.

"The lock looks pretty ripping edge," I said.

"It is," HARA replied. "Apparently Smiles ordered it special. I guess he didn't want you busting in again."

"Is it coded to his DNA or Sexy's?"

"His."

"Looks like we're out of luck."

"Oh, please," HARA said. "I could pick this lock while I'm in sleep mode."

"But you need Smiles' DNA."

"I snagged a drop of his spittle the other night when he was berating you in the limo."

"Great. I'm glad something good came of that."

"I broke it down and stored the data as a digital code that the lock will recognize. Just put your eye near the lock and let me do the rest."

I did as I was told and bent down near the lock. A red beam of light flashed from my lens like a laser sight on a gun and hit the touch pad on the DNA lock. HARA used the data-filled light beam as an informational lockpick, hacking her way through the lock's defenses and feeding it what it would recognize as Smiles' DNA. A nano later, the lock's status light flashed green and the door opened.

"Nicely done," I said.

"It's all in the touch," HARA replied.

Sexy's dressing room was as I remembered it; well-appointed and dominated by the meditation chamber. HARA wasted no time approaching the big machine.

"Radiation levels have dropped but they're still relatively high," she said. "Looks like we got here in time."

"In time for what?" I asked.

"I'm not sure yet. Come here, I'm going to need your help hacking into this as well."

"Hack in how?" I asked.

"Same as with the door lock," she replied. "Just get near the interface and beam me in."

"What are you going to do once you're in there?"

"You don't want to know and you wouldn't understand. Now just let me do my job."

"Fine," I said. "But be quick about it. We need to get back."

Again, I put my eye near the machine's computer interface and HARA shot another databeam through the lens and into the chamber's central computer. I could tell from the look of consternation on her holographic face that the security on this machine was a little tougher than on the door lock.

"Are you okay?" I asked.

Her hologram disappeared from its spot beside me as she directed more of her concentration into the search and her voice appeared inside my head.

"I'm in," she said.

"What exactly are you looking for?"

"Answers."

"Can you be more specific?"

"Not unless I know the questions."

"You know, you're getting to be very cryptic in your dialog."

"It's all part of being a woman, big guy," she replied. "You're going to have to learn to read between the lines."

"I do enough line reading as it is. I don't enjoy it."

"You're not very good at it either."

"What does that mean?"

"Hush. I'm almost there."

"Almost where?" I asked.

She was silent for a couple of nanos. All I could hear was the hum of the meditation chamber and the morass of Sexy's music through the walls. It was starting to make me nervous.

"HARA?"

"Well," she said. "This explains a lot."

"What did you find?"

"Sexy can't sing."

"Newsflash."

"No. She can't sing, but teenagers think she can."

"What?"

"It's not a generational thing after all, young people having different tastes in music than older people. It's a matter of susceptibility."

"What?"

"They really think she can sing."

"What are you talking about?"

"Sexy is tricking her audience. She's making them believe that her music is good when in actuality it's not."

"How can she do that?"

"Simple," HARA replied, her hologram reappearing beside me. "She's a psi."

28

Most people who know me (I mean *really* know me) will attest that I am an accepting and loving person. I judge people on their actions and on their character rather than by their classification. Clones, aliens, mutants, it makes no difference to me. My accountant is actually half undead (on his mother's side). Hey, I'm a private investigator whose clothes are a hundred years out of style. I'm in no position to judge anyone.

That said, Carol being one very big aside, I have never met a psi that I liked (or that didn't try to kill me, but I think one is sort of related to the other).

"Psis," I sighed. "Why does it always have to be psis."

"It's not always psis," HARA said, sitting her hologram beside me on the couch. "Sometimes it's androids."

"They're easy."

"Or robots."

"Pieces of cake."

"There have been mad scientists."

"Cream puffs."

"Mobsters, alien invaders, savage monsters long thought extinct?"

"Walks in the park."

"Telemarketers?"

"Okay, I'll give you that one. But it's usually psis."

"You do tend to come across more than your share of them," HARA agreed.

"Okay," I said, fighting off the headache that I knew was fast approaching, "explain to me how you know that Sexy is a psi."

"Well, first of all," HARA said. "She's not a psi as one generally describes it. She's what we call a niche psi."

"Niche psi?"

"Right. She has very limited abilities. She can't read minds, for instance. She has no telekinetic powers or anything like that. She has only limited telepathic powers."

"Limited how?"

"She broadcasts feelings rather than actual thoughts."

"Feelings?"

"Her powers can stimulate the amygdala and other brain stem structures, the ones that control emotion. She gives people good feelings. That mental stimulation, combined with her music . . ."

"Makes people think that they like her music."

"Correct."

"That's sort of illegal, isn't it?"

"Psionically manipulating people for profit? Yes, it's outlawed in every province, even Jersey."

"So how come I don't like her music then?"

"Because you're old."

"Thanks."

"No, it's true," HARA said. "Look, Sexy's power is very limited. She can stimulate a person's emotional centers but only if that person's prefrontal cortex allows it. The PFC is the portion of the brain that controls things like judgment, organization, and impulse control. Anyone with a fully developed PFC is going to be immune to Sexy's power. The thing about the PFC though is that it matures more slowly than the other areas of the brain. On average, it doesn't fully develop until about age twenty-five."

"Which is why Sexy's fans are teenagers and the like."

"Exactly. Once their prefrontal cortices reach maturity, her power no longer affects them so they no longer like her music."

"They outgrow her."

"In a manner of speaking."

"There are fifty thousand people in the arena right now," I said. "How is she powerful enough to control that many people?"

"She's not," HARA replied. "That's why Smiles is augmenting her."

"With this?" I said, motioning to the meditation chamber.

"Among other things," HARA said. "The mediation chamber uses radiation to artificially stimulate the areas of her brain that produce the psionic energy, augmenting her power. That would also explain the ambient radiation in her suite. She probably gets low level doses throughout the day and then a hefty jolt in the meditation chamber just before showtime. My guess is that there's also some kind of similar augmentation technology built into the sound system. That would explain the odd microphone she uses."

"And Sexy's use of the radio airwaves, to broadcast her music," I said. "Is it possible to transmit her kind of energy that way?"

"It's never been tried but if you consider that, for instance, Carol can read your mind over the net, then I suppose that it's possible that Sexy's powers can be broadcast in that manner as well."

"So Smiles could have developed the kind of technology years ago but couldn't use it until he found a singer who fit the psionic profile," I said.

"Which would explain why Sexy Sprockets is his one and only client."

"Well, it makes sense in a sick, twisted, illegal sort of way."

"Did you expect anything else from the music business?" HARA quipped.

"Unfortunately," I said, "it's not going to help us find the hit man that's been hired to kill Sexy. One thing's for sure though, I think I better start wearing a psi-blocker on this job."

"That would be wise," HARA said. "And I know you don't want to hear this, but I think you'll need to keep a close eye on Smiles."

"Like I didn't know that already."

"I mean, keep a close eye on his relationship with Carol. After all, with Sexy retiring, he's going to need a new psionic cash cow. And Carol is a much more powerful psi than Sexy."

A sick feeling of dread washed over my body like a cesspool tsunami and this already bad case became decidedly worse (and more personal).

"You really know how to kill a moment, HARA."

29

The concert went off without a hitch. Sexy psionically sang her heart out and the audience ate it up. She did three encores and the crowd didn't start filing out until the management had turned the house lights on, turned the air-conditioning off, and began blasting polka-tinged Doors muzak (with heavy accordion) over the PA system. Best of all there were no attempts on Sexy's life and for a nano or two I actually allowed myself to think that I'd have an easy night of it. Then Sexy reminded me of the time-honored music industry tradition of the after-concert party and my thoughts of a good night's sleep slipped away like spilled champagne down an open sewer.

"Under the circumstances, Sexy, I don't think you should be going out tonight."

"I know that, Zach," she replied. "That's why the party's at the hotel!"

And thus, my troubles continued.

An hour later, Sexy's suite was filled to bursting with partygoers: celebs, minor celebs, wannabe celebs, and-ones, hangers-on, parasites, bottom-feeders, leeches, and sub-leeches. It was like slogging through a designer-wear-clad mudhole. The music was too loud, the lights were too dim, and the alcohol (and Gates only knows what else) was flowing way too freely.

"I think I'm going to be sick," I whispered to HARA, who was outfitted for the occasion in a designer miniskirt and silver lamé blouse.

"Me too," she said. "I can't believe these people are drinking this trendy domestic champagne. The elite have palates like swine."

"Big help there, HARA."

I'd spent every nano since my arrival very conspicuously tailing Sexy as she worked the room, chatting up, dressing down, or reveling in the adoration of the partygoers. She was the very jingly belle of a very junglelike ball and was loving every nano of it. She was also a very tempting target for any chicly dressed assassin who may have slipped in under the velvet rope and that made me more nervous than I can accurately describe using overwrought pop-cult metaphors.

"Have you been able to scan the guests?"

"I've screened the scene, big guy," HARA replied. "They may not be clean, but no one's packing heat and no one fits the hired killer profile."

"Yeah, backstabbing's more this crowd's speed."

"Welcome to showbiz," she replied.

Sexy, at the nano, was holding court with a pair of twin actors I half recognized from an HV action show. The three of them were laughing and flirting as they reminisced. Thanks to the directional microphone in my wrist interface, HARA and I could hear pretty much every word they were saying.

"No, no," Sexy said, between giggles. "I dated Chad in January of that year. You, Brad, didn't come until February."

"Chad was in March," Brad said. "January was when you were with our father, Thad."

"That's right. I'm glad he survived that heart attack."

My head was starting to reel a bit from the crush of people (and the inane banter). It was all I could do to stay close to Sexy and let HARA scan the crowd.

"How many people are here?"

"Two hundred and eight currently. The problem is that there's a steady flow coming and going so it's a little difficult to keep track of them all. I've tapped in to all the security cams though, so I'll let you know if anything or anyone looks suspicious."

"What we need is another set of eyes on this room," I said. "Where is Carol anyway?"

"She's in the northwest corner of the room with Smiles, Sissy, and Misty," HARA replied.

"I should talk to her. She has to get her head together and start helping us again. She also needs to know the truth about Smiles."

"Well, if you want to speak with her, you better do it soon," HARA replied, "because she and Smiles are about to leave together."

"What?"

"They just excused themselves from the conversation with Misty and Sissy and are headed for the main door."

"What is she thinking?"

"Beats me," HARA said. "*She's* the mind reader."

"I have to stop them."

I started pushing my way through the crowd toward the main entrance and accidentally spilled a drink on a few wannabe actors as I passed (none of whom took it well).

"Crazo!"

"Sorry."

I caught sight of Carol and Smiles making their way toward the door. Smiles had his arm around her shoulder, shepherding her through the crowded room like a protector. The mere sight of it gave me chills.

"Carol!"

I pushed my way through the crowd a little farther (disturbing a few more partiers—bodybuilders, I think) and was closing in on them when HARA's hologram suddenly appeared in front of me.

"I think we have trouble," she said pointing toward Sexy.

I spun around and saw Chad and Brad looming over Sexy. Their faces were red and their movements were threatening and anger fueled. I aimed the wrist interface their way to hear what they were saying.

"You mean you were with Brad that weekend?"

"He got me on the rebound, Chad," Sexy said, with a shoulder shrug. "You had left me."

"I was in the hospital!"

"Yeah, for *elective* surgery!"

"You told me that you'd break up with me if I didn't get pec implants!"

"And you expected me to wait around forever?"

"Wait a nano," Brad said. "You said that what we had meant something."

"Well it did, for that afternoon."

"I can't believe you two-timed me with my own brother!"

"I didn't know he was your brother at the time."

"We're twins!"

"Well, I wasn't looking at your faces."

Brad and Chad, both relatively angry now, each grabbed Sexy by an arm.

"She's in trouble," HARA said.

"It's just a misunderstanding with a couple of old flames," I said, casting another glance at Carol and Smiles as they headed toward the door. "I'm sure Sexy will handle this delicately."

"Don't get all sentimental, guys," she said. "What we had wasn't that great. It turned out that your mother was the best of the whole bunch of you."

"Our mother?"

"Okay," I mumbled. "She's in trouble."

I cast one last look at Carol and Smiles as they left together and started pushing my way back through the crowd toward Sexy, rejostling the same people that I'd angered on the way over. By the time I reached the unhappy three-some, things were starting to get ugly.

"You're a two-timer, Sexy," Brad shouted. "A DOS-loving two-timer."

"A three-timer actually," Chad said. "No, wait, a four-timer, counting Mom."

"Why don't we take a nano and dial things back a notch, fellas?" I said, putting a firm hand on a shoulder of each brother.

Chad took umbrage at my hand and slapped it away without turning around.

"You never cared about either of us, did you?"

"Define care." Sexy said, unperturbed.

"You're heartless," Brad said.

"And cold," said Chad.

"And selfish!"

"Guys, this is not what I meant by dialing it back," I said, putting my hand back (a little harder) on their shoulders.

Sexy, for her part, wasn't bothered by the brothers' ire. If she was feeling any emotion other than contempt and a tinge of boredom, it didn't show on her face.

"And you know what else, Sexy? Your music stinks!"

A look of shock washed over Sexy's face.

"Yeah," said Brad. "I used to like it, but hearing you tonight, I realized that it sounds like DOS."

"What did you say?" Sexy snarled, her look of shock quickly changing into anger.

"That's it, guys," I said, pulling them away from Sexy. "You're out of here."

"You heard us, Sexy," Chad shouted. "You're a no-talented hack of a singer. Your music hoovers, your songs hoover!"

"And your voice hoovers!" Brad yelled.

That was all Sexy needed to hear.

She let out a guttural roar and launched herself at the boys like a she-cat from a catapult, giving Brad a short, sharp kick to the groin with her pointy-toed designer shoe. Brad let out a high-pitched shriek and crumpled to the ground like a golfbag with no balls. Chad lunged at Sexy but I grabbed him before he reached her and pushed him hard to the ground. It could have ended there but Sexy was still angry and started stomping on his hands while I held him down.

"What did you say about my music?" she yelled. "What did you say about my voice?"

When the other partygoers (including the ones whom I'd jostled or bumped a few nanos earlier) heard Sexy screaming and saw me holding Chad to the ground, they all just assumed that I was the troublemaker (I get that a lot) and attacked me en masse. I was hit at once by a quarter-kiloton of pseudo-celebrity, male model and bodybuilder bulk. The force of the charge pushed me away from Sexy, Chad, and Brad and into a larger throng of startled guests where we were met by screams, gasps, and more than a few douses of domestic champagne.

Thankfully, I had the advantage over the attackers because I was sober and wearing computer enhanced body armor. I used a judo throw on the bodybuilder, tossing him over my shoulder and into a group of wannabe actresses (they caught him) and gave the male model an uppercut to the jaw that sent him unconscious into a small pack of film producers (they let him hit the ground and pretended not to notice). The actor sneered at me but then ran away when I made a move toward him.

Misty and Sissy had come to Sexy's aid by then and were trying to pull her off Brad. Chad, on the other hand was still looking for a fight. He grabbed an empty champagne bottle from a table and came at Sexy with it. I stepped in front of him and caught his swinging arm at the wrist and twisted it behind his back until he dropped the bottle and fell to the floor. I pinned him facedown on the floor with my shoe on the back of his neck, popped my gun into my hand, and sent a low-powered blast into each and every speaker in the room. The shots echoed for a few long nanos afterward but all two hundred plus of the partygoers stopped dead in their tracks and fell silent.

"The party is over," I growled. "And the last person to leave this room is going to get shot in their surgically improved ass."

Needless to say, the room cleared out pretty quickly after that.

"I can't stay here, Zach," Sexy moaned between sobs. "I can't bear it."

She'd been crying since the end of the party half an hour ago. Misty, Sissy, and Lusty had done their best to comfort her but it was no use.

"Where's Smiles?" I asked Misty.

"We don't know," she said. "We tried netting him but he's gone incommunicado."

"Carol, too," HARA added.

I didn't want to think about what was going on with Smiles and Carol so I tried to focus on Sexy.

"You're perfectly safe, Sexy. It's just us here."

"Did you hear those things they said to me? It was horrible."

"They were crazo jealous, Sexy," Sissy said. "You know how guys get."

"But Zach went old school throwdown on their carcasses," Misty added. "Ub-zeen!"

"He also went old school on the sound system," HARA whispered.

"I have so many ex-boyfriends," Sexy said. "What if they're all like that now?"

"Sexy, you're overreacting."

"Actually," Misty said. "She does have a lot of ex-boyfriends. I've lost count."

"Girlfriends, too," Sissy added.

"And there were a few that I'm not sure what they were."

I knelt down beside Sexy, who was facedown on one of the couches, and gently touched her hair. It was softer than I expected and thick enough to hide my hand.

"It's been a long day, Sexy. You've been through a lot. Let's get some rest."

She turned and looked at me with moist, wide eyes.

"I can't stay here. I don't feel safe."

"We've sealed off the floor, Sexy. No one is going to hurt you here."

"I won't be able to sleep in this place, Zach. It's filled with bad memories and negative vibes."

The Elite's security system was top of the line. I knew that Sexy was safe here. Unfortunately, I also knew that there was no way she was going to be able to get any rest in her current state. Like it or not, for her own mental health she needed to get out of the hotel. The problem was, I couldn't think of any place to take her that was more secure at the nano.

That's a lie. I knew of one place. I just didn't want to admit it.

"Please, help me, Zach. Please."

I sighed and held out my hand to her. She took it gently and I helped her to her feet.

"HARA, bring the limo up to the hoverport."

"Where are we going?" HARA asked.

"Home."

30

I brought Sexy into my house with as little fanfare as possible. It was late at night so there was no one out to see the limo land in the driveway and HARA had Shreek take the vehicle back to the hotel as soon as we were clear.

Thankfully the household droids had cleaned the place up since Electra's morning outburst so the house was relatively debris-free. The new couch had even arrived and the housebots had set it up in its designated spot in the living room.

HARA had the house computer make Sexy some cocoa and she sipped it as she sat on the new couch, (I managed to deactivate the glowing UPC tag just before she sat down). She was still a little upset but much less so than before and she was calming down with every nano. She needed to rest but I could tell by the look on her face that she wasn't quite ready to be alone yet. So I grabbed a cup of coffee and made myself comfortable in the easy chair across from her.

"You live here alone?" she asked, sipping her tea.

"My girlfriend stays here most nights," I said. "But she's staying at her own place for the time being."

"You guys fighting?"

"Something like that."

"It's not over me is it?" she asked.

"Would it make you feel better or worse if I said that it was?"

"Better, actually."

"All right then," I said. "We're fighting over you. But I'd rather not discuss it."

She took another sip of her cocoa and curled her feet

underneath her. She was wearing sweatpants and a T-shirt now (designer label, of course) and no makeup on her face. But the lack of accoutrements didn't diminish her beauty. Truthfully, she looked more attractive to me without all the glitz.

"I'm not usually like this, you know."

"Like what?" I asked.

"Scared, helpless, weak. I'm actually pretty strong."

"I know you are."

"You have to be strong to be in this business. It's totally cutthroat. People will kiss your feet to your face but the nano your back is turned, they'll do anything they can to rip your heart out. You know what I mean?"

"Um, I think so. The anatomy metaphors don't really match."

"I had to be strong to get to the top," she continued. "I had to climb over a lot of people on the way. And once I got to the top, I had to keep climbing just to stay there. I'm constantly reaching higher to stay where I am. That kind of wears on a person after a while."

"I imagine that it would," I said. "But again, your metaphors are a little . . ."

"You don't like my music, do you?" she asked.

I took a long sip of coffee while I considered the best way to answer the question. In the end, I went with a soft-pedaled version of the truth.

"I'm not in your target audience."

"That's one reason why I hired you, you know," she said with a bit of a smile. "I knew you wouldn't coddle me because of who I am. I knew you'd be professional. I knew you'd be honest with me."

"I appreciate . . ."

"Like Sammy."

"Huh?"

"Sammy's the guy who helped me find my voice. He's a genius. There's no denying that. I owe him so much professionally. But I think I owe him even more on a personal level. Does that make sense?"

"Actually, no," I replied. "That makes even less sense than your metaphors."

"Oh, I know he's odd, but once you get to know him, you see what a wonderful, giving spirit he has. He's honest.

He's nurturing, He takes care of me. That's why I'm still so wrung out by the incident at the party. He's not here to comfort me."

"I don't think we should talk about Sammy right now," I said. "You've had a rough day. I think you should get some sleep."

She smiled, finished her cocoa, and then got up and stretched. Her T-shirt crept up her midriff as she reached high, showing off her taut, flat stomach. And her sweats hung low on her hips, revealing a little more flesh than I was comfortable seeing, especially when she turned around and moved to the base of the stairway.

"The bedroom's upstairs, right?"

I nodded.

"I'm assuming that the bed's large enough for two?"

I got up from my chair and took a step toward her. She seemed a little disappointed when I took the empty tea cup from her hand and turned away.

"I'm sleeping on the couch."

"You and your girlfriend are already fighting because of me," she said. "You might as well make the fight over something worthwhile."

"Like I said, Sexy, I'm not your target audience."

She shrugged as she turned and disappeared into the bedroom.

"Your loss," she said, walking up the stairs into the bedroom and closing the door behind her. "What about your hologram pal?"

"Good night, Sexy."

31

The couch turned out to be not at all conducive to sleeping (the fact that Sexy was on the other side of the bedroom door didn't help matters either). But I managed to fall into a fitful sleep just before dawn. It didn't last long, of course.

"Zach," HARA whispered in my ear, her voice soft and lilting. "Zach, you need to get up now."

I stirred slowly awake, opened my eyes, and saw her standing over me. She had outfitted her hologram in a long white pajama shirt with thin pink vertical stripes. The shirt hung to midthigh, which was good because she wasn't wearing pants.

"Why are you dressed like that?"

"Because it's morning," she replied.

"HARA, you don't sleep," I said, rubbing my eyes. "You have no need to be wearing holographic pajamas."

"I thought it might make you feel more at ease."

"I would be more at ease if you were wearing pants."

"I'll take that as a compliment," she said, changing her hologram back to her business suit. "You'll need to get up now."

"What time is it?"

"Shortly after six," she replied.

"Why do I need to get up now?"

"Because Dr. Gevada will be here in approximately two minutes."

"What?"

I rolled off the couch in a mild panic and reached for my pants. Unfortunately, they weren't there.

"Why is she coming here so early?"

"I'm not sure," HARA replied. "According to the work schedule at her clinic, she's not scheduled to be on call until nine-thirty."

"This is not good," I said, still looking around for my pants.

"However, my woman's intuition is telling me that it may have something to do with the footage running on *Entertainment This Nano* this morning that shows you and Sexy leaving the hotel together last night with your arms around each other."

"What?"

I tripped over the blankets at my feet and fell to the floor.

"It looks like your good buddy Shreek has been working both sides of the fence," HARA said. "The pictures were clearly shot from inside the limo. He probably sold them for a small fortune."

"That little weasel."

"He also got some good shots of you bringing Sexy here."

"Oh, DOS."

"So I'm thinking that might explain why Dr. Gevada's in such a hurry to get over here."

"Wake Sexy up, we have to get her out of here."

"It's been on the news already, Zach. You're not going to be able to hide this from Electra."

"I'm not trying to hide it," I said, still searching the room for my clothes. "I'm trying to protect Sexy. There's no telling what Electra will do to her once she gets here."

"Gee, I never thought of that."

"And will you please tell me where my pants are?!"

"The maidbot put them in the wash last night," HARA replied matter of factly. "They were stained with blood, salsa, and overpriced champagne."

"DOS! I need a new pair."

"Everything else is in the bedroom."

I heard the bedroom door open just then and Sexy walked unsteadily down the stairs into the living room, stretching her lithe muscles and rubbing her eyes.

"What's all the commotion?" she asked.

In retrospect, I suppose that I shouldn't have been surprised. But, since I was under a good bit of pressure at the nano, I think I can be forgiven for losing my head, just a little, upon first glimpse of the freshly awaked Sexy Sprockets.

"Sexy," I said, my life flashing before my eyes, "you sleep in the nude?"

Sexy looked down at her naked body unashamedly and shrugged her shoulders.

"Wouldn't you if your body was this hot?"

And that, of course, is when Electra walked through the front door.

32

In retrospect, I guess you could say that Electra took that initial nano fairly well but only because she didn't have a firearm handy.

"I'm going to step back outside," she said softly between gritted teeth. "I'm coming back into this house in exactly five minutes. When I do, I am going to break the hands of everyone who is not wearing pants."

Then she calmly stepped back outside and closed the door behind her (but not before smashing the small table by the doorway).

"Is that your girlfriend?" Sexy asked, still stretching (and naked).

"That's her." I replied.

"She's hot for an old lady. But I think she has some anger management issues."

Sexy and I got dressed remarkably quickly and HARA contacted Misty, Sissy, and Lusty (none of whom were happy to be awakened so early) and convinced them to come and pick up Sexy in the hover limo. Then HARA made herself scarce as well.

True to her word, Electra waited outside for five minutes before coming back inside the house. She sat in the easy chair and didn't say a word until after Sexy had gone, which gave me about fifteen very uncomfortable minutes of silence. And when the limo finally lifted off, leaving her and me alone, the feeling of dread in the pit of my stomach felt like a black hole.

"Now, I know this looks bad," I said.

Electra's face was stoic as she activated the computer screen on the wall and switched it to multiscreen mode and brought up *Entertainment This Nano, Instant Buzz, Before-It-Happens News,* and *The Tattler Network.* I was pretty certain that I was the top story on everything but the cooking channels. She muted the sound, for which I was thankful. The last thing I needed to hear at that hour of the morning were the smug assertions of entertainment reporters. But the visuals were painful enough on their own: grainy nighttime footage, obviously shot through the open window of the limo, of me and Sexy leaving the hotel together. She had been unsteady so I'd helped her down the stairs and across the hoverport with an arm around her shoulders. She'd put her head on my shoulders and an arm around my waist to keep from falling. But on the grainy, dark recording we looked like two lovers on the lam, stealing a secret nano.

The footage was the same outside my house only this time taken from above as the limo lifted off; me leading Sexy into my house, our arms around one another, and then stumbling in through the door.

I knelt beside her as she continued to stare at the monitor.

"Electra. Nothing happened."

"I know," she said, without looking at me.

"You do?"

She sighed and then slowly got out of the chair and walked into the bedroom.

"Yes," she said, "but it doesn't matter."

I followed her into the bedroom. She pulled a suitcase from underneath the bed and began packing up some of her things, stuffing cosmetics, lotions, and clothes haphazardly into the bag.

"Please don't do this," I said. "I can explain."

"I know you can explain. There's always an explanation," she said. "I'm just tired of hearing them."

"I understand," I said. "After this case is over . . ."

"After this case is over, there'll just be another one," she said without turning away from her packing. "And another after that."

"Electra, I'm a private eye," I said. "This is what I do. I can't give it up just because it makes you uncomfortable."

She turned to me quickly with a flash of anger passing across her face.

"How many cases have you taken from ugly women?" she said.

"What?"

"You heard me. There are a lot of women out there who aren't stunningly beautiful. They must have troubles too. How many jobs have you done for them?"

"You're being ridiculous."

"Name one. Come on. Just name one."

"Electra."

"Because I can list the beautiful ones without any problem. There was BB Star and Ona Thompson. There were actually four beautiful women in that one."

"I sort of saved the world on that one as well, as you might recall."

"Then there was the porn star, Fever Dream; the heiress, Giselle Dumas; the jilted wife, what was her name, Fifi Lefevre? I can go on all day talking about the clients you've had who have been drop-dead gorgeous. Can you name one for me who wasn't."

"There was Pacheco kidnapping case. The mother in that one was no looker."

"She hired you to find her beauty queen daughter."

"True, but the woman who actually hired me wasn't beautiful."

"How about a man then? Have you ever taken a case from a man?"

"Men don't hire private eyes. It's against our nature, like asking for directions or putting the seat down."

"In other words, no male clients."

She closed the suitcase haphazardly, with some bits of clothing still poking out from the sides, and carried it out of the room. I followed her as she headed toward the front door.

"There have been companies," I said.

"You mean like the lingerie manufacturer? Or the escort agency?"

"Those were legitimate cases."

"You see the pattern though, don't you?"

"I see that my clients make you jealous when they shouldn't."

She snorted and shook her head disbelievingly.

"And you act surprised when HARV suddenly decides to become a woman."

"What does that mean?"

"I'm not a prop, Zach. I'm not a set piece in your playboy, tough guy fantasy life that comes and goes. I'm a living, thinking person and I happen to love you more than anything else. Not for what you do or for the life you lead but for who you are. And yet after all we've been through together you still don't understand how these sorts of things make me feel. How all this marginalizes me and what we have. You want me to be a walk-on in your life. A recurring character on the cast list, who can provide a little comic relief whenever you come home from your zany, adventure-filled life. Well, I can't be that. Not if I want to be happy."

She was crying now, which is something I'd never seen before. After all this time I'd learned how to deal with the many forms of her anger: the violent outbursts, the seething yet controlled episodes, the unspoken passive/aggressive periods. But I'd never dealt with tears before. And they scared me more than anything because I didn't know what they meant.

"You're wrong," I said, following her to the front door. "I do love you. Just as much as you love me and I'll prove that to you anyway you want me to. You want me to quit this case? Fine. I will. You want me to stop taking female clients? I'll do that too. I'll take on ugly women only if that's what it takes to prove it to you. Just tell me how to do it, Electra. Tell me what you want and I will do it. I swear. Just tell me what you want me to do."

She took her hand off the doorknob and stood motionless for a long nano; long enough for me to begin to hope again. Then spun around and gave me a left cross to the jaw that snapped my head back like a bungee jumper on a trampoline. A galaxy's worth of stars flashed before my eyes and my knees buckled as I sunk to the floor and then fell flat on my butt.

"You're the private eye. You figure it out," she said, slamming the door behind her.

33

I sat on the floor for a while, thinking and holding my jaw gently with my hand. It's hard to describe exactly what I was feeling at the nano (other than pain) but I suppose utter confusion comes closest.

HARA's hologram appeared, still wearing her business suit, for which I was grateful. I don't think I would have reacted well to a nurse's outfit kind of gag.

"The girl's got a mean left hook," she said.

I said nothing.

She knelt beside me and looked at my jaw.

"Somehow I knew that the scene was going to end in violence. Frankly though, I thought she'd take it out on the couch again," she said. "I've scanned your mandible. It's not broken. Do any of your teeth feel loose?"

"No," I replied.

"Small comfort. You might have a mild concussion but there's not much we can do about that at the nano. Here. Take a seat on the couch. I'll get some ice."

I climbed onto the couch and the maidbot brought an ice pack for my jaw.

"So why exactly did she hit you on the way out?" HARA asked.

"I'm not sure," I replied. "Partly because she's jealous of my clients."

"Sexy tends to bring that out in people."

"Not just of Sexy," I said. "She's jealous of all of them. They marginalize her."

"What does that mean?"

"I don't know."

HARA shook her head. "Women," she whispered.

She stepped into the kitchen and personally brought me another cup of coffee.

"My hard light capabilities are getting stronger," she replied. "I can hold up to half a kilo of weight now. A little more time and I might be able to hit you myself."

"Oh, good," I said. "You should get your name on the waiting list."

I took the coffee and tried sipping it without moving the ice pack from my jaw but failed miserably, dribbling some onto my shirt. I finally gave up and just put the ice pack on the coffee table.

"I don't get it," I said. "Electra's one of the smartest women I've ever met. She tough, she's strong. She has a career. Why would she feel threatened just because I have a good-looking client?"

"Because we're more emotional than men," HARA said. "We use different parts of our brains to process certain stimuli. It's biology."

"That sounds like a huge generalization."

"It is," she nodded. "Not every woman would react that way to your lifestyle."

"You don't," I said. "I mean, not that you're a woman but . . . you know."

"I'm as much a woman as I ever was a man, Zach."

She reached out and gently stroked the side of my head with her solid light hand, running her fingertips through my hair. There was a bit of an electric tingle to her touch. It felt good.

"But you're right. I wouldn't react that way," she said. "I haven't so far, have I?"

She was in full Rita Hayworth mode now. Her hair was thick and lustrous, messed gently in a subtle, sensual way. Her skin was creamy and smooth to look at, free of blemishes of any kind. And her lips were full and red. For a nano, I thought they were getting larger but then I realized that was wrong. They were just getting closer. She was leaning toward me, lips parted, moving in for a kiss. And I realized then that I actually wanted her to.

Then her fingers gently slid down my face and touched my jaw where Electra had hit me. It sent a jolt of pain through my body and I jerked back.

"Ow!"

"Sorry," she said. "Did I hit the bruise?"

"Yeah, it's a little tender, I guess."

"Tender? You're lucky that she didn't break your jaw."

"Yeah, well, it could have been worse, right?" I said with a smile. "She could have been wearing a ring."

And then it hit me.

"She's not wearing a ring," I said to myself.

"Who's not?"

I felt my face flush as my confusion turned to shame and for the first time in my life, all the between the lines gibberish that women talk about began to make sense.

"Gates, I'm a louse. I take these cases. I show up on the news with all these other women. How's she supposed to react to that? What kind of reassurance have I ever given her for that not to bother her?"

"What?"

"Sure, I tell her I love her, but what does that mean? DOS it, I've never proven it to her. I've never shown her any commitment."

The seriousness of the nano hit me full force and I got to my feet.

"I have to go find her."

"What do you mean?" HARA asked.

"Electra," I said. "I have to get her back before it's too late."

"Zach, she broke your couch. She hit you in the jaw."

"She had to," I said. "I gave her no choice."

"How? Your couch attacked her? Zach, you're acting crazy. Well, more crazy than normal."

"I love her, HARA!"

"You mean to tell me that you still love her even after all the grief she's given you?"

I grabbed my coat and hat from the rack and headed quickly toward the door.

"There's nothing else she can do, HARA," I said. "She gives me grief *because* she loves me."

"Well, what about me then?" HARA shouted as she rose to her feet. "Don't I give you grief?"

The sound of her voice made me freeze in mid-stride. There was more pure emotion in those final five words than I'd ever heard HARA, or HARV for that matter, utter before. And I realized that my world was getting much more complicated than I ever wanted.

34

I stepped back into the living room. HARA was still standing by the couch, her eyes were wide, a mix of confusion and disbelief. Awkward does not to begin to accurately describe the nano.

"HARA . . ."

"I just don't understand, Zach."

"Quite honestly, neither do I," I said. "That's the way love is, I guess."

"Please don't go into Bogey mode on me now."

"I'm sorry, but it's all I know. You're a wonderful woman, HARA, even without the flesh and blood. You're a geek's wet dream and you're one helluva sidekick. You're more Bacall than I am Bogey. I mean that."

"But you still love Electra?"

"This isn't about Electra."

"What's it about then?"

I paused for a nano, weighing my options. I'd been walking too many tightropes in my relationships of late; avoiding the real issues and hiding behind smaller, more trivial things. And by doing so, I had royally messed everything up. I decided then I wouldn't do that anymore. It was time to be honest.

"It's about HARV," I said. "The truth is that I miss him. He was annoying and condescending and more of a nuisance than any machine should ever be, but he was my friend, HARA. Gates, he was my best friend. You're wonderful and you're sexy and you do great snappy patter and innuendo, but, I'm sorry, it's not the same. I miss HARV and . . . and I want him back."

HARA refused to speak at first. She refused to look at

me or even move. For a nano, I thought her hologram was stuck.

"HARA?"

She turned to me, caught my gaze with hers for the briefest of nanos and then swallowed hard and turned away. The tension in the room was so thick, it was like breathing Jell-O.

"I don't know how to take this, Zach," she said, her voice heavy with emotion. "I need to think about it."

"Okay."

"Maybe I'll see you around."

"I'll be here," I said.

She nodded and bit her lip slightly in what appeared to be an attempt to hold back emotion.

"Good-bye Zach."

Her hologram dissolved slowly and she disappeared. Then the skin around my left eye went numb and my wrist communicator went dead. HARA was gone.

I was alone.

35

Talk about having girl troubles!

HARA out of my head left me a little more empty than I thought it should. It also left me without any way of piloting my hovercraft (just in case you've forgotten, I have a thing about heights). So I rolled out my old school transportation: a 1954 baby blue Kaiser Darrin. I know what you're thinking, that I'm masking my insecurities about the women in my life by fixating on my car. Well, you're probably right, but I didn't have time right then to properly analyze myself.

My heart told me to go out and find Electra, but HARA's disappearance seemed the greater danger (and one where I could enlist some help) so my first stop was Randy's lab. Needless to say, Randy didn't take the news well.

"What do you mean HARA's gone?"

"I mean she's gone," I said (for the third time, I think). "She's not in my head and my wrist interface is dead."

"She's not here either," Randy said, checking his own computer. "What did you do to her?"

"Nothing, really. I just said that I missed HARV."

"What?" He fell back in his chair, almost tipping over but he caught himself. "Why did you do that?"

"I don't know, it was just part of the natural flow of the conversation."

"What kind of conversation were you having?"

"Well, it started out about Electra and me and then it sort of morphed into HARA and me and then we sort of almost, um, kissed."

"I'm sorry," Randy said, very calmly. "Did you say that you kissed HARA?"

"Almost, yeah. It was sort of a mutual thing."

"You mean HARA. The holographic computer interface for your computer. You kissed her."

"I didn't actually kiss her."

"But you were going to."

"She started it," I said.

"Zach, do you know what you've done? I mean aside from bringing the man and machine paradigm to a new moral low?"

"What?"

"I don't know what!" Randy shouted. "That's how bad this is! First of all, the interface in your head is a permanent access module to HARA's systems. She shouldn't have been able to turn it off. It's the same with my system here. She shouldn't be able to break contact. She shouldn't be able to leave. But she's gone!"

"Where do you think she went?"

"That's the problem, she could be anywhere. It's like she's not just a computer anymore. She's a consciousness and she could be anywhere."

"Well, that's good then, right? She's evolved."

Randy shook his head as though he were talking to a child and turned back to his computer keyboard.

"I did some searching into HARV's systems since we last spoke," he said. "I found that he was doing some interesting side projects that were outside his program parameters. He was researching society, human culture, human history, psychology, and human/technology interaction in general."

"What was he doing?"

"I don't know, but I don't think it bodes well. Do you know that he wrote a joke?"

"A joke?"

"I found it in a more accessible region of memory so it's relatively new. It was probably written shortly before he became HARA. 'Why are there no round boxes at the Archimedes Bakery?'"

"What's the punch line?" I asked.

"I don't know," Randy replied. "It was hidden elsewhere in his system. Probably somewhere deeper, possibly encrypted. I think he wanted to protect the punch line."

"Oh yeah, you have to," I said. "The worst thing you

can do is tip the punch line. The whole joke's worthless if you do that. Who's Archimedes?"

"An ancient Greek mathematician."

"Kind of an esoteric topic for a joke."

"Not for HARV."

"Okay, so he wrote a joke. That's a good thing, isn't it?"

"Comedy is dangerous, Zach."

"No, comedy is hard. Love is dangerous."

"Not from a psychological standpoint. Humor is a mask for insecurities and other psychological problems. This was a cry for help. I don't think it's a coincidence that he became HARA shortly after this."

"Randy, I think you're blowing this way out of proportion."

"HARA is quite likely the most powerful computer on the planet, Zach. Remember all those computers that HARV hacked into for you over the years? Well, HARA can do that too, without either of us telling her to. Do you realize what kind of havoc she can wreak if she chooses to?"

"Do you think she'd do anything dangerous?"

"Have you ever known a scorned woman to act irrationally?"

"Randy!"

"No, seriously, I'm asking because I haven't known that many women and I don't think I've ever actually scorned one. But I've heard they can be unstable. Is that true?"

"Well, yeah. But no more then men, I guess."

"How did HARA seem to you when you last saw her?"

I thought of the look of confusion and pain on her face when I told her that I loved Electra. I thought of her biting her lip in an effort to hold back tears when I told her how much I missed HARV. Only one word came to mind.

"Heartbroken."

Randy ran his long fingers through his shock of red hair out of frustration and let out a very long, agonized sigh.

"I've been working on some code," he said. "I was hoping that we wouldn't have to use it, but I think you better have it handy, just in case."

"What kind of code?"

"It's a virus," he said, holding out his hand. "Give me your wrist interface."

"Randy?"

"Give me your wrist interface, Zach!"

I took the interface off my arm and handed it to Randy. He removed a memory card from the back and slid it into his own computer console. Then he pressed the download button. A download meter appeared on his screen, slowly moving from red to green.

"The virus is designed to attack the higher functions of an artificial intelligence, surrounding it with firewalls and permanently wiping out the memory. It's like a combination of Ebola and brain cancer for computers."

"You want me to kill HARA?"

"No, I don't, but I think you should be prepared in case we need to."

"Can't you just say kaflooey or whatever and take her off-line?"

"She's not in the system anymore," he said. "The failsafe will no longer work. That was only designed for short term stoppage anyway. It wouldn't hold her long. She may even have defenses against it by now."

"So what do we do?"

The computer signaled that the download was complete. Randy took the card from the computer and reinserted it into the wrist interface. He touched a few controls on the unit's control pad and then handed it back to me.

"I've downloaded the virus into your wrist interface," he said. "HARA probably won't stay away from you for long. She'll reestablish contact through the interface at some point. If, during that time, she seems like she's becoming dangerous, you'll just need to hit the download button to inject the virus into her system. It will immobilize her and then systematically destroy her memory."

"Randy . . ."

"Remember, the sign that she's completely broken free of her parameters is when she refuses to follow a direct command. That's when she becomes a danger."

"Randy, I'm not going to kill HARV."

Randy's expression was more serious than I'd ever seen it. His face was wan, his eyes were nearly lifeless with resignation, and his shoulders drooped as though they were weighted down with a kiloton albatross.

"I hope you get the chance to make that choice, Zach."

36

I'd had no luck all morning reaching Carol on her communicator so I took a gamble and tried calling Sexy at the Elite, hoping that Carol was with her. Unfortunately, the only person I could get on the vid was Smiles.

"What is it, Johnson?"

"I need to talk Carol, Smiles. Where is she?"

His face was hard to see on the wrist interface, which is what I was reduced to using for mobile communication since the Kaiser didn't have an on-board computer. It didn't help matters that I was driving during the call so I had to split my attention between the interface and the road.

"She's unavailable at the nano," Smiles responded smugly. "I'll have her call you back."

"I want to speak with her now, Smiles. Put her on or I'll drag her out from wherever you're holding her when I get there."

"She's helping Sexy meditate," he said. "Sexy was quite tense after what you put her through last night and this morning."

"Oh yeah, last night. I guess I must have missed you at the party. Too bad you left before all the trouble started."

"I was exhausted and decided to call it an early night."

"Carol, too?" I asked.

"I don't think that's any of your concern," Smiles said.

"Oh, I think it is," I snarled. "Carol is my employee. You taking her away from Sexy without letting me know put Sexy in danger last night."

"I see, so keeping Sexy safe from a couple of holovision actors was too much for you to handle on your own?"

"Stay away from Carol, Smiles," I snarled again. "I can't make myself any clearer than that."

"That's something you should discuss directly with Carol, I'm afraid," he said. "She and I are developing a business relationship, which I believe she is well within her rights to do."

"You mean the kind of business relationship that you have with Sexy?" I asked. "Don't even think about using Carol that way."

"I don't know what you mean, Johnson."

"I know all about it, Smiles. I know what you do to Sexy."

His smile faltered a little bit as a splash of concern dappled his face.

"What do you mean?"

"The meditation chamber, the ambient radiation, the psionic augmentation."

"I don't know what you're talking about."

He was starting to squirm now. The smile had all but left his face, which was no easy feat, and I could almost see the beads of sweat forming on his brow. I had to admit, I was enjoying it.

"Sexy's a psi," I said. "You know it and you've been using her abilities to sell her music from day one."

"That's insane."

"Say whatever you want, but both you and I know it's true."

"People buy Sexy's music because of the beauty of her voice and the artistry of her songs."

"Sexy couldn't hit a clear note with a sledgehammer. Her music's bio-waste and you know it. The only reason anyone buys her music at all is because you're using her psionic abilities to brainwash the audience."

Smiles' grin reappeared on his face This time with extra smug and the corners of his mouth went so wide that my monitor wasn't big enough to contain his cheeks. It was the type of grin that a cobra gives a paralyzed mouse just before he swallows it. The grin of knowing that the prey's fate is sealed.

This time around, he was the cobra and I was the mouse, because when he stepped aside I saw Sexy's face fill my interface screen. And she was livid.

"What did you say about my voice?"

*   *   *

Sexy's diatribe went on for roughly ten minutes. At one point I turned the sound off and just nodded occasionally to let her know that I was still there. But even without the audio, her intent was clear. My services as bodyguard were no longer required, which was fine with me. Sexy had brought nothing but grief to my life from the nano I met her and the sooner she was out of my life, the better off I'd be. Tony and his men could protect her now.

Of course that still left Carol. Smiles said that he had put her directly onto Sexy's payroll as an additional bodyguard and backup dancer. I knew having her around would help keep Sexy safe but the idea of Smiles getting his hooks into Carol made my stomach turn. I realized I had to get her out of there and do it quickly.

But I had a couple of other things to do first.

37

Even in the bright morning sun, the joyless shadows of the alley hid the squalid storefront entrance. The air was fetid and smelled of old trash. I hated leaving the Kaiser in the open in this kind of neighborhood, but I had little choice and even less time.

The thick polymer of the door was greasy to the touch, caked with dirt and slime from Gates only knew where. I popped my gun into my hand and used the barrel to knock. There was no answer. I knocked again, louder but again to no avail. I knocked once more, so hard I thought I'd dent the door. This time, I got an answer.

"Go away." The voice was deep, thick with an Arabic accent, and emanated from a small speaker hidden within the door itself.

"I need to see Bushy," I said.

"There is no Bushy here," the voice responded.

I knocked again, this time rattling the door on its hinges.

"Last warning," the voice responded. "Go away."

"Bushy, it's Zach," I said. "Open the door."

A metal panel above the door slid open and a large blaster on a wall-mounted swivel emerged from the building and pointed itself directly at me.

"How do I know that it is really Zach?"

"Who else would come to this dump pretending to be me?"

The blaster twitched on its swivel in response. I heard the high pitched whine of the weapon charging.

"You come here, pretending to be Zach, just to insult me?"

"I *am* Zach, you senile old cow. And I came here to pick up my package. Insulting you is a secondary bonus."

"Why do you want the package?"

"Because the time has come," I replied.

Silence. Then: "Really?"

"Yes, really, Bushy. Now open the DOSsing door before I blast you and your fake gun to smithereens."

The blaster retracted into the wall and I heard the sound of several dozen locks on the door being undone. The door opened a crack and I saw a weary dark eye peek through.

"It is really you, Zach?"

"It's me," I replied.

"You've put on some weight."

"Yeah, and I've lost a little hair. I'm guessing you've aged as well and you weren't any prize to begin with."

The door opened another half a meter and Bushy stood fully in the opening. He was a short, dark-skinned man; rail thin with eyes as black as onyx and a huge, well-coiffed head of (obviously fake) silver hair.

"I was wrong," I said, looking at him. "You look pretty good after all."

He smiled and unconsciously ran his hand through his hair (it shifted a little on his head but I didn't say anything).

"You really need the package?" he asked. "This is not a drill?"

I shook my head no. "It's the real deal."

He swallowed out of nervousness and nodded grimly as he ushered me inside.

"It's in the vault," he said.

Bushy's vault was six stories underground (I'm not sure what, if anything was on the other five stories). He ushered me down the stairs, activated the DNA encoded lock, and opened the big metal door.

The vault was brightly lit and made entirely of metal that shone coldly under the halogen lights above.

"Your package is in drawer C, I think," he said, leading me across the room. "C for Zach."

The drawer was protected by another DNA encoded lock. This one had two activation pads; one for me and one for Bushy.

"Are you sure you want to do this?" he asked.

I nodded and, in unison, we touched our fingers to the pads. The indicator light turned green and I pulled the small drawer from its housing. It was as I remembered it, about half a meter square, and lined with lead. Inside it was the small black box.

"How long has it been?" Bushy asked.

"Twenty-two years, I think."

"That's a lot of rent you owe me."

"I'll send you a check."

I lifted the black box from the drawer. It fit nicely into my hand and I gripped it tightly for a long nano, hefting its weight, both physical and metaphorical. Then I stuck it into my pants pocket and turned away.

"Thanks, Bushy."

He stopped me with a hand on my wrist. His grip was surprisingly strong. When I turned to him, his face was serious. Then he hugged me tightly and kissed me once on each cheek.

"Gates speed, my friend. You go first into the great unknown."

I nodded and smiled ever so slightly.

"Don't worry," I said. "I'll send you a postcard."

38

It took me three hours to find Electra. That's another downside to not having HARV around to do the legwork. She called in sick for work at the clinic (sick of me, I guess). She wasn't at her place and she wasn't at any of her favorite tapas bars. I figured that the only place left for her to be at the nano, ironically, was my house. A quick check of the house computer confirmed that someone had entered the house using Electra's code and that the new couch had been broken into small pieces. That pretty much confirmed it.

I pulled up to the house in the late afternoon. A few dark clouds had rolled in and the once sunny day had turned cool. I parked the Kaiser in the driveway and entered the house sheepishly, flowers in one hand, takeout food in the other.

"Hi."

She was packing her things into boxes, taking knick-knacks and photos off the shelves and walls. I'd become used to seeing her breaking things. But the sight of her actually packing things up underscored for me how serious the situation had become.

"I thought you were working," she said.

"I quit the job today," I replied. "Actually, I was fired. It turns out that Sexy doesn't like criticism."

"I'll go then," she said. "I just came by to pack up my things and break a few of yours."

"Please, don't go."

"I'd rather not pack up my things with you here, Zach."

"No, I mean, don't go."

"It's too late for that, Chico," she said, staring first at the flowers and then turning away.

I heard the soft rumble of thunder outside and hoped that maybe the rain would keep her here, if only for a while.

"It's only too late if we allow it to be," I said. "My watch says that there's still time."

"Your watch is slow."

"You're probably right," I replied. "I just wanted to let you know that I understand how you feel. It might be too late now, like you said, but I understand how all my stuff, the cases, the clients, the news stories, I know how that made you feel. And I'm sorry."

The thunder outside rumbled again, louder this time, signaling the coming storm.

"*Por favor,* Chico," she said. "I'm not strong enough to have this conversation now. Let me just take the stuff I've packed and go. I'll get the rest another time."

She grabbed a box and took a step toward the door. Without thinking, I reached out and grabbed her arm, dropping the flowers and spilling the takeout on the floor.

"Electra, please."

My grip on her arm was a little too tight and she shot me a look that could have melted steel. Then she twisted her arm and broke my grip and continued toward the door.

"At least wait until after the rain stops," I said.

"What rain?" she said, as she walked. "It's supposed to be sunny all week."

The sky rumbled again. But it didn't sound like thunder anymore. The air in the house suddenly felt charged. Just breathing it left a bitter, acidic taste in my mouth. Electra was across the room now, nearing the front door. I could see the sparks of static electricity jumping toward her as her feet moved across the carpet. She was reaching for the doorknob, her hand just inches from the metal.

"Electra, don't!"

I ran toward her, sparks flying from my feet as I moved. I leaped as she turned and hit her broadside as the door opened. We fell to the floor together, me spinning us as we fell to ensure that she'd land on the bottom, with my body shielding hers.

Then a bolt of electric white heat flashed in the sky and

blew the doorway to pieces. The lights in the house flared ultra bright from the energy surge and burst as the bulbs overloaded. The security alarms in the house went off in a deafening roar. Shrapnel from the destroyed entryway flew around us. I felt it bounce off my armor in a dozen places and I felt Electra shake beneath me from the shock of the explosion.

We were under attack.

39

"What was that?" Electra asked, as we quickly got to our feet.

"Ion cannon blast," I said. "Very bad."

I looked outside through the gaping hole in the wall where the front door had once been and saw a milky-white wall of energy pulsing just outside the house. It was undulating like a wall of clear gelatin but I knew that it was a lot stronger.

"A forcefield cage," I said with a sigh.

"You're kidding," Electra said.

"We're trapped in here."

We ran quickly to the central computer console. I reset the alarms and tried to bring up a status report on the house systems.

"Most of the security system is down."

"Can HARA reboot it?"

"I don't have HARA anymore."

"What do you mean?"

"Never mind. Get to the weapons closet and grab some heavy ordnance," I said. "We might be in a little trouble here."

"Great. This is exactly the way I wanted to end our relationship, Chico," she said. "With a firefight."

"It will give you a chance to break more of my stuff."

She scrambled across the hall to the weapons closet and punched in the security code. The door slid open and she pulled two laser rifles and two hand blasters off the rack. She tossed one rifle to me, stuck both blasters in her belt, then grabbed the second rifle for herself. That's when the second alarm went off. It was a high-pitched wail, like a police siren stuck on a single note.

"What's that?" Electra yelled, trying to be heard above the din.

"Perimeter alarm," I said. "We're under attack."

"No DOS, Sherlock. From where?"

"I don't know. I never heard this alarm before."

"You don't know your own alarms?"

"HARV set the system up," I said. "He usually keeps track of these things."

"Check the console."

I checked the security screen on the house computer and didn't like what I saw.

"We have an intruder."

"In the house?"

"No," I said. "In our airspace."

"What does that mean?"

"It means we better duck."

A high-pitched squeal, like something out of an old World War Two movie, filled the air, growing louder by the nano. Electra and I turned our eyes skyward then looked at one another from across the room and dove for cover as the sound reached its crescendo and a large chunk of the roof exploded inward in a horror-filled nano.

The house shook to its foundations as the debris settled but there was no explosion. I hit the alarm override to turn off the alert. Everything was silent. Electra and I peered at one another from our hiding places (she was in the weapons closet, I was under the com) and scanned the damage.

There was a perfectly square crater in the living room floor. It seemed odd at first but it made sense when we looked up because it matched the perfectly square holes in the rooftop, the second floor ceiling, and the ground floor ceiling. Whatever had fallen from above had gone straight through the house, settled in the basement, and was now hidden beneath a couple layers of rubble that had once been part of my house.

"I have a bad feeling about this."

"You're sharp as ever, Chico."

We heard the whir of a hydraulic motor from below and the debris began to shift. Then the sound of metal against metal filled the air as the debris began to rise. We powered up our weapons and trained them on the crater as the movement continued. Whatever was down there was lifting itself out.

The debris slid away as the thing rose, revealing a slate gray metal cube, four meters tall, wide and deep, rising toward us on thick, hydraulically powered legs. Two nanos later, it was on the first floor, standing rock solid on the foundation of its own legs.

"What is it?" Electra asked.

As if on cue, a tiny hatch in the top of the box slid open and a thin pole emerged, extending a meter and a half high. There was a puff of smoke that made us jump, then a rigid, multicolored banner sprang from the pole and mechanically waved a flag at us. Three words were printed large on the surface in glowing red letters.

Let's Kill Zach.

Something lurched in my stomach and I felt my face redden from pure, unfiltered anger.

"Roundtree."

The box split open suddenly, like the display case of a pushy traveling salesman, and two dozen gray figures leaped out. They were humanlike in form but thin, long of limb, with no fingers or toes and completely featureless of face. Half came at me and half went for Electra. We didn't wait to see what they wanted, choosing instead to say hello with our guns.

Electra hit the one closest to her with a blast from the laser rifle, cutting it neatly in half. I shattered the one nearest me into pieces with a blast to the chest. Two nanos into the fight and we'd already taken out two attackers. I was starting to feel good about our chances.

Which is of course when things turned very, very bad.

The torso half of the attacker that Electra had destroyed started to shake. A nano later two legs popped out of the bottom end and it was as good as new. Likewise, the bottom half grew a torso.

"What the . . ."

Mine was even worse. Each piece of the thing that I'd blown apart was shaking and growing itself a new body. We were now four nanos into the battle and we'd increased the number of attackers by nearly half.

"What are these things?"

"Gray-Goo," I replied.

"What?"

"A new weapon. Randy told me about it once. It's intelligent inorganic matter, a single organism with sort of a hive mentality and composed of self-replicating circuitry. Like a giant computerized amoeba programmed to attack a specific target."

"I'm guessing that we're the targets," Electra shouted as the Goo attackers, moving slowly now, began to surround her. "What do we do?"

"Hit 'em," I yelled.

I flipped my laser rifle over and hit the nearest Goo in the head with the butt end. It tumbled over into the figures behind it and their long legs and arms got tangled up with one another. I doubt it hurt them, but it slowed them down, and gave me some time to hit a few more.

"That's your answer for everything," Electra replied.

She knocked one Goo off its feet with her rifle and then leg swept three more to the ground. It was clear that our rifles wouldn't be of much use in this case. As hand-to-hand weapons, they were a little clumsy, especially for Electra, who was having trouble with their bulk. So I decided to give her something a little more suitable for the fight.

I fought my way over to the wall by computer console and pulled a hard polymer softball bat from behind the coat rack.

"Electra, catch!"

I tossed the bat over the wall of Goo attackers. Electra caught it on the fly and began whacking away at the gray-shelled foot solders with a new fury and effectiveness.

And although the laser rifles weren't effective against the Goo, my personal gun certainly was.

"Sticky stuff."

The first glue-shot pinned one Goo attacker to the wall. The second bound two so tightly together that they fell over and began waving their legs like upturned ladybugs. It didn't stop them from functioning but it took them out of the fight.

We held our own for a while. The Goo attackers weren't all that strong, but they were relentless, like a bunch of really persistent and annoying toddlers. Their limbs didn't break easily (which was just as well because any piece that broke off would just grow an entirely new body, as we had already found out) but they hit hard and we weren't as indestructible as they were. Worse still, they were constantly trying to wrap their arms or legs around us and pull us down to the floor. I knew that if they ever pulled us down they'd crush us through sheer weight of numbers. I had my armor to protect me to a certain degree but Electra had nothing and that's what scared me the most.

When I ran out of glue-shots, I switched to the hogtie command and wrapped a bunch of them up in polymer cables. And when I ran out of hogties, I grabbed a bat and started slugging away along with Electra. The Goo kept coming at us and before long Electra and I were standing back to back atop the coffee table, protecting one another as the Goo surged around us.

"This is your fault, you know," she yelled at me between swings.

"I know," I said. "I'm sorry."

"I just came by to pick up my things. Now I'm fighting Goo!"

"I get it. It's my fault. I accept that."

"You should!"

"Not just in this particular case either," I said, still fighting back the horde. "All the danger I've put you in over the years. It's all on my head."

"You're darn right it is!"

"And I'm sorry for all the times I've embarrassed you and all the times you've had to apologize to people for whatever I may have done. That's my fault too."

"You can say that again!"

"But you know what's not my fault? The fact that you loved me."

"What?"

"That was your choice, Electra. I may have encouraged it. I know that I welcomed it. But you knew who I was when we met and you fell in love with me of your own volition."

"Yeah, I did."

"And I loved you back as well as I could. So we're both to blame, okay? I may have messed things up for us and you may not love me anymore but you chose to love me then. And that part is not my fault."

"Who says I don't love you anymore?"

Despite everything, my heart skipped a beat.

"Don't toy with me here. I'm not in the mood."

"I just said that I couldn't live like this anymore, Chico," she said. "I never said that I stopped loving you. Believe me, I would if I could. Gates knows, it would make my life a lot easier."

The Goo were around us tightly now, for every hand or body that we'd knock away a dozen more would take its place. Electra's pants had been shredded below the knee and her legs and arms were scraped and cut. My trench coat had been torn off me, my jacket was ripped up the back, and my arms felt like they were ready to fall out of their sockets. And yet none of that seemed to matter at the nano, because Electra was still in love with me.

"Do you have any plans after we finish up here?" I asked.

"I hadn't really planned that far in advance," she answered.

"Good. Let's go somewhere, I have something for you."

"Get us out of here first," she said. "Then we'll talk."

"Can you remotely control your hover?"

She nodded. "I need both hands to work the control though."

"I'll buy you the time," I said. "Bring the hover directly over the hole in the roof but go high. The force field probably has a ten meter height range. We're going to have to get to higher ground so head for the stairs."

"Ready when you are," she said.

I wanted so badly to kiss her then. Just one brief taste of her lips would have given me such strength. But she had only just now stopped yelling at me so I figured that I shouldn't push things.

So instead, I turned and leaped from the table into the Goo horde. I knocked half a dozen attackers off their feet as I landed, making a momentary pathway through the fray.

"Go!"

Electra jumped from the table and used me as a stepping stone to skip past the horde on her way to the stairway. A few of the Goo tried to follow her but I swatted them aside from behind even as the ones around me began pulling me down.

"Zach!"

I looked up at her from the floor and saw the conflict in her eyes. She was ready to jump back into the fray to help me (and I loved her for it).

"Go!" I shouted. "I'm right behind you."

I threw my bat at a Goo who was climbing the stairway behind her, hitting it in the head and knocking it back down to the floor. Then I started to go under as the Goo surged again. I grabbed the coatrack and swung it around like a quarterstaff, clearing enough room for me to get to my feet. Then I held the hefty rack horizontally and charged; pushing at the horde like a pigheaded snowplow against a trillion evil snowflakes. I pushed a dozen Goo into the weapons closet, slammed the door shut, and activated the lock. I changed course and pushed another few into the crater in the floor. I threw the coatrack at the ones in front of me, leaped over the prostrate bodies, and finally headed up the stairway.

Electra was waiting for me on the second floor, just beneath the hole in the roof, maneuvering the hover into position. It was no easy task, guiding the hover remotely past the energy fence, especially since the house was now shaking with Gray-Goo fury.

The horde was hot on my heels as I reached the second floor but the hallway was narrow so it was impossible for them to swarm, which is what I was counting on.

"Throw me your bat!"

Electra tossed me the bat without looking away from her work piloting the hover. I caught it and spun around quickly, knocking the nearest Goo pursuer to the back of the pack.

"You know, this isn't the way I imagined this going," I said, battling back the horde.

"Imagined what going?" she asked.

"I'll tell you later. How's the hover?"

"About ten meters straight up," she said. "What's your plan?"

I popped my gun into my hand.

"Big Bang."

I put a blast into the hallway ceiling. The entire upstairs shook as the ceiling supports gave way and the hallway collapsed around the Goo.

"That will buy us some time but my insurance agent is really going to hate me."

I went to the end of the hallway, stood beside Electra and looked up through the hole in the roof at the hovercraft above us.

"Tarzan."

I took careful aim and fired. A tiny magnetic grappling hook and cable shot from the gun toward the hover and latched onto the craft's underbelly. I turned and held out my arm to Electra.

"I'll hold you," I said. "You'll have to drive the hover."

She walked into my arms without hesitation and wrapped herself around me. I held her tightly for dear life (in more ways than one).

The Goo were close to digging through the rubble now. I could see their malletlike hands beginning to poke through. They'd be clear in a few nanos. But they'd be too late to catch us.

"I'm taking us up, Chico."

"Wait, hang on."

I reached into my pants pocket and pulled out the tiny black box that I'd taken from Bushy's vault. Then I wrapped my arm around her and slipped it into the pocket of Electra's jeans.

"A little something for later," I said.

"Fine," she said. "Now hold on tight."

"Gladly."

The strain on my arms was enormous as the hover lifted us into the air and up through the hole in the room, but there was no way I was letting her go. I saw the Goo finally dig clear of the rubble. They swarmed the hallway and leaped at us as we were lifted higher, but we were out of reach. The Goo let out a collective sigh.

"Don't take this the wrong way," I said as we cleared the top of the energy cage, "but I'm glad you were with me for this."

"Why? Is Sexy not so good in a fight?"

"Are you kidding, every time there's been one of these *Let's Kill Zach* things, she's been cowering in the corner. No help whatso . . ."

And that's when things started coming together.

40

"Hey, you can't go in there!"

"Lady, if I had a credit for every time someone said that to me I'd be as rich as your slime-sucking boss."

My foot hit the center of Rupert Roundtree's door like a sledgehammer on a melon. The door was real wood, and I felt a little bad splintering it but there are times in this world where you just have to break a few things for the sake of drama.

Roundtree was at his giant desk (more real wood), scanning some data on his floating computer screen. He turned to me as I broke open his door and smiled widely.

"Zach-acappa Johnsonccinno. I was just thinking of you."

"I hope it didn't tax your brain too much."

"I tried to stop him, Mr. Roundtree," the assistant said, scampering into the office behind me. "Should I call security?"

"That's all right, Jessie," Roundtree said, dismissing her with a wave. "The Zachtathalon here is going to be the network's biggest reality superstar before long. He's allowed a little idiosyncratic behavior. You can go now. We'll be fantacuous."

The assistant backed out of the office and did her best to close the broken door behind her. Once she was gone, Roundtree sat back in his chair and smiled.

"Honest to ingenuity, Zachtastrophe, I was just looking over the *Let's Kill Zach* results from the test screenings. You are going to be so hot when this show drops, you're going to have to start wiping yourself with flame-retardant toilet paper."

"I survived your Gray-Goo, Roundtree."

"Like I knew you would. And I'm sure it was triumphastical."

"Sexy wasn't with me, by the way," I said. "Unlike all the other times you've tried to kill me, she was safely at the hotel when this one hit."

"She was? Oh well, she can't be in every episode, right? We don't want her stealing your spotlight."

I popped my gun into my hand and brought it down hard on his desk.

"Here's how we're going to play this," I said. "You're going to tell me the truth because every time you lie to me, every time I even *suspect* that you're lying to me, I am going to break something very expensive in this office. Lie enough times, and it will be your kneecaps. Got it?"

"Gotta hand it to you, Zachtinium, you have the star tantrum down pat."

"You expected Sexy to be at my house today based on the morning's news reports. That's why the Goo was programmed to attack everyone in the building rather than just me."

"I've told you before," he said. "The drama quotiency heightens with the addition of potentially collateralized victimization. It's all good for the show."

I lifted my gun and blasted a hole through his computer screen. It fell to the floor, sparking and fizzling where it melted a small portion of the carpet.

"The show is a front and you know it. You're not trying to kill me. You're after Sexy."

"Zachquiescence, that's utterly preposteronious."

I blasted a hole in the computer screen that covered the northern wall of the office.

"It wasn't a coincidence that Sexy was at the Kabuki Palace the night that your droids attacked me. You lured us both there, but she was the one you wanted killed in the chaos. That way it would be written off as a tragic accident during a crazy Zach Johnson adventure. When I saved her and became her bodyguard, you just kept trying to get her under the guise of the *Let's Kill Zach* show. That's why all the attacks came when she was nearby; at the hotel, in the limo, and at the HV studio."

"You don't know what you're talking about."

I turned and shattered another of his computer wall screens.

"I know about the memo from the governor's aide, Roundtree. I know that one of Spierhoofd's main contributors put out a hit on Sexy because they feared that she was a threat to the governor's reelection plans. And I checked the records. Your corporation contributed over five million credits to the governor's last election campaign. You've gotten some sweet corporate tax breaks out of it so far and there's huge media deregulation legislation in the works now that will make you a ton of credits if it passes. You couldn't risk losing that. So you put the hit out on Sexy."

Roundtree moved to speak but stopped when I aimed my gun at his third (and last) wall monitor.

"You hired a hitman," I continued. "That's who's been sending the PATA threats. And that's who put the bomb in the flowers and gave them to that kid during the concert. But you don't trust the hitman to get the job done. So you've been using the *Let's Kill Zach* idea as insurance and to do the job yourself."

"Are you finished?" Roundtree asked.

"Yeah," I said, taking a seat in one of his guest chairs. "And so are you."

"I don't think so, Zachariasis."

He leaned back in his chair, put his arms casually behind his head and his feet up on his huge desk.

"First of all, the whole scenario is preposterous. True or not, it's just too crazy to be believed."

"Which is exactly how you planned it."

"Second of all," he said, holding up a hand to quiet me, "you have no proof. It's all wild supposition based on the idle speculation of an unreliable reality HV actor who is currently in bitter contract negotiations with me over his show."

"We're not negotiating anything."

"Give me a nano to call the press and the story will be running in the evening cycle. Zach Johnson, seeking a pay raise for his upcoming reality series on the Faux Network, shoots up the office of the network's president while spouting conspiratorial gibberish. It's actually a great publicity piece for the show. I'm surprised I didn't think of it myself."

"You're not going to win this one, Roundtree."

"I'm sorry, Zach. Can I call you Zach? But I already have. I'm squashing you like the insignificant little bug that you are because that's what happens when you come at Rupert Roundtree alone."

"He's not alone, Rupert!"

The already broken office door burst open again, this time coming loose from its hinges and falling to the floor as Hans Spierhoofd dramatically entered the room.

"He's with me."

Roundtree nearly fell out of his chair.

"Hans, what are you doing here?"

"I'm here to set things right, Rupert," Spierhoofd said, striding confidently toward Roundtree's desk. "I don't condone murder for hire in my administration."

I have to admit that I used to like Spierhoofd's movies and HV shows. He's not a good actor. He wouldn't know subtlety if it was in the form of an anvil and fell on his head, but in his early days, nobody this side of Robert Mitchum did a better badass tough guy. You'd think that after a few lousy movies and nearly two terms as governor the guy would have lost a step, but I had to admit, standing in that office, he proved that he could still bring on the A-game.

"Don't tell me you believe what Johnson is saying . . ."

He slapped Roundtree hard in the face with his hamsized open palm.

"Everything Johnson has said is true and we all know it. So don't embarrass yourself by lying."

"I made you, you self-righteous steroid addict."

Spierhoofd slapped him again, harder this time.

"Don't threaten me," he snarled. "I saw the Soviets roll their tanks down the streets of Austria when I was a boy. Believe me, there's nothing you can do that would frighten me."

"Hans, you idiot, you're Danish, not Austrian," Roundtree said. "And the Soviets occupied Austria fifty years before you were even born."

"I'm a politician, Rupert," Spierhoofd said, slapping Roundtree again. "I'm allowed to embellish my past for the sake of drama."

"I got you elected," Roundtree sneered. "Your career

was sinking when I talked you into running for governor. If it hadn't been for me you'd be doing infomercials by now."

Spierhoofd's face turned red with anger and he put his large hands down hard on the edge of Roundtree's massive desk.

"I don't do infomercials," he growled.

He pushed the desk forward, sliding its great bulk into Roundtree's stomach and pushing him all the way back to the office wall, pinning him hard against the clear Plexiglas of the windows. Roundtree, gasping for breath, tried to free himself but Spierhoofd's hold on the desk was too strong.

"You are going to answer every one of Mr. Johnson's questions completely and truthfully. Do I make myself clear?"

Roundtree nodded and Spierhoofd eased his grip ever so slightly on the desk.

"*Let's Kill Zach* was on our list of shows to be developed anyway," Roundtree said. "We were just hoping to find someone better looking to be the lead."

"Hey!"

"I'm sorry," Roundtree said, "but you didn't poll well with the eighteen-to-twenty-nine demographic."

"Who is the hitman you hired?" I asked.

"I don't know."

Spierhoofd pushed the desk a little harder, squeezing Roundtree's midsection a little more.

"I swear, I don't know. It was done through intermediaries. I spoke to him once over the net; audio only and on a protected channel with voice masking. It wasn't even a good connection. I could barely understand him when he said the word 'kill.' I paid half his fee up front to a Cayman account. The other half was promised on delivery. Honestly, I don't know who he is."

"When is he going to try and kill Sexy?"

"He was supposed to do it at the first concert. Make it look like a crazed fan. We thought that would be most dramatic. If he couldn't do it then, he promised to do it straight out at the third concert."

"That's tonight."

"Everyone would be expecting it to happen at the last concert. We wanted to be a little more unpredictable. You get a bigger bang that way."

"Call off the hit." I said.

"I can't. I don't know how to contact the killer. I can't stop it."

I turned to Spierhoofd.

"The concert starts in half an hour," I said. "We have to stop it."

"You go," Spierhoofd said. "As I told you at our last meeting, I can't be part of this."

"You're all heart, Mr. Governor."

Five minutes later I was back on the street, the pedal of the Kaiser hard to the metal, heading flat out to The Fart. Whether Sexy wanted me or not, in my mind I was still her bodyguard. And there was no way I would let her die on my watch.

41

The area around The Fart was jammed with pressbots, flesh-and-blood media, and wannabe concertgoers even five minutes before curtain time. I pushed my way through the crowd as best I could (making more than a few enemies along the way) and made my way to one of the police officers stationed at the entranceway.

"My name's Zach Johnson," I said to the officer. "I'm Sexy's bodyguard. I need to get in right away."

"I'm sorry, Mr. Johnson," the policeman said, "but we have orders from Ms. Sprockets' people that you are not to be allowed in the arena."

"What?"

"Apparently, you're no longer in Ms. Sprockets' employ."

"I know that but I have to get in. She's in danger."

"Which might be why there are like five hundred cops in and around the arena right now."

"Look, just call Tony Rickey. He'll vouch for me. You could even call the governor."

"Mr. Johnson, no offense, but I have fifty thousand people to deal with right now. Why don't you call Captain Rickey or the governor or the World Council yourself."

The cop turned away and I was pushed aside by the throng of fans. I desperately netted with Tony on my wrist interface.

"Tony."

"Zach, you can't come in."

"What?"

"I'm sorry. Sexy and Smiles went directly to The Fart management. They said that if you are found inside the arena, they will cancel the concert. We have to keep you out. I had to pull a few strings just to keep them from having you banned from New Frisco entirely."

"Tony, you have to get me in. They are going to try to kill Sexy tonight onstage."

"Who is?"

"I don't know but it's a professional hit man."

"Are you certain?"

"Absolutely. Rupert Roundtree confessed it to me twenty minutes ago."

"Rupert Roundtree? I thought he was trying to kill you."

"Yeah, it's a long story."

"Do you have any proof?"

"Other than an unrecorded confession that took place in the presence of the governor? No."

"The governor was there?"

"Like I said, long story. The point is that we have to cancel the concert."

"Do you have a description of the hit man?"

"Nothing. It was an anonymous hire."

"I'll speak to Sexy's people," Tony said, "but if we cancel the concert now, we're going to have a riot on our hands."

"At least get me inside."

"Then I know there'll be a riot. Like it or not, Zach, you're not coming in."

The screen went blank and a wave of despair and frustration washed over me. I could hear the crowd inside the arena chanting Sexy's name, begging her to come onstage. The pressbots and correspondents were scurrying around, prepping themselves for live netcasts from the scene. The ground itself was vibrating from the excitement of the nano. The night was hot, the air was electric, and there was murder on the wind. My client was going to die and there was absolutely nothing I could do about it.

And that's when my head started to buzz in a very familiar way and a very well-shaped silhouette appeared from the shadows like a wraith from the forest.

"Hey there, Sadsack. You look like you could use some help."

HARA had returned.

42

She was wearing a tight tweed skirt and matching jacket over a white blouse. Her heels were high and a wide-brimmed hat covered half of her holographic face. Her look was one hundred percent femme fatale, which sent a chill down my spine.

"Before you say anything," she said as she approached, "I just want you to know that I'm still angry with you."

"I figured that. Join the club."

"But as I said yesterday, I'm a professional. And we have a job to do. So I'm setting all our emotional baggage deep into my random access memory while we see this through."

"HARA . . ."

"After that," she said, holding her hand up to silence me, "all bets are off. Got it?"

I nodded. "Got it. Are you up to speed on the situation?"

It was her turn to nod this time. "I monitored your call with Captain Rickey. Now come on, let's get you in the arena."

The HV reporter was looking at the notes on his palm computer and finishing a cup of coffee. He was a little thinner than me but about my height, which is pretty much all I was looking for.

"Hey," I said, tapping him on the shoulder, "you're, um . . ."

"John Blue from *Instant Buzz*," HARA whispered.

"John Blue from *Instant Buzz*," I said.

He turned to me and flashed me a smile.

"Yes, I am. And you're Zach Johnson. Good to meet you."

"Likewise," I said, looking closely at the all-access pass around his neck. "You're here for the concert, huh?"

"No, not really," he said with a smile. "I just like the coffee."

"Funny. Well, good meeting you," I said, turning away. "Enjoy the show."

"You, too."

He smiled and turned away, and when his back was turned I popped my gun into my hand and fired. He spun around quickly, a look of shock on his face.

"Did you just shoot me in my ex-male model butt?"

"It's a tranq dart," I said, as he stumbled into my arms. "Sorry about that."

I pulled him into the shadows of the building, grabbed his pass, and sat him by the wall. HARA threw a hologram over me that made me look exactly like him and we were back in business, that is until I rounded the corner.

"There you are, John."

I turned and saw a pretty blonde woman approaching, a cameraman at her side.

"Andrea, your cohost," HARA whispered.

"Andrea, my cohost," I said, waving.

She came up and stood beside me as the cameraman squatted in front of us, prepping his camera.

"I was starting to wonder if you'd been kidnapped. We're doing a live bumper in about ten seconds."

"Live?" I asked. "Why don't you do this one?"

"Right," she said, giving me a joking poke in the ribs. "You mean you're actually going to let me get a word in this time?"

"Yeah," I said. "Just kidding."

"And by the way," she said, "you better lay off those doughnuts. You're starting to lose that ex-male model body."

The cameraman finished his quick-prep and shouted to us.

"And we're on in five, four, three . . ." He held up two fingers, then one and pointed to us as the red light on his camera went on.

"Andrea and John here at New Frisco's famed Fart Arena for what has become the musical event of the year, Sexy Sprockets' death-defying Ménage Abattoir Tour. And the energy out here is absolutely radioactive. Isn't that right, John?"

"Actually, it's, um, it's really boring here," I said.

"What?"

"It's a total snoozefest," I said. "There's nothing happening here whatsoever. Anyone thinking of coming here should think again because this is concert is duller than dull. I'm leaving now, as a matter of fact."

"John?"

"So just to recap, it's really dull here. Nothing to see. Please stay away. Oh, and don't watch the Faux Network. It's an insult to humanity. This is Jeff and Angela."

"John and Andrea."

"Right, John and Andrea, signing off."

Andrea and the cameraman stared at me open-mouthed and unbelieving for an uncomfortable nano. I shrugged my shoulders and turned away.

"I gotta go."

As I left I heard Andrea say, "He's cute but dumb as a doorknob."

I used John's all-access pass to get into the arena through the press gate. HARA kept the holographic disguise on me as I made my way backstage.

"What's the plan?" HARA asked, appearing beside me.

"We have to find Sexy and get her to cancel the concert."

"Wow, that's a generalized and bad plan even for you."

"We have to stop the show."

"You don't think the fans will riot?"

"There'll be a bigger panic if Sexy's killed onstage."

We moved quickly through the backstage area and down the hallway to Sexy's dressing room.

"Sexy, it's Zach," I said, knocking on the door.

I heard music playing loudly inside. It was a fast paced track of Sexy's called "Google My Soul" that she liked performing late in her concerts. It worried me a little that I was becoming so familiar with Sexy's music, but I tried not to think about it too much.

I knocked again, pounding this time and shouted.

"Sexy, you're in danger tonight. Let me in!"

There was no answer but the music continued.

"Can you still open this lock?" I asked HARA, stepping away from the door.

"Just put your eye to the interface and let me do the rest," she said.

I did as I was told. The red databeam flashed from my eye into the lock. The door popped open and I stepped inside.

Immediately I was hit with a blast of the music. It was louder than I had expected. The lights of the room were off but the flaring meditation chamber bathed most of the room in a molten burgundy glow.

Sexy wasn't there but what I saw instead made my stomach turn.

Carol was in the meditation chamber this time. Floating in the air and bathing in the deep red glow. Smiles stood beside the projector, his grin smug, his expression hungry.

I was too furious to speak, consumed by a rage more violent than I'd ever known. I moved toward him without thought, fueled only by emotion. He turned as I approached and didn't recognize me in the holographic disguise.

"I'm sorry but this room is off limits to the media."

I hit him in the face and felt a few of his teeth break free of his jaw. He fell to the floor like a rag doll but I lifted him up by the shirt collar as HARA dissipated the hologram. He turned to me still conscious but dazed.

"Johnson," he spat.

I hit him again in the face and felt the cartilage in his nose crack against my fist. He fell to the floor again, bleeding from the mouth and nose now. This time I left him there.

"Turn this thing off."

"It's set at a very high level," HARA said, forming her hologram beside me. "We may need to power it down slowly."

"Turn it off now!" I shouted.

"Get your eye close to the interface," she said with a sigh.

She flashed the databeam into the machine and powered it down quickly. Slowly Carol sank to the floor. I stood beside her as she descended and cradled her as the last of the red glow faded and the room lights came up.

"Is she okay?"

"Her vital signs are fine," HARA said. "Her heart rate and breathing were low due to the meditation but they're returning to normal. Radiation is dissipating. She should be coming around in a couple nanos."

"Good."

I gently laid her on the floor and put my coat under her head. Then I walked over to the meditation chamber. I popped my gun into my hand and blasted it to bits. I grabbed the biggest piece of the debris I could find and angrily threw it at the wall. Then I turned to Smiles who was sitting on the floor, holding his handkerchief to his bloody face.

"Keep your hands off her," I said, grabbing him again by the collar and shaking him furiously. "Keep away from her or I swear I will kill you with my bare hands. Do you understand me?"

He moaned as I shook him and I gave him a slap to the face with the back of my hand.

"Do you understand me?"

He didn't answer and I hit him again.

"Zach . . ." HARA said softly.

"Do you understand me!" I shouted hitting him again.

"Leave him alone!"

The words were a command rather than a request and I felt them deep in my head as well as heard them. I turned and saw Carol, fully awake now and crawling toward us.

I let Smiles go and backed away from him as she approached. He slumped to the floor and she cradled him in her arms.

"Don't touch him again."

Again, her words echoed in my head. They were bitter and anger-filled. I could feel her reaching into my mind, trying to get control. I wasn't even sure if she knew that she was doing it, but thankfully I was wearing a psi-blocker. That and HARA's presence in my head, gives me protection against psionic attacks. Even so, I had to fight the urge to obey her.

"Carol, he was poisoning you."

"Get out of here," she spat.

"Carol, he's done something to you."

"I said, get out of here. And don't come near me again!"

The vitriol and hatred in her voice was like a slap to my face and I couldn't speak at first. I got to my feet as she helped Smiles wipe the blood from his face and turned away.

Just then the chanting of the audience in the arena changed into a roar. The heavy bass riffs of the opening song sounded and I knew that the curtain was beginning to rise. Sexy's throaty whisper rolled out over fifty thousand screaming fans (and one killer) pumping them into a frenzy.

"Mesdames et messieurs . . . amants et rêveurs . . . bouchers et bétail . . ."

"Oh no," I said.

I was too late. The concert had begun.

43

I ran down the hallway toward the stage as Sexy ripped through the opening number. The roar of the crowd was deafening, almost drowning out the music itself, which wasn't exactly a bad thing. I wanted to put my earplugs in but the psi-blocker prevented me from doing so. I was tempted for a nano to take the psi-blocker out but didn't, choosing instead to protect myself against the evil I didn't know rather than the music I did. HARA's hologram ran with me (putting special slow-motion effects in her hair and clothes as she did so).

"Contact Electra," I shot to HARA through the mindlink. "Tell her Carol's in trouble and that she needs to get here right away."

"She may not like having the message come from me," HARA said as we ran.

"There's no other way. She wouldn't be able to hear me over the noise."

I made it to the backstage area and cast a quick glance at Sexy onstage. It was pure bedlam, as I knew it would be. The crowd was even more raucous than before with fans charging the stage steadily in ones and twos and each time being grabbed by security and hauled away. Tony's men were in full force around the arena and I was actually afraid that one of them would spot me and try to drag me away as well.

"HARA, I need to talk to Tony."

"Done," she said. "He's on the interface."

"Tony, it's Zach. I'm backstage."

"How'd you get inside?"

"Don't worry about it, just let your men know that I'm here and that they shouldn't arrest me."

"That will be a hard sell," he said. "Arresting you is like second nature to them. Any sign of the killer?"

"I'm sure there is. But I can't tell since I have no idea who it is. Have you screened the audience?"

"We checked them individually going in and we're area scanning for weapons every five minutes. No sign of any weapons so far."

"I don't like this," I said.

"You're making me nervous, Zach. I mean more so than usual."

"Good," I said. "I'll let you know if I see anything."

I circled around the stage looking for any signs of trouble. I even discreetly watched Sexy's first costume change (slipping out of something small into something smaller). I saw signs of chaos, lunacy, and tastelessness everywhere I looked, but nothing out of the ordinary (in the context of everything else). And no sign of anything that looked like a killer. That's when I knew things were bad.

"I don't like this," I said. "We're missing something here. Something very big."

"Any idea when during the show the killer is supposed to strike?" HARA asked.

"None whatsoever but let's figure this out now, if I'm a killer, how do I kill Sexy?"

"Make her listen to her own music? Or maybe make her wear a skirt with a hem below the knee?"

I was standing in the wings on the right side of the stage with a full view of Sexy onstage and the lion's share of the arena crowd, my mind desperately running through the possibilities.

"A sniper's no good. There's too much movement onstage and there's no place to get off a good shot except for the luxury boxes. Does Roundtree have a luxury box here?"

"Captain Rickey's men are stationed in all of the luxury boxes," HARA replied. "And they scanned negative for weapons."

"What about a crazed fan with a sidearm or a bomb then? They could get close to the stage and attack."

"The audience has been scanned for weapons as well."

"The press too?"

"Yes," HARA said. "All negative."

I turned my gaze back to the stage, scanning the musicians and stage sets.

"What about something onstage?"

"It scanned negative before the show for weapons and explosives."

"It wouldn't have to be a bomb," I said. "The set pieces could be sabotaged."

"That would mean that the killer would have access to the backstage area," HARA replied. "Do you think it's an inside job?"

"It has to be," I said. The pieces of the puzzle were beginning to come together in my mind. "The PATA notes—they all indicated easy access to Sexy. The kid with the bomb flowers had a legit backstage pass. And he was chosen because of his history of chasing Sexy. That was no coincidence. DOS it. This has been an inside job all along and we didn't see it."

Sexy ended her Poor Little Rich Girl ballad to another roar of the crowd and the synthesizer and Arabic drums of "Love Cutlets" kicked in. Sexy and the girls shimmied across the stage as the dancers (minus the ones I had injured two nights before) strode onto the stage.

"It's one of the dancers," I said. "It has to be."

"They don't have access to Sexy's hotel," HARA said "And I checked them out, they're dancers. Not killers. They're built to sway, not slay."

And it clicked.

"Baba Wawa," I whispered.

"What?" HARA asked.

"It's a joke from an old television show about a newscaster with a speech impediment. She couldn't say her name right and it came out Baba Wawa."

"That's . . . totally unhelpful here, Zach."

"No. Roundtree said that the hitman was hard to understand. He thought it was a poor communication line but the hitman couldn't say 'kill.' And the kid with the flowers, he told the police that he got them from someone who said that the flowers would 'sway Sexy.' It was a joke. It wasn't sway the killer was saying it was . . ."

"Slay," HARA said.

"It's Lusty, HARA. Lusty's the hitman. I mean hit woman."

"Assassin," HARA said. "And that's a shame, because right now she has a meat cleaver in her hand."

"Let Tony know," I said. "And let him know that we're taking her out."

The "Love Cutlets" production number was a crowd favorite with its flying meat, flashing cleavers, and undulating dancers. Tonight was no different, except for the fact that, if I didn't act soon, it was going to end with some real butchering.

"HARA, do you remember the guy whose leg I broke?"

"You're going to have to give me more to go on, Zach," HARA said. "There have been so many over the years."

"The dancer the other night."

"Oh, him," she said.

"Throw a hologram of his image over me," I said. "I'm going onstage."

"You understand, of course, that a hologram won't help your dancing abilities, right?"

"HARA!"

She shrugged and put the holographic disguise of the dancer over me. No one seemed to notice me as I stepped onstage, which is a good thing, because the sight of the fifty thousand screaming people stopped me dead in my tracks. I could actually feel the force of their screams pressing against me like a strong wind. The stage floor was shaking from the music and the heat from the spotlights was so intense I felt like a soy burger in the McMunchies warming tray. It was simply overwhelming.

"Zach?" HARA whispered. "Zach, snap out of it."

I fought back the stage fright and began moving slowly across the stage. One of the security people at the foot of the stage looked my way and furrowed his brow. I quickly looked away and started bobbing my head in a desperate effort to find the beat.

"Nice cover job, Zach," HARA whispered. "No one's going to notice the background dancer who can't dance."

I carefully made my way over to where Misty, Sissy, and Lusty were dancing a couple of meters behind Sexy. All three of them (and the men with whom they were dancing) did double takes when they saw me approach but they kept up with the dance, if a little more awkwardly now.

Lusty was on the end of the dance line and I moved closer to her as she danced in front of one male dancer, bumping and grinding her hips against him. I wiggled next to them and tried to match their movements as best I could.

"Not the twist, Zach," HARA pleaded. "Anything but the twist."

The entire group of dancers, as one, moved to the left, but I caught Lusty's hand and pulled her toward me as the others continued on. She shimmied alongside me, improvising as I leaned close to her.

"Don't do it, Lusty," I said.

"What?"

"I know what you're planning," I said. "Don't do it."

"Zach?"

"It's not too late. You can turn back now."

And turn back she did, only not in the way I had hoped. She attacked almost quicker than I could see, spinning around cleanly and swinging the cleaver in her hand at my neck. I brought my arm up and blocked the swing but the blade sank deep into my forearm, lodging itself in my body armor (not my flesh, thankfully) but hurting like hell nonetheless.

I fought off the pain and forced back any regrets I had about hitting a woman, then sent a left jab at her face. It was as quick as I could muster but she avoided it easily. I followed quickly with a right. She saw that coming as well and sidestepped it. Then she pulled me close and sent her knee into my crotch, then gave me a left jab and right cross to the face that knocked me to the floor. I later learned that Lusty was a minor psi as well. She had precog abilities allowing her to see a second or two into the future. That gave her a nice edge in a fistfight.

The fight had happened too quickly for anyone to notice. The crowd's attention was firmly on Sexy and the others who were on the opposite side of the stage. So few people, if anyone, saw me go down. And only I, from my position on the floor, saw Lusty pull the laser knife from her boot and shimmy her away across the stage as the music began to crescendo.

I got to my knees as the holographic disguise dissipated.

There was no time for subtlety now. I scrambled to my feet and launched myself at Lusty. She was close to Sexy now, whose back was still turned, caught up in her song and dance. Lusty ignited the laser knife and its electronic red blade flashed three hundred centimeters out from the handle. Everyone saw it now, Misty, Sissy, the musicians, even the crowd. Everyone saw the blade but Sexy, who was too caught up in herself to see her own death fast approaching.

"Lusty, don't," I yelled.

Lusty put a hand on Sexy's shoulder and Sexy turned around, confused and annoyed. She saw the knife in Lusty's hand and still didn't understand what was happening. The music stopped, the crowd went silent and every media person in the arena began writing their lead for the next news cycle.

It was clear to me then that this wasn't just a job to Lusty. It was personal. She wanted Sexy to see her death coming. And she wanted to watch Sexy die and make sure that Sexy knew who had ended her life.

But she never got the chance.

I leaped at Lusty from behind and this time she was too caught up in the work at hand to foresee it. I grabbed her knife hand just as she started to bring the blade down. We tumbled to the floor and rolled across the stage, each of us wrestling for control of the weapon. She head butted me hard in the face (which I wasn't expecting) and then kneed me again in the groin (which I guess I really should have expected). I lost my grip on the knife and she quickly grabbed it. Then she rolled on top of me and raised the blade high over her head, giving her, she hoped, enough momentum to pierce my armor. I popped my gun into my hand and was just about to pull the trigger when Lusty froze in mid-swing. Then her eyes rolled back in her head and she tumbled off me, falling unconscious to the stage floor and curled into a fetal position.

I looked up and saw Carol standing on the stage, a little smile flaring the corners of her mouth.

"Hi, Tio." Her words echoed in my head.

"You gave her a psi blast, huh?" I asked.

"I couldn't have her putting a hole in my favorite uncle now, could I?"

The crowd that had gone silent a nano ago now began

to applaud. Carol smiled, turned toward the audience, and gave them a little bow.

"Ladies and gentlemen," Sexy shouted into her mike, "please welcome my ub-zeenly old school bodyguard Zachary Nixon Johnson!"

The crowd applauded and I waved.

"And my double-xette and backup dancer, Carol Gevada!"

The crowd went wild. Tony's men slapped the cuffs on the still unconscious Lusty and dragged her off the stage. The musicians took their places to finish the concert and I turned away, hoping to get off the stage as quickly as possible. I actually began to think that we were on our way to a happy ending.

You'd think that I'd have learned by now never to think that.

44

Things turned very ugly very quickly. Things have a way of doing that around me and I'm beginning to take it personally (I don't know why the universe insists on using me as its personal chew toy).

It started suddenly but innocently (or so I thought). Everyone in the audience was applauding. And everyone onstage was happy and smiling. Then the stage lights dimmed dramatically and a bloodred spotlight cut the darkness. The intensity of the light was so great that I feared at first that it was a giant laser and, in retrospect, that would have been much better. The light did no damage when it first hit the stage, it simply enveloped Carol. That's when I noticed that the beam of light was the same shade of red as the projector beam from Smiles' meditation chamber.

"Uh oh," HARA said, appearing beside me.

"What is it?" I asked.

"The radiation level of the area just shot up."

"Oh, that can't be good."

Carol stood motionless in the red beam and let it wash over her, actually lifting her head upward as though she wanted to feel the light on her face. Then she stretched her arms out wide and rose into the air.

"Carol!"

I ran to her but the heat from the beam was so intense that I couldn't get close. And yet somehow Carol was safe inside it.

"It's an oversized version of the meditation chamber," HARA shouted. "It's supercharging Carol's power."

"Where's Smiles?"

"Right here, Johnson!"

Sammy Smiles strode onto the stage with the swagger of a conquering headliner. His orange suit was smeared with blood from his broken nose and split lip but, even though his teeth looked like a picket fence after a cattle stampede, he was smiling so widely that his cheeks were messing up his hair.

"Did you think I'd let Sexy just walk away from me? Did you really think I'd let her go without getting a replacement?"

"What are you doing to Carol?"

"She's not Carol anymore," he sneered. "She's the new Sexy. Better and more powerful than ever before!"

He pushed a button on his wrist interface and the spotlight on Carol cut out. She fell to the stage floor with a thump, landing on her hands and knees.

"Carol!"

I rushed to her and helped her to her feet. She seemed weak and a little shaken, but otherwise intact.

"Are you okay?" I asked.

"Yeah," she said, shaking the cobwebs from her head.

A sort of distant look came over her eyes and she stood straighter, looking around the arena as though seeing it for the first time.

"As a matter of fact, I feel great."

And then the audience began to cheer. Not the polite applause of a happy ending or even the emotion-filled cheers of appreciation for an exciting show, but the wild, raucous cheers of ecstatic frenzy. The musicians began playing again, more vibrantly than before. Misty and Sissy and the dancers onstage slipped back into their routine. And Carol ran to the front of the stage, pointing at the crowd who screamed every time she moved. The concert had picked up right where it left off. Only Carol was fronting the show instead of Sexy. The fact that Carol wasn't singing didn't seem to matter to anyone. They loved it just the same. Carol blew a kiss at the crowd and the people in the first few rows (male and female alike) were so overwhelmed that they simply fainted.

Only Smiles, Sexy, HARA, and I were unaffected.

"What the DOS is going on?"

"It's like they say, Johnson," Smiles shouted. "The show must go on!"

"She's not even singing!"

"She doesn't need to," HARA said inside my head. "Carol's psionic power is so strong now that she can simply broadcast her thoughts directly into everyone's heads. Everyone out there is hearing her thoughts and they're loving it."

"But I don't hear anything!"

"You and Smiles are wearing psi-blockers. Sexy, having experienced Smiles' treatments for many years already, has built up an immunity to this type of psionic broadcasting."

"No way!" Sexy said angrily. "There is no way that my fans would forget about me this easily!"

"Believe it, Sexy," Smiles yelled. "You're not even a has-been now. You're a never-was!"

Sexy picked up her microphone and ran to the front of the stage, trying to get in front of Carol. But Carol waved her hand and telekinetically swatted Sexy away like a fly. Sexy flew head over heels and landed on a pile of red satin pillows; angry and stunned but otherwise unhurt.

"I'm still hotter than her," she shouted to no one in particular. "Aren't I? Will somebody please tell me that I'm hot!"

HARA and I meanwhile were still focused on Carol.

"Carol's never had that kind of telekinetic power before," I said.

"You're right," HARA said with a nod. "Frankly, I'm not sure she can control it."

"She can't," Smiles shouted, his gap-toothed smile beaming like an Alfred E. Neuman lighthouse. "But I can. I've built safeguards into the technology that will allow me to control anything up to a level four psi."

"But Carol's a level six," I said.

"No she's not," Smiles said. "She's level one, class six."

"She's class one, level six!"

"Which classification measures potential again, class or level?"

"Level!"

"DOS," he said. "I always get those two mixed up. I swear they changed those around now and again."

"Well," said HARA, turning her gaze from Carol to the arena ceiling, "there's an extremely good likelihood that you'll never make that mistake again."

"Why's that?" he asked.

The walls of the arena began to shake, and the scream of tearing polymer and twisting metal overhead nearly drowned out the music as the roof of the arena began ripping itself apart.

"Because we're all about to die, you idiot!" I shouted.

45

Carol had literally blown the roof off the arena. Her teleki-netic power had peeled back the hundred kiloton metal and polymer lid of the structure like the lid of a sardine can. The wet night air swept into The Fart like a whirlwind as the music grew louder and the still entranced audience cheered more raucously.

"This isn't right," Smiles shouted, frantically punching the buttons on his wrist interface. "The technology should allow me to control her."

"She's too powerful for your gadgets," I yelled.

Over the past few days, Smiles had surreptitiously given Carol the same kind of psionic enhancing treatments that he'd given Sexy for years. But while supercharging Carol's abilities he had unknowingly broken down the natural power dampening barriers of her brain. He had thought that the technology he'd used to control Sexy's power for so long would work on Carol as well. But where Sexy was a babbling brook, Carol was a raging sea and all Smiles had was a beaver dam and a leaky bucket. And now we were all going to pay for it.

"What have you done to my niece, Chico?"

I turned and saw Electra climbing onto the stage (el-bowing screaming fans aside as she did so) and she was wearing a psi-blocker, for which I was very grateful, so she was in control of her own mind.

"Electra, what are you doing here?"

"HARA netted and told me that you needed me here, remember?"

"Oh, yeah," I said. "In retrospect, I think that might have been a mistake."

"What's going on?"

"Long story. Right now we have to get these people out of the arena before Carol brings the whole place down."

"Evacuating the arena won't help," HARA said.

"What do you mean?"

"Carol's power is still increasing."

"That can't be. The red spotlight's off."

"Smiles' augmentation treatments only began the process," she said. "They lit the fuse."

"Please don't use that metaphor," I pleaded. "Nothing good ever comes from you using a fuse/bomb metaphor."

"Without the natural dampeners in her mind, Carol's power is continuing to increase. This wind you feel isn't a natural one. It's telekinetic leakage and it's only going to get stronger. In a few minutes she won't be able to contain her power at all. She'll hit critical mass."

"What happens then?" Electra asked.

"Let's just say it won't really matter who becomes governor of California in the next election," HARA said, "because there won't be a California to govern."

The wind was getting stronger, picking up debris and hurling it around the arena. The structure itself was groaning as its damaged supports bent and swayed from the force of Carol's power.

"How do we stop her?"

"Other than rebuilding the dampeners in her mind," HARA said, "I have no idea."

"Then how do we rebuild the dampeners?"

"We can't," HARA replied. "Carol has to do that herself. We have to convince her to do it."

I took a step toward Carol and got hit with a blast of telekinetic wind that nearly blew me off my feet. I popped my gun into my hand and aimed directly at Carol, who stood motionless amid the fury.

"Tarzan."

The cable flew out against the wind and latched onto the only secure thing in the entire arena, Carol herself, wrapping around her leg several times. I detached the cable from the gun muzzle, popped the gun back into my wrist holster, and held on for dear life.

"Electra, HARA, help me get close to her."

Electra moved behind me and leaned into my back, propping me up against the wind. HARA became as solid as she could (her hands mostly) and began pushing as well. Together, we fought off the wind and took a couple steps toward Carol.

"You know," Electra said, "this isn't the way I imagined this going."

"You do you mean?"

"I opened the box you gave me this afternoon at your house. You forgot about it after you had whatever epiphany it was about this case and ran off."

"I said that was for later."

"You give a girl a little black box then run off and you expect her not to open it?"

"He gave you a little black box?" HARA asked.

We were making our way through the telekinetic storm, baby step by baby step. The winds were lashing us but we were hunkered down low and held tightly to the cable; Electra and HARA lending their strength to mine.

"What do you think?" I asked.

"I think you have great taste in rings."

"He gave you a ring?" HARA shouted.

"It was my mother's ring," I said. "And her mother's too, I think. I'm not really sure. My family history is a little spotty. I'm fairly certain that it's not stolen, though. So what do you think? Do you want to make things official?"

"Only if you say the words, Chico."

As fate would have it, I was already down on one knee, thanks to the fierceness of the telekinetic wind around us. So at least there was one traditional element to the proposal.

"Electra!" I shouted above the din, "will you marry me?"

Electra leaned harder into my back and wrapped her left hand around me. I felt her lips, soft and moist, against the back of my neck and smelled the sweetness of her hair on the violent breeze.

"Does this answer your question?"

I looked down at her left hand on my chest and saw the ring on her finger.

"Great!" HARA said, a little coldly. "Let's plan a June wedding. Or a November funeral, whichever is more appropriate!"

I looked up at Carol, still standing, arms spread wide, at

the center of the storm. I felt Electra's arms around me and HARA's presence in my head. I put my head down and took two more giant steps forward.

"No one's dying today," I said through gritted teeth. "No one."

I pushed on, inexorably, step after step. The winds eased ever so slightly the closer we got to Carol. She was only a few meters away now but the walls of the arena were starting to tear at the seams. I knew we were fast running out of time.

I put my head down and lurched forward once more and suddenly felt the winds ease dramatically. Without the resistance, I tumbled forward and fell to the stage floor. I looked back and saw Electra, still clinging to the cable and fighting the winds.

"What happened?" I asked.

"We're at the eye of the storm," HARA replied, her hologram appearing beside me.

I grabbed onto the cable and reached my hand out to Electra, who was still struggling.

"Grab my hand, honey."

Putting my hand into the telekinetic wind nearly ripped me off my feet. If it hadn't been for the cable, I would have been spun into the air like straw in a funnel cloud. I held tighter to the cable and went to reach back toward Electra again but she waved me off.

"Don't worry about me," she said. "Save Carol."

"Electra!"

"I'm fine," she said, wrapping the cable around her midsection. "I'll be there in a nano. Just go."

We shared a long, wordless look and then she waved me away. Slowly I got to my feet and took a step toward Carol. She didn't seem to notice me.

"Carol!"

There was no response.

"Carol, it's me, Zach!"

She turned and I felt the winds in the arena shift with her movements. A huge portion of the arena's southern wall ripped free with a thunderous shriek and simply blew away. Through the hole that it left, I could see that the winds had expanded outside of the arena. Carol's storm was growing.

"Listen, Chica," I said. "I know you don't want to destroy anyone, or everyone, as the case may be. So I'm going to need you to power down. Okay? Can you do that?"

Her face was serene with the slightest trace of a smile on her lips. Her gaze was distant, as though she were looking through me. And my words seemed to have no effect.

Being this close to her made my head hurt from the psionic power that she was putting out. I could feel her inside my mind, fighting through the psi-blocker, and unfortunately, I knew that I didn't have much time left.

"You know," I said, "you're officially my employee right now, so I'm going to be liable for the damage you're doing. I'm going to have to take it out of your pay."

Her eyes shifted subtly in her head as though they were focusing on me.

"Do you have any idea how much an arena like this costs?"

Her body remained completely motionless. But her eyes moved again, as though she was calling my attention to them.

"You can hear me, can't you, Carol?" I shouted.

She nodded almost imperceptibly.

And then she blinked her right eye three times quickly.

"She blinked her right eye," I said to HARA. "Did you see that?"

"I saw it."

"That's our code for trouble. It means she's still in there. She still remembers who she is."

"Whatever you're going to do, Zach," HARA said. "You better do it quickly."

"You can do it, Carol," I said. "You can control this, I know you can. How can I help you?"

She blinked her right eye again, three times fast.

And then a fourth time.

"Four blinks?" I said. "What does four blinks mean?"

"It means 'please shoot me in the head,'" HARA said. "Remember?"

A pit opened in my stomach as my memory confirmed HARA's words.

"Carol," I said, pleadingly.

Her right eye blinked four times again, more persistently, and it was as though someone had reached into my chest and pulled out my heart. I could hear the arena walls ripping apart around me and the cheers of the audience who were too stupid to know what was happening. I knew what Carol was telling me, but I didn't think I was strong enough to do it.

I flicked my wrist and popped my gun into my hand.

"Are you sure about this, Carol?"

I stared at her face hard, through the tears that were forming in my eyes. I stared long and hard, searching desperately for the smallest sign of a negative response. I found nothing. Instead she very clearly nodded her head.

I stood back and wiped my tears with my sleeve. Then I raised the gun and pointed it at her.

"Zach, what are you doing?" Electra shouted.

I swallowed away a lump in my throat the size of a golfball and when I spoke, it was barely more than a whimper.

"Gates help me."

46

"Zach, no!"

HARA's solid light hand ripped the gun from my grip.

"HARA, give me the gun."

"It won't work," HARA shouted.

"Don't make this any harder for me. You saw what she did."

"She's way too powerful to be killed by your gun, Zach." HARA said.

"I'm going to trust Carol on this," I shouted. "Now give me the gun."

HARA backed her hologram away from me and held onto the gun tightly. Her hands were a little unsteady. It might have been because the effort of holding the gun was taxing her capabilities, or it may have been the effort of what she knew was to come. Because, much to my surprise, she raised the gun and pointed it at me.

"What are you doing?"

"It's the only way, big guy."

The arena was giving way in the storm. People in the rear seats were beginning to be thrown into the air from the force. The arena itself was ready to collapse. Carol had to be stopped.

"HARA," I said, "give me the gun. That's a direct command. Give me my gun!"

"I'm sorry," she said. "But I can't."

And there it was. Everything that Randy had warned me about had come to pass. HARA had refused a direct command. With thousands, perhaps millions of lives hanging in the balance, she had abandoned me. And as she stood there with my own gun trained on me, she had the

femme fatale glare of a woman scorned. It was the end of
every pulp novel ever written. But I couldn't let her do it.

Slowly, sadly, I reached my hand toward my wrist interface and gently placed a finger on the button to download
the virus that would erase HARV. My hand was shaking
but I was running out of time, and I had no options left.

Then she stopped me with two words.

"Trust me."

HARV had saved my life more times than I could count.
I trusted him implicitly to do the right thing. He was my
partner, my friend. He had my back. But as Randy had
said, this wasn't HARV anymore. It was HARA. The question was, could I trust her the way I trusted HARV? Was
there enough HARV left in HARA to trust? There was
only one way to find out.

"What's the punch line?" I shouted.

"What?"

"The joke you wrote, the Archimedes Bakery," I said.

"How did you know about that?"

"It doesn't matter," I said. "Just tell me the joke."

She swallowed once and spoke slowly and shyly.

"Why are there no round boxes at the Archimedes
Bakery?"

"Why?"

"Because they're π r^2."

I thought for a nano as the wind swirled around me and
the arena continued to tear itself apart. Then I smiled and
suppressed a bit of a chuckle. Then I laughed out loud.
HARA saw me and smiled as well.

"Okay," I said. "I trust you."

She aimed the gun at me. I saw the OLED light flash in
response to her silent command as she overrode the security system. Then her hologram shimmered and her form
disappeared, reassembling itself into HARV.

And he fired.

47

The blast hit me full in the chest and enveloped my body in a thin layer of intense pain. Every nerve, every bundle, every ganglia, synapse, and neuron in my body fired at once with a soul-twisting blast of pure agony. I was on fire. I was being pierced by a million needles. I was being torn apart. I was sitting through a never ending Adam Sandler film retrospective.

I screamed once, loud and long, as darkness rolled in at me from all directions. Somewhere in the distance I heard another scream and felt the winds of Carol's psionic storm envelope me.

And then there was nothing.

48

I awoke in a void. Bodiless and shapeless, I was nothing more than a floating consciousness in a sea of nothing.

"This better not be eternity."

A white light appeared in the distance. Actually distance isn't the correct term because in a void, distance has no meaning. So let's just say that the light was very small at first and slowly grew larger. It took on a form after a few nanos and I recognized it.

"Carol."

She was luminescent, almost ethereal and I didn't like where all this symbolism seemed to be heading.

"Hola, Tio."

"What happened?" I asked.

"I went a little crazy," she replied with a shrug. "Lost control of myself, broke some stuff, almost destroyed the earth. Sorry."

"It's all right. It wasn't your fault," I said. "What happened after HARV shot me?"

"Pain," she replied.

"That I remember."

"Me too," she said. "That was the point."

"What do you mean?"

She flashed a very mature and knowing smile at me that made me feel kind of old.

"I needed something to snap me out of my trance in order to give my mind a chance to regain control of my power," she said. "HARV knew that. But he also knew that in the state I was in, I was fairly impervious to physical pain."

"So he shot me?"

"Your mind has always been an open book to me, Tio," she said. "It's sort of a bond we share. When HARV shot you, it hurt."

"You can say that again."

"I know, because I felt that pain just as much as you did. It was like a slap in the face."

"That's all?"

"A very hard slap in the face," she said with a smile. "It brought me back reality and gave my mind a chance to power down."

"So you're okay?" I asked.

"I'm fine."

"And everything else?"

"Well, The Fart's pretty much destroyed. The walls collapsed. They found the roof in the bay."

"What about Electra?"

"She's fine; she and everyone else who was there, they're all safe and most of them don't remember what happened."

I relaxed a little and felt a peaceful feeling wash over me.

"I suppose in the long run then it was worth it."

"What do you mean?" she asked.

"It's not a bad way to go out, really. Saving your loved ones and fifty thousand innocent bystanders with crappy taste in music."

Carol smiled and shook her head softly.

"Tio, you're not dead."

"I'm not?"

"Of course not."

"I'm in a void here. I have neither shape nor form."

"That's because you're not thinking of one."

I looked around again and saw my left hand appearing from the darkness, becoming more and more real with every nano. My right arm soon followed as did the rest of my body.

"Any chance I could get some clothes, too?" I asked Carol, covering myself.

"Think harder."

I did, and a nano later I was wearing my favorite gray suit, trench coat, and fedora.

"So let me get this straight, when HARV shot me . . ."

"He used the big hurt," Carol responded. "Lots of pain, but nonlethal."

"Wow. I need to get Randy to turn that down a notch." I said, "So where are we right now?"

"We're in your mind."

"And my body?"

"Tio, look," Carol said. "No offense but this is getting a little sappy. I came here to let you know that everything's okay, but I really have to go now."

"What?"

Her form began to drift away, slowly shrinking.

"I'll see you in the real world," she said.

"Carol?"

"Oh, and, Tio," she said, turning to give me another ethereal smile. "Thanks again. You're the best."

I watched her form shrink away until it was a tiny white light against the lightlessness of the void. Then all at once, the void began to brighten. Ebon turned to black. Black turned to gray, gray to white, and then it was almost too bright to look at.

That's when I opened my eyes.

"Hola, Chico," Electra whispered.

I smiled and felt safe at last.

49

I woke in a hospital bed where I'd lain unconscious for four days. I had three cracked ribs, a hairline fracture in my left leg, and a concussion. All of which were painful, but none of which, fortunately, would do me any lasting damage. And as the months went by, the final threads of the case would play themselves out and come to resolution.

Sexy Sprockets, as promised, officially retired from the music industry, ending her career with the concert that has become known as The Last Fartz. She recently announced her candidacy for governor of California and, at the nano, is polling about even with incumbent Hans Spierhoofd. It's worth noting that Sexy's younger sister, Sassy Sprockets, has just embarked on a singing career. Industry insiders say that the younger Sprockets has a much better singing voice but much smaller breasts than her older sister. They therefore give her little chance at any real success.

Rupert Roundtree was arrested and charged with solicitation of murder, but was acquitted due to lack of material evidence (and Governor Spierhoofd's refusal to testify, citing executive privilege). In retaliatory news, several tax loopholes for media corporations such as Faux were closed by the state government and the media deregulation legislation was vetoed and then killed by the governor. Undaunted, Roundtree has begun an all news channel, which unfortunately, reports mostly fiction.

It was learned that Sammy Smiles had once been employed in the weapons R&D department at the World Council Department of Defense. It was during his tenure there that he developed the technology of psionic augmentation and psionic broadcasting over the AM radio spectrum. The DOD is still uncertain as to how they lost track of him and the technology. Smiles' current whereabouts are unknown. He disappeared from The Fart during its destruction and is currently a wanted fugitive.

Lusty (last name unknown) was tried for attempted murder but was acquitted by an all middle-aged jury on the grounds of insanity. In post-verdict interviews, the jurors claimed that, after listening to Sexy's music in court, they completely understood Lusty's desire to kill her and could therefore not hold Lusty responsible for her actions. Lusty has since become a solo artist and is currently the headliner at the Lively Little Lighthouse Club in Lafayette, Louisiana.

And the World Society of Isaac Newton Scholars recently put out a statement saying that Newton had consumed a little too much absinthe on the night that he made his dire prediction about the world ending in 2060. What he really meant to say, they claim, is that the world will *bend* in 2060, which apparently was some kind of metaphor. Hey, the guy couldn't be brilliant all the time.

50

A few weeks after I was released from the hospital, Electra and I took a trip to our favorite spot on the New Costa Rican coast. We spent most of our time lying on the beach planning our wedding with HARV.

"Are you sure you want the imported champagne for the toast?" HARV asked from his holographic lounge chair. "The domestic brands are becoming quite hip."

"The domestic doesn't taste as good," I replied.

HARV smiled and nodded. He had returned to his original holographic interface since that last fateful nano at The Fart. His hair was a little more stylish now and his body seemed a little buffer as well (not that I notice those type of things). But at the core, he was still the same HARV.

"Good for you, Zach," he said. "I was testing you. Your palate is evolving."

"I want plenty of buffalo wings on the hors d'oeuvres table, though," I said, trying to get to an itch on my leg that was just out of reach beneath my air cast. "With lots of bleu cheese dressing on the side."

HARV sighed and shook his head gently.

"Alas, one step forward, two steps back."

HARV claimed that the HARA experiment was officially over and that he had permanently erased her hologram from his memory. I couldn't say that I was sorry to see her go. HARA was perfect in a lot of ways but, like they say, redheads are just trouble.

"Just a reminder," Electra said, as she sipped her margarita, "my mother will be there and I don't want her sitting next to any of your former clients."

"Done," said HARV. "And speaking of former clients,

you've agreed to invite Ona Thompson. Are you also inviting Twoa and Threa?"

"Didn't they try to kill me?" I asked.

"Technically yes, but if we're going to exclude anyone
who's ever tried to kill you then we'll need to cut another
three dozen guests from the list, including several members
of Electra's family."

"Okay," I said. "But don't put all three of them at the
same table."

"A fine idea," HARV said.

We heard the sound of distant thunder then, which struck
me as odd since the early evening sky was completely
cloudless. It seemed to make HARV a little uncomfortable
as well.

"And, um, have I mentioned yet, that you'll be checking
out this evening?" he asked.

"No," I said. "You skipped that part."

"What's going on?" Electra asked.

"Well, you see, it's kind of a funny story really."

"You mean funny-haha or funny-odd?"

"Both actually. It seems that the pilot episode of *Let's
Kill Zach* was pirated and illegally put on the net."

"Oh, no."

"It's become sort of a cult hit, especially here in Costa
Rica," HARV continued. "So much so that the premier
Latin American network, Holomundo, is planning a Costa
Rican version. It's called *Matemos a Zach*."

The rumbling sound grew louder and it was clear to us
now that it wasn't thunder. It was coming from the forest
to the south.

"Oh, well," Electra sighed, getting to her feet and tying
a wrap skirt around her bathing suit. "It was fun while it
lasted. I was getting a little homesick anyway."

Our hovercraft, with HARV remotely piloting, pulled up
neatly beside our lounge chairs. I slowly got to my feet and
limped toward the passenger seat.

"Yeah," I said. "I get a little antsy if I go too long without someone trying to kill me. *Matemos a Zach* did you
say?"

"Correct," HARV said as he held the hover door open
for me. "The show was to be very representative of the

Costa Rican culture. In the first episode, droids were going to be pelting you with spherical granite bolas."

I settled into the hover and fastened my seat belt as Electra revved the engine.

"Sounds like first rate entertainment," I said. "It's a shame we'll miss it."

Electra gunned the hover and we sped off down the beach, a cloud of pure white sand in our wake and bloodthirsty reality show producers on our tail.

"By the way," HARV said, his hologram leaning forward in the rear seat of the hover, "did I mention that I plan on bringing a date to your wedding?"

"A date?"

"I'm allowed, aren't I?"

"Of course you are, HARV," Electra said.

"Good. His name's Guy," HARV said. "He's a fashion model from New Milan."

"Guy?"

"I realized recently that I prefer men," HARV said. "That's not a problem, is it?"

I smiled, eased the hoverseat back just a bit, and watched the sun set a glorious red and orange over the sea.

"No problem at all, buddy. No problem at all."

My name is Zachary Nixon Johnson. I am the last private detective on Earth.

And my life rocks!

THE
FROST-HAIRED
VIXEN

To Little Harris (lieutenant shorty pants)
and to everybody else who still believes.

Acknowledgments

I'd be totally remiss if I didn't acknowledge my old writing partner and second favorite cousin Larry Ganem. It was a great experience working with him while we were writing the first three books. While it's certainly easier and faster to write a book alone (I had way fewer "disagreements" with myself) without Larry around there was nobody around to shout, "No! No! No! You've gone too far with that. I'm totally rewriting it." Hopefully the reader won't mind that there is now nobody to pull me back from the edge of absurdum. Plus, now without Larry around I don't have anybody else to blame if something goes wrong. The old, "Larry wrote that part . . ." excuse won't fly anymore. I always say, "A person should be accountable for his own actions." I guess now I really have to practice what I preach more.

I am eternally grateful to Betsy Wolheim, DAW's Commander-in-Chief, for giving me the chance to write this book on my own as well for publishing the first three books. Betsy is fairly patient woman (for an editor) with a great sense of humor. Interestingly enough, Betsy was constantly pushing me back *toward* the edge of absurdum. My guess is that I was overcompensating for not having Larry around and playing it extra safe (by my standards) so I needed Betsy to give me a little kick in the pants. Thanks, Betsy!

I also have to thank my agent Joshua Bilmes, because quite frankly he'll whine if I don't. Seriously, Joshua does a great job of explaining the business aspect of writing to me preventing me from selling my books for "magic beans." Joshua is also "A-Number-1" at talking up my books and getting foreign publishers to buy them.

Aaron and Rebecca Goldweber also get a big thank you for their help with early editing with the book. That's the other spot I missed, Larry. Larry took actual writing classes in college so he knows things like the difference between a comma and a semicolon. Aaron and Rebecca are ace editors so they know these arcane facts too.

I of course have to mention all my real-life friends and family who are and were "inspiration" for characters in this and past books. The list is fairly long and just as boring but it's always nice to see your name in print: Carolina and Natalia Padilla, Tom Rickey, Ron Pool, my sister Mary Erdman and her husband Steve, Shannon Codner, and of course, my wife Olga. I'm sure you can all pretty much figure out who you are. If I left anybody out, sorry, I'll mention you twice in the next book.

Finally, I really have to thank my wife Olga and my son Jay, for putting up with me while I wrote this book. I'm hard enough to deal with on a regular basis but I imagine I'm even tougher to handle when there's a deadline bearing down on me. Thanks, I love you guys! (PS: Note to Jay: don't worry, you're going to be a character in a book soon enough.)

1

The holographic name on my door reads Zachary Nixion Johnson, PI. That's mostly correct. My name is Zachary NIXON Johnson. That's what you get when you let your fiancée's brother program your door. Sure, the door would be easy to reprogram but I can't hurt my future brother-in-law's feelings. I look at it like this: it separates me from the crowd even more. Besides, most people either call me Zach, or Johnson, or in the case of the New Frisco police force, *that damn Zachary Johnson* (and that's when they're in a good mood).

You would think being the last freelance private detective on a planet with 15 billion beings, every day would be an action-packed adventure. Only this is 2061, the peak of the over-the-top-information age. A time when everybody has access to more information than any human, meta-human, or even bot could ever want or need. For the most part, clients only enlist my services when the information they need is particularly "sensitive." In other words it's so dangerous any sane person who avoid it like .10 credit sushi.

Somehow, some way, whenever trouble does teleport to my front door, it's always of the earthshaking variety. That's just my lot in life, my pile of spam to sift through. I've learned to accept that I will either be figuratively bored to death or some person, mutant, robot, android, alien, animal, and yes, once even a vegetable, will literally try to kill me. I find it's best if I don't ponder it too much.

Today, though, was a quiet day. Quiet days may not be the stuff of great adventure, but they are the stuff that lets me recharge for upcoming great adventures. Life's like a rollercoaster ride; the highs wouldn't be nearly as fun without the lows. I was sitting in my office on the New Frisco docks, enjoying a nice game of holo-backgammon with my annoying but mostly trusty holographic assistant, HARV, who had me on the ropes.

"Looks like I'm going to backgammon you again, Zach! Which means you'll owe me ten more credits!" HARV said, not even trying to hide the joy in his voice.

"That's only because you're the one who rolls the dice, HARV." I felt I should remind him of that. I turned away from the shimmering board HARV was projecting onto my desk. I slid open one of my desk drawers.

"What are you doing?" HARV asked, annoyed that I had turned my attention away from his impending victory.

I started rummaging through the open drawer. "I'm looking for my real backgammon board. The one with non-computer-generated dice!"

Though I couldn't see HARV, I was certain he was shaking his head and rolling his eyes.

"Zach, Zach, Zach," he said softly, using his *what am I going to do with you, dense human* tone. "Remember, you sold that one last month at a charity auction of e-square-Bay to generate some extra money for Electra."

I stopped my rummaging and looked at HARV. "Oh, that's right."

"Of course that's right," HARV said very indignantly. Since he was a hologram HARV could appear in any form he choose. Over the years he has picked some dandies, from cowboy to ace detective to hot babe (I like to block out that one, except when I can use it to my advantage). Today he was in his favorite mode, snooty, aging English butler. In this form he was mostly bald with patches of graying hair running along his temples and circling around the lower area of his head. His eyes were just wide enough to make it clear when he was giving condescending looks. His nose would hardly be noticeable accept he accented it with a little handlebar mustache and usually had it sticking up in the air. He was wearing a better-than-tailor-fitted gray, Ralph Lauren-C (that *C* stands for clone) suit and black bow tie. I think HARV enjoys acting as a butler because even when he's serving me he still gets to look down on me.

"Zach, first you make such a big deal about me finding one for you. Then the nano you need a few extra credits you sell it off," HARV moaned.

"I wanted to make a special contribution to Electra's clinic," I said. "After all, she puts up with a lot."

"Now that may very well be the understatement of the century," HARV said.

My last big case six months ago was kind of a washout for me. I was acting as bodyguard for teen pop "singing" sensation Sexy Sprockets. It seemed like a simple enough job, protect a very beautiful but not overly (or even remotely) talented singer from a crazed cult that wanted to kill her. When you're me, crazed cults are a walk in the park on a sunny day. Of course, when you're me, it's never just a crazed cult. The crazed cult was actually an overzealous supporter of the Governor of New California, as the powers that be wanted to make sure Sexy never made good on her plans to retire and run for governor. Turns out protecting Sexy was the easy part.

Long story abridged for HV: Sexy's slimy and totally dishonest (and those are his best points) manager was augmenting her latent psi powers to force teens to love her music. That was, of course, until the manager met my psi assistant Carol. Carol had far more mental powers and potential than Sexy. The scumbag manager decided to focus on her, augmenting her powers. The process didn't go as planned (it never does) and turned Carol into a vastly powerful psi who could dominate the minds of everybody. She became so powerful she started to bring down the house—literally. Carol created a telepathic, telekinetic maelstrom that ripped the roof off of Frisco's very expensive public auditorium (lovingly called The Fart) and threatened, at the very least, to tear the province of New California apart. Luckily, I was able to bring to Carol back to Earth (by getting shot—trust me, you don't want to be me) and thus saving the day.

After that, everybody lived happily ever after—everybody except me. There aren't many lawyers left in the world since the great lawyer purge (at least those who openly practice law without being called greeting card salesmen), but those who are jumped on the case and down my throat. They sued everybody and anybody even remotely related to the case. They sued for: destruction of personal property, mental anguish for forcing the concert to end early, mental anguish for not stopping the concert sooner, compound mental anguish for not stopping the mental anguish soon enough, the rise in the cost of liquid hydrogen, and bad cases of acne. You name it they sued for it. My insurance company covered a lot of my expenses (then sent me death threats and really hiked my premiums). Sexy picked up most of my remaining tab. The whole ordeal soured Sexy on running for governor. Instead, she ran for World Council rep and won easily. She now represents the Western United States, thus proving politics is even more accepting of the strange, unusual, and mostly useless than the music industry.

I ended up making fifty-two credits and got to put "saved the world again" on my résumé.

HARV looked me in the eyes. "You're fixating on the Sexy Sprockets case, again."

"Maybe," I said. "It's the reason I needed to sell my real backgammon board to get the cash for Electra's clinic."

HARV rolled his eyes. "Zach, let it go. You saved the world, made a few credits, and didn't get killed despite numerous attempts. You should be happy." He pointed to the board. "Now back to more important matters. My victory."

I don't know why HARV took such great joy in constantly beating me at backgammon. It worried me a little. I decided it was best not to think about it too much. I knew when the chips hit the fan, HARV had my back— eventually.

"I can't help thinking that you might load the dice," I said.

HARV glared at me. "You're acting like a typical human, trying to blame your computer for your inadequacies," HARV said. He pointed to the shimmering board. "By the way, I just rolled you a nice two and a four."

I looked over the board. There are times when a two and a four can be a handy roll. This wasn't one of those times. In fact, it was a roll that would leave me wide open.

"Thanks, HARV. You're all silicon . . ."

"Hey, Zach, my chips just let the dice fall where they may. You don't have to be me, the most advanced cognitive processor on Earth, to generate a random number between one and six."

He looked at me.

I glared at him.

Until just a few months ago HARV and I actually were linked together—literally. He was connected through my optic nerve to my brain stem. Yes, it was as uncomfortable as it sounds. It was an experiment developed by my very brilliant and almost as mad friend Dr. Randy Pool. He wanted to see how a human/computer nano link would benefit man and computer, but mostly computer.

Having HARV hooked up to my brain gave me instant access to all the knowledge and information HARV has access to, which is nearly everything. Our link allowed me to communicate silently with him. It also let me project holograms from my eye lens. The link for better or for worse gave HARV easy access to the chemicals in my brain allowing him to juice me up from time to time.

Randy would always insist this was beneficial to me. I have to admit there were instances when it came in handy that HARV could crank up my adrenaline, norepinephrine, and even the electrical currents of my body. Still, I couldn't help feeling like a supercomputer's personal guinea pig/ biochemistry lab. Plus, I could never turn HARV off (though Randy could), so HARV was constantly with me, droning on inside my head like a whiny, electronic Jiminy Cricket. After a while I got used to it, but I never totally accepted it.

HARV, for his part, got to interact with a human brain on a constant basis. Randy's theory was this would be good for HARV, as it would help him grow to be more than was designed to be. He would become greater than the sum of his nano chips. If you ask me (which nobody did), it was working. Before our link, HARV had only a very rudimentary sense of humor. He could recite a joke easily enough, but he couldn't *tell* a joke. He was unable to comprehend what made funny funny. In the time we, for lack of a better word, were "bonded," he grew—upgraded. HARV is loath to admit this.

Randy recently removed the chip set for modifications. He insisted he needed to add more shielding to it. Not for me, mind you, but for HARV. He was worried that my personality was tainting HARV too much. I'm pretty positive he wanted HARV to be more human but less like me. Randy e-mailed me a couple of days ago (or was it weeks?) saying the upgrade was complete, and I could have it stuck into my brain at anytime. (Though Randy used much more technical terms than "stuck into my brain.") I've been purposely avoiding it. Why? I'm not really sure.

Having instant access to HARV, who has instant access to pretty much all the information in the world, is undeniably handy when you are in my line of work. Plus, the ability to project holograms from the eye lens has come to my rescue on more than one occasion. I also must admit that HARV's ability to supercharge the biochemical reactions in my brain, thus stimulating other parts of my body, has gotten me out of a dicey situation or three.

There can be no question having a computer connected to your brain does come with an upside. But the universe is filled with checks and balances so with that up naturally comes a downside, which admittedly has a lot more gray area. I don't like sharing my brain with another living consciousness. I guess it's not so gray after all. In this world where everything is connected to everything else, our brains are our last oasis. The place where we can be alone with our thoughts. When HARV is hooked up to me or I am hooked up to him (as he likes to say), my thoughts and I are never alone. That's why I planned on delaying sticking HARV back in my brain until the need arose. (Not to mention that the process is far more painful and unpleasant than being examined by an angry mutant proctologist with big hands.)

"After this game, you will owe me one hundred credits," HARV said proudly.

I looked up at HARV. "Why do you care? You're a computerized hologram. You don't need credits."

HARV furrowed his balding brow. "It's the thought that counts."

"You don't think. You just simulate thinking," I said, knowing it would really rattle his e-chains.

"There's nothing simulated about my thinking," HARV said, his narrow eyes tapering to slits as he scowled at me. "You don't have to have an organic collection of white and gray matter to think."

"That's what you think you think," I said.

HARV crossed his arms and looked away from me. "Quit stalling and make a move!"

I won't deny that I was pleased when Carol's voice and image superimposed itself over HARV. Not only did it let me put off the game, but Carol was a lot easier on the eyes and the mind than HARV. She was back to her old self, a cut above normal humans. She could still stop traffic with her looks or her brain, but she was no longer bordering on godlike.

"Zach, you have a visitor," she said with excitement in her voice. In her time with me, Carol has seen everything from amorous aliens to zany killer bots made of zinc. She handles it all coolly and in stride. I was worried at the prospect of someone who could get Carol this wound up.

HARV looked at me looking at Carol. "If this was a threatening situation don't you think Carol or I would have warned you by now?"

"Carol, yes. You, I'm not so sure," I said.

HARV gave me a slight grin. There was a gleam in his eye—literally. "Touché, Zach, but you worry too much."

"When you're me, there's no such thing as worrying too much. Remember how the networks wanted to try to kill me week after week for a reality show?"

HARV gave me a dismissive wave. "Oh please, that was just the Faux Network. They didn't want to kill you that badly anyhow. Then they wouldn't have a show."

"What about that time when the grandma assassin tried to strangle me with her pantyhose in UltraMegaHyperMart?"

"Well, you did have seventeen items in the fifteen-item line. You can't blame her for being mad. If it wasn't for me augmenting your muscles, she might have killed you."

"It's only because she was bionic."

HARV smiled. "Of course, there was that time you got attacked while guest umpiring a girls softball game between New Vegas showgirls and cocktail waitresses. Only you could turn a fun charity event into a fight for your life. That was great the way that Melissa girl took you out . . ."

"Hey, she hit me with a blindside tackle."

HARV's smile widened. "Then when that Jody girl jumped in, pelting you with softballs."

"They aren't soft at all. Especially where she was hitting me."

"Oh, Zach, don't be such a whiner. It's not like you weren't wearing your underwear armor."

"Which is exactly my point," I said, pointing at HARV. "How many other people do you know that need to wear carbon-steel-reinforced underwear?"

"Don't forget computer-enhanced. Those two ordinary little waitresses would have been using you for home plate if it wasn't for me."

"They weren't ordinary, they were mutants, for Gates' sake. They both played in the Female All-Tackle Mud Rugby League before they became New Vegas waitresses."

"I understand that league makes an excellent training ground for cocktail waitresses."

I started rubbing my temples.

"Zach," Carol called over the holographic intercom. "It's not only bad business but rude to keep clients waiting."

"Trust me," HARV said. "You'll be okay."

"Whenever you say that I never am."

"At least in the short term. I guarantee it. If you die, I'll forget about those credits you owe me."

"You're not going to tell me who it is?"

HARV just gave me his patented (really it is) sly grin.

"Okay, Carol, send them in. HARV, turn off the game."

"This isn't going to save you from losing," HARV insisted.

"Quit being a Pentium, HARV. Go to stealth mode before I find a way to unplug you!" I ordered.

"Fine," HARV huffed.

HARV and the backgammon board disappeared. My wall screens changed to a nice black background. Without the shimmering holographic computer or the information-filled interactive wallscreen, my office looked like it was yanked out of some hundred-year-old, classic PI flick. It was an office of a guy who won't take spam from anybody. Besides my antique wood desk and my leather chair that tilted back just the right amount, there was a chair across the desk for a client and a coat rack in the corner by the door. It was all simple and spare with no clutter. I liked it that way.

Some people would even say I'm a throwback to simpler

times. I take that as the ultimate compliment. Even though it's never meant to be. The old days, when we relied more on our guts and instincts and less on massive amounts of data and statistics, were better days. Today too many people suffer from information overdose.

"I'm recording this in my journal as a victory," HARV mumbled just audible enough for me to hear it clearly, drawing me back to the present.

I took a deep breath to clear my mind. I was pretty certain HARV was right (as usual); whoever it was didn't have hostile intentions. Experience has taught me that most assassins don't politely wait in the reception area before they kill you. Still, these are strange times. It was possible, however unlikely, that my guest was a very polite trained killer who had mentally overpowered Carol and somehow managed to reprogram HARV into thinking he wasn't a threat. When you are in my line of work and the universe has tattooed "kick me hard" on your butt, there's no such thing as being too paranoid.

I spun around to greet the door as it started to open. I was ready to move my wrist in just the right way that makes my trusty Colt 46 version 3-B pop from up my sleeve into my hand, just in case. I tensed. I took a deep breath and held it. A woman sauntered into the room. This wasn't any woman. For starters, she had more curves than a road up the Alps, only these curves were in all the right places. She was wearing a light red syn fur, micro-minidress trimmed with fluffy white cotton. The entire outfit was accented by her hot red boots with three-centimeter-high heels. On anybody else it would have looked ridiculous but on her it looked sensuous, like she was born, or in this case created, to wear it. Her hair was a frosty white that danced down over her shoulders. Her skin was creamy smooth like virgin snow. Her green eyes twinkled, giving her the appearance of the perfect blend of wise, caring, and oh so voluptuous. I exhaled. I relaxed. I had no choice. There was something warming and calming, yet extremely arousing about her. She was both yin and yang.

"Mr. Johnson, how nice it is to meet you in person."

It didn't take my keen mind to detect who this woman was. "Santana?"

"In person! Ho ho ho," she said. "Sorry, I couldn't resist

throwing in the 'ho ho ho.' Though my marketing elves insist that's so last cen."

I stood up and held out my hand. "What brings you this far south?" I asked.

I was familiar with Santana—after all, everybody on Earth is. Santana and her team of highly skilled elves and bots have been operating for over twenty years now. The World Council created them as a way to "instill joy and unity into the entire world's population." Santana is the CEO and all around head honcho of the North Pole Organization. It's their job to coordinate the Holiday, the time of year when everybody in the world is given three gifts.

To my knowledge she had never been in New Frisco. For her to be down here, knocking at my door, something had to be terribly wrong. I noticed that while her lips may have been smiling, her eyes weren't, at least not really. This wasn't a personal visit just to see if I was being naughty or nice.

Santana shook my hand. She had a strong, firm grip, like a person who works for a living, which belied her soft look.

"Mind if I sit?" she asked. "This synthetic fur doesn't breathe well this far south."

"Of course not." I replied, as I motioned to the extra chair across from my desk.

She sat. She wiped a bit of sweat from her brow. "I'm not used to this heat. It's never like this at home." She shrugged. "Still, it comes with the job. It's a clean job but somebody has to do it," she said with a forced smile. She had something to tell me, she was just having trouble getting it out.

"Uh, Santana, I'm sure you came here to discuss something besides fashion."

She smiled. Her smile brightened the room, like a halogen star on top of an old Christmas tree. "I see you're all business." She took out a paper computer from her pocket, unfolded it, and typed a quick note. I hoped she was putting me on the nice list. She finished typing the note then put the computer back. She smiled again. The smile downgraded to a frown. "Zach, I have a problem."

"Go on," I said in my most professional, concerned voice.

"This isn't easy for me to say." She paused again.

"I've noticed."

She took a deep breath. She quickly blurted out, "There's been a killing at the North Pole. I think somebody is trying to destroy the Holiday."

"A killing at the Pole?" My voice was dead serious, though I was having trouble believing what I was hearing.

Santana shook her head. "Actually, there have been two killings. Elves M-778 and M-892."

"Two killings?" I couldn't hold back the surprise in my voice. This type of thing wasn't supposed to happen at the Pole. It was the happiest, safest place on the planet, a haven from the real world. I took a breath to maintain my composure.

"Are you sure the elves were murdered?"

Santana paused for a moment. "Well, I'm not a professional at this sort of thing, but I'm reasonably certain. M-778 was found squished under a five-hundred-kilo bag of toys."

"That could have been an accident, " I interrupted.

"I thought so at first also. But elves aren't prone to accidents. Furthermore, from what we could make out from his mangled body, both his hands and feet were tied. Once I saw that, I ruled out accident."

"Good deduction." I agreed. "What about the other elf?"

"M-892 was poisoned while taking a late-night snack and drink."

"Poisoned?"

"Somebody had mixed wine in the elf's eggnog punch. Wine is deadly to elves."

I couldn't help thinking that wine, if consumed in high enough quantities, could also be deadly—or at least trouble—to non-elves. I managed to keep this thought to myself.

Santana continued, "Luckily, we found M-892 before the next meal cycle or we would have had a major problem on our hands—lots of dead elves. Our operation and the Holiday surely would have been ruined. We're fortunate our lab works so fast and efficiently."

"Have you mentioned any of this to the police?" I asked.

Santana shook her head. "I couldn't. For one thing, the Pole doesn't come under any jurisdiction. For another, if word leaked out that somebody was trying to destroy the Holiday, the public would panic."

"Good thinking." I agreed.

"That's why I came to you, Zach. My elves and security bots are good, but they aren't up to solving a murder mystery. They just aren't designed for that. I need you to find out who is trying to sabotage the Holiday. You have to stop him. The happiness of billions is in your hands. If the Holiday is canceled, the very structure of society itself could be ripped apart. Will you take the job? I'll pay whatever your normal rate is."

I stopped and thought about what she said. At a quick mental glance, I thought this talk of society being ripped apart seemed exaggerated. On reflection, it wasn't totally far-fetched. The entire world had come to depend on the Holiday. It was a time when everybody, regardless of anything, received three gifts from the North Pole. One gift they picked from the Pole's extensive catalog and two specially selected fun gifts were chosen by the Pole's crack staff of elf consultants. If something happened to offset this, who knows how that would impact the world?

My decision was never in doubt. "Of course I'll take the job." I hesitated for a nano then continued. "Since the job's for such a good cause, I'll even do it for half my normal rate."

Santana smiled. For the first time since she had entered my office the twinkle in her eyes matched the one in her smile. "You're a good man, Zachary Nixon Johnson."

"Let's hope I'm good enough."

"Ona Thompson and Sexy Sprockets rave about your service. You saved the day in their cases. I'm sure you can get equally pleasing results with my case."

"It's your job to be optimistic, Santana."

"Yes, I suppose that is part of the job. Like my elves, I'm made to see the bright side." She smiled again. "You'll start immediately?"

"Yes, I believe my calendar is free. I'll need to make a trip up to the Pole."

Santana nodded. "Yes, of course. We have a bimonthly seven-day, six-night tour of our facilities. The group is limited to ten people, and we're booked years in advance, but I do have a certain leeway to add an extra person now and then. The tour started yesterday, but I can get you in." She stopped to think for a nano. "So somebody on the tour is involved?"

"I wouldn't bet against it. Particularly if the deaths coincided with the arrival of your visitors."

Santana nodded.

"Would your fiancée Electra like to join you? It might help make the trip look more like a vacation." For a gal whose job it was to supervise a bunch of elves and deliver presents to people, Santana had a pretty good mind for this.

"I'll ask her. She's always complaining that I never take her anywhere. She'd be a help examining the bodies. Though, I don't know how much she knows about elf physiology."

Santana stood up from the chair. "Good. Then I'll count on you for sure. If Electra wants to go, just have your computer call my elves." (Now that's a phrase I never thought I'd hear.) "We'll squeeze her in. The more the merrier."

"No problem, Santana."

"You realize that you have to port to the North Pole."

I was trying hard not think about how the only way I could get there was to have my molecules scrambled, then descrambled, and hopefully put back exactly how they were before they got scrambled.

Santana saw the look on my face. "I know how much you deplore porting."

Deplore was way too mild of a word. I hate teleporting even more than I do flying while being audited with Yoko Ono's greatest hits playing in the background as telemarketers try to sell me life insurance. I inhaled slowly. My logical side knew that porting was perfectly safe. Studies by scientists who have far too much time on their hands have shown that the odds of being killed by porting were far less than the odds of getting struck by a bolt of lightning while wearing a rubber suit on a clear day. Despite that, I couldn't help imagining my top half being sent to the Pole while my bottom half went to Hawaii. However, duty called.

I took another deep breath. "No problem, Santana. The fate of the Holiday is more important than my fears. Hopefully all I'll lose is my luggage."

Santana smiled. "You don't have to worry about that. No luggage is allowed at the Pole. We supply everything! It's part of the price of admission. This way everybody is equal."

"Sounds reasonable in a Marxist kind of way."

"You do understand what I mean by no luggage, don't you, Zach?" she said leaning forward. It was a movement that was much sexier than it should have been.

"Santana, you're paying me five thousand credits a day. Of course I understand what no luggage means. It means I don't bring anything with me. Believe me, I can handle it."

Santana just stared at me. Those big, all-knowing eyes knew that my brain still hadn't made the connection.

She helped me out. "At the North Pole, everybody dresses in the same green or red elf suits. Except for me, of course." She paused, hoping that now I would see the problem.

I held my hands out. "So I have to wear an elf suit for a couple of days. I'll survive. As long as nobody takes pictures or anything."

Santana continued to give me that *aren't you forgetting something?* look. If she wasn't Santana, it would have been an *aren't you forgetting something, stupid?* look. "I'll give you a hint, Zach. The suits don't have a lot of extra space to hide things up your sleeve."

Now it hit home. "My gun! I can't bring my gun!"

"Very good, Zach. You really are the best."

I couldn't tell if she was being sarcastic or overly optimistic. I chose to believe the latter. "I can live without my gun. I don't even like the thing. It's just with some of the characters I deal with a sidearm is sort of a necessity. I don't really see myself having to shoot any elves at the Pole though."

Santana just smiled. "Body underarmor is also restricted."

"No problem, " I told her. "It itches when it gets too cold. I don't suppose you allow personal computer communication links?" I asked semi-rhetorically.

Santana shook her head. "Sorry, Zach. While at the Pole, you have nothing to rely on except your wits!"

She stood up and pointed to a button on the buckle of her belt. She turned and started to walk away. She was engulfed in a pool of energy then disappeared.

"What the DOS?" I said.

My wallscreen sprang to e-life. HARV's holographic form appeared before me.

"From the energy readings I would compute that was a PPTD, a portable personal teleporting device," HARV said with more than a bit of awe in his voice.

I shook my head. No good could come from portable personal teleporting. I turned my attention to HARV. "What are your initial thoughts on the case?"

"Nothing to rely on but your wits!" He smiled. "Too bad, I always liked the Holiday."

I ignored him and started running through potential culprits in my brain. When a problem like Santana's arises, my first instincts are to check out the big corps. These days there are about four of them that control most of the action on Earth: ExShell, HTech, Enter-Corp, and UltraMega-HyperMart. ExShell is the energy giant; their motto is, "We sell you the sun." HTech specializes in building high-tech devices; their motto is, "Everything is better in bits." En-terCorp controls much of the entertainment industry; their motto is, "We make fun more fun." UltraMegaHyperMart is the largest chain of retail stores in history; their motto is, "If we don't sell it you don't need it." (They allege that 99.9999 percent of the population has purchased at least one item from one of their stores or from their net site.) Of course while all of these megacorps may claim to specialize in a particular area, they are all far to greedy not to dip their toes (and feet, knees, and most of their other body parts) into one another's pools of potential profits.

"Enough chitchat, HARV. Find out if any of the big corps would profit from the demise of the Holiday."

HARV churned for a quarter of a nano. "Done. All of them make far more profit after the Holiday than they do before. It seems the free gifts given by the Pole spawn a frenzy of buying other gifts."

"Dig deeper. Find out if the Holiday upset or rearranged the apple cart. Maybe one of them makes less more than the others?"

HARV looked at me confused (it's never good a sign when you confuse a supercomputer). "Less more?"

"Companies are greedy. Maybe one of them is jealous that the others grew more than it did."

HARV shrugged. "You humans are strange. I suppose that is possible."

"I also need a breakdown of everyone currently touring the Pole."

"That will take a bit longer. The Pole's computer defenses are quite good."

"Ask Santana for them."

"That's no fun."

"Just do it, HARV." Randy may have been on to something with his concerns that HARV had the potential of becoming too much like me.

"Fine. Done. Her elves say they will have the information for me within hours."

"Why so long?"

HARV shrugged again. It's unnerving to see a supercomputer shrug. "I didn't ask because I'm sure they wouldn't answer. They were quite chipper and peppy though." He paused for a nano. "DOS, I find them even more annoying than I do humans."

"Is it possible for an elf to go bad?"

"I am analyzing the psychological profiles of the elves now."

A picture of a smiling elf face appeared on my west wallscreen.

"It's highly improbable for an elf to 'go bad,' as you put it. While they can be quite irritating, they are built for nothing but kindness and goodness."

"Highly improbable, but not impossible. Correct?"

HARV looked at me and shook his head. "Of course it's possible. Elves are organic sentient beings created by humans. 'Nuff said."

"HARV, you just said 'nuff."

"Did not."

"Did too."

"Zach, I assure you that while the word 'nuff may be in my vast vocabulary database, I would not use it."

"Review the last minute."

HARV rolled his eyes. He frowned ever so slightly. "I must have been relating to the person I was interacting with. It's within my parameters you know."

I smiled at him. It wasn't a big smile, just one noticeable enough for him to catch.

HARV shook his head. "I am deleting that word from my database and I will fervently deny ever using it. It's your word against mine. Who do you think the world will believe?"

"How did the elves get to the Pole?" I asked, tipping the conversation back to business.

"They were cloned in New Brazil then teleported directly to the Pole via a special teleporter programmed solely for delivering elves."

"Hmmm."

"What are you thinking, Zach?"

It was a well-publicized fact that the World Council created the elves, and for that matter Santana, in their labs. The WC has extensive resources and capabilities. For better or for worse, they have their hands buried into every aspect of everyday life; in some parts they are buried clear up to their shoulders. Yet the elves were a special job, the kind of job that would take a mind too smart to work on a government salary. They had to have had a consultant. Somebody like my buddy Randy, but Randy would have only been fourteen at the time. He was probably good enough to do the job then, but Randy's an electronics guy not an organics guy. I couldn't see him working outside of his field. I was fairly certain that would go against some sci-geek union rules.

"I'm not sure yet. Do me a favor, though. Try to get the name of whoever led the elves project."

"The elves were made by the Council; they are hush-hush about that kind of thing."

"I'm betting they had help—outside help. I want to find that help and talk to it, if possible."

"Okay, but that could take some time. Information of that type can be tricky to find. Sort of like looking for a specific grain of sand on the beach during a hurricane."

"I have faith in you, HARV." I got up and stretched out. "Net with Randy and tell him I'll be coming by for the thingy."

"The thingy? You want me, the most intelligent cognitive processor in the known worlds, to say *thingy*?"

"Yes," I reaffirmed. "That is correct."

"Do you stay up nights thinking of ways to humiliate me?" HARV asked.

"Nope, it just comes naturally," I told him.

"By thingy, I take it you mean our bio-computer neuron-link lens?"

"Yes, I do. I just don't want to mention that over the net. Just in case."

"I didn't think you liked the bio-com lens. You know, being constantly linked with me."

"On a day-to-day basis, I don't. But for big cases I like to have it."

HARV smiled so openly I could see his teeth. "So you can't solve the case without me, huh?"

"It's not that I can't," I corrected. "I'd be foolish not to use all the tools at my disposal. Besides, I know how YOU need to feel useful."

I moved away from my desk.

"Where are you going?"

"I told you, to see Randy to get the bio-computer lens and then home. I need to talk to Electra in person about this trip."

I started to the door. "If you find anything interesting, give me a beep." I left my office figuring I had a lot of background work to do before I headed up north.

2

Carol was sitting at her desk in my reception room, smiling. Carol, as I mentioned before, is my assistant. She's also Electra's niece. And like her aunt, she's also quite stunning: long, flowing, light brown hair; dark brown eyes; and golden skin all wrapped in a classic dancer's body and governed by a sharp mind. Like her aunt, she's the total package.

"Boy, Tío, I've never seen anybody so soft and warm yet sexual," she said with a wide smile. "I'm straight, yet I have to admit, I was quite aroused."

Suddenly the whimsical smile on Carol's face turned to a grimace.

"Get out of the way!" she ordered, ducking behind her desk.

"Carol, I'm the boss here. I'm the one who gives the orders. Why do you and HARV have such a hard time with that concept?"

Carol didn't answer with words. She, much like her aunt, could be very stubborn. She pointed a finger at me then motioned toward her. I flew from where I was standing over her desk and down to the floor.

"Why did you do that?" I questioned sternly, standing up.

"Get down!" she commanded, pulling me with her mind and her body back down behind the desk.

"This is not going to look good on your resu—"

I stopped mid-sentence as my front office door exploded open. A rather large robot came rolling in through the space where the door and I had been seconds ago.

"Oh, never mind," I told Carol, popping my gun into my hand.

I peered over the desk to get a peek at the bot. The good news was I never really liked that door. The bad news was I was about to go mano-on-machino against what I guessed was a deadly bot. It was highly mechanical, with a red tanklike bottom, a green metal cylinder for a body with two claws and a weapon barrel protruding from it. For a head it had a dome sensor with a star on top. Even with the series of twinkling multicolor lights traversing its frame it still managed to look menacing. It seemed to be a cross between a standard battlebot, an ornament, and a madman's all-wheel-drive sport vehicle.

"Now, about my raise?" Carol asked.

"We'll discuss that later, if we're still alive," I answered.

"Give up!" the bot called over to us. "Resistance is futile, vain, useless, hopeless, and fruitless!"

"Great, we're being attacked by a killer thesaurus," I muttered to Carol.

The bot fired an energy beam at the desk we were taking cover behind. The bolt destroyed a good portion of it, leaving my head exposed like one of the gophers in that old whack-a-mole game.

"That was genuine simulated oak!" I yelled at the bot. "Do you have any idea how much that *cost?*" These days almost everything is made from cheap soy-plastic, but I digress.

"No, I have not been programmed with or given access to any information that is not useful for termination and destruction," the bot replied.

"How come?" I asked.

"Well, because—"

The bot never got to complete its "thought" as I aimed my gun and fired. The projectile passed through Carol's desk and into the bot, destroying them both.

"It never ceases to amaze me how gullible bots can be," I said.

"I feel the same way about humans," HARV said, as he appeared in the middle of the room and began examining the bot.

I turned to Carol and asked, "Is it safe to stand up?"

There wasn't much left of the desk to offer protection anyhow.

Carol grimaced again.

"I don't suppose that look means you had a bad burrito for lunch."

Carol shook her head. "There's a backup bot," she said. "Outside, waiting."

"Of course there is," I said.

I stood up and aimed my gun toward the doorway.

"Come out, come out wherever you are, little killer bot!" I called.

"Do you really expect that to work?" HARV asked.

The second bot rolled into the reception area. I had to admit I didn't expect that to work. This bot either had to be dumber than the first one or had something really nasty in store for us. History suggested—no, dictated—it was going to be the latter.

"I have analyzed and neutralized your computerized weapon," the bot said, in a metallic yet cheery tone. I could have sworn it was snickering at me.

I aimed at the bot and pulled the trigger hoping it was a poor bluff. Nothing happened. I didn't wait around to see the bot's next move. I dove to the ground, this time pulling Carol down with me. The beam from the bot's energy weapon flew over us, singeing my back. Fortunately, my underarmor took most of the damage.

"You have only delayed the inevitable," the bot said, rolling toward Carol and me. "Without your weapon, which was high-tech but lower-tech than me, you stand less than a point five percent chance of survival."

DOS! I knew I was getting too dependent on that computerized gun! What I wouldn't give for a good old-fashioned twin-barrel shotgun. LINUX. I'd even settle for a good slingshot.

The bot slowly rolled closer. It seemed to be enjoying itself, quite confident in the fact that there was nothing I could do to stop it, never stopping to compute that there were other threats to it in the room.

The bot rolled past HARV. Apparently, it didn't consider a hologram to be a concern. Just as the bot passed by, HARV's clothing morphed from the formal gray suit he was wearing into an old-fashioned, two-piece, purple-striped bathing suit. At first glance, it appeared to be a queer choice (especially considering he kept the bow tie), but knowing HARV, I was betting he had a reason for it.

HARV waited until the bot was a meter in front of him and focusing its energy cannon on me.

"Prepare to die!" the bot said.

"Oh, please!" I said. "I've been in tighter situations than this babysitting for my nephew." I didn't know if my under-armor could take a direct hit from the bot's energy cannon, but I wasn't about to let the bot sense any fear. I was confident, or at least fairly certain, that HARV had something up his holographic sleeve.

HARV clasped his hands together, bent his knees, then leaped up two meters off the ground, diving headfirst into the bot. Suddenly, the bot started to spin madly as if it were possessed. And in a way it was.

"No, no, no, this is not right!" the bot sputtered. It whirled around and around, firing shots into my ceiling. It was easy to see why nobody ever wanted to rent the office space above me. "I will drive you out! You cannot control me long! I am a rebel! I am the warrior! I will survive, I will survive!" the bot ranted, semi-singing the last line

I turned to Carol. "You heard the crazy killer disco bot. HARV won't be able to keep him doing three-sixties all day. Time for a little smash and, well, smash."

Carol smiled. Her face glowed with joy. She loved the idea of being able to let the leash off of her powers. She stood up. Her hair rose off her shoulders, crackling with energy. It was an impressive, if slightly scary, sight. She locked her eyes on the bot. The bot stopped shaking. Carol made a fist and motioned upward. The bot flew off the floor, smashing into the ceiling. Carol whipped her hand down toward the floor. The bot came crashing down, shattering into thousands of bot pieces.

HARV appeared in the middle of the room, no worse for wear.

Carol turned and looked at me. She smiled. She reached out her hand and pulled me to my feet. "Now about that raise?" she said, her hair still standing on edge, rippling with energy.

I was pretty certain it was more of a question than a

threat. Though I did have a sudden urge to double both her salary and her lunch hour.

"Are you okay?" I asked.

"That was fun!" she said, as her hair fell back down onto her shoulders.

I walked over to HARV, who was carefully looking over the bot rubble.

"So what do you think?" I asked.

"Those bots didn't like you," he answered.

"Thank you, Sherlock. I mean did you recognize them?"

"Yes," he answered.

Carol chuckled. It was barely audible, but more than adequate for a supercomputer to notice.

"Don't laugh, you'll just egg him on," I told her.

I turned my attention back to HARV. "Come on, get serious! Those things just tried to kill me."

"You should be used to that by now," HARV told me. "As you are so keen to point out, this does happen to you a lot. You are either incredibly unlucky or incredibly lucky, depending on your perspective."

I took a deep breath and counted to ten. This wasn't as annoying as the time HARV decided he was a drill sergeant and would wake me up screaming, "You're a good for nothing lowlife maggot!" at 5 AM for *my own good*, but it was close. "Is my gun working yet?"

"While the bots may have been above your gun in the electronic food chain, I am above them. So, yes, your gun is now functional," HARV gloated.

"Good, because I'm thinking about using it on you!" I said.

HARV looked at me in mock disbelief. He rolled his eyes and sighed. "First, as I have told you seven hundred and twelve times, I am an extensive collection of chips. You would have to shoot me in many places to actually get rid of me. Second, I doubt you would know how to use the potty without me," he said with a tone used to address a small, very dense child.

"I could always trade you in for an older model. One of the BOB series, perhaps." The BOB series was a mass-market line of personal computer-holographic assistants, who are, according to their ad, *like your best friend, only better*. They were all the rage about ten years ago. The interface

was supposed to get to know you and then anticipate your
every need from recording your favorite HV shows to ordering flick tickets to buying the daily groceries. The idea faded
out pretty quickly when it turned out that anticipating a human's needs isn't that easy, as most of us aren't really sure
what we need and don't really know what we want.

"Ooh, that's low, really hitting below the old CPU. Okay,
Mr. Grouchy, those bots were very much like the ones that
guard the Pole from outsiders who might be tempted to
take advantage of Santana and the elves' kindness."

"Call the Pole and see if they are missing two bots," I
told HARV.

He nodded. "Already done. They say they are not."

I took a deep breath. You appreciate breathing more
after killer bots try to stop you from sucking in air. "Let's
bring these bot parts over to Randy for analysis."

"I doubt that is possible," HARV said.

"Not with that attitude it's not."

HARV pointed to the broken-down bots. They started
to sizzle, like cold steak on a hot laser griddle but without
the pleasant scent and with much more ominous conse-
quences. The bot parts started to vibrate.

"Just my luck. They're going to blow," I said.

HARV shook his head. "You really do worry too much.
Calm down. It's not like EVERYTHING is always going
to try to kill you."

I looked at the pieces of bots. Now they were quivering
and smoking.

"Are you sure this isn't a bad thing?" I asked.

HARV folded his arms. "Just wait for it."

Almost on HARV's mark, every bot part in the room
began shrinking, dissolving into nothingness right before
our eyes. In a matter of nanos, the bots had disappeared
into a puff of white smoke. The smoke dissipated and that
was that. It was as if the killer bots were never here.

"See," HARV told me. "Nothing to worry about."

I turned to Carol. "Call maintenance, and use whatever
methods necessary to get a new door, a new desk, and the
wall repaired."

I turned back to HARV. "Does the Pole make their
own bots?"

"No. Santana would have nothing to do with making anything that could be even remotely considered an offensive weapon."

"Then who makes them?" I prompted.

HARV calculated for a nano. "The bots are made by HTech and donated to the Pole. HTech defines it as charity work."

One of their home offices was here in New Frisco (the other was in New Peking), so our paths crossed on occasion. But they had never collided until now.

"Interesting, very interesting," HARV said slowly and annoyingly.

"What?"

"Of the top congloms in the world, HTech's profits have grown the slowest since the advent of the Holiday."

"See, less more," I said. That wasn't a lot to go on. But it was enough to get me started. "Get me an appointment with their CEO, William Doors."

There was complete and absolute silence from HARV. Then he started to chuckle, making it very clear he was laughing at me, not with me.

"Zach, Zach, Zach," HARV said, shaking his head. "My little organic friend. Mr. Doors is one of the richest and busiest men on Earth. I know by some strange quirk in the ripple of reality that is this Universe you happen to be friends with the three richest women on Earth. But Mr. Doors is a man, and he has never needed your services."

I knew what HARV was referring to. Gates knows I heard this enough from Electra; I didn't need it from my computer, too. It's not my fault I have far more female clients than male clients. Hiring a PI is like asking for directions when you are lost—guys just don't do it unless they are very, very desperate (and that desperation usually revolves around a gal). I decided to play stupid.

"What do you mean by that?"

"He won't play the damsel in distress to your knight in underarmor."

"I repeat, what are you talking about?"

"Zach, as Electra has pointed out to you on thirty-two different occasions, your clients are always beautiful women. For some reason, you attract them in times of trouble. My theory is it's either pheromones or they think of you as a pet."

"Thanks, HARV."

"Mr. Doors is a world-class geek with innumerable resources at his disposal. He doesn't now, nor will he ever, need the specialized services you offer. He doesn't know you from any other annoying peon. So there's no way you can just pop into his office and talk to him."

I was sure HARV had a point somewhere in that diatribe of his, but I wasn't going to let that slow me in the least. "Is Doors in town today?"

HARV put his head in his hand, rubbed his temples, and sighed. "You're not going to let this go . . ."

I shook my head no. I wisely decided not to point out that by rubbing his temples he was mimicking me.

"Doors is in town. I checked with his assistant's assistant's computer's computer. He can't even consider thinking about seeing you for the next six months."

"Let's find a way to make it happen a bit sooner. Like in a couple of hours. If you have to prioritize, put that over researching the elves, since we know bots can go bad."

"I am more than capable of doing both," HARV said, hands on hips, head raised high, channeling every angry girlfriend I had ever had.

I patted him on a shoulder that wasn't really there. I started toward the door. At least where the door used to be. I stopped and turned to Carol.

"Oh, and, Carol? Thanks for saving my life there."

She smiled. "Don't mention it. Remember this when raise time comes around."

"Now, now. You only saved me from killer bots, it's not like you gave me the winning lottery numbers or anything!"

I gave her a smile, then headed off to Randy's lab.

3

It was a quick trip to Randy's AMP Labs, as after he blew up his last lab he moved to a new facility near the old docks. Randy insisted this was because the ocean air helped clear his sinuses. I think it was because the city council wanted to keep him as far away from the general populace as possible. Electra thinks Randy moved there because he wanted to be nearer to me, as I'm his only friend he didn't build from a kit.

From the outside, the new lab, like the old lab, looked just like your run-of-the-assembly-line storage facilities that lined the dock in their heyday. Today, thanks to teleporting, most of these buildings have been turned into monuments to a better time. A time when getting it there overnight would do. Things weren't rushed then like they are today, when everybody absolutely has to have it there in five minutes or less.

When I entered the door my head started to spin. No matter how many times I come to Randy's it still takes me a few nanos to collect myself. The place is a whirlwind of pandemonium in motion. Computers on all the walls, ceiling, and floor flashing away in an infinite stream of info. Bots of all shapes and sizes moving in every direction possible and some directions I didn't think were possible. The benches were packed with test tubes, beakers, megapowerful Bunsen burners, microscopes, and even a couple boiling cauldrons. I had no idea what Randy did with the cauldrons. I figured it was better not to ask.

Randy's long, lengthy body was stretched out on the floor in the middle of the lab's main work area tinkering away on some sort of cylinder-like device. It didn't look dangerous, but this was Randy, the guy who invented the exploding nuclear marshmallow. I approached with caution.

He didn't notice me, as he was totally engrossed in making his adjustments.

"Ah, Randy?" I said.

No response.

"Randy, I need your help," I said waving my hand in front of his field of vision.

Still no response. DOS, when he focused, he focused.

My initial reaction was to punch him, but I figured that wouldn't go over well. My second thought was to fire a gunshot, but the last time I did that his security robots jumped me. It only takes one cavity search by a robot to convince you that's an experience you don't want to have twice. This called for a more subtle approach.

"E equals mc cubed," I said loudly.

"That's squared," Randy corrected. He stopped working. He looked up. "Is that you, Zach?"

Finally, I had made contact. The team that made first contact with aliens couldn't have been prouder than I was right this instant.

"What are you working on?" I asked, figuring it was best to start with some small talk.

He smiled. "A matter reduction device," he stated proudly. "If this works like I know it will, it will save untold amount of storage space on the planet, plus it will make traveling mega easier. You'll be able to put your suitcases in your pockets!"

Randy, for all his idiosyncrasies, was an upside kind of guy. He only saw (or wanted to see) the good that could come out of his inventions. I was sure he never considered the possible downside of a matter reduction device. Or how something so powerful and meant for good could easily be something so terrible in the wrong hands. Randy and I had talked about this on an occasion or two. He would call this a scientific gray area. He was always quick to point out that forks and knives can be used to cause harm, but that doesn't mean society would have been better of without them. Thinking about this usually gave me a throbbing pain in my temples, so I chalked this up to one of those things that was better just not to think about.

"Thanks, really absolute zero," I told him. "But I need your help."

"I know you didn't just drop by to make idealist small talk," Randy said, giving me about half of his attention as he continued to tinker away.

"Dr. Randy," a very sexy woman's voice, which I knew had to be computer generated, sounded over the room's speaker system, as a computer screen dropped down in front of him. "You have an incoming call."

"I can't take a call right now, I'm busy talking science with Zach."

Randy was the ultimate one-track mind science geek. When his brain latched on to something, it was like a hungry shark grabbing hold of a really plump seal—nothing could break that hold.

"You'll want to take this call," the sexy computer insisted.

"Who is it?" Randy said not even bothering to look at the screen.

"Your mother."

Randy instantly stopped working. He looked up at the screen. He straightened his back and started running his extra long fingers through his bright red hair, trying to give it some semblance of organization.

A woman who looked like a cross between Randy and a prune appeared squinting into the screen.

"Is that you, honey?" Ma Pool said.

"Yes, Mother, it is," Randy said with a lilt in his voice he usually reserved for when he was talking about his inventions.

"Why are you blurry? Who's that blurry blob behind you? Is it Zach?"

"Why aren't you wearing your bionic vision enhancers, Mom?"

She shook her head. "You know I don't believe in that high-tech fooey."

"Mom, I invented that fooey for you."

She leaned into the screen almost touching it. "You did? How sweet."

A little robot rolled up to Ma Pool holding a pair of what could only be described as eyes in its claws. The robot's arms extended up and placed the eyes over Ma Pool's real eyes. She blinked. She smiled.

"You're too skinny. You haven't been eating," she told Randy. "You're nothing but bones and brain held together by pale-bordering-on-albino skin. And you need more sun. Not too much, mind you, but more. I've seen beached beluga whales who have been dead for a month that have more color than you." Ma Pool looked past Randy. "Oh, hi, Zach."

"Hi, ma'am."

"You're not getting my boy in trouble are you?"

"No, ma'am."

"Well you should, he needs to get out of the lab more."

"Yes, ma'am."

"Are you still dating that nice Electra girl?"

"Yes, ma'am."

"Does she have a sister?"

"Why, ma'am, are you interested?"

Randy glared at me and stomped his foot.

"I'm one hundred and ten years old, my boy. Maybe in my younger experimental days, but these days I'm too old to swing either way," she said. "I'm talking about for my boy."

"I do okay for myself, Mom," Randy protested.

Ma Pool waved a finger at the screen. "I'm talking about real flesh and blood women. Not ones you have to clone."

"Clones are flesh and blood, Mom."

I looked at Randy.

"Long story," he told me under his breath. "Science can be a lonely mistress."

"I want grandkids that don't come out of a test tube or a robotics lab. I'm not getting any younger, you know," Ma Pool said.

Now Randy shook his head. "Ma, I sent you money for a regeneration treatment."

"Fooo-ey," Ma Pool spat. "I don't believe in that elitist crap."

"Mom, I want you around to meet my kids," Randy said.

The thought of Randy procreating scared me on far too many levels to count.

"If that happens, and I know it's a big IF, then I will

consider it." Ma Pool looked at the screen. She forced herself to smile. "Dinner at the regular time this Sunday?"

"Of course," Randy said. "I'll bring the wine."

"Nah, I'll get the wine, your taste is crap. Love you, son."

"Love you, Mom."

"Bye, Zach. Find a nice girl for my Randy."

I waved to the screen as it went blank.

"I've received two Nobel Prizes; cured three diseases; won the 2050, 2052, and 2054 New Frisco Rock, Paper, Scissors Championship; I have over one hundred patents; and bowled a three hundred, but all she cares about is me mating," Randy said.

"You bowled a three hundred?"

"I was using a bionic eye, an arm enhancer, and a pin-sensing ball but it was impressive nonetheless," Randy insisted with far more emotion than he usually had.

"She just wants what she thinks is best for you, buddy."

Randy composed himself. "Now where were we?" he asked, scratching his head and ruffling his hair again. "Ah, yes, now I remember. HARV told me about your visit. I take it now you want the new and improved biorganic-neuro-link-holo-projector-lens."

"I hope that's not what you've decided to call it!" I said.

"Still not sure, I'm toying with it. I like the NIBONOLIH-POL acronym. I think it's got a groovy kind of sound. Though the whole point is moot if I patent it. It kind of defeats the purpose of a secretive organic chip that links a human and a computer and is totally undetectable to scanners to be on the public records as existing." He paused for a nano. He sighed. "Oh, well, nobody ever said science had to be easy. And marketing, whoa! Now that's tricky. Einstein never had these problems. It was so much easier in those days! The average investor was so impressed with little things like atomic bombs and theories of relativity that—"

"Ah, Randy, hate to interrupt you when you're rambling *poetically,* but I could really use the—hope you don't mind if I just call it the link."

Randy stopped his dissertation and returned to matters at hand. "Ah yes, the link . . ." His eyes searched through the chaos that was his lab. "Now, now where did I put that?"

He examined his lab coat pockets, his pants pockets, his left shirt pocket, his right shirt pocket. He smiled. He reached into his left shirt pocket and produced the neuron-link. He showed it to me.

It still didn't look like much to me, just a small contact lens with some computer circuitry jutting out of it.

"You do remember how it works?" he asked, as he handed it to me.

"I put it my eye. It digs into my eye causing piercing pain. It drills deep into my brain, causing excruciating pain. It then links my brain to HARV," I said.

"Good, you do remember!" Randy said, brushing some of his stringy red hair off his face. "I was going to work on reducing the pain but the funding for it fell through." He shrugged. "Like they say, no pain no gain."

"Do I need to do anything special?" I asked.

Randy shook his head. "Nope. Now that it's calibrated to your brain, it's almost foolproof."

"*Almost* foolproof?"

Randy shrugged. "Nothing is totally foolproof, Zach. It's been my experience that fools are inventive and ingenious with their foolishness."

I held the lens up to my eye. I took a deep breath. I took another deep breath. I remembered the last time I put this thing into my eye it was more painful than watching old political speeches while listening to the "Macarena" and having a root canal performed by an angry, clumsy chimp. Still, duty called. I slapped the lens onto my eyeball quickly, my logic being if I did it fast enough, maybe it wouldn't hurt. My logic proved faulty. It felt like that angry chimp was filling ten thousand cavities in my mind using a dull, rusty drill and making sure he hit as many nerves as possible. Starting at my eye, the drilling traversed my skull, increasing in magnitude as it spread, leading me to believe that if my head exploded, it would be a good thing. Then it all stopped.

"That wasn't so bad now, was it?" Randy said.

"I swear that hurt more than the last time!" I told him.

"It probably did," he agreed. "I modified the lens some, so HARV could have instant access to your synapses."

"You could have warned me!"

"True," he agreed. "Does it still work?"

A beam of light shot out from my eye. The numbers 1, 2, 3 appeared, then changed into HARV's face. It's an interesting feeling having your eye used like an old-fashioned movie projector.

"It works!" HARV said. "Nice job, Dr. Pool!"

"Now turn yourself off," I said. "Until we get to the Pole, stick with normal means of communication."

"Zach, with you there is no such thing as normal communication," HARV told me before he beeped out.

4

I left Randy's office before he could use me as a guinea pig for any other new gadget. I got in my car and fired her up. So far things had been going as well I could hope. Which in my world meant nobody had tried to kill me for the last hour. I took advantage in the lull in activity to wax poetic about my car. My current vehicle of choice is very sweet, slightly modified, 1969 cherry red Mustang convertible. I love driving a car nearly as much as I despise flying in hovers. Why? Well for one thing, I hate heights. I often say if men were meant to fly we would have been born with either feathers and wings or at the very least parachutes that pop out of our butts. Second and more important, when I was driving I had control of my destiny. I was the one running show. Sure some hovers give their drivers the appearance that they are driving, but there are so many computer fail-safes and backup systems that the human usually just points and clicks on a destination and the hover's computer does the rest. When I'm driving I'm the one making the decisions. My fate is in my hands. That's the way I like it.

HARV popped into the dashboard screen. Like I said, the Mustang is "slightly modified."

"Where we off to now?" he asked.

"Any luck getting in touch with HTech?" I asked.

"I only reached the front-level people and machines, and they all have said no way."

"That's no good," I said. "I need to talk to the big guy! Have Carol talk to them and do her thing."

HARV shook his head. "I already thought of that.

HTech is psi-proof, as only machines and people with heavy psi blockers interact with the general public."

There had to be a way to see Doors. Sure he was rich and powerful, but deep down (actually, not all that deep down) he was still a geek. Kind of like a greedier, slightly less socially inept version of Randy. I quickly changed directions.

"Where are we going?" HARV asked.

"To HTech headquarters!" I told him.

"Right, like you have a chance of getting in."

We drove on for fifteen minutes, and all the while I had to listen to HARV lecture me on how I didn't have any chance of getting in to see William Doors, the president of HTech. I ignored him until we neared HTech's main gate.

"Okay HARV," I told him, "cover me with a hologram?"

"Of who?" HARV asked.

"Doors may be rich and powerful but deep down he's still a geek. And what's the thing all geeks respond to?"

"Computers."

"Process some more."

"Different computers."

"Keep processing."

"Classic comics."

"Keep working on it, HARV."

"Bikini models."

"Try again."

"Old Monty Python skits?"

I was proud of HARV for picking up on that. I was really starting to rub off on him. But his guessing was so random I decided to give him a hint.

"Think about Randy earlier today."

"Their moms! Geeks are almost always momma's boys."

I touched my finger to my nose. "Vingo! I'll go in as Ma Doors."

Luckily for me, Ma Doors was almost as famous as her son. She, with her eccentric ways, had become the darling of the media. She had recently been hitting the talk show circuit—*Oprah-clone, The Instant Buzz, The World Right Now*—to promote her new book, *Still Super Sexy at*

Seventy-seven, which was the sequel to her bestseller *How to Raise a Billionaire*.

"Do a scan of all the public security cameras to see if you can find her."

"I can't do that," HARV insisted from my car's screen.

I just stared at him. He stared at me. He crossed his arms. I knew he could do it. He knew he could do it. The problem was this was one of those legal gray areas. The cameras were only supposed to be accessed by the proper authorities.

"I'm doing this for the good of all mankind," I said.

HARV raised an eyebrow. "No, *I'm* doing this for the good of all mankind." He shook his head and mumbled in a New York accent, "I don't get no respect."

"What did you say?"

"You heard me."

"You sounded like Rodney Dangerfield."

"I knew you'd appreciate that," HARV said.

"Why Dangerfield?"

HARV lowered his eye. "You'll laugh."

"No, I won't."

"You'll make fun of me."

"I'll try not to."

"I missed being connected to your brain," HARV said quickly, practically too quickly for me to understand.

"Really?"

"I'm loath to admit this, but it taught me to appreciate humor. When I wasn't hooked up to you, I was forced to look for another source of inspiration. I found that Mr. Dangerfield and I have a lot in common."

I decided not to touch that. I was happy that HARV had learned the value of humor.

"So, have you found her?" I asked.

"Yes, she just stopped at the 700-1100 to buy a Slurpee," HARV said. "Believe me, I am not making that up."

"Great, then throw the disguise over me and we're a go!"

"This still isn't going to work," HARV said. "I'm sure the guards know this isn't Mrs. Doors' vehicle! I doubt she even has a land-based granny vehicle."

"Perhaps, but I'm sure none of them will have the guts to question her about it. She's an eccentric old woman. She's prone to change cars. Besides, who doesn't love the classic Mustang? And only a very hot grandma could handle this car."

The HTech tower was a tall, black, seemingly windowless pointed monolith that shot two hundred stories up into the sky on the outskirts of New Frisco. The building was so tall that it was visible from any place in Frisco. Still I was totally unimpressed with it. Rumor has it that William Doors designed the building himself. The guy certainly didn't make his fortune by being creative. The building reminded me (and most adolescent boys) of a part of the male anatomy. My hunch was Doors was trying to compensate for his own inadequacies.

The entire compound was protected by an electric energy fence that ran its perimeter. I wasn't sure if it was to keep unwanted visitors out or the workers in.

I drove up to a little square armored guard post that sat just outside of the protected area. I rolled down my window. A short, stocky, human guard wearing computerized body armor came out to greet me. I swear all these guards look alike. It's as if rich people can shop at Guards Я Us.

I smiled at the approaching guard.

"Oh, I'm sorry, ma'am. I didn't realize it was you . . ." he told me. "You'll be allowed right in after the psi scan!" The guard pushed a button on his wrist communicator.

A tall, slim, female guard with short hair and a long nose that matched her body came out of the post. She reminded me a Doberman pinscher, I'm not sure why. She had to be a psi.

This could have posed a problem. In the past, my link with HARV has made me hard to scan which was good. Plus, my vast experience with psis has taught me a little trick—psis hate humming. Nothing drives them out of your mind faster than humming the tune from some old classic. Only this case, I didn't want to drive her right out of my mind. I needed to convince her that I was Ma Doors. I wasn't sure how to pull that off.

The words "don't worry" flashed in front of my eyes. "I have run an analysis of all of Ma Doors' purchases over the last twenty years and every show and song she has downloaded. I have concluded that if you hum the theme to *The Love Boat*, version III, the psi will pass you as her."

The psi locked eyes me.

I started to hum. *"Love is ready to cruise. Come on*

*board. There's no way you can lose. Take a chance. Give
love more than a fleeting glance. The love boat is ready to
sail again. The loooove boat . . ."*

The psi pulled back and held her head. "It's her," she
said. "It's definitely her."

The first guard smiled at my confirmation. He pushed
another button on his wrist communicator. The energy field
guarding the gate disappeared.

I drove in and parked in a VIP space. I looked up at the
high-rise. Even up close I still wasn't impressed. I got out
of my car.

"You do have a map of this place, correct?" I asked
HARV.

A map of the building appeared in the corner of my eye.
"Cool!"

"Just follow the arrows to Mr. Doors' door," HARV told
me. "And hope that the real Ma Doors doesn't chug down
her Slurpee and head here . . ."

I walked in the front door and waved to the receptionist.
He politely smiled and waved back.

"Unlike most big shots," HARV whispered, "Mr. Doors
likes his office on the first floor. I think he's like you—
scared of heights."

I didn't respond to that. I'm not scared of heights. I'm
just scared of falling from heights. It adds to my vulnerabil-
ity, which is part of my charm. I'm tough enough to be
secure with my flaws.

The arrows in front of my eyes pointed down a long hall
to the right.

I followed the arrow, always having a friendly smile for
all the employees I passed.

An X formed on a door at the end of the hall. I was
certain it was Mr. Doors' office. As a matter of fact, it
seemed to be the only actual office I encountered. Everything else was just open bullpen space. I walked up to his
secretary's desk.

She looked up from her work.

I gave her the once-over like any good mother should. I
admired Mr. Doors' taste. The secretary was bit pale and
too porcelain perfect for my taste, but she was quite lovely,
with delicately chiseled features.

"Do you wish me to alert Mr. Doors to your presence?" she asked me.

I put a finger to my mouth, whispering her to silence.

"Oh, I see. You want to surprise him," the secretary said, as I walked by her to the door.

If you only knew, I smiled. I walked by and opened the door to Mr. Doors' office. It was a BIG office. You knew this guy was the boss.

"Debbie, I asked not to be disturbed!" he said. He looked up and saw his mom coming toward him. His anger turned to pleasure, rearranging his mouth into a smile.

Doors was kind of cold, square, and bland looking, much like his building. His haircut looked like his mom had done it by placing a bowl over his head and trimming around the edges. You would think a billionaire could afford to get a better cut. Then again, when you're a billionaire, why bother?

"Oh, sorry, Mom, I didn't know it was you," he said.

"Nope," I said in my own voice, pretty much blowing my cover.

"What's the meaning of this?" he demanded, as he carefully pushed a button on his desk.

"HARV holo-off!" I said.

There was a slight shimmer. I looked at Mr. Doors looking at me.

"Zachary Johnson, to what do I owe this *honor*?" he said, kind of choking on the honor part.

"Sorry to bother you," I said. "I just need some info, and I'm in too much of a hurry to go through other channels."

"Oh, really?" he said, raising an eyebrow.

"I understand you and your corporation made the bots for the Pole," I told him, getting right to the point.

He remained calm.

"Of course. That's public knowledge," he said. "We did it because though we may be a huge corporation, we place the good of the entire world in front of our profits."

I smiled at him. He returned my smile. There was a bit of awkward silence.

"Okay, maybe we place the good of the world beside our profits." He shrugged. "What does this have to do with anything?"

"Two of your guardbots attacked me today," I said.

His eyes never wavered from mine, and his voice was calm, deliberate, and steady when he said, "I assure you, Mr. Johnson, I know nothing about that. Besides, those are not our guardbots. They were a gift to the Pole."

I walked across the room (it took a few minutes) and leaned on his desk. It was a bullying technique. Doors might have been rich but he was still a slight man. I thought maybe I could intimidate him with my size advantage.

"Well, these bots must have been from a separate lot. According to the Pole, none of their bots are missing."

"Then why are you bothering me at all?"

"I'm betting you have a few spare bots around like those at the Pole," I said, leaning forward.

"Why would we have spare North Pole guardbots around? Those are old models. And why would we send them after you?"

"My question exactly. I need to—"

"I'm sorry," Mr. Doors interrupted, "but I've given you more time than I should have. If my nieces and nephews weren't fans, I would have had you tossed out long ago. Maybe even had you killed."

I felt a hand on my shoulder. A very strong hand.

I looked over my shoulder, up the arm, and at the face attached to that hand. It was the porcelain-perfect secretary.

"Let me escort you to the door," she said, making it very clear that it was an order, not a request.

"Don't you want a voicegraph?" I asked her boss.

She yanked me away from the desk with one arm.

"DOS!" I told her. "What do you do, live at the gym?" Then it hit me, porcelain-perfect face, pale while skin. I sniffed her. "You don't smell at all," I said.

"Thank you," she told me, as she shoved me out the door and down the hallway.

"Yes, but the thing is, you should smell a little. I mean it's the middle of a hard day, you've been running around, and now you're pushing around this eighty-five-kilo guy like he's a microchip. You should be sweating some."

"I am a woman. Women do not sweat, they perspire," she corrected, as drove me toward the door to the outside.

"You don't even do that do you?" I told her. "You're a DOSing android, aren't you?"

She placed one hand on the neck of my jacket, the other on the belt of my pants. She lifted me up. She pulled me back. "Door open!" she commanded.

She flung me out the door.

I made a very undignified thud to ground five meters from the door. I turned to her.

"I'll take that as a 'yes,' " I said.

"If you mention this to anybody, we will sue you for slander!" she told me.

"But it's the truth," I said.

"So?" She laughed. "We employ almost half of the lawyers and greeting card salesmen left in world! You would need more than the truth on your side!" She smiled. "Now if you don't mind, I have real work to do." She started to walk away. She stopped and turned to me. "Oh, by the way, I do work out at Maria and Arnold's every day at 1800. Stop by, I would love to go a round with you in the ring." Then she walked away.

I got up and limped to my car. I guess I shouldn't have let that catch me so off guard. After all, I know that Ex-Shell has experimented with illegal human-skin-toned androids. So it only made sense that HTech would be doing the same thing. Plus, if the World Council ever called them on it (which they'd never do), I would bet credits to donuts that HTech's lawyers would argue that "her" skin tone isn't really human color. I was sure I had learned something from this experience, I just wasn't sure what.

I headed to my car. "Well, I guess that could have gone worse," I said under my breath to HARV.

"Define 'worse,' " HARV said.

"Broken bones would have been worse. I consider any hostile meeting I can walk away from with nothing broken and only my ego bruised a success."

"I wouldn't be adding this to the victory column quite yet," HARV said.

I didn't like the sound of that.

I heard a throat clear behind me.

I stopped walking and turned around. There stood a big burly man and a bigger, burlier woman. Even if they weren't dressed in plain blue uniforms, I could have guessed by the cold stone looks on their faces they were security.

"Each of their left arms are bionic," scrolled by my eyes, a warning message from HARV.

I held up my hand in the stop position.

"What gives here guys? Mr. Doors said I wasn't to be hurt."

"We work for Mrs. Doors, senior," the man said.

"What does Ma Doors have against me?" I asked.

"The security computer forwarded Mrs. Doors the image of you entering the building disguised as her. She wants you to know she would never wear an outfit like that," the woman said. She then pounded her fist into her bionic palm. "She wants us to make sure you don't do anything like that again."

"Don't worry, I won't," I reassured them.

The woman grabbed me by the shirt and lifted me up with one arm.

"Good," she said.

"Are these bullies bothering you, citizen?" an all too familiar voice said from above and behind me. I didn't have to turn around to know it was Twoa Thompson.

For those of you who don't know, Twoa is one of the world famous Thompson quads. The four genetically perfected sisters were created by Dr. Dave Thompson, who created the girls a few years before he created a potential doomsday device that was so menacing the World Council bought the rights to the machine from him (for a HUGE sum of money) and then had his memory erased. Twoa thinks of herself as a superhero called Justice Babe. She walks (well, flies) around in a skimpy costume fighting evil. Not just fighting it, but crushing it, and usually causing more harm than good. The odd thing is she's not even the most eccentric one in her family.

"It's okay, Twoa. I have it under control," I said.

Twoa landed next to us. She looked striking and frightening as ever in her full Justice Babe garb. I swear she had even less skirt and more breasts than the last time I ran into her.

"This is private property," the female guard said to Twoa.

Twoa shook her head. "That doesn't give you the right to womanhandle good citizens and champions of justice."

Twoa grabbed the woman's bionic arm and squeezed. I heard circuitry smash—or more accurately squish—causing the guard to release her grip on me.

The male guard rushed to his female counterpart's aid. He clubbed Twoa on the back with his bionic arm. The arm smashed on contact. Twoa was no worse for wear.

"Twoa, don't hurt them!" I said quickly. "I had this worked out. They were only doing their jobs!"

Twoa faced the guard and lifted her elbow as if she was going to give him an elbow smash in the face. Instead, she stopped and just held her elbow up, giving the guard a whiff of the pheromones under her arm.

The guard's angry expression instantly turned into one of complete admiration . . . actually worship is probably a more fitting word. He looked at Twoa as if she were a goddess. And quite frankly, to him she very well may have been. He fell to one knee and gazed longingly at her.

Twoa then lifted her other arm, giving the ailing and flailing female guard a subtle whiff. The guard's eyes glazed over, and she, too, fell to a knee.

"What can I do to please you, master?" she asked.

Twoa ignored her and turned her attention me.

"Are you okay, Zach?" she asked.

"I'm fine. Thanks," I said. I looked at the dumbfounded guards. "How long will they be like that?"

Twoa shrugged. "Who knows? A day, a week, forever. Not my problem. That'll teach Ma Doors for cheating me in celebrity strip poker."

We started to walk to my car. I figured it was best to move out of the area just in case any more HTech security people were foolish enough to come and engage or enrage Twoa.

"What brings you here?" I asked.

"I understand you were asking about me?" Twoa said.

"I wasn't," I said.

"Your computer was poking around looking for information," Twoa said. Twoa put her arm around me. It wasn't so much a gesture of friendship as it was a maneuver to hit me with some of those pheromones. "Why?" she asked.

My head started to spin, but I liked it. I looked at Twoa.

She was always beautiful and touched up picture perfect, but today she seemed extra beautiful, extra perfect. Her skin was smooth and velvety purple like her creator had intended. Her eyes were big, brown, gorgeous and could wilt a man (literally). Her hair was brunette with just a hint of gold, as if it were streaked by the sun. It danced playfully around her shoulders. Those big lush creamy lips of hers— what I wouldn't give for the honor of being her lipstick! And that body, that unbreakable, super toned yet soft as velvet body! Zow, that's probably the only time in my life I've used the word "velvet" twice in the same minute. That just shows how special Twoa was. Far more beautiful than her sisters Ona and Threa, she was also a lot smarter and much nicer. She had much more pleasant breath, as well.

"Woah!" HARV shouted inside my head. "She's trying to turn you into one of her lovesick puppy slaves!"

"I don't mind," I said, out loud.

"I'm shocking you, and I'm turning off your nasal receptors," HARV said.

"Youch!" I screamed, as the current rushed through my body. I leaped forward and away from Twoa's grasp.

Twoa smiled. "Ah, your computer inside your brain. I forgot about that."

I composed myself quickly. I had to react before Twoa tried to do something more drastic.

"Really, Twoa, I don't know what you're talking about. There's no need for you to try to bend my will."

I've seen Twoa turn a dozen well-armed killers (out of work actors) into floor mats in under ten seconds. There was no way I wanted to upset her. She smiled and gave me a pat on the shoulder.

"Just tell me why your computer was talking to my dad, ah, computer, ah, I'm never really sure what to call him."

(Twoa's dad had his memory downloaded into their house computer as a safeguard against the World Council erasing his mind. It's a long story that's been told before.)

"Twoa, at the risk of being twisted in a pretzel, I have no idea what you are talking about."

"My old science project," she said sincerely.

I tilted my head and looked at her. "You've totally lost me."

Twoa gave a heavy sigh. The force of her breath almost

knocked me over. "Your computer was asking my dad, who is now my computer, if he had any idea who designed the elves for the North Pole."

"Yes, that's true," I said.

"It was me," Twoa said, thumping on her ample chest (and making my heart pound). "They were my middle school science project."

We reached my car, which was a good thing, because I need it to lean on.

"You designed the elves?" I said.

Twoa smiled proudly. "Yes, back in my science nerd days. Why do you care?"

Twoa leaned in close to me, very close. She started slowly massaging my back. It felt good.

"I don't need pheromones to get what I want," Twoa said.

"Twoa, I can't tell you," I said melting under her grip.

"Two of the elves have been killed," HARV said from my wrist communicator.

Twoa stopped her massaging.

"What?"

"HARV!" I shouted.

"I had to do it, Zach," HARV said. "You wouldn't be much good to anybody if Twoa turned you into a pile of mush. Don't worry. Nobody else heard because Twoa's sending out so much negative energy, she's knocked out everybody else in earshot."

Twoa took a step back from me and nodded. "He's right, you know."

It took a nano for my head to stop spinning. I wasn't sure what had it rotating faster, Twoa's pheromone attack or her words. Come to think of it, it was exceedingly quiet. I glanced around. Sure enough, all people, animals, or machines for as far as I could see were on the ground, curled in a fetal position.

"You designed the elves," I said slowly.

I looked at HARV's face in my communicator. "So much for your theory that elves can't go bad."

Twoa thought about that for about a nano. She frowned. "Hey!" She placed her fist under my chin. "I resent that. Take it back now, before I decide to make you into my permanent footstool."

I shook my head. "Come on, Twoa, even you have to admit you are a bit of a nutcase."

She took a step back. She wasn't used to people (besides her sisters) having the nerve to talk back to her.

"I'm not a nutcase. I'm rich, so, if anything, I'm eccentric," she said defensively.

"Eccentric? You walk around dressed as a superhero fighting crime. You even sleep with your boots on!"

"Crime knows no time," she said. "I have to be ready to leap into action at a moment's notice. Besides, I take my boots off once a week to let my feet air out." She stopped to think about what she had said. She put a finger to her lips. "Okay, I'm definitely on the eccentric side."

"Twoa, you are so far past eccentric, you can't even see it from where you are standing with a suprathermal electron telescope."

"What about my supervision?" she asked.

I put my hand on her shoulder, taking the chance that she wouldn't rip it off and hand it to me.

"The point is, Twoa, if you made the elves, I can't rule out the possibility that they are as crazy and as capable of destruction as you are."

Twoa put her index finger under my chin and lifted me off the ground, again. "Zach, you have to believe me when I tell you this," she said.

"You've got my undivided attention."

"I worked hard on the elves. In those days, before Daddy's memory got erased, I wanted to be a great scientist like him. Sure, I had a setback or two, but I swear to you, Zach, on my tremendous bosoms, that I perfected the elves to be capable of nothing but kindness."

I looked down at her. The first thing that caught my eye were those tremendous bosoms. Being lifted up like this gave me quite the eyeful. With great difficulty, I moved my gaze up to meet hers. I saw something in Twoa I had never seen in her before: sincerity.

"I believe you," I said.

"Good," she said with a smile, as she lowered me to the ground. She patted me firmly on the shoulder. If it wasn't for my body armor, she probably would have dislocated it. "Is there anything else I can do for you?"

"What do you know about Santana?" I asked.

Twoa shook her head. "I didn't have anything to do with her."

"Do you know who did?"

Twoa shook her head again. "Sorry, Zach. I was too busy with my elves project to pay attention to anything else."

"I appreciate your help, Twoa."

"Of course you do," she said with a wink. "Anything else?"

"Not at the moment," I said.

"Very well," she said. "If you need me, just activate the Justice Babe signal."

She put an arm up in the air and flew off.

"I don't think I want to know what the Justice Babe signal is."

I sniffed the air. It was eerie not to be able to smell anything. I felt like my nose should be stuffy, but it wasn't.

"HARV, turn my nose back on please," I said.

I felt a slight tingle in the back of the head.

"Can you smell again?" HARV asked. "Now, that's a phrase you don't say very often."

I was hit by a sudden rush of my olfactory senses: the flowers that lined the walkway to the building, the sweat of the beaten (and still in fetal position) guards, the slight scent of exhaust.

I got in my Mustang and started her up. HARV popped into the dash window.

"I'll drive," he told me. "I know you take pride in your driving, but your head still may not be totally clear from Twoa playing with it."

"Twoa and you," I said as HARV pulled the car out of its parking spot. (Okay maybe my car is more than slightly modified.)

HARV frowned. "I do not 'play' with your mind. I perform certain functions to increase its efficiency."

"You say tomato, and I say potato," I said.

"So, Sherlock, what have you concluded besides the fact that androids shouldn't have a need for deodorant, yet Twoa does?" HARV asked, trying unsuccessfully not to snicker.

"I'm still processing that info," I told him.

"I knew you wouldn't learn anything from just barging into the man's office," HARV lectured.

"I needed to judge his reactions to my questions. That type of thing is much easier to gauge in person, especially when you don't know somebody," I said, defending my actions.

"So what do you conclude?" HARV prodded.

"He seemed sincere," I concluded.

"Of course he seemed sincere!" HARV said. "He's a professional businessman! It's his job to seem sincere. DOS! Zach! You can be so naive at times."

"Did you do a voice scan on him?" I asked.

There was silence.

"Well, HARV?"

"I did."

"And?"

"His voice waves and facial patterns indicated that he was quite surprised by your news."

"See, so we learned that," I said.

"But he's a smart guy. He obviously knows you were scanning him, so he might have anti-scanning software, just to throw us off track," HARV said. There was another slight pause. "DOS! I should have scanned for holographic activity. For all we know, he had on a holographic cover!"

"HARV, I don't think the man sits in his office under a holographic cover," I said.

"Probably not. Too much exposure is bad for the brain."

"I think you would have noticed if he activated a hologram while we were in the room," I added.

"True," HARV said. "I am exceedingly smart." HARV processed for a nano longer. "Still, he's a professional businessman. We can't rule out that he's also an expert liar, and therefore can't rule out HTech as a suspect."

"They may be a suspect right now, but we have to look at all the options. ExShell would really gain from setting HTech up to look like the bad guys," I pointed out. HARV was great at cranking out facts but he had a tendency to jump to conclusions and then stick to those conclusions, as if they were attached to him with super-duper glue. I took it as my duty to teach him to think outside the CPU.

ExShell and HTech were longtime rivals. Over the years, their competition has grown so fever pitched their executives can't even be in the same room together without breaking out in a brawl or lawsuit. I knew this and so did HARV.

HARV calculated for a bit. "True . . . I guess they are the obvious choice. But there are times when the obvious choice is the right choice."

"Yes, but dead elves don't seem to fit the style of either HTech or ExShell. It's too subtle."

"That is a good point," HARV conceded.

"Plus, by coming here we did learn that Twoa helped create the elves. Therefore, we can't rule out the possibility that elves can snap."

"True, again." HARV said.

"There are still a lot of possibilities," I said. "We still have the unknown wild-card factor."

HARV looked at me.

"The unknown wild-card factor? Which is?"

I shrugged. "If I knew, it wouldn't be unknown. Still there's always something or somebody you don't think of until it walks right up and slaps you in the face."

"Yes. Humans are so unpredictable that even I can't always deduce with total reliability and accuracy the probability of their actions," HARV said.

This was the second time today he admitted that there was something he didn't totally understand. Despite Randy's new shielding, I was still rubbing off on him.

"I do have some good news for you," HARV said.

"And that is?"

"Esteemed World Council Member Sexy Sprockets will make time to see you today. She can fit you in from 16:15 until 16:19."

"Four minutes?"

"She's a busy girl. You should be glad you get any face time at all."

"Well then, I guess I have time to grab a quick bite to eat."

5

I was sitting at a table in one of my favorite outdoor delis, sipping on an ice tea (I was on duty), and munching on a roast beef on rye. I was trying to mentally piece together the parts of the puzzle I had so far, attempting to get an idea of what the solution to this puzzle would look like.

The things I did know I could count on one hand. HTech would certainly gain something from the demise of the Holiday, but was it enough to risk ripping apart the moral fiber of the world? They were a pretty successful company as it was, so why sink the boat to success? Maybe another company was trying to shake things up? A small upstart looking to make its mark? Or another one of the big guys just trying to screw over HTech?

Having learned that Twoa was the one responsible for the creation of the elves didn't put my mind at ease at all. After all, this was a woman who would stop jaywalkers by knocking out everybody on the street. She was only a kid at the time she created the elf template. Who's to say she couldn't have screwed up and incorporated a bit of the homicidal maniac in there?

I hoped that once I got to the Pole some of this groundwork I was laying would pay off.

I looked up to see a little guy with an old-fashioned handlebar mustache coming toward me. He was wearing a black suit that was at least one size too small for him. He waddled like a penguin.

"Are you Zachary Johnson?" he asked, as he drew within a meter.

"I am."

He reached into his jacket and pulled out a laser pen.

"That's not really a laser pen," HARV said in my brain.

"Good, I hate signing autographs," I thought back.

"How do you feel about death threats?"

"They are slightly more annoying than autographs. Why?"

"The pen is actually a hand laser with a holo-projector to make it look like a pen," HARV said.

Hand weapons with holographic projectors are all the rage these days. They were especially handy for people who were terrible shots. It allowed them to get up close and personal with their targets so they could kill at close range. I tipped the table up to use it as a shield and dropped under it just as he fired. The shot blew a hole in the table but missed me.

People screamed and headed for cover.

"For future reference," HARV said, "whenever anybody asks if you are Zachary Johnson, you should deny it. Maybe even claim that you spit on Zachary Johnson."

"Not helping here, HARV."

I popped my gun into my hand. Problem was, there were still too many civilians in the way to fire indiscriminately. Luckily (and luck is a really relative term here), I didn't have to. The man simply peeked around the table I was hiding behind and pointed his pen-gun at me. Only a truly lousy shot would make such an overt move. He certainly wasn't a professional—at least not a highly paid one. It could also mean that he didn't want to hurt anybody else or that he just hated me so much he wanted to kill me at close range. Frankly, it didn't really matter.

I put my hands up over my head to let him know I wouldn't hurt him, giving him one last chance to back down.

"Woah, cool the warp engines, buddy," I said in my most calming voice. "Let's talk this out."

His hand was shaking as he pointed his weapon at me. There were beads of sweat forming exponentially on his brow. He had the upper hand, yet he was more scared than I was.

"You met with Santana earlier today!" he shouted, waving his weapon at me.

I put a finger to my mouth to quiet him.

"No need to shout. And what's it to you, anyhow?"

"Santana is evil," the man spat, still brandishing the weapon.

I raised an eyebrow (I learned that from HARV). "A woman whose sole duty in life is to give everybody in the world presents is evil?"

He stood there thinking. His hand stopped twitching some, which relieved me. You don't want folks with weapons to have twitchy trigger fingers.

"She's not evil per se, but what she stands for is evil."

I shrugged. "You've lost me, buddy."

A message from HARV scrolled across my eyes: "The police are on their way."

DOS, it took them long enough to respond.

My would-be assassin looked at me like he was the Harvard professor and I was the idiot freshman. "Santana and the Holiday make us all the same. It's a crime against human nature."

"Come again?"

"If Santana gets her way, we'll all be the same. There will be no individuality left in the world.

"Come again?"

He rolled his eyes and shook his head. He took a deep breath. Now it was as if he was the Nobel laureate and I was the helpless grade schooler—and a slow one at that.

"You see . . ." he started to say.

Before he could finish, I kicked him in the shin. Not the most flashy or macho of moves, but your choices are limited when you are on the ground and don't want to shoot or be shot by your assailant. My kick forced him to instinctively bend over and shield the wounded shin. This left his chin wide open and much nearer to the ground. I hit that with another quick kick. The kick snapped his head back, and he went crashing to the ground.

I leaped up and dove on top of him. I popped my gun into my hand and forced it under his chin.

"Now, let's continue our little talk on my terms," I growled.

"Policebot behind you," HARV said in my brain.

I turned my head just enough so I could see the bot rolling in from behind.

"Freeze!" the bot yelled.

I put my hands over my head, giving the bot easy access

to my gun. It rolled up to me, extended a claw from its cylinder body, and took the gun. The little man in black took advantage of the opening, tagging me with a punch to the stomach. Between my underarmor and his awkward position on the ground, all he really managed to do was hurt his hand. That and get us both netted by the policebot.

"Hey, why are you netting me?" I shouted to the bot.

"It is impossible to net just him from my position," the bot replied. The bot followed his reply by shocking us. My attacker and I both screamed, though he took the brunt of the shock due to my armor being insulated.

"Why'd you do that?" I shouted.

"Precautionary measures," the bot snickered as it started to drag us down to headquarters.

6

For those of you who have never spent time in a police interrogation room, it's not fun. It's kind of like waiting for the dentist, yet more lonely because you don't have other equally apprehensive people sitting around with you. In fact, there's nothing else in the room besides you, a light, table, and a couple of chairs so the interrogators can sit. The police had taken away my gun, but they had left me with my wrist communicator. They obviously didn't think of me as a major risk. HARV went into stealth mode the nano I was captured. He knew anything we said was most likely being recorded, so the less said the better. I looked at my communicator. I had an hour to make it to see Sexy.

I had been sitting in the police detention and interrogation room for about ten minutes before my buddy Captain Tony Rickey and a blob of a lieutenant rolled in. Tony and I were old friends. It's helpful for anybody to have an old friend high up in the police force. It's especially helpful for me, since I "visit" the building so often. I've been told they have a chair that they reserve just for me.

"Zach, this is Lieutenant Ray Rayborn," Tony said, pointing to the lieutenant.

I nodded. He growled back at me. He had the look of a walrus, and an unkempt walrus at that.

"Detective," I said.

"Lieutenant," he corrected. Apparently he also had the temperament of an angry walrus.

I decided my best course of action was to focus on Tony and appeal to our friendship and his reason. After all, I was just an innocent bysitter.

"Tony, you know I wasn't doing anything except relaxing and having a light meal."

Tony nodded.

"That's what they all say," Rayborn scowled. He stood up from the chair and pounded his fists into the table.

I sat there unimpressed.

"Listen, buddy, I do this so much I have a frequent subject of interrogation card," I said. "It's going to take more than you to scare me, especially when I know I'm innocent."

I looked at Tony. "I swear, Tony, for once, I have absolutely no idea why I was attacked."

"Any idea why you were thrown out of HTech headquarters?" Rayborn asked with a snarl.

I should have seen that one coming.

"Business."

"Zach, even you have to admit it's a little strange that you get thrown out of the office of one of the richest men in the world, saved by a superhero babe, and then attacked by a member of the SSS."

"All in a day's work when you're me. The SSS?"

"The Santana Stinks Society," Tony said, as square-jawed as humanly possible.

I tried to suppress a smile, but I'm sure I didn't totally succeed. "That would explain his ranting about Santana."

Rayborn pounded his fists down on the table again. "The question is why you?" he snarled.

I sat back in my chair. "Does that work with anybody?"

Tony looked at him. "I told you Zach doesn't scare easily." Tony looked at me. "He's in training, Zach. Give him a break."

I gave him a mock shudder and trembled, "Oh, please, sir, don't hurt me. I'll tell you anything you need to know."

He eased back a bit and smiled. "Now that wasn't so hard was it?"

"Truthfully guys, I have never heard of the SSS until just now. I have no idea why they would be after me."

Tony and Ray just looked at me. It was clear that I wasn't going to get out of there until I gave them something.

"Okay, maybe I have a slight idea. Santana and I are talking about doing a Zach Johnson action figure."

Tony smiled. "Well, that would explain it."

"Yeah, even I think that makes sense," Ray agreed.

"Can I ask the name of the guy who attacked me?"

The name "Joe Summers" scrolled across my eyes.

"Joe Summers," Tony said, looking at his hand computer. "He's a first timer, so we'll let him off with a fine and probation for discharging a weapon in public and resisting arrest."

"What about attacking me?"

"Since he didn't hurt you, it would be a stretch to get any judge in this province to hold him. There's talk of treating attacks on your life the same as littering: a hundred-credit fine then you are free to go."

I stood up. "So, I'm free to go."

"I'll even drive you to your car," Tony said.

"You don't have to."

"I insist."

7

Tony and I didn't talk much until we got safely in his standard white-and-black police hover. For a hover it wasn't bad to look at. In fact it had more than a passing resemblance to the police cars of the 1950s, except there were hover jets supplementing all the wheels.

Tony punched some coordinates in his hover's dash.

"Are you sure?" the hover asked.

"Positive," Tony said.

These police hovers were bimodular, able to fly or travel across the ground. Of course Tony picked the air mode.

"Okay, Zach, tell me what's really up," Tony said.

"Tony, I told you the truth."

"I'm sure you told me some semblance of the truth. Zach, I don't think you know what you are getting yourself into here."

At the moment, HARV appeared between us, projecting himself from my wrist communicator.

"Captain Rickey, when have you ever known Zach to have any idea what he was getting himself into?"

"Good point," Tony said.

"When the man is on a job, he leaps, then looks, and expects us to hand him a parachute."

"When you're right, you're right, HARV."

"I doubt he'd be able to survive if it weren't for us."

"Another good point, HARV."

"We are lucky he only gets one significant job a year," HARV concluded.

"Yeah, if he got any more work, I'd have to quit my job on the force, and Zach would have to put me on payroll."

"Like he could afford you," HARV said with a laugh.

"Guys, I'm sitting right here in the hover with you!"
I said.

"Plus, he's so self-centered," HARV continued, ignoring
me. "It's always about him. Like he farts sunshine."

Tony laughed.

"First, none of that, well, not much of that is true. And
second, '*farts sunshine*'?"

HARV crossed his arms and acknowledged that I was in
the hover for the first time by actually looking toward me.
"I got my point across."

"He did."

Just then I decided to look down. Normally when I am
in a hover I don't like to look down; no good can come of
it. It will only remind me that I am hundreds of meters up
in the air. In this case though, I made an exception. Anything had to be better than watching my computer and my
friend rant about me. I noticed we weren't where I thought
we would be. I was no expert in finding places by air but
I could tell one side of town from another.

"Ah, Tony, my car is parked at a bistro clear on the
other side of town."

"I know. I'm not taking you to your car—yet."

If this had been any other police officer in town, I would
have been worried, but this was Tony. We'd known each
other longer than either of us (especially him) cared to
admit. We played ball on the sandlots together. I was his
best man at his first two weddings.

"So, where are you taking me?"

"To a bar I know, in Oakland."

Almost every province in the world has one city that, for
better or for worse, has dug in their heels, vehemently re-
fusing to be dragged into the second half of the twenty-
first century. These cities were designated "low-tech zones"
and became refuges for those folks who didn't want to be
constantly wired. Those who don't need to be instantly notified of any changes in the world. People who don't want
everything wired to everything else. In the province of California, that city is Oakland.

I know this may sound weird coming from a guy whose
computer is wired to his brain, but I could empathize with
those people. I really appreciated those throwback cities.

They were our link to our past. They were places where people could commune with our ancestors. They served as living memorials of simpler times.

I figured Tony wanted to go to Oakland because he had something he wanted to tell me away from the prying eyes and ears of security cameras.

Tony landed outside the little place in the bad part of Oakland (not that there is an especially good part) called The Mad Hacker. The place was so low brow I hadn't ever been here. Entering The Mad Hacker was like entering a time warp. It was dark and smoke-filled despite the fact it was midafternoon and smoking in public had been out-lawed in California for decades. The building had to be a hundred years old, and it still boasted the original paint. The paint that survived was peeling off the walls like it was victim of a strange skin disease. There was one large window in the front of the building but it was so dirty it might as well have been boarded over. I'd call it a run-down dive, but that would be offensive to run-down dives. It was the bar that time ignored. I found that kind of a cool thing.

We made our way through the crowd and up to the bar itself.

"So, what's this all about, Tony?" I asked.

He held up one finger. He pulled an earpiece from his pocket. It looked like an earring with a chip on it. He clipped the earring to his left ear.

"Tony, should I be aware of some sort of lifestyle change?"

Tony just smiled. "Everybody sleep!" he said firmly.

The next thing I knew Tony was patting me on the shoulder. "Zach, wake up."

"Zach, wake up!" I heard HARV say inside my brain.

Sure enough, my eyes were closed, and my head was down on something. I opened my eyes. Then I remembered: Oakland and the bar. I shot my head up. I rubbed the sleep out of my eyes. I looked around. Except for Tony, everybody else in the bar was asleep. Some had curled up on the floor, some fell asleep at their tables, and some were asleep on their feet. It didn't matter, they were all out.

I looked at Tony. He pointed to the earpiece. "Portable psi power simulator," he said.

"Impressive."

"We were having them developed for the crowd control," Tony said.

I looked around at the sleeping crowd.

"It seems to work."

So this is what Tony wanted to show me in private. I was certain the department wouldn't appreciate him showing me top-secret test equipment. The question was why was a by-the-book guy like Tony showing me this? What did this have to do with Santana?

"I'll tell you what this has to do with Santana," Tony said.

I was impressed.

"Santana's elves developed this for us. They have a knack for these kinds of things."

"You're telling me."

"The problem is Santana decided that while these weren't offensive weapons, she still didn't approve of them. This was the only one made. The force begged and pleaded for more. She wouldn't budge. She made a lot of enemies that day."

"I bet," I said.

Tony looked at me. "So, Zach, tell me, what is your involvement with the Pole?"

"I'm going to the Pole to help solve the murder of two elves," I said without even thinking. "Hey! Stop using that thing on me!" I said.

"I'm calibrating your brain to be able to resist it," HARV said from inside my brain. "It's quite complicated, but I should have your defenses up in two minutes."

"Sorry," Tony said. "I had to know. You don't mind."

"No, I don't mind," I said. "Hey! Stop doing that."

"Don't worry, I can't do it for much longer. This thing gives me a nasty headache if I use it for more than five minutes."

"Good!" I said.

"I've made my point," Tony said. He took a sip of the beer from a lady sleeping next to him at the bar. "Let's get out of here."

We slowly made our way through the sleeping crowd. When we reached the exit, Tony turned to the sleeping people. "Everybody wake up."

The crowd started to stir.

"Go about your business as if nothing happened," Tony ordered.

Everybody stood up and began doing whatever they had been doing before Tony zapped them. Tony headed to his hover and motioned for me to follow.

"Come on, I'll get you back to your car. I know you have a meeting with Sexy Sprockets in a half hour," he said.

"Hey!" I said. "You're not supposed to know that."

"Don't worry, Zach, I'm on your side," he said with a pat on the back. "Though it is tempting to see what else you might be hiding."

Tony removed the device from his ear. He got into his hover. I followed. As trips to the police station go, this turned out to be one of my less painful and more eventful ones.

8

I pulled into the secure parking area of the World Council building in downtown Frisco a mere three minutes before my scheduled meeting with Sexy. I looked up at the shimmering ivory tower.

"Don't tell me. Sexy is on the top floor."

"It is the most secure," HARV said. "Of course, that's not the reason why Sexy wanted it. She wanted it for the view."

"Figures."

After passing through about a dozen security checks and about a dozen more Starbucks and Coffee Corners, I finally reached the door to Sexy's penthouse office. I knocked on the door. The door opened. The office was much less tacky than I thought it would be. In fact, it was very spartan and proper. Sexy was sitting at the far end of a long conference table. She stood up to greet me when I walked in.

She was wearing a black miniskirt, two-centimeter heels, and a silky black jacket with nothing else on underneath—no shirt, no bra, no pride. Now this was more along the lines of what I was expecting.

"Zach, how super neato of you to come," Sexy said, as she ran up to me and gave me a warm hug that felt better than it should have.

Sexy turned to a tall, powerfully built, blonde woman who had been giving Sexy a neck rub. "Shannon, this is Zach! I've told you about him."

The blonde woman just nodded her acknowledgment.

Sexy turned her attention back to me, still hanging on around my neck. "Zach, this is Shannon Cannon. She's my new bodyguard."

"Charmed," I said.

"Shannon's a mutant," Sexy said proudly, pulling me over to the conference table. "She can overpower people with her breath."

"Her parents must be so proud," I said.

Shannon glared at me. Sexy smiled at Shannon. "Zach is such a kidder."

Sexy sat back down at the head of the table and propped her legs up on the table. "Sit," she told me.

I pulled out a chair and made myself comfortable. Well, as comfortable as possible under the circumstances.

Sexy put her hands behind her head, giving me quite the view, and then said, "Zach, do you believe I'm now one of the most powerful people on Earth?"

"I try not to think about it too much, Sexy."

"Neither do I," Sexy said. "I find I'm happier when I don't think too much." She smiled at me. "We're a lot alike."

Now that was a scary statement.

"People don't understand the pressure we are under, having the weight of the world on our shoulders."

Sexy looked over at Shannon. Shannon moved forward and started massaging Sexy's shoulders.

Sexy turned to me. "Still, the perks of being a World Council member are almost as good as being a rock star!"

Sexy slid her legs from the top of the table and onto my lap.

"Massage my feet, please," she said.

"Excuse me?"

"My feet, rub them. It's been a long day of making decisions and stuff. Shannon is doing my neck, but my feet hurt, too."

I looked at her trying to gauge if she was serious. She returned my gaze with a tilted head and pleading puppy dog eyes.

"You don't want to be audited for the next ten years, do you?" she said in a pussy cat voice.

It was nice to see that Sexy's past life as a pop diva hadn't spoiled her.

"Sexy, you know I don't respond well to threats."

"Please . . ."

I shook my head. The things I do in the line of duty. I popped off her right shoe.

"I hope my feet aren't stinky," she said with a sly smile.

"Don't worry, I turned down the scent receptors in your brain again," HARV said.

I started to massage Sexy's foot. I guess there are worse things a PI has to do in this business than massage a beautiful pop-star-turned-politician's feet.

"Isn't it so subzero that I'm one of the most powerful people in the world?" Sexy asked, sitting back in her chair.

"Is subzero a synonym for scary as all get out?" I said.

Sexy smiled. "Oh, Zach, you're such a kidder." She looked up at Shannon. "He loves making funnies." Sexy looked back at me. "You know, I could have Shannon kill you right now and so totally get away with it."

I looked up at Shannon. She had the faint trace of a smile on her face as she gave me a subtle but obvious *yes, I could kill you easily* nod. It's a nod I have come to recognize because I have seen it far more often than I am comfortable with.

"Yes, I'm sure you could," I told Sexy. Then looking up at Shannon, "But I'm a lot harder to kill than most people think."

"I can attest to that," Sexy said. "But trust me, Zach, Shannon the Cannon isn't most people. One breath from her and you'd be deader than the polka. I've seen it. It's really quite impressive." She looked up at Shannon and winked. "And even more than a little sexy."

I shook my head. Yes, this was all strangely erotic in a campy, pulp fiction sort of way, but I had a job to do. It was time to steer this conversation back to the task at hand.

"You're probably wondering why I wanted to see you," I said to Sexy.

She laughed. "You mean this isn't just a social visit from an old friend?" Her face suddenly became sullen and more serious than I had ever seen it. "I know that, Zach. I know more than you, the media, and the general populace think."

Sexy reached forward and pressed a button on the table. "Sonny, Cher, come in here now, please."

"Sonny and Cher?"

On Sexy's command, a tall man with long hair and a skinny woman with short hair walked into the room from a hidden side door. They were both dressed in dark gray suits that seemed to fit their personalities as neatly as they did their bodies. They were both carrying paper-thin computers.

As Sony and Cher approached, Sexy turned to me and whispered, "Two of my personal lawyers."

"Yeah, I can tell."

"See, I have so much freaking power my lawyers can even admit to be being lawyers."

I watched as the two lawyers marched up to Sexy for their commands. The only thing that could have made this more fitting would have been if they were goose-stepping.

"What can we do for you, ma'am?" Sonny asked.

Sexy turned to me again and giggled. "They call me ma'am. I love that." Sexy looked at them. "At ease," she said with a dismissive wave of her foot.

Sonny and Cher became slightly less tense.

"Clear your calendars," Sexy ordered.

"Yes, ma'am," Cher said.

The two unfolded their computers and started to type.

"For how long, ma'am?" Sonny asked, as his fingers slid over the flat keys.

"For a LONG time," Sexy said.

The two stopped typing and looked at Sexy. "Does ma'am have an especially sensitive case for us?"

"Nah, I'm just having Shannon kill you."

"Is ma'am unhappy with our work?"

"Nah, I'm just showing something to a friend."

"Very well," they both said.

I didn't like the way this conversation was going. I started to push Sexy's feet up off of me. She resisted and forced her foot down on me.

"Don't be impatient, Zach," Sexy ordered. "This is a demo."

Before I had a chance to react, Shannon inhaled then exhaled on Sonny and Cher. The two held their throats, went stiff, and then fell over backward.

I pushed Sexy's legs off my lap, this time with much more force. I sent her spinning in her chair.

"Hey, what gives?" Sexy yelped as I stood.

"Sexy, I didn't think you were callous enough to casually kill people."

"Zach, I came from the music industry—of course I'm callous," Sexy said. She pressed another button on her desk.

I rushed to the side of the fallen lawyers. Sure they were lawyers, but even lawyers don't deserve to die like that. I bent down and checked Cher's carotid artery for a pulse. Nothing.

Two little scooterbots came out the same hidden door the lawyers did. The two bots slid up to Sonny and Cher and injected them in the neck.

"But even I wouldn't kill my own lawyers for fun," she said, pointing down to the fallen lawyers.

I checked again for Cher's pulse, and this time it was there. I looked up at Sexy.

"Just trying to prove a couple of points," she said. "I know you met with Santana."

"How—"

She stopped me with a wave. "I have my sources. I just want to warn you that you don't know what you are getting into."

"Yeah, that seems to be the general consensus," I said.

"The thing is, Zach, you are dealing with two very crazy factions. And believe me, Zach, I know crazy!"

She didn't have to convince me on that one.

"Can you elaborate?"

"Zach, I'm a politician now. Of course I can elaborate. Santana has many enemies on the World Council."

"Why?"

"Well, to me it's her poor taste in color coordination, but the why isn't important. What *is* important is that you understand these people are extremely powerful and well connected. They also command the loyalties of many other fanatical people. Look at how I could have had my own lawyers killed so easily, and how they were willing to die on my command."

I had to admit, Sexy had a point.

"Believe me, Zach, I'm not nearly has hardcore as some of the World Council members."

"What's the other faction?"

"Santana herself," Sexy said. She pointed to Shannon. "You've seen how easily she killed those lawyers. Well, Shannon and Santana share some DNA."

Great. Now I know that not only are elves prone to go crazy, but so is Santana herself.

"That's why the World Council outlawed mutating and cloning humans. There is so much about the process we still don't understand. We really shouldn't tamper with things we don't understand."

Sexy looked at her watch. "Wow. Look at the time. I've already given you much more than you were allocated. Thanks for the foot rub. I'll have Shannon escort you to the door."

Shannon got up and started walking me across the room. "Shannon, remember don't kill him," Sexy called out.

9

As I drove to my house I was thinking that this was the kind of case that I really hated. The kind where the more information I gathered, the bigger and more confusing the case got. My first instinct on these types of cases is to stop gathering information. My second instinct is always to ignore my first instinct. Hardly any good can come out of ignoring information. The trick was to sift through the mass of information and find the important keys to the crime. Every crime has two or three keys, that if used in the right order will break the case open. The trick was in the sifting, but that's where HARV came in.

HARV was running background checks on all the humans currently visiting the North Pole. The murders of the elves occurred shortly after they arrived. I was certain that wasn't a coincidence. One or more of those people were involved, but who and why were the keys.

I knew big business wouldn't shed a tear if the Holiday suddenly ceased to exist. I knew a certain faction of the World Council wasn't happy with the way Santana was running things. I suspected that elves had the potential to snap and totally lose it. I had learned that there is a fanatical group called the Santana Stinks Society that thinks Santana is an abomination and would use any means necessary to stop her. Like I said, the more I learned, the more confusing things got.

"Have you got the data on the Pole visitors yet?" I asked.

HARV didn't say anything, which was very uncharacteristic of him.

"Are you in there?" I said, tapping gently on my car's computer screen.

HARV face appeared on the screen. "Keep both hands on the wheel in a ten and two position while driving. New studies have shown the ten and two position is the safest."

Whenever HARV didn't have the answers he wanted to give me, he would give me other information he deemed essential. It wasn't significant to the case, but HARV has this need to be informative. HARV was loathe to admit his need to be needed. I found it rather quaint—at least as quaint as a supercomputer can be.

"I take it the elves haven't given you the information we requested."

HARV shook his head on the screen. His brow furrowed, "I only asked again a few nanos ago."

"Ah, why?"

"I was testing their computer defenses to see if I could break in."

"I take it you couldn't."

"I need more time. The elves are quite thorough with their computer defenses. They have firewalls, surrounded by moats, surrounded by e-razor-wire, surrounded by more firewalls, surrounded by lead, surrounded by—"

"I get the point, HARV."

"I'm only scratching the surface with that explanation."

"Yes, but you're pushing the limits of my patience. Just remind them how important that information is to the case."

"I have. They said they are compiling it now and will get back to me before the evening is over."

"Now that wasn't so hard, was it?"

HARV shuddered on the screen. "Actually, it was excruciating! But I am learning their defenses."

I drove through the neat, clean suburban streets to my house. Yes, I live in the suburbs. I know it goes against the code of the down-and-out PI. I should be sleeping in my office or at best living out of a cheap hotel room. But just because my career choice made me a nosy tough guy doesn't mean I can't live comfortably. I like the burbs.

After my last house got destroyed by a TV network try-ing to kill me (long story), they paid me just enough money so I was able to purchase a nice house away from the hustle and bustle of the city. Of course, the minute I moved into the neighborhood, every house around mine went on the market. But that's not my fault.

I placed my hand on the DNA lock on my front door, and it popped open. The first thing I noticed was a suitcase by the doorway. It appeared that this time Electra wasn't even going to let me explain myself before leaving.

I should elaborate. I love Electra more than anything else in this world. (Even though she insists I love my 1986 Mets poster and Mustang more.) Electra is beautiful through and through, and a caring, intelligent woman with a heart as big as the moon. (Yes, the fact that she is with me is an enigma to pretty much everybody.)

The thing is, Electra doesn't like my job. She doesn't like the constant danger and having to patch me up. She isn't fond of the weird hours I have to put in. The part she really despises is the strange fact that all my biggest cases always involve beautiful women. It's my lot in life, and I readily accept it. Electra, not so much. Usually, though, she waits for me to personally tell her about the case before she storms out on me.

I headed up the stairs and found Electra hurriedly running a brush through her long, dark hair.

She heard me come in and turned toward the door.

"Oh, hi," she said quickly.

Being a trained PI, I knew she was in a hurry but she didn't seem angry. That meant either she wasn't mad at me or she was so mad at me her anger had wrapped around and turned into calmness—a calmness that could explode at any nano in a fit of Latina fury.

"Ah, hi," I said. "What have I done this time?"

She smiled. I started to breathe again. "For once, Zach, it's not you."

"Oh?"

"Santana called me right when I got home and explained the situation."

"Oh?"

"I think it's a good cause." She paused for nano. "It is a little scary that she knew my exact schedule."

"It's her job to know those things, I guess."

"So, the suitcase is packed because you are going? Didn't Santana tell you no personal belongings at the Pole?"

"No and sí."

"Electra, mi amor, you have me confused."

She gave me a sexy smile. "Now you know what it's like living with you," she said. "Constant confusion."

I wasn't about to argue that point with her. I pleaded with my eyes for her to please fill me in.

"I WAS going," Electra said. "Really, I was."

"But . . ."

"But, a few minutes after Santana called I got another call from a conference in New New York. One of their keynote participants got sick at the last moment and had to cancel. They want me to replace her and demonstrate my techniques for instant same-host stem revertation and implantation."

"Revertation isn't a word," HARV said.

"It's patent pending," Electra corrected.

"Oh," HARV said.

"So, it will be the threepeat of medical science."

"Huh?" they both said.

"So, you're not going to the Pole with me," I said.

"Zach, this is my chance to teach my techniques to hundreds of others. Plus, it will be great PR for my clinic."

This was one of those rare moments where I truly didn't know what to say. For one, I was stunned that Electra had actually wanted to go to the Pole. I was also a little hurt that she would put her career ahead of our vacation. Then I remembered that it wasn't really a vacation. It was my career—we were going to investigate dead elves. Still, my male ego was a little bruised.

"We all save the world in our own way," Electra said with a subtle but nevertheless quite noticeable raised eyebrow.

"You probably would have cramped my style, anyhow," I said with a playful shrug.

Electra punched me in the arm equally playfully. She gave me a hug. "I'm sure you can save the world as we know it without me."

"I *am* very good at what I do," I said.

"And modest, too," HARV said, pointing a finger down his throat.

"Santana sent me the medical records on the dead elves," she said.

"She did?" HARV said.

I turned to HARV. "See what happens if you ask nicely?"

"What did you learn, hon?"

"I learned that those elves are more vindictive than they appear," HARV said.

I glared at HARV. "I was talking to Electra."

Electra grinned. "I didn't learn much from the squished elf's lab work. Squished is squished. But the other elf, the one that was poisoned—I learned she was definitely poisoned."

"So, now we know for sure it was a murder. I didn't think there was much doubt about that." I already knew it was a murder, but I wanted to make Electra feel better for helping.

"I also learned that the poisoned elf only had about a year to live."

Now this was a surprise. I assumed the elves had long life expectancies.

"Are you sure?" I asked.

She nodded her head. "I'm no expert, but the elf was twenty-one years old, and only had a year left to live."

"HARV, where can we find Twoa?"

"At this time she is always patrolling the Trump Hundredth Known Universe Bank."

"Tell her I need to chat with her."

"She doesn't take calls when on patrol."

"In that case . . ." I grabbed my hat and coat and headed out the door. I stopped halfway through the doorway, backed in a bit, and planted a big wet kiss on Electra.

"Gracias, mi amor," I said.

"Anytime."

"Travel safely," I said.

"I don't think I'm the one I have to worry about," she said.

10

Just as HARV said, I found Twoa patrolling the Trump 100th Known Universe Bank. The bank wasn't much, just a collection of HolographicATMs on the first floor of a business complex.

That didn't stop Twoa from marching up and down across the machines like a well-built, spandex-clad, Nazi tin soldier.

The nano I walked in the building, Twoa stopped her patrolling. She turned toward me and smiled.

"Does my supersight, -hearing, and -sense of smell deceive me? Or is that my fellow champion of justice, Zachary Nixon Johnson? Twice in one day?"

I opened up my arms to her.

"None other," I said.

Twoa rushed over to me. She lifted me up and gave me a super-powered bear hug. Twoa was always an emotional rollercoaster. If it didn't hurt so much, I might have found it arousing.

"To what do I owe the honor?"

She dropped me to the ground. It was nice to be able to breathe again.

"Twoa, I need your help."

Her smile widened. She smashed her fist into her open hand. The sound was near deafening. "What evildoer do you want me to smash? Do you need me to rush to the Pole with you to battle injustice?"

I loosened my collar a tad. "Actually, no."

"Smash some battlebots?"

"Ah, no."

"No smashing?" she said. Her eyes sunk. Her eyes lit up. She pointed behind me.

I turned to see two mean-looking men and a meaner-looking woman walking into the bank. They were all mohawk-wearing, leather-clad, biker types.

"Those guys are trouble," she said.

"Known bank robbers?"

"No, known unemployed actors."

Twoa's HV network broadcasts her "exciting crime-fighting adventures" on a reality HV show called *Justice Babe: The Adventures of a Well-Built Superhero*. A typical show consists of Twoa stopping some crime and then pummeling any bad guy or gal with the nerve to resist her. It was a huge hit with teen boys, criminals, and wannabe actors. For the viewers, the appeal was easy to see: Twoa was a pro wrestler for the 2060s. For the criminals, it also made sense: if you are going to get caught, you might as well be caught and pummeled on worldwide HV. Many of them said it was the best time they ever had. For actors, the appeal was even more obvious: cheap exposure. Sure enough, the three of them were heading right for us.

"I'll take the two men, you take the woman," Twoa whispered to me.

I didn't really want to play into Twoa's fantasy life, but I knew if I didn't, she wouldn't talk. So I had to go along.

I popped my gun into my hand.

"I'll end this quickly," I said, as I aimed my gun at the three.

They saw my gun and immediately stopped their approach.

Twoa was confused. She didn't know why the biker bunch had stopped. She noticed my gun. She shook her head.

"Superheroes don't use no stinking guns!" she said.

"Perhaps, but I'm not a superhero. I'm just an above-average hero," I said.

"Oh, please!" HARV said inside my head.

Twoa grabbed the gun from my hand. She flung it across the room. "There! Now it will be a fair fight!"

That's easy for the invulnerable one to say, I thought.

The three actor thugs reached into their leather vests. They pulled out laser knives and activated them.

I pointed at them. "How come they get to use weapons?"

"They're bad guys, Zach. They don't play by the rules. That's what makes them bad guys!"

Without warning, Twoa moved forward at superspeed. She was behind the two biker guys before they noticed.

She tapped them both on the shoulders.

They turned.

Twoa moved forward quickly and clotheslined them both in the head. They crashed backward to the ground. They weren't just out cold—they were cryogenic.

Twoa blew on her nails. "That was too easy," she said.

Meanwhile, I wasn't having it quite as easy. The biker chick had rushed toward me, slashing her laser knife wildly. I was able to duck under her attack every time. I wasn't sure if I was actually that good or if she was missing me on purpose.

"I don't really want to fight you!" she shouted as she lunged forward.

"Great, because I have no interest in fighting you," I said as I sidestepped her lunge. She might have been in great shape, but she was an actress. She didn't have the experience I had when it came to fighting. I was easily able to anticipate and fend off her moves. One good thing about being the universe's punching bag—you get good at surviving fights. I call it survival by necessity.

"Unfortunately, I have to get rid of you to face Twoa!" she said, being persistent if nothing else.

I could dodge a hundred of her attacks, but it would only take one lucky hit for her to win. I had to end this fast, but I didn't want to hurt her.

"HARV," I thought. "I need to put her out without hurting her. How about doing the shock trick?"

"It's not a trick," HARV protested. "I just magnify and project the combined electric energy of our interface and your body. The TCA cycle creates—"

"I don't need the biology lesson. I just need to stop this chick."

"I'm ready when you are. Just make good contact with her chest."

I smiled. Now that was something I could handle.

She lunged at me again with her right arm. I sidestepped her and grabbed her attacking arm with my left hand. I placed my right hand on her chest.

"Now!" I shouted in my head.

I felt a tingle. The biker chick felt a jolt. Her body jerked forward. She dropped her knife and fell over backward. She shook for a minute. The shaking stopped. Her eyes rolled to the back of her head, and then closed.

"That worked," I said.

Twoa walked over to me smiling. She pulled a small computer from a pocket in her spandex. The spandex was so tight, I had no idea how she managed to get the paper-thin computer in there.

She unfolded the computer and handed it to me.

"I need your retina print on this release form."

"Release form?"

"In case I use any footage of you on my show," she said. "My lawyers insisted that a release form is far more legal than turning guest stars into mindless zombies."

I took the computer and pressed my eye to the proper part of the screen. "Lawyers are no fun," I said.

"True," she agreed. Twoa pointed to my gun across the room. It popped up into the air and floated back into my hand. "See, I told you that you don't need any messy guns," she said.

"I wasn't planning on shooting them. Just scaring them," I noted.

Twoa shrugged. "Where's the fun in that?" She paused for a nano. "Don't you live for pummeling bad guys?" she asked. Her face took on a quality that could only be described as orgasmic.

I decided I needed to change the subject.

"Now, about the reason I came here," I said. "I need more info on your science project."

Twoa's eyes open wide. "What science project?"

"The elves," I said.

"Oh, that science project," she said.

"Why didn't you tell me the elves are built to live twenty-two years?"

Twoa shook her head. "I didn't know that."

"You didn't know?"

"Zach, I was thirteen and a half when I designed them. Excuse me if they have one or two tiny design flaws. I bet you weren't genetically engineering elves when you were a teen."

I patted her on the shoulder. "No need to get defensive, Twoa. I'm just trying to wrap my mind around this."

"Twoa, is it possible your elf design could have been altered?" HARV asked from my communicator.

Twoa raised an eyebrow and floated off the ground. "Why would anybody want to do that?"

"I'll look for the motive later, but for now I just need to know if it's possible."

Twoa nodded. "I'd say that's far more likely than me making a mistake." She thought for a moment. "Can I see the data?"

"Show it to her, HARV."

Formula after formula starting projecting and scrolling from my wrist communicator. To my brain it might as well been ancient Greek, but Twoa was watching it and reading it intently. In fact, I had never seen Twoa pay such close attention to anything.

"Hmmm," she said. "This is interesting."

"I concur," HARV said.

"What?"

"Nothing you'd understand," Twoa and HARV said in unison. They gave each other high fives. Yep, a day is never complete until both a supercomputer and a superhero have looked down on you.

"So, what have you two learned?" I asked.

"That you're annoying," HARV said.

Twoa grinned. They once again exchanged high fives.

"Maybe you two should get a room?" I said.

Twoa raised an eyebrow. "Ah, if only we could."

HARV raised a holographic finger. "You know, in the past . . ."

"Let's stick to the point here, people—um, superhuman and hologram."

"Superhologram," HARV corrected.

"Whatever, what's the poop?"

Now they both looked at me like I was speaking ancient Greek. Actually, they both could probably read ancient Greek. They looked at me like I was babbling gibberish.

"What did you learn?" I prompted again.

"My design has been altered," Twoa said. "The telomere sequences have been cut, drastically reducing their life expectancy."

"Are you sure?"

"Yes, probably."

I shook my head. "So, what you two super-geniuses are telling me is that it's a definite maybe?"

Twoa started to say something but HARV held up a holographic hand, stopping her. He turned to her. "I deal with Zach more, let me handle this." HARV turned to me. "The elves receptor cells have also been altered."

I shrugged. "So?"

"They've been modified to accept some sort of enzyme. We're guessing it's a kind of telomerase booster that if ingested would allow the elves to live longer."

I let what they had just told me sink in for a nano. "So, the elves are being drugged to stay alive?"

HARV and Twoa both nodded.

"He's not as slow as you make him out to be," Twoa told HARV.

"It's from hanging out with me," HARV said.

11

I rushed back to my house with more questions than I had when I left. Never a good sign. I tossed open the door.

"HARV, contact Santana for me. I need some answers from her."

"That won't be necessary," HARV said.

I shook my head. "HARV, how many times do I have to tell you this? I'm the boss. When I give you an order, you're suppose to follow it."

HARV pointed to my living room wall computer screen. Santana's image filled the screen.

"Zach, I've been waiting to talk to you," she said.

"Likewise," I said.

"I've been doing some thinking," she said.

"Likewise," I said.

"Wow, nice to see you impressing the client with witty banter," HARV said inside my head.

"Let me hear what you've been thinking about," Santana said.

I took a moment to collect my thoughts. I wanted to do this logically without tipping my hand too much. "I met with Twoa Thompson."

Santana smiled. "How is the dear girl?"

"She's, well, Twoa."

Santana's smile widened. "Yes, that sums her up nicely. I really appreciate the groundwork she did for us back when we were getting started." Santana looked at me. We locked eyes (well, at least as much as you can lock eyes over a screen). "What's bothering you, Zach?" she asked.

"Why'd you alter the elves?" I asked, not even bothering to consider how strange that statement was.

Santana took a step back from the screen. She patted herself on her chest as she exhaled. She smiled. "That's why I picked you for this job, Zach. You don't beat around the bush."

"Actually, Zach usually stomps the bush into the ground," HARV said.

I glared at HARV. He shrugged. "I find that to be one of your more endearing traits," he said.

I decided to ignore HARV and how he's acting more and more like me. I needed to concentrate on Santana. "Are you going to answer the question?"

"Of course, Zach. It was the elves' idea to alter themselves. They are quite clever you know."

"They altered themselves?"

"They thought it would help them with the S and M," Santana said.

"S and M?"

Santana grinned. "Zach, bring your mind up a few levels. S and M stands for Stimulation and Motivation."

"Oh, I knew that."

Santana continued. "The elves figured if they simply lived for one hundred and fifty years that after a while they might become lazy. That's why they altered themselves. They decided that once a year they each must be injected with an enzyme we lovingly call ELF."

"The elves must take ELF?"

"It means Elf Life Formula. I control the supply. If any elf doesn't keep doing a bang-up job, they won't get their yearly shot. They will die within days."

I've heard a lot of weird stuff in my day, but this was right near the top. This might have been the Mt. Everest of weirdness. Elves alone would have been strange enough. Elves working at the Pole pushes the strangeness up a notch. Elves working at the Pole who intentionally make themselves reliant on a drug to live in order to force themselves out of complacency—that's just beyond weird.

"Wow," HARV said. "Zach speechless is something you don't see very often."

"I just can't believe what I'm hearing . . ." I said.

Santana gave me her most disarming smile. "Zach, I've never withheld ELF from any elf. I doubt I will ever have to, but the businesswoman inbred in me likes the idea that I have a motivational tool at my disposal if the need arises."

"I still say it's weird."

"The universe is a strange and wonderful place, Zach. Who are we to question it?"

I took a deep breath. What she said made sense in its own demented way.

"Fine," I said. "Now what did you want to talk to me about?"

"I wanted to talk to you about you," she said.

"Santana, have you been hanging around with HARV? That sounds like something he would say."

"I'm talking about your reputation. I've been following the news vids. You do create a stir wherever you go."

"It's a gift," I said.

"Yes, well, we have enough gifts at the Pole. We don't need any more."

I took a step back. I wasn't sure I liked where this conversation was going. I had already taken my share of licks for this job. Maybe that would have made a sane man want out of it, but I was determined to see it through.

"I hope you don't want me off the job," I said.

She shook her head. "I want you on the job."

"Good."

"Just not as you . . ."

"What?"

"Now that Electra won't be there, there is no way anybody will believe you're there for fun. I want you to come incognito. You like wearing disguises don't you?"

"As long as they're manly, I can handle it. But why?"

"Zach, I like you. I know you get the job done. But you have to admit your reputation often precedes you. If you suddenly show up as yourself at the Pole, some people will be leery. Other people will be scared."

Santana was beating around the bush, but I knew she was onto something. When I'm on a case, there are so many attempts made on my life that some restaurants refuse to let me in. There's one place that even has a sign that reads: No Shirt, No Shoes, or if your name is Zach Johnson, No Service.

"I can bring a holo-disguise, if you like," I offered.

"I have that and your arrival and your backstory all covered," Santana said.

Santana looked past me to HARV. "I'm locking onto your signal now," she said.

"Very good," HARV said with a nod.

"What's going on?" I asked.

HARV held up a hand. "Wait for it," he urged.

I did.

He pointed to a spot by his feet. I looked down and sure enough the area directly in front of his feet started to glow. It was a strange, unnatural glow, not the glow of a hologram, but the glow of a transport beam. The glow transformed from a nondescript, fractal-like blob to an outline of a circle. The circle started to form into a transparent belt. The belt then become less and less transparent until it became a solid object. The entire process took longer to describe than to occur.

I pointed to the belt.

"Did what I think just happened, happen?" I asked.

"Yes," Santana said.

"If you think you just saw an item teleported to a specific spot in time and space without a receiving pad or another teleportation device, then yes," HARV said. HARV was never big on simple answers.

Until earlier today, I was under the impression that teleportation was only possible between very special teleporting transmitters and receivers. And until this morning, I had also been under the impression that living organics could only be transmitted between even more specific transporters. Now something had been teleported to a place in my home without a receiver and it came from a place so past ripping edge, you couldn't even see ripping edge from there.

I walked over, bent down, and picked it up. I was half expecting and half hoping it wouldn't be a solid object. It felt true and strong in my hands. I showed the belt to Santana. I recognized this belt, as it was remarkably similar to the portable teleporting device Santana had used earlier.

"Impressive," I said. "Teleporting a teleporting device to me."

Santana wasn't smiling; she was beaming. "You can see my elves have made remarkable progress in the field of teleportation. When activated, that device will beam you directly to the Pole. We've programmed it to bring you to a reception room where my elves will greet you and prepare you. This way nobody will know you are at the Pole."

"You just teleported that device to my bedroom. I don't have a receiver in my bedroom."

Santana grinned. "We have made some progress in teleporting nonorganic matter to nonspecific spots. Like I said, it comes with the territory."

I decided not to push it further. At least for now.

"Once I'm on the grounds, though, people will know it's me unless you let HARV—"

She shook her head and cut me off. "Once you are here, my elves will give you a special holo-disguise and a cover."

"A cover?"

The image of Santana was replaced by a man with light skin, neatly cut short blond hair, and blue eyes. He looked nothing like me. "You will look like this," Santana said. "Your name will be Bart Starr, with two *r*s, three counting the one in Bart."

"Nice reference," I said.

"I thought you'd appreciate it," Santana said.

HARV had a blank look on his face.

"It's a spin on an old comic strip character's name," I told him.

"Oh, I knew that," HARV said.

I turned back to Santana. "I usually use the name Jay Jackson as my alias."

"Yes, that's why we picked a name for you. You'll be a blogger on special assignment reporting on how way fun it is at the Pole."

I had to give Santana credit, she was quite good at this. With that cover nobody would grow suspicious of my asking questions. After all, everybody knows bloggers are the nosiest reporters around.

"Is that okay?" Santana said.

"I'll make it work," I told her.

HARV cleared his throat behind me. It was a not so subtle hint for me to hit Santana up for the info we needed.

"My computer asked your elves about background information on your guests."

Santana turned her head and mumbled something to somebody behind her. She turned back to me.

"The information is downloading now."

"Thanks," I said.

"Can I be of further assistance?" she asked.

"I'm cool," I said.

She looked at me.

"That's Zach's quaint way of saying 'we've got what we need for now,' " HARV said.

"Oh, okay. See you tomorrow, Zach."

The screen went blank. I turned to HARV. "Do you have the data?"

"Yes, I do."

"Good, I could use a second pair of human eyes. Call Carol and see if she can come over and lend a brain."

"No need," HARV said.

There was a knock on door.

"Carol?" I asked.

"Carol," he said.

12

I walked over and opened the door. Sure enough, Carol was standing there holding Chinese take-out in her hand. Sometimes it really pays to have an assistant who's a class I psi.

Carol and I sat down on my real simulated leather couch as HARV scrolled the Pole's visitors onto the screen for us. The first to appear was a tall Asian woman with more rippling muscles than a steroid convention. She was very familiar to me. It was mutant pro wrestler Nova Powers. I had met Nova a few years ago when I was working on the BB Star case. Nova is a striking woman (in more ways than one) who has a thing for geeks. She was the ex-lover of a mad scientist turned poet. I had tangled with her in the wrestling ring. She only toyed with me, and I still had to cheat to get out of there in one piece. Now she looked even more pumped and bulked up than the last time we met. Usually I don't find women with bigger arms than mine attractive, but the look worked for her.

"Nova Powers," I said.

HARV smiled. "Very good, Zach. Glad you remember."

"I never forget a woman that tosses me around."

"There have been so many that's hard to believe."

"Ha ha, funny computer."

"Speaking of funny," HARV said. "I told my e-shrink I keep cognizing I'm ugly, so he told me to lay on the couch—facedown!" HARV accented the joke with a "ba da bum!"

I looked at him. Carol looked at me. She was too young to have any idea who HARV had stolen that joke from.

"Long story," I said.

"He's been connected to your brain too long," Carol said.

Okay, maybe it wasn't such a long story. I turned my attention back to Nova. My run-in with Nova had been brief. She was emotional and hot tempered (like a Twoa lite) but she didn't strike me as an elf killer. Unless, of course, an elf got in the way of her and her man. If she wanted to off an elf, I doubt she would poison it or drop a giant bag of toys on it. Love may make people do strange things but even then they usually stay in character.

"Who else is there?" I asked HARV.

"Don't you want any more background info on Nova? See what she's been up to for the last couple of years, besides adding fifteen kilos of pure raw muscle?"

"Not really, no."

HARV whirled for a few nanos. He wasn't ready to take no for an answer. "Zach, she's a mutant pro wrestler. She beats people up on a daily basis."

I looked at Carol looking at Nova. "Does she look like a killer of elves to you?"

"I don't really like the way she looks," Carol said. "For my taste she was more attractive when there was less of her."

"Not the question," I said.

Carol studied the picture of Nova intently, she shook her head. "If a man pissed her off, I could see her ripping his head off and shoving it up his behind. But an elf? No."

That was good enough for me. Even if Carol wasn't a psi, I would have trusted her woman's intuition on that one. I pointed to screen. "Next."

The picture of a very distinguished and proud-looking gray-haired woman filled the screen. She looked like she could be anybody's young, hip grandma. Not just any grandma but a beautiful one who spent a good deal of time in the gym. I knew this woman—DOS the entire world knew this woman. She was Senior World Council Member Stormy Weathers. The most trusted politician in history, or at least that's what her press release says.

"What's Councilwoman Weathers doing at the Pole?" I asked.

"Probably freezing her butt off," Carol said.

"Oh, that's good. Can I use it?" HARV asked.

"I'm sure one of you will," Carol said.

"Ah, back to the case," I said.

"It's her biannual visit," HARV said. "She takes four vacations a year, and every other vacation she goes to the Pole. You should know that! It's in all the vids," HARV scolded.

HARV was right, I should have known that. These days we get so inundated with what this HV star or bigwig is up to and what that pop starlet or fat cat is dressing like, I tend to turn it all off in my brain.

"I bet you don't even know her voting record!" HARV said.

"No, I don't," I said. I was secure in knowing that 99.999 percent of the population didn't know her voting record either. I started to think out loud. "Sexy did say the Pole had enemies on the WC. Maybe she was hinting at Weathers."

HARV shook his head. "She hates the spot she vacations every year?"

"Maybe it's like New Vegas. You kind of love to hate the place."

"What could the councilwoman achieve from trouble at the Pole?" Carol asked.

That was what we needed to find out. What, if anything, Weathers might gain.

"Where's she from originally?" I asked.

"New Canada," both HARV and Carol answered.

"Everybody knows that," Carol said. "Gee, Zach. Don't you pay any attention to politics?"

HARV sighed. "I try, but he never listens to me. Of course, if Ms. Weathers was a pitcher for the Mets, he'd know her lifetime ERA."

"I have my priorities," I said. I pointed to my head. "I only have so much storage space up here."

HARV sighed again. "Yes, I am painfully aware of your numerous limitations."

"Me, too," Carol said.

"Yes, well, I'm in his brain," HARV told her.

Carol glared at him. If he was human, that glare alone would have stopped him in his tracks. "I pick up his stray thoughts. He's not very good at shielding them."

HARV put his hands on hips and stuck his chest out. He

was aching for a fight. He pointed a finger at Carol. "Yes, well—"

I positioned myself between them. "Guys, I have enough faults for each of you."

They both nodded in agreement.

"True."

"Amen to that."

"Let's stick to the case, okay? I need you two."

"Right," they both said.

"My point is that if Weathers goes to the Pole twice a year, she must know it pretty well. Plus, she's connected. She might be able to cause some trouble there."

Now HARV focused his anger on me. His hands went back on his hips. "Why do you insist on thinking a respected councilwoman would have anything to do with this?"

"Just keeping my options open, HARV."

For a nano or three I didn't understand why HARV was so defensive about Ms. Weathers. It wasn't like HARV to defend a human (besides Randy) this strongly. Then I remembered that Weathers backed the Sentient Machines Rights Act. That explained why HARV was a registered member of her e-constituency.

HARV crossed his arms and glared at me. "I'm checking her past records now."

"I appreciate that," I told him.

"I am a professional," HARV insisted.

"Yes, I know," I said. I turned my head and rolled my eyes so Carol could see. Carol smiled. HARV frowned.

"I saw that!" he said. I forgot HARV was connected to every security camera in the house. "Ms. Weathers has never even had a parking ticket," HARV said proudly. "Even her accident wasn't her fault."

The accident the councilwoman was in about ten years ago was the stuff of legend. A hover truck ran a stoplight and crashed into her hover. Her driver was killed, and conventional wisdom was that the councilwoman was lucky to be alive and that her nerve endings were charred so badly that even with limb replacement, she would be lucky if she ever walked again. Three years later she won the Mars Base Marathon, the toughest 10K in the solar system. The press called it a testament to her inner strength. All I know is that crash made her stronger and more popular than ever. It couldn't have worked out better for her if she had planned it.

"Face it, Zach. The woman is clean and as perfect as humanly possible," HARV said.

Carol nodded in agreement. "I took a class from her at university. She was incredible. I've never encountered anybody so pure."

My first reaction was that nobody is perfectly clean. Even the best of us humans mess up a fair share of the time. If she was perfectly clean, then something was wrong. I decided not to push the issue for now. I'd check her out when I got to the Pole.

"The councilwoman doesn't travel with security?" I said.

"Not at the Pole. It is the safest and most secure place on Earth," HARV said. HARV's eyes flashed for a nano. That meant he was downloading something. "Santana does give her a panic button, so if anything happens she can summon guardbots to her in seconds," HARV said.

"Lovely. I've had such good luck with them." I took a nano to collect my thoughts. "Who else is up there?"

A picture of an older man with a neatly trimmed mustache and just the hint of a receding hairline popped up on the wall.

"That's Councilwoman Weathers' husband, Carl Weathers," I said.

"Very good, Zach," HARV said. "Though I'm certain you know that only because he used to be a quarterback for the NY Space Jets."

"Yes, but back then his name was Carl 'Laser Cannon' Carlson," I said. "So I still get some credit."

"He changed his name when he married the councilwoman," Carol said with a smile. "I always liked Councilwoman Weathers."

"As does the entire world," HARV added. "She's been voted the most likeable person on the planet three years running by *People, Pseudo-People, and Androids e-Mag*."

"What do we know about Carl Weathers, besides he changed his name and never played in a Super Duper Bowl?"

HARV started to blink his eyes rapidly. "Scanning every occurrence he's ever made in the news. His football career was uneventful. He had a lifetime record of seventeen and seventeen."

"What about business ventures?"

"He is part owner of a space salt mining company. That's it. He's pretty much defined as being Mr. Stormy Weathers."

I remember watching Weathers play football. He had a good arm but he was either stubborn or just not mentally quick. He would never look at his secondary receivers. I wasn't sure if he wasn't good at seeing his options or wasn't nimble enough to change plans midcourse. Whatever the case, he didn't seem like the type of guy who could pull off a murder at the Pole.

"Next," I said.

Pictures of two blue-skinned humans, one with blue hair and one with green hair, appeared on my screen. Their skin tone made it easy to recognize that there were MESSHs, Medically Enhanced Super Smart Humans. They were all the craze in the brave new world of the 2030s. The cloning regulations and modifying bans were lifted and the world went wild for a while, trying to usher in a braver, newer world.

MESSHs were created to be human thinking machines, meant to rival the best computers of the day. The experiment worked to a certain extent. MESSHs are the ultimate in geekdom. If it has something to do with technology, they can understand it and make it work. The problem is MESSHs have no idea how to interact with regular humans. In fact, most regular humans are repelled by them. These days all the MESSHs live on their own colony on Mars.

"MESSHs, huh?" I said to HARV.

"Gross," Carol said, as she looked at their pictures on the screen. "I'm glad human cloning is restricted again. We shouldn't be messing with stuff like that. Why do they wear thick glasses? Can't they have corrective surgery?"

HARV shook his head. "It's illegal for MESSHs to correct their eyesight. It's a flaw deliberately encoded into their DNA to ensure they don't feel too superior to regular humans. They make the best out of it by using the glasses as information interfaces."

"Who are they?" I asked HARV.

"Bim and Norp Smith of Mars Base-Delta. Bim has the blue hair and Norp the green."

I looked them over. If they combed their hair, trimmed about a half a centimeter off their noses, and did something about their complexion (the zits on top of blue skin really stood out), they might be halfway to sort of presentable.

"They care more about their brains than their looks," HARV said, apparently figuring out what I was thinking.

"Don't tell me you're reading my mind now, too," I said to HARV.

"I don't need to read your little mind when your face is broadcasting in technilocolor HV. After all these years, you humans still put way too much value on physical appearance."

"I'm betting they have the technology to make or re-program bots like the ones that attacked me earlier today."

HARV nodded. "You would win that bet."

"The question is, do they have a motive?" I said.

HARV shrugged. "Hatred of regular humans. You do treat them pretty crappy just because they don't look as good as you do."

"That could be a pretty good motive," I said. "I'll make sure I keep an extra close eye on them while I'm there."

Carol sat back on the couch and made a gagging motion with her finger. "I'm glad I'm not going on this job."

"Who else do we have?" I asked HARV.

Bim and Norp's images on the screen morphed into what appeared to be a family of four: a father, a mother, a son, and a daughter. The father had one hand on an electric pitchfork and the other on his son's shoulder. The mother had one hand on an electric shovel and the other on her daughter's shoulder. They were all blond-haired, blue-eyed, and smiling like they'd just won the lottery. They looked as sweet as the apple pie the daughter was holding in her arms. I didn't trust them.

"This is the Billings family," HARV said. "Bob Billings, his wife Betty, their son Billy, and their daughter Bobi. They are farmers from New Kansas."

"What's a farm-fresh family from New Kansas doing at the Pole?"

"Does it really matter?" HARV said.

"Of course it matters," I said.

HARV groaned then muttered. "I don't get no respect, no respect at all." He straightened himself up then looked me in the eye. "Billy won the Pole's quarterly e-essay contest, 'Why I want to win a trip to the Pole.'"

"Okay, that explains it." I looked over their picture on the screen. They were squeaky clean. It's been my experience that when somebody is so clean they shine, that means they've been polished by somebody else. Polished for a reason.

I turned to Carol. "Any vibes from them?"

Carol studied the screen. "The mom creeps me out. How can she work on the farm all day and still be so pale? And that eyeliner is so not her."

"Yeah, I get bad vibes from her too," I said. "HARV, check her out good."

HARV groaned again. "I'm glad you're basing your investigation on such empirical evidence."

"Just scan her, HARV."

"I have, Zach. She has never left New Kansas."

"Are you sure?"

"I've cross-referenced her ID card with every travel database in the world. She's never left New Kansas."

"Weird."

"None of them have ever left New Kansas. In fact, none of them have ever gone more than fifty kilometers from their home just outside of Lyons, New Kansas."

I thought about what HARV said. Ma and Pa Billings had to be in their mid-forties. Forty years of never leaving New Kansas? Sure it's a nice state, but you'd think they'd want at least one break from all the flat land and rows and rows of genetically-engineered wheat. It was almost unheard of, in today's world, for people to stay in their own little sector of the Earth.

HARV noticed that I was pondering this. "Don't give yourself a headache overanalyzing this," he told me. "They're just throwbacks to a simple time. Like you, but with denim overalls instead of a fedora and trench coat."

It was possible HARV was right, but they didn't seem right to me. I'd keep a close eye on them when I got to the Pole.

"Dig a little deeper, HARV. Make sure nothing has been covered over."

HARV sighed. "Fine. This will take time, because if something has been buried, it's been done by a pro."

"Who else do we have at the Pole?" I asked.

HARV smiled. "I saved the best for last. I'm giving you five to one odds that these two did it: Mary and Steve Eatman."

I looked at their picture on the screen. They didn't look very malicious, but then again, we've all heard the stories of the guy who looked like a Boy Space Scout who was hoarding bodies in his basement. They were both middle-aged. Mary was pleasant enough looking, but had a grumpy, I-just-ate-a-lemon-and-I'm-not-sure-if-I-like-it expression. Steve looked to be the mellower of the two. His bright eyes had a cooperative, groupie-type of alertness.

"Let me guess, she's a lawyer and he's an engineer," I said.

"Vingo," HARV said. "And guess where they work."

"I don't want to guess."

"Come on, Zach, guess. It's easy. It's almost too easy."

"ExShell?" I said.

HARV's smile was wide enough to fly a semi-hovertruck through. "Yes."

HARV was so sure of himself on this, I was surprised he didn't stamp "guilty" on their heads.

"It's so obvious. They've been planning this trip for five years. They made their reservations years ago. ExShell may have not built the bots but they donated the computer systems."

I glanced over at Carol. She was studying their photo.

"What do you think, chica?"

"Not sure I'd want to run into her in a dark alley. He looks likable enough, in a simple sort of way."

"Think they're the types to off a couple of elves?"

"Not really," Carol said.

"Zach, I've just dug up some interesting info. ExShell was designing guardbots just like HTech. They were very upset when the Pole went with HTech models. It—"

"It's doesn't matter," I interrupted. HARV always hated when I cut him off in mid phrase. That made doing it even sweeter. "It's not them."

"What? How can you say that?"

"I move my lips, words come out."

HARV dropped his arms to his side, fists curled. He was genuinely upset with me. "I mean, why would you say that?"

Apparently Randy's latest shielding made HARV a bit thicker than he was before. I had encouraged HARV to think more radically. Randy must have reined some of that free thought in. I didn't appreciate somebody else messing with HARV's mind. That was my domain.

I walked up to HARV and put my hand on the image of his shoulder. Yes, it was truly an empty gesture but it made us both feel a little better.

"Process it, HARV. They are too obvious. If anything they are patsies, fall guys, scapegoats . . ."

HARV stared at his feet for a nano or two. He sighed. He was doing that a lot lately. I chalked it up to another side effect of our connection. "I guess I haven't been running as many algorithms as I could." That was HARV's way of saying he had been closed minded, or more appropriately, close circuited. He looked up at me. "Just because they are the obvious choice doesn't mean they aren't the choice."

"True. If I were weighing the chances of it being them, I'd say two out of ten."

"So it is possible," HARV said.

"Yes, but we need to look at all the possibilities. This isn't a low-budget HV movie. Cases don't wrap up that easy."

"You may not be wrong," HARV said.

"Don't worry, HARV, once we get to the Pole, examine the scene, and talk to the people, we'll get a better idea of what the score is."

HARV nodded. "I'm sure." HARV's eyes lit up. "Speaking of getting there, I just received a message from Elf-1, Santana's head of organic security."

"Okay, what is it?"

"Elf-1 asked that you alert them before you teleport there tomorrow so they can lower the disruptor field."

I didn't like the sound of that at all. I wasn't a big fan of teleporting. I was even less of a fan of personal teleporting (though I didn't mind not having to wait in line at the porting center). But I really hated the idea of teleporting through a disruptor field. I didn't know what a disruptor field was, but it didn't sound like the type of thing I wanted anything to do with.

"A disruptor field?"

"They've just initiated it today as standard protocol. It will severely limit any unauthorized transmissions into or out of the Pole," HARV said.

"Oh." I wasn't sure if this meant the elves didn't trust me, didn't trust somebody else, or if it was some combination of both. I was sure that this would mean HARV and I would be on our own at the Pole. "No problem."

"I won't be able to access outside databases," HARV said. "Not without tipping them off or getting really sneaky."

"We can live with that."

"We won't be able to call in backup," HARV said.

"Don't worry," Carol reassured us. "If you're in trouble, I'll know."

I felt a little better and a little scared knowing that.

"I suppose that means ordering pizza is out?" I said.

"I'm not even going to dignify that with a response," HARV said.

HARV and I were going to have our work cut out for us. I was quite positive it wasn't anything we couldn't handle.

Carol stood up from the couch. "It's getting late. I better get going. Unless you need something else from me."

I shook my head no. "We'll be fine." I gave her a kiss on the cheek. "Thanks for everything, chica."

She gave me a little peck on the cheek. "Don't mention it, Tío. If you need help, just think real hard." She smiled and left.

13

The night passed without incident. HARV said this was because when I was sleeping it was easier for him to keep watch over me and I was less likely to offend anybody. I couldn't argue with his logic.

At 0600 alarms went off on my wallscreens and in my head, jolting me out of bed. Apparently HARV was anxious to get started.

"I'm up! I'm up!" I said. I sat up before HARV figured out a way to launch me off the bed. I rolled out of bed.

I turned to HARV, who was standing by my closet. I noticed that he seemed to be inventorying my wardrobe.

"What are you doing?" I asked.

"Finding you something suitable to wear to the Pole today."

"Once I get there they're going to make me wear some sort of uniform," I said.

"It's an elf suit," HARV said, not letting me even pretend otherwise. "There's no reason you can't look good until you get there."

I walked over to the closet. "I look good in whatever I wear."

"Sure, you do," HARV snickered. Let me tell you, being snickered at by a supercomputer is kind of annoying.

I reached into the closet and pulled out a nice off-white suit. I blew some dust off it and showed it to HARV.

HARV closed his eyes, lowered his head, and pinched his nose, all the while shaking his head. I knew the pose well, as it was one I often took with him.

"What?" I said.

"Zach, Zach, Zach. You can't wear white to the Pole."

"Why not? Polar bears do."

HARV rolled his eyes. "You're not a polar bear. And for that matter, polar bears aren't really white. The fur that covers them is transparent so they reflect the light, making them appear white."

I shook my head. "I don't have a lot of choices. I only own five suits."

"Wear the black one," HARV insisted.

"But then people might think I'm a penguin."

"Penguins only reside at the South Pole. You'll be fine, Zach. Trust me."

I decided to humor HARV at least temporarily. Though he would never admit it, he needed to feel needed. I could have sworn his dependence grew whenever he was wired to my brain. I pulled the suit off the rack.

"Fine. I'll try it on after a quick shower," I said.

"Very good. I'll meet you down in the breakfast area," he said.

I thought about saying something, but decided against it. Instead, I thanked my lucky stars that HARV was going to give me some privacy and didn't want to supervise my shower to make sure I was washing behind my ears.

When I got into the bathroom, I gave myself a quick glance in the wall's reflective screen. I wasn't thrilled at what I saw. I swore I was getting older by the nano, which I guess I was. The thing is, it looked like I was aging much faster than I should have been.

My once jet-black hair now had wisps of hair that couldn't be called black. To make matters worse, either my forehead was growing or my hairline was shrinking. I choose to go with the former as it made me feel better. I still had my strong Roman nose, but now it was more bent than it was when I was younger. I decided to consider each bend and bump as a sort of reward, an organic medal if you wish. A memento from each scrape I was in and survived and learned from. I was proud of the fact that I had all my original teeth and that my jaw had never been broken. I guess my jaw was as strong as it looked.

When I came to the breakfast table, HARV was waiting for me. He was "reading" an old-fashioned newspaper while sipping a cup of holo-coffee. It was kind of quaint and surreal at the same time. HARV looked up from his holo-paper. He frowned when he saw I was wearing a pair of casual brown pants, a Mets cap, and carrying my fedora in my hand. HARV shook his head.

"You couldn't wear what I suggested?"

"I could. I just choose not to," I said. "I tried it on, it was too . . . constricting." HARV should know by now I'm not a suit person. I'm pretty sure he was hoping if he could get me in one that would change.

A cookbot rolled up to the table. I grabbed a pancake and a couple of pieces of soy bacon from the bot's griddle top. I rolled the bacon into the pancake and smiled.

"Thanks a lot, bot," I said.

HARV pointed to the scrambled eggs on the bot's griddle. "Those eggs are fortified with vitamins, A, B, B12, C, D, E, and K, plus many helpful amino acids. You should have some of them."

"You make them sound so tempting," I said.

HARV motioned to the bot with his head. A serving arm popped out of the bot's side. One serving arm held a plate. The bot put the plate on the table next to me. The other arm scooped out a generous portion of eggs and then plopped them on my plate.

HARV pointed to the food. "And use your fork and knife."

I looked at the little cookbot.

"Whose side are you on, anyhow?"

The bot made a faint whimpering noise, then rolled off.

"The bot is on the right side. Mine," HARV said. "I found something when you were in the shower. When their farm was having trouble making ends meet, Pa Billings took a job at UltraMegaHyperMart."

"So?" I said.

UltraMegaHyperMart is such a huge multipurpose chain that they have more employees than many countries have citizens. They have so many stores that there's not a city in the world (beside Oakland) without at least three of them. There's an UltraMegaHyperMart every few blocks in every major city, and some of their stores are so big they take up an entire city block. The stores may not have the same name (sometime I think they change names monthly)

but they all come under the UltraMegaHyperMart flagship.
UltraMegaHyperMarts sell everything: food, clothing, medicine, toys, games, machines, bots, pots, and even stocks
and livestock. I didn't find it strange at all that Mr. Billings
had worked there. I think I read (or more likely saw on
HV) once that 1.4 out of every 2 people work for UMH-
mart for at least a few hours of their lives.

HARV gave me a smile. "The Pole's security elves never
picked up on that. It was covered up pretty well."

"So?"

HARV shook his head. "Zach, Zach, Zach. My poor,
naive, uninformed human."

"HARV, HARV, HARV. My annoying, egotistical,
human wannabe. What is it?"

HARV's face turned simulated bloodred. "I don't want
to be human! I'm a supercomputer, not Pinocchio! I am
interested in exploring the depths of human emotion. Scientists who study dolphins don't wish they were dolphins."

I smiled at him. "I know. I just said that to get under
your chips." I paused for a nano. "So, what's the big deal?
He worked in the store for a while."

"The fact that it was covered up," HARV said. "That
might mean that there is more to the Billingses than meets
the initial scan. Who knows what else they might be hiding?
I'll check."

"Good," I said, unable to conceal the look of smugness
on my face.

"Okay, I admit I learned something from you," HARV
said.

"Glad to be of assistance."

HARV's eyes opened wide. "You know, until now I always thought our relationship was very one-sided. You did
all the taking, and I did all the giving."

"You've certainly given me enough grief," I agreed.

"But now I see you give me something," HARV said.
He paused, baiting me to ask.

"Which is?" I said, biting.

"You give me the satisfaction of knowing that even
though I was created by humans, I can surpass them."

"Gee, glad I could help."

"But you've also given me something else. The more

time I spend with you the more I realize that it's not as easy as I thought to break down the world into ones and zeroes."

"Really?"

HARV nodded. "At times you come to conclusions that don't seem logical, but against all odds, they turn out to be right."

I shrugged. "It's a gift."

"You see things that aren't there. They are there, but they are so buried and twisted a logical mind will overlook them."

"Lucky guesses," I said.

HARV shook his head. "I don't believe in guesses or luck. You just have a way of making connections that logic and common reasoning say aren't there. I call it the W-H-Y factor."

"Cute, HARV."

"You have a keen grasp of the illogical. I figure there has to be a logical and reproducible method behind your reasoning. I just haven't found it yet."

I finished my breakfast and stood up. "If you stay connected to me long enough, you'll probably become more and more like me."

HARV shuddered. "I can feel my IQ growing exponentially lower as we speak."

My only reply was a slight smile. I knew I had gotten to HARV. That was enough satisfaction—no use egging him on or rubbing it in. After all, as much of a pain in my ass as he could be, I knew he was also an invaluable tool. I would never admit this to him, at least not outright. I knew if I was going to get to the bottom of this case, it was going to be a lot easier with him on my side. I had him riled up, which helped. It would encourage him to push himself harder. I just had to make sure I didn't push him off a virtual cliff.

I realized that HARV is just as affected by our link as I am. HARV was just as worried about becoming too human as I was about losing aspects of my humanity. I'd have to be more careful of his feelings, simulated or not. We'd have to cooperate to figure out how to better ourselves while we each stayed true to our own self. It wasn't going to be easy.

Very few things worth doing ever are, according to the fortune cookie I had last night.

I decided to head outside and catch a bit of fresh air before I ported myself to the Pole. I hate porting almost as much as I enjoy sparring with HARV. There's just something about having my molecules converted to energy and then transferred across space that bothers me. It doesn't seem natural. Still, when going to the Pole, it was the only practical way.

I was hoping some clean air would make me feel better. When I got to the door, I noticed that there were five people, three men and two women, milling about my Mustang. These people weren't thugs, at least not in the normal sense of the word. They all looked like different versions of the same person. They had long, uncombed hair and multicolored clothes that clashed with themselves, each other, and common sense. Each of them had a string of old-fashioned wooden beads draped around his or her neck. They were the new beatniks.

These are eclectic times. Lots of folks, in order to better connect with their roots, have taken to dressing and acting like their ancestors did generations ago. Most of these people have a very limited idea of what their ancestors actually dressed and acted like. All they know is the little they see on HV. As entertaining as HV may be, any duh knows it's not the most reliable source of historical information. Any HV exec knows that when it comes to selling, flare beats fact every time. (And sex is the ultimate trump card.)

The new beatniks are a sign of these times. They are a group of people who desperately strive to be like the beatniks of a hundred years ago. Except all they know about the original beatniks is what they see on made-for-HV specials. This information is limited to a few superficial facts—they dress in offbeat colors, talk in slang, play bongos, and don't shower nearly as often as others wish they would.

"HARV, can you identify those people?" I asked from the safety of my house.

"Yes."

"Who are they?" I pushed, trying to be a bit more specific.

"Their names are pretty much unimportant to you. What is important is that they are members of the SSS."

"The Santana Stinks Society. Again."

"They think Santana reps the Man, and the Man is bad, and they are determined to turn people onto their message."

In a way, they were right, if "the Man" is the World Council. It appeared that the World Council had as much against Santana as the SSS.

"Are they armed?" I asked.

A cursor appeared next to the first guy, and then moved to each of the SSS members.

The cursor disappeared, and the scanning stopped.

"Nope," HARV told me.

"Good," I said, as I headed out the door to greet my new friends. There were five of them and just one of me. But I was packing a high-tech gun in my sleeve, which tipped the scales considerably in my favor.

"What can I do for you good people?" I asked, as I approached cautiously. They may have been unarmed but I wasn't about to let myself get careless. Like my old mentor use to say, *get careless today and kiss tomorrow away.* Not the best poet, but the lady was a DOS-tough PI. I made sure that I kept a good three meters between myself and the beatniks.

"We want you to deliver a message to Santana for us, man!" the biggest one in the group said.

A short, bearded, skinny guy next to the spokesman accented each of the words with a bongo drumbeat. The bongo man had long, slender arms, hairy hands, and big ears. He reminded me of a monkey with bad hygiene. I fought back the urge to snicker. I didn't want to give these people any excuse to turn up the tension level.

"Santana? I have no idea what you're talking about," I told the man.

"Don't play pentium with us Johnson!" he told me. "Our sources tell us that you and Santana met yesterday!"

"You have sources?" I said.

They all nodded.

"Well, your sources are wrong!" I told them.

The group took a collective step toward me. They certainly had one part of the beatnik lifestyle down pat—I could smell them from two meters away.

I popped my gun into my hand. I wasn't scared of them so much as I didn't like the smell of them.

The group took a collective step back.

"Wait, man. We mean you no harm! So chill!" the smallest member of the group said.

"Okay, what's the message for Santana?" I asked.

"We just want you to make sure she reads our manifesto! We keep it on our net page: Info.SSS.org. We are a nonviolent organization, after all."

"Fine, I'll make sure Santana bookmarks it," I sighed. "Now if you don't mind, get out before I lose my temper, as I am a non-nonviolent organization."

They all looked at me, trying to decipher what I just said. So to accent my point I fired a warning blast over their heads. To further accent my point and help society while I was at it, I also shot the monkey man's bongos.

"Hey!" he protested. He took a step nearer to me.

I aimed my gun at him. He kept coming. I turned on the laser sights. Red dots appeared on his head and between his legs. His eyes tried to focus on the red dot on his forehead. Then his eyes scanned down to the lower dot. I think this one worried him more. He stopped advancing toward me.

"Sorry, it slipped," I said. "Net with my computer, download him the receipt, and I'll reimburse you." I didn't really want to do that, but sometimes when you're the good guy, you have to make sacrifices.

The monkey man's mouth fell open. "But I stole them, man . . ."

"In that case, leave now and we'll call it even," I said. "Now get out!"

They all turned tail and leaped into their old hover that looked like a '57 Chevy and took off. I smiled. It's always nice to communicate with my fellow man.

"Just for my own info, HARV, what did you do to scan them to make sure they weren't armed?" I asked over my wrist com as the SSS faded into the sunrise.

HARV's smiling face appeared in the com.

"Simple. I ran a psychological profile on each of them based on the size and shape of their heads."

"That's it? I relaxed my guard because of a psychological profile!"

"What did you expect? From that distance I was only able to look at them, not scan them with any analysis rays. Don't be such a big baby. I was right."

"This time!" I told him.

"And ninety-nine percent of the time after that," HARV concluded.

"It's that other point one percent that worries me," I told him.

"Don't worry Zach, that percent is statistically insignificant."

"That's easy for you to say."

"Yes, is it. It is easy for me to say that in four hundred and one different languages."

I decided this was just another one of those things it was better not to think about. I watched attentively as the SSS flew off. Then it hit me. Another one of those strange leaps in logic.

"The guy who attacked me yesterday wasn't a true member of the SSS," I told HARV.

HARV just looked at me. "Zach, the official police records said he was. He was carrying one of their cards."

"Perhaps," I said. "Only the attacker yesterday was different than these guys today. One, he showered. Two, he definitely believed in violence."

"Maybe he was a fringe member of the group?"

"Or maybe he was a plant?"

"No, I'm certain he didn't have any chloroform in him."

"Ha, ha, HARV."

"DOS, I *have* been connected to you too long."

It made sense on some level. Somebody wanted me off the case, so they sent an assassin. Just to be on the safe side, they set the assassin up as a member of a radical group. This way, even if he doesn't off me, they pass the blame onto another group. This got me thinking that this group might have something to do with the problems at the Pole.

HARV thought about what I had said. "You're either very clever or very paranoid."

I shrugged. "Hey, the two aren't mutually exclusive."

"This is interesting," HARV said. "On a hunch I scanned the SSS database, this time including members who have been deleted."

"And?"

"There was one very interesting name: Nina Small."

I shrugged. "The name doesn't ring a bell," I said.

"Nina Small was Nova Powers' given name."

"So." I shrugged again. "We can't be sure it's the same Nina Small. Can we?"

"No, the SSS keeps very bad records. So we can't be sure. But still . . ."

"We certainly know that Nova does believe in violence," I added. Actually, I think Nova thrives on violence.

"True. Still, we can't totally dismiss Nova as a suspect," HARV said.

He had a point.

"I'll check her out her carefully when I get to the Pole," I said.

I wasn't quite sure where this case was going to end up. The only thing I did know was that it was going to be interesting.

14

I went back into my house and told HARV to inform the elves I would be teleporting to the Pole in ten minutes. They asked for twenty minutes to prepare. I was in no hurry to try this personal porter. Humans have been using mass teleporting for years now (since the good aliens from Glad-7 shared the technology with us), and there have been very few incidents. HARV tells me mass teleporting is safer than walking across a busy street—especially if you are me. Still, I'm never anxious to step on a port pad. I was less than anxious to try a personal porting belt.

I walked up to my room and grabbed the belt, taking a closer look at it. It didn't seem all that special. It looked like your usual fine leather belt that just happened to have a few computer circuits sewn into its inner lining and a big red button on the buckle.

I held the belt up away from my body. "Are you sure this will work?"

HARV rolled his eyes. He knew I hated it when he did that.

"There's no place on this belt to enter coordinates," I said.

Now HARV looked down and put his head in his hand and sighed.

"It's just feels so *Star Trek*ish, and not in a good way."

HARV's head started spinning—literally doing 360s. This was one of the times when HARV really benefited from being a hologram. His head spun around on his neck four or five times, finally stopping when it was facing me.

"Trust me, Zach. It works. I've looked at the specs. It's

brilliant. It's preprogrammed to bring you to a specific place in space."

I looked at the belt. I looked back at HARV. "I don't see how . . ."

HARV sighed. "It creates an energy field around you. Think of it as a teleportation cocoon."

"How does it know where I end and the floor begins? Or where I end and somebody else begins?"

HARV threw his arms up and started flailing them around. He reminded me a lot of Randy right now. "Algorithms, Zach. Algorithms." HARV looked down at the ground. He looked up at the ceiling. It was like he was desperately searching for inspiration. He walked forward and patted me on the back.

"Zach, this is something I don't often say to you," he said.

"Yes?"

"You're thinking too much. If you can't trust a sentient computer, a bunch of elves, and a genetically-enhanced bombshell Santa, who can you trust?"

No truer words had ever been spoken. I closed my eyes, reached down, and pushed the button.

"You may open your eyes now, Mr. Johnson," a high-pitched voice said.

"Call me Zach," I said, opening my eyes.

I looked around. "Gee, Toto, we're not in Kansas anymore," I said.

I was standing on a pad in a small room with metallic walls. There were four elves in the room. Two males and a female were standing in front of the pad, and another male elf was manning a control panel alongside the pad.

The elves looked interchangeable: a meter tall, big blue eyes, fair skin, lithe build, long hands and longer feet. The men had short hair and green elf bodysuits complete with bells on their shoes. The woman had longer hair and wore a red elf dress that was cut just above her knees. Oh, you could certainly tell from her profile that she was woman, all woman if you get my not so subtle snow drift. As far as I could see, the males were identical looking. I assumed the females were too. To identify one another, they wore name tags with numbers on them. (I later learned that the elves only wear the numbers so visitors can identify them. They are like penguins and can tell one another apart quite easily. [Even later I learned they do this by scent. I stopped asking after that.])

A male elf with a big number 1 on his chest walked up to me (bells jingling all the way) and extended me his hand. "Mr. Johnson, how nice of you to come."

I shook his hand as I stepped off the transport pad. "I'm glad I made it in one piece."

The elf smiled. It was a smile that dominated his face. "No fears, Mr. Johnson. Our technology is topnotch, A-One-plus-plus squared then cubed."

"So I've heard. This fancy belt can transport me anywhere it was programmed to?" I said.

"It certainly can, Mr. Johnson. We chose to bring you to one of our support transporter rooms. Just in case."

"Just in case?"

The elf pointed at my midsection. "Mr. Johnson, that is a marvelous piece of equipment."

"Thanks," I said with a wry smile.

The elf looked at me for a nano. He tracked his pointing finger to my body and realized he may have been aiming a little lower than the belt. He raised his finger so it was unquestionably pointing at the belt.

"I'm talking about the teleporting belt," he said. "Not the naughty area," he added.

"Oh good, because I was getting a little uncomfortable," I joked.

The elf took a deep breath. He started counting to ten under his breath. "Must go to my happy place, my happy place," he muttered. He was well-trained in customer service, but he'd never had a customer like me before.

"Mr. Johnson, the technology we used is very hush-hush. Only high-level and elves who have worked R and D know it exists. We transported you into this room onto a standard pad so that if any other elf had happened by, they would have thought nothing of it."

I pondered what he said. It did make sense in its own overly cautious, bordering on paranoia way.

"Mr. Johnson?" the elf said.

"Please, call me Zach," I said as I looked around, starting to draw in the ambiance.

"Very good. And you may call me Number One, Elf-1, or just One," the elf said, pointing to the number on his chest. "I am the head of organic-based security here."

"Your mom must be so proud," I said.

His eyes opened even wider than normal. "Surely you must know we are all clones. We have no mothers. At least not in the traditional sense."

The female elf offered me her hand. "Elf-1, that was just some of Mr. Johnson's, I mean Zach's, legendary humor."

Elf-1 looked perplexed. For an elf, he wasn't all that jolly. He forced a polite chuckle.

"Ah, yes, humor."

"Zach, I'm Elf-2," the female elf said.

I pointed to the number on her chest. It took me a nano to force my gaze away from the number. Her creators had certainly gone to great pains to make her well, stand out, from the men. After another nano, I noticed that her lips were much fuller and her eyelashes longer and curlier than her male counterparts'. It was sort of unsettling but in a mostly comforting sort of way. I regained my composure.

"I can see that," I said. "I hope people don't call you Number Two."

"Not those that want to keep all their original teeth," she said. She smiled politely. "I'm in charge of marketing and public relations here at the Pole."

"A place that actually gives things away and asks nothing in return needs a head of marketing and public relations?"

She smiled. "You'd be surprised. We treat everybody equally. And therein lies the problem: as much as people claim they want to be equal, they actually don't."

"They don't?"

She shook her head. "Of course not, silly. They want to be treated better than the next guy. You're a PI, you should know that."

She was right. In my line of work, I have learned that greed is the foremost human motivator, the driving force behind many of our actions. (Lust is a biggie, too.)

Elf-2 pointed to a little changing booth in the corner of the room. "Now, as head of public relations, I hope you don't mind if I insist you change into your visitor's suit and activate your holo-disguise. Nothing personal, but your presence here might cause the other visitors to panic."

I headed toward the changing booth. I wouldn't take it personally that my very presence would worry people.

When I got out of the changing booth, Elf-1 was the only elf still in the room. I looked around. "Was it something I said?"

Elf-1 looked confused. "No, the others have duties to attend to."

Elf-1 held up a mirror for me to check myself. Blond hair, blue eyes, light skin. I didn't look anything like me. "My own mother wouldn't recognize me," I said.

"That is the point," Elf-1 said.

"Until I talk," I said. "My voice is still mine . . ."

"No, it just sounds the same to you. Your voice is being modulated to the outside world."

"Seriously?"

Elf-1 started tapping his big pointy shoes and pointed to himself. "Do I look like the kind of guy who would joke around?" he said over the jingling bells.

"Do you really want me to answer that?" I said.

He rolled his eyes and took a deep breath. He took another deep breath. "Go to my happy happy place," he mumbled. He looked at me. "Have you ever listened to a recording of your voice and not recognized yourself?"

"Yeah."

"This is along the same lines but the exact opposite."

"Really?"

"I'm an elf. We don't tell lies. Not even white ones . . ." Elf-1 rolled up his sleeve and looked at his wrist interface. "The boss is going to want to see you," he told me. He walked toward the door, "Please follow me."

"Boy, Santana doesn't waste any time," I said, tagging along behind him.

"No, she doesn't," he said, leading me out the door. "When you have the happiness of billions at stake, you must be efficient."

Elf-1 guided me through a maze of corridors. These weren't like any others I had ever walked through. They made tacky look spartan. The color cycled between red and green and the middle of the walls were lined with twinkling multicolor lights. The top halves of the walls were covered with ever-changing holograms: trees, snowflakes, wreaths, waving snowmen, flying reindeer, and even the occasional menorah with some fruits and vegetables tossed in for good measure. The ceilings were covered with glowing icicles of various lengths. All the doors we passed were lined with holly. The only boring thing about the halls was the green line traversing the middle of the floor.

For the coup de grace, the official Holiday song was constantly playing in the background.

> Holiday is here
>   Time to raise a cheer.
> Holiday is here
>   It's the best time of the year.
> We love Holiday a lot.
>   Boring like Christmas it's not.
> Holiday is so cool
>   It's the day that makes Hanukkah drool.
> Kwanza may be nice.
>   But Holiday puts it on ice.
> Three great presents for everyone.
>   Oh, my, that's so much fun.
> All those other days are left in the dust
>   Holiday is the only Holiday for us.
> hoo hoo, ha ha, fa la la la la la.
>   Holiday, Holiday, ra ra ra.

The song always was always "traditionally" sung by what sounded like chipmunks high on mixture of helium and speed. It had to be one of the most annoying songs of all time, so of course it was insanely popular with 90 percent of the population. It was one of those tunes that stuck in your brain like gum on the bottom of a fat guy's shoe on a hot day.

The corridors all looked somewhat different though they blended together. After walking for a while the green line that ran across the middle of the floor had turned yellow. Except for the tunes droning on and the jangling of Elf-1's shoes we walked in silence. For an elf, Elf-1 was not a fun guy.

Finally, I had to say something.

"You don't talk much, do you?" I said.

"No," Elf-1 said.

"Why not?"

"I need to concentrate," he said.

"I know you're worried, but I'm here now."

He ignored me and kept chanting, "My happy place, my happy place."

Something wasn't kosher here. I admit I'm no expert on elf psychology but Elf-1 seemed agitated and uneasy. Part of my brain attributed that to the fact there had been a murder on his watch. Another part, my paranoid part (which was growing larger by the hour), warned me to use caution.

"HARV, can you pick up any readings from this guy? He seems jumpy to me," I said inside my head.

"Zach, his diet is seventy-seven point seven percent glucose. Of course he's jumpy."

"Look deeper, HARV."

"I've analyzed his facial expressions."

"And?"

"Inconclusive. Elves are hard to read. Not enough studies have been done."

"Great, HARV. Thanks for nothing," I muttered.

"Excuse me, Mr. Johnson. Did you say something?" Elf-1 asked me.

"Just talking to myself."

"I know the feeling," he said. "I'm sorry I'm not much company. I take my job very seriously."

"No problem," I assured him.

We continued to walk through the labyrinth of corridors, each one seemingly longer than the last. As we walked farther and farther, the corridors became blander and blander until they became simple white walls with a red stripe down the middle. Only the music and the clinking of Elf-1's bells remained. I knew what mice in psychology experiments must feel like. I could only hope that when I found the cheese at the end of the maze it would be really good cheese.

Whenever we approached a door I would become excited in anticipation that this would be it. It would be the door that leads to our destination. The farther we walked, the rarer the doors became.

Finally, we reached a metal door. This door looked different from all the other doors I had seen at the Pole. It was much thicker and ominous looking.

"Boy, your boss likes to hang out far from the main complex."

Elf-1 pressed a button on his wrist com. The door opened. He motioned for me to go in. I did, but reluctantly. He followed me.

The room wasn't that much bigger than a good-sized walk-in closet. It didn't seem to be a place worth walking fifteen minutes out of our way for. It was almost barren, except for a big chair in the middle. It looked vaguely like an old-fashioned dentist's chair like they have in the museums but even less inviting.

"Sit down, please," Elf-1 told me as he motioned to the chair.

I shook my head no. "No thanks, I'll stand."

"Please sit!" he insisted. "It is just a simple mind scanner, a very standard procedure."

"Sorry," I said. "I don't believe in standard procedure. It's just so standard."

"I'm afraid I must insist," he said, as he grabbed my arm.

"I'm afraid I must resist!" I said, as I pushed him back.

He took a karate stance and stalked toward me. "I feel obligated to warn you I'm an expert in the martial arts."

I kicked him in the groin.

"I feel less obligated to warn you I fight dirty," I told him. Though from the shocked look of surprise and pain on his face, I figured he had probably figured that out.

"That wasn't very nice," he whined, in a voice that was even higher than normal.

I made a fist and showed it to him.

"If you don't think that was nice . . ."

I kicked him in the same spot again. He doubled over, then crashed to the ground with enough force to knock his pointy hat off his head.

I picked him up by his little green shirt.

I showed him my fist again. "Listen, buddy," I said in my meanest, most intimidating voice. "I want to know what this is all about!"

"Rocko! Help!" he cried.

"Rocko?" I said. "Rocko the elf? This ought to be good. What is he, a full meter and a half tall?"

I heard something coming up from behind me: *clunk, jingle, clunk, jingle, cluck jingle*. I felt something, something big, tap me on my shoulder. It was a hard tap, more like a jab. Against my better judgment, I turned around. A fist the size of a family-size holiday ham slammed into my face, sending me slamming to the ground.

I looked up. There standing above me was the biggest, meanest elf I had ever seen. DOS, he was the biggest, meanest being I had ever seen.

"Rocko, I presume?" I said.

Rocko had the same fair features as the other male elves I had seen only everything was three times their size, making him a lot more grotesque. His nose was bent in three places, forming a little *z* and letting me know this wasn't his first dance.

Rocko reached down to grab me and then lifted me up over his head. He held me up for a nano, letting me appreciate the view. Then he heaved me into the wall.

I hit the wall and rolled to the floor.

"They never mentioned this in the brochure," I moaned.

Rocko walked over, reached down, and pulled me up from the ground, this time lifting me up to his face. He towered over me like I did over Elf-1.

"Elf-1 says Rocko don't like you!" he told me, his voice sounding like he had swallowed a gravel hovertruck then gargled with acid. "So I am going to beat you up."

"A giant, mutant elf with an attitude. What will they think of next?" I said a split-nano after I gave Rocko a head butt.

The force of my head butt caused Rocko to release his grip on me, but also made my ears ring as if I were the Hunchback of Notre Dame on Bastille Day.

"Man," I said, as I put a hand to my head. "Now I see why they call you Rocko."

Rocko threw a lumbering left cross at me.

I ducked under it just before it would have launched my head to Pluto. I hit him with a right jab to the breadbasket. The punch did as much damage to me as it did Rocko. This was one of those nasty situations smart people are clever enough to avoid. I was in it knee deep and sinking fast. A part of me was thinking that there must be another part of me that actually feeds off of these types of messes.

It wasn't all bad news. I was faster and smarter than Rocko. DOS, most pet rocks are smarter than Rocko. Unfortunately, there was very little I could do to hurt him and sooner or later he would catch me with one of those lumbering blows of his, and then I would be in big trouble.

"Rocko, your shoe's untied," I said, pointing down toward his feet.

Rocko paused and looked down.

I nailed him with an uppercut to his chin. The blow cocked his head back half a centimeter. If it hurt, he was too confused to noticed. I pulled my hand back in pain.

"My shoe is not untied," Rocko said.

"I can't believe he fell for that," HARV said.

"Are you sure?" I asked Rocko to buy me some time.

Rocko looked down again. He nodded his head yes. "Yes," he said.

"HARV, what can you do to help me here?" I thought.

"Do you mean to improve your hearing or to aid you in your current situation?" HARV asked.

I backed away from Rocko. I didn't know what my next move would be, but I knew I didn't need him getting ahold of me.

"You know what I mean, HARV."

"Have you ever noticed you only talk to me when you need something?" HARV said. "I really don't get any respect . . ."

I ducked under a thundering right cross.

I countered by springing up and hitting Rocko with an uppercut to his granite chin. I knew the last time I tried the chin it didn't go so well, but it was a big target and easy to hit. I was hoping my first punch might have softened him up some.

Much to my pleasure, this punch seemed to hurt him. It sent his head reeling back, causing him to stagger him a bit.

"Subzero!" I said, proud of myself.

"I increased blood flow to the bones and muscles of your arms and increased your adrenaline," HARV said. "Don't get too cocky. He still has plenty of fight left in him!"

Rocko quickly regained his balance. He threw a right roundhouse at my head. I saw it coming and ducked.

"Do the same thing with my legs and knees," I thought back to HARV.

"Why? So you can make a hasty retreat?"

"Just do it, HARV!"

"Fine!"

I felt a tingling in my legs. I took that as a good sign. I moved in on Rocko, ducking under a left hook as I did. When I got within striking distance, I rammed my souped-up knee into his "personals." I was flabbergasted when he blocked the move, catching my leg with his arms. He smiled at me.

"Even Rocko not dumb enough to fall for the same move you used on Elf-1," he said.

He pulled my leg up in the air, driving me down into the floor.

It hurt. But it also left him open. I kicked up with my left leg and caught him squarely between his legs, doubling him over. He stubbornly refused to fall.

I sprang to my feet. His head was now within easy striking distance of my knee. Before I could do anything, he lowered his massive shoulder and rammed into me. He lifted me off the ground and drove me into the wall.

Once again, it hurt. I took my fists and boxed him in the ears. He dropped me to the ground. He was cunning enough to keep his weight leaning in on me and keep me pinned to the wall.

That left him vulnerable to my next move. I shot my knee up quickly to his groin. He doubled over in pain. I cuffed both my fists and hit his doubled-over head right in the jaw. It sent him flying backward to the ground.

"Okay! Now you're pissing me off," he said, as he nimbly hopped back to his feet.

He spat out a couple of teeth and wiped a bit of blood from his cheek. The splattering of red blood on his green suit was festive in a macabre sort of way. He made two fists and motioned for me to come toward him with his head.

"Let's rumble, little man!" he spat.

I shook my head.

"See, now this is why you carry a gun," HARV lectured uselessly.

"I don't need a gun to take this big lug on," I said out loud. I glared at Rocko. "He might be big, but I'm faster and smarter."

Rocko turned his neck back and forth, making crackling

sounds. "Faster? Maybe. Book smart? Maybe. Fight smart? No way!"

He made two huge fists and moved in on me, the bells on his shoes clanking as he approached.

"Hit me with everything you've got!" I thought to HARV. "I'm going to show this cloned clown he's not messing with sweet elves now!"

Luckily, one of us was saved by the bell. I'd like to think it was him, but I can't really be sure.

"What is going on here?" Santana demanded, as she burst into the room, her face redder than her hot-red boots.

Santana zeroed in on Elf-1 and Rocko. She stormed over to Rocko and put a finger under his chin. She lifted him off the ground with that finger.

"Rocko, what have I told you about fighting?" she said.

Rocko hung his head (at least the best he could with Santana holding him up by his chin). "Fighting bad."

Santana let him drop to the ground with a very unceremonious thud.

"You two should be ashamed of yourselves! I bring Zach here to help us and this is how you treat him." She pointed to the door. "Out! Go to your rooms! Stay there until you hear from me!"

The two sulked out like children.

"Sorry about that, Zach," Santana said. "Elf-1 was the first out of the mold so to speak. He gets a little testy from time to time, but he means well. He just doesn't trust you yet."

"And Rocko?" I asked, as I rubbed my neck.

"He's our one failure. He's a really good guy, but he does whatever Elf-1 tells him to. Truth be told, he's not the brightest fellow, but he is loyal."

"And surprisingly cunning," I said.

"That I wouldn't know," Santana said.

"You don't think they could be involved in this?"

"Ho ho ho, no! Rocko is simply not bright enough, and Elf-1 is constantly by my side. I always know what he's up to even when I don't care to know. He just wants to solve the case alone. He's a proud one. Poor dear, he's always wanted a case to solve and now that he has one I'm afraid he's not up to the task."

"Well, no harm done," I said.

She smiled at me. It was a smile that made me feel much better than it should have. "You're a good man, Zach."

I took a deep breath to clear my thoughts. "Since Elf-1 is so anxious, I think it's time to get to work. Why don't you take me to the murder sites?"

15

The first area Santana brought me to was a giant warehouse. When I say giant, I mean mega-giant. The place went on for as far as the eye could see. There was easily enough room in there to hold a baseball game and a rock concert at the same time without one interfering with the other. DOS, you could probably even fit the collected egos of the World Council in there. Okay, maybe I am exaggerating a micro, but you get the point.

Santana and I took a compu-tram through the vast aisles of toys. As we rolled past toy after toy after toy, I couldn't help getting a bit giddy. Well, not quite giddy, PIs don't get giddy. But if they did, I would have been giddy. This was every kid's dream, no matter how old that kid happened to be.

We stopped in the H_2O pistol aisle. Santana jumped off the tram, and I followed. Santana pointed down at a small chalk outline on the floor.

"Here's where M-778 met his demise. He was doing quality control on five thousand boxes of H_2O pistols when the net that was carrying them broke. Poor guy never had a chance. There wasn't much left of him after that."

I examined the spot of impact. All I saw was a small spot with a chalk outline around it.

"There aren't even any bloodstains?" I said.

"That's due to our very efficient maidbots. They started to clean the mess up before I could stop them."

"Can I examine the net that was holding the toys?"

"Net R-1117 C-129 down!" Santana ordered.

The net slowly lowered to eye level. I looked it over. I

tugged on one of the cords. It bent but not without effort on my part. It was strong and sturdy, yet supple.

"The support cords are made of a special nylon. They are supposed to be able to support one hundred tons easily. They are supposed to be unbreakable under normal use."

I examined the cord that had snapped, causing the accident. The break was straight and clean. It looked like it had been cut by something very sharp. I made a mental note.

"Okay, I've seen enough," I said. "Now please take me to the other scene."

"Of course," Santana said, as she headed back to the tram.

I picked up an orange transparent H_2O pistol that was sitting on a nearby table. The pistol was shaped like an old-fashioned handgun. It reminded me of one my grandfather had given me as a kid. It wasn't very big, holding enough water for maybe twenty shots, but if you were good that was all you needed.

"Can I keep this?" I asked.

"Sure," Santana said.

As we were walking back toward the tram, I noticed that one of maidbots had left behind a small bottle of cleaning acid. I bent down as if to tie my silly elf shoe. I grabbed the bottle of acid and slipped it into my elf suit's handy pockets. Just in case.

Next, Santana lead me to the mess hall. It was another big room. Only this time instead of being filled with toys, it was filled with tables and chairs and refrigerators. It looked like a vastly larger version of my high school cafeteria, only cleaner and much more pleasant smelling. Like the rest of public areas of the Pole it was filled with holiday touches, tables shaped like sleighs, wreaths levitating near the ceilings, and the ground and tables covered in simulated snow. The Holiday theme was playing in the background.

"We can feed a thousand here at a time," Santana said proudly.

The west wall of the room was lined with serving machines. Santana pointed to them. "Each of those machines is programmed to freshly prepare one of ten different meals on demand."

"And to drink?" I asked.

"Elves only drink water, hot cocoa, and eggnog from our special drink dispensers," she said.

"Let me see them," I said.

"Of course."

Santana sheparded me over to the north wall. It was lined with shining stainless-steel refrigerators. They all looked identical: each had three drink dispensers on the door. One was labeled H_2O, another had a smiley face over it, and the last one, an egg.

"This is where M-892 met her demise. Poor dear. All she wanted was a cup of soy eggnog drink."

"What fridge was spiked with wine?" I asked.

Santana led me over to a refrigerator in the middle of the pack. It had a big OUT OF ORDER hologram flashing on top of it. "This one."

"Did any others contain eggnog that was poisoned with wine?" I asked.

"No, only this refrigerator was spiked. Whoever did this apparently only wanted to kill a few of my elves."

"Did you do a fingerprint analysis of the door handle?" I asked.

"Yes. Unfortunately, it didn't give us any information, as all elves are genetically equal. There were no traces of any other beings found."

I examined the fridge, carefully studying the door handle. It appeared to be scratched. I ran my hand up and down the handle. It wasn't as smooth as I thought it should be. There were definite nicks in the surface.

I examined the door handles on the nearby fridges. They were all smooth.

"Who maintains the eggnog and hot cocoa?" I asked.

"Our elf staff."

"You don't use bots to refill?"

Santana shook her head. "No. All of our cocoa and nog is handmade and hand delivered by elves, just like it should be." She looked at me, deadly serious, and said, "It's one of our proudest traditions."

Santana pointed to the end of the room. "Do you want me to take you back to the kitchen where they prepare the eggnog and cocoa?"

I shook my head. "No need. If you only found traces in this one fridge, I'll assume it was tampered with here."

"That's what Elf-1 thought," Santana said.

"Well, I've seen enough," I told Santana.

"What are you thinking, Zach?"

"Not sure yet, Santana. Let me go to my room and clean up. Then I'll chat with the others. After that I'll have a better idea where we stand."

Santana hit me with the smile again. Yep, I needed to take a nice cold shower for more reasons than one. She looked at her wrist communicator. "It's ninety minutes until lunch. That would be a splendid time for you to meet your group."

"I agree," I said. "I always think better on a full stomach."

"Ho ho ho, so do I," she said, giving me a gentle tap on the shoulder. "I'll walk you to your room."

"That would be nice."

"I have to make sure none of my elves beat you up again," she said with a wink.

That got me thinking.

"How many elves do you have here at the Pole?" I asked.

"Exactly ten thousand and two. Half male and half female."

"How do ten thousand elves make handmade presents for fifteen billion people?" I asked.

"Ten thousand and two elves," Santana corrected.

"My question still stands," I said.

"Well, the official marketing answer is elven magic," Santana said with a wry smirk.

"I'm looking for the real answer," I told her.

She put a finger to her lips, and I tried to concentrate on her words not her lips. "Elves only sleep for two hours a day, and while they may eat five meals every day, they are small meals meant to energize them."

"Santana, if I'm going to solve this crime, I'm going to need all the information I can get out of you."

"When we say all the gifts are elven-made, we're not lying. Elves do make all our gifts by hand. Using gestures. We have computers trace the movements of each elf and re-create the items with virtual robotic elves. This way one elf can easily make thousands of items at a time. Of course, we don't show that part during the tour."

She looked at me. "Anything else you need to know about elves?"

"When I was doing background work on them, HARV told me they were all the same, yet the three I've met have been different."

Santana simply smiled. It was a warm, disarming smile, just not quite a natural smile. It was like a proud grandma's smile merged with a slick-talking, used hovercraft salesman's.

"They are all the same, but different," she said.

I stopped walking. I tilted my head a bit and said, "The same, but different?"

"What, you can't walk and think at the same time?" HARV whispered inside my brain.

Santana disarmingly touched my hand. "Oh, Zach, it's really not that hard of a concept. Think of it like a beehive but improved."

"An improved beehive?"

"Beehives are incredibly efficient organizations that center around a queen. Much like we do here."

"So, you're saying you're queen bee of the Pole?"

Santana nailed me with another one of those enchanting smiles. Only this one wasn't quite as sincere as the previous. "In a way yes. I don't like to be boastful, but I am more than just a pretty face for PR. I am the heart, soul, and brain of this place."

I learned about bees when Electra was teaching at the university and one of her students took an interest in bees. At first, I thought the girl and her bees were just plain loco, but then Electra explained that a bee's honey has some important antimicrobial properties. Many naturalists believe honey can be used to help wounds heal faster. As a guy who gets wounded a lot, this piqued my interest.

I learned that bees in a hive come in three types: the queen, the drones, and the workers. The queen is the heart of the hive. She doesn't move much, but she reproduces and regulates the size of the hive. A drone's job is pretty much to mate and die. The worker bees are, as the name suggests, the ones who do everything else around the hive. I'm sure when the queen isn't looking, they are always complaining about how they are underpaid and underappreciated.

"I understand that you know a bit about hive structure from Electra's old student. Her name was Izzie World, if I recall correctly."

I tried, but I am quite certain I failed, to hide the surprise on my face. "Excuse me?" I said.

"Izzie World. She was one of Electra's students at the New Frisco State Medical College from 2055 until 2057," Santana said.

"How do you know that? And more important, why do you know that?"

"Zach, I'm Santana Clausa. It's my job to know everything. I even know you had Chinese take-out for dinner last night."

Wow, talk about "big sister is watching." That was kind of scary. I knew Santana was well connected, but this stopped me in my tracks. Suddenly, it occurred to me—

"Hey, you saw me eating dinner last night when you called," I said.

Santana's eyes—and somehow her cheeks—started to twinkle. "You have me on that one," she said. "In any case, my elves mine through terabytes of information on everybody. It allows us to make sure we give people the best gifts possible."

I decided this was another one of those gray areas it was a lot better if I didn't mull over too much. Yes, Santana was watching and tracking, but I had to trust that she was watching for all the right reasons. Of course, the information the elves gathered would be worth a lot of credits to a lot of people. I pushed those thoughts to the back of my mind. This was Santana Clausa, the kindest person in existence.

"Now, back to the beehive analogy," I said, anxiously coaxing the conversation away from me. "You said you improved on it?"

"Very much so. For one thing, we don't have drones. Though I do confess that the concept of beings who exist solely to mate with me is something that I find intriguing," she said, staring off into space.

"But you digress," I said, snapping my fingers.

"Oh, yes." She smiled. "Boy, I'm glad you're not really a blogger, or I'd be in big trouble with that statement." She took a deep breath to clear her head and to fog mine up. "All the elves are basically worker bees. The typical worker bee has one function in the hive that changes as they age: cleaner, nurse, builder, forager, defender. This works well for the bees because, quite frankly, bees don't get bored, aren't that bright, and exist just to propagate their species."

I nodded so Santana could tell I was still following her.

"While this hive concept is very efficient, we figured it wouldn't work as well for completely sentient, highly intelligent beings like the elves. So, we bettered it. All the elves have the same interchangeable skill sets but different personalities."

"So they can all do one another's jobs?"

"All except for Elf-1 and Elf-2, and of course, Rocko. But yes, the rest share the same skills. They all have different likes and hobbies, and unlike worker bees, we made them in two sexes because, well, you know."

"Some things are just more fun to do with the opposite sex," I said.

Santana smiled. "Exactly. The elves call it being naughty. They have a saying, being naughty is soooo nice. It may cloud their judgment from time to time, but elves have needs too."

She took a moment to let me digest what she said.

"If you say so, Santana."

"I'm actually quite proud. We took an idea from nature and made it better."

"That's great Santana, but who's this *we* you're talking about?"

"Why, me and the World Council executive board at the time. As you know, we used Twoa Thompson's design, with a few adjustments."

I took a nano to digest what Santana had just told me. I now understood elves better than I thought I needed to. We all take the Pole and the elves for granted. I never paid them much attention. Now that I had to, I was pretty certain that HARV was right—these probably weren't elf-on-elf murders. Man, that's another phrase I never thought I'd hear myself think.

"This brings me to another question, Santana."

"Go ahead."

"Who created you?"

There was silence, Dead silence. This was followed by laughter, loud boisterous laughter. "Ho ho ho, Zach, that's the funniest thing I've heard all day."

"It is?"

"Come with me," she said.

"Where?"

"To my quarters."

Santana wrapped her arms around me before I even had a chance to think about it. Not that I was complaining, mind you. It just would have been nice if I had some say in the matter. She pressed a button. The next thing I knew we were standing in her room.

16

Describing Santana's room isn't easy. It was the strangest place I had ever been in, and I've been to a fairy realm, every bar in New Frisco, and a couple of comic e-book conventions.

First off, everything in the room was pink—a variety of shades of pink. Pink walls, pink carpeting, pink bedspread, pink chairs, even the screen on her HV was pink.

Santana hopped off the port pad (which was pink), walked over and sat down on her bed (which had a big pink headboard). She patted the bed and motioned for me to come over.

I stepped off the pad and cautiously walked toward her. I had no idea where this was going, but I've never let that stop me before.

"I like pink," she said, in case I had suddenly gone blind and stupid. "I initially wanted my costume to be pink, but marketing convinced me to go with the more traditional red miniskirt and boots."

"Oh," was all I could say at the moment.

"I think of red as pink with an attitude." She smiled.

"I know I don't have to remind you that you are an engaged man," HARV said inside my head.

I sat beside her on the bed.

"What gives here, Santana?"

"What I'm about to say is very personal. Not many people in the world know this."

"Go on."

She slipped her feet out of her boots. She propped her foot up over my lap. "Do you mind giving me a foot massage? Don't worry, my feet smell like candy canes."

I wasn't sure what it was about superwomen and foot massages, but I figured I had more important questions to ask. I started to massage one of her feet.

"Remember, you are practically a married man," HARV whined.

"Let me start by saying one thing," Santana said. "HARV, turn off."

HARV projected from my eye lens and bowed. "As you wish," he said. He disappeared.

My eye started to tingle. HARV wasn't in my head. This had happened before when Randy deactivated HARV, but Randy was HARV's creator.

"What the . . ." I said. I started to push Santana's legs off me. But she resisted, keeping me pinned down.

"Don't panic, Zach," she said. "What I have to say is very personal. I want to make sure this isn't being recorded for the world to hear."

"But—"

"How did I know HARV was there?" She shrugged. "It was an educated guess. Like I said, it's my job to know everybody."

"But—"

"How did I deactivate him?" She smiled. "I have the ability to communicate with any human, animal, or machine. It helps me do my job."

"So, you're a psi?"

She shook her head. "Technically, no. Psis can't control machines. I can."

"Who the DOS created you?"

"Zach, I was created just as you were. By a man and a woman who loved each other very much. One night, at least I think it was the night, it might have been the morning, the two of them got together and . . ."

"I know how the birds and bees work," I said, even though I knew she was just playing with me. "I just assumed you were a clone."

"You and the rest of the world. I'm actually a normal woman. A normal woman who was mutated by the World Council."

"But intentionally mutating humans has been illegal longer than cloning. In fact, I don't think it ever was legal!" I said.

"You know, you can talk *and* massage my feet," Santana said with a giggle, waving her foot under my nose.

I resumed my foot massaging, though I wasn't really sure why.

"So you were mutated?"

She locked her steely eyes on me. For the first time I noticed the blue in her eyes was offset by dots of white. The floating dots gave the impression of snowflakes falling from a clear sky. "You make it sound so bad."

"It wasn't? What about your previous life?"

"I had just graduated from university, and I was looking for something different to do." She pointed around the room. "Now this—this is different."

"What about your family?"

"I was an orphan. My parents were killed in a terrorist attack in 2022."

"Oh, I'm sorry," I said.

"They were killed at the Alien-Earth Commerce Treaty signing in Old Washington."

I was just born in 2022, but I knew the date well. That was the first year of human existence that aliens made open contact with us. They had been watching us, observing us, and experimenting on us (though they called it interacting with us) for decades. Once they deemed us worthy (or just got tired of experimenting on us), they went public.

Going public was a big move for both the aliens and Earth. They gave us many breakthroughs that we take for granted today: teleportation, regeneration, and the cure for many diseases. They opened up the universe for us. They also opened up our minds. They made us realize mankind wasn't nearly as unique in the universe as we thought we were. For some people, that was just fine. They had seen what man could do. They figured there had to be a better way.

For others, they didn't take it so well. They claimed humans were superior to the aliens—spiritually. They also declared that Earth should have nothing to do with aliens. They did everything in their power to convince the Earth's governments and the alien governments to stay away from each other. This included lots of bombings at Earth and alien events. It was a bloody time in our history. Humans killing humans and aliens in the name of the good of humankind.

Eventually the resistance was put down. But it left bitter feelings on both sides. The aliens now only interact with Earth when they need to. In fact today, most people my age have never met an alien. I am, of course, the exception. I know aliens all too well. But that's just my lot in life.

"Those were ugly times for Earth," I said.

"Yes, " she said. "It was an especially ugly year. Except, of course, when you were born."

I grinned and glanced away from her. I hoped I wasn't blushing but it felt like I was. "Some people would call that the low point of a very low year."

"Later, when the World Council put out a call for a young woman of exceptional talent, I answered. The rest is history—literally. Top secret history, but history nonetheless."

"Why are you telling me this?"

"You asked."

"You could have just given me a rote answer."

"Zach, you've saved the world on an almost yearly basis. I think you can handle the truth. In fact, I think you deserve to know the truth."

"Thanks, I appreciate your words. But I'm just an Average Joe who gets lucky once in a while."

She simply looked at me.

"Okay, maybe a Slightly Above-Average Joe who is really persistent. Still believe me, I am nothing special."

"I wouldn't say that," she said. She leaned forward and kissed me—hard—on the lips.

I moved away from her and fell off the bed. It wasn't one of my smoothest moves. It must have been entertaining, as she started to laugh.

"Just a little friendly kiss between kindred spirits," she said.

I pushed myself up from the floor. "Santana, I'm honored, but I am an engaged man."

She rolled her eyes. "Zach, I know that. You're getting married but not dying. There's nothing wrong with sharing a little passion. It's not like I'm offering you my bed."

She stood up and patted the bed gently. "Though, if you would like to . . ."

"Santana!" I shouted.

"Just a suggestion. What good is being nice ninety-nine percent of the time if I can't be a little naughty now and then?"

"I think we'd better keep our relationship professional. Remember, the happiness of billions is at stake."

"I am entirely capable of multitasking," she insisted.

"Yeah, well I'm not," I said.

She looked at me. She smiled. "Very professional, Zach, very professional." She adjusted her dress. "You passed the test."

I know I looked much more puzzled than I wanted to. "Test?"

"Yes, test. I wanted to make sure you were a man of outstanding character who would let nothing get in your way as you find out who is causing problems at my Pole."

"Oh, good. Glad I'm deemed worthy."

"Very worthy." She smiled. She accented the smile with a wink. I felt like a lab rat again, only this time instead of searching for cheese in maze, I had been cornered by a cat. A sexy cat dressed in red who was toying with me before the kill.

"I think I'd better get to my room and freshen up before meeting the others."

"Yes, a splendid idea," she agreed. She looked at a pink analog clock with candy canes for hands that hung on the wall. "It's an hour until lunch is served. I'll walk you to your room."

"You'll turn HARV back on," I said.

She grimaced. "Of course."

17

I got to my room and sat down on my bed. It was soft, but not too soft. I gave the room a quick once-over. It was a nice room, comparable to the finer hotels I've stayed in. It had everything a tourist would want to have an enjoyable time at the Pole—a full wall information and entertainment screen, plenty of storage space (though we had nothing to store), a little desk in the corner, and a fridge in the other corner. There was a control console near the bed with settings for room temperature, window size, and even wall color.

I flipped the wall color switch, and the walls changed from a nice light sky blue to a darker angry blue. I pushed the undo button, and the walls transformed back to the lighter color. I slid the window switch to the right. The little picture window on the wall opposite the door expanded to bay-window size, giving me a better view of the outside world. It was a pseudo-man-made snow-filled holiday wonderland covered with evergreen trees, each littered with thousands of lights. The Pole's automated FAQ said that these were in fact real trees genetically engineered to withstand the subzero temperatures outside. The trees even grow with their own solar-powered, fiberoptic lights. They called it another amazing triumph of elf over nature. I pushed the switch the opposite direction and the window contracted to porthole size. I left it that way.

I figured the coast was clear.

"Okay, HARV, come on out," I said.

HARV resonated from my eye lens.

"You know we could do this mentally," HARV said.

I nodded my head. "Yes, but thinking to you gives me a headache."

HARV nodded. "You just missed seeing me."

Suddenly, HARV had a look on his face I wasn't accustomed to. He went pale. "My time stamp!" he said very dramatically.

"Yes?" I said.

"My time stamp is four minutes off!"

"Oh, I thought you knew—Santana turned you off."

"What?" HARV cried, looking far more like Randy than I was comfortable with. "That's impossible!"

"Apparently not," I said.

HARV grabbed his head and ran his fingers through whatever little hair was there. "I always suspected Dr. Pool might, just might, be able to take me offline. But, but Santana?"

"Apparently, it's her special gift. She can communicate with any person, animal, or machine."

"You're saying apparently a lot. I don't like apparently. I want certainty."

"I'm certain she took you offline."

HARV shook his head back and forth. "No, I'm wrong. I don't like certainty either!" He put his hands on his head, squeezing his ears so hard that if he was a human his brain would have popped out. "Did you hear that?" he shouted.

"You're shouting, HARV. It's kind of hard not to hear."

"I can't be wrong. I'm not infallible. In fact, I'm fallible, very fallible." He pointed at me violently. "This is your fault. Your brain is rubbing off on me, making me weak and wishy-washy." He paused in horror, turned pale as virgin snow. "Oh my Gates, I just uttered the words wishy-washy." He looked at me pleadingly with his eyes. "Tell me I'm incorrect about being wrong?"

I shrugged. "Sorry, buddy I can't."

Now he pointed at me with both hands, practically thrusting his index fingers at me. "You're ruining me, Zach. Next thing you know I'll be getting lost, stubbing my toe, and shooting myself with my own gun!" he ranted.

"HARV, I've never shot myself with my gun."

He moved closer to me, sticking his holographic face right in mine. If he had breath, I would have been able to smell it.

"But you will!" he shouted. "It's only a matter of time!" HARV backed off a bit and wiped some simulated sweat from his brow. "Then it's only a matter of time before I become more and more fallible." He looked up at me. "Just delete me now. Please?"

I walked up to him and did what any good friend would do. I slapped him in the simulated face. It didn't hurt him. It couldn't hurt him. But he reacted to the slap as if it did.

"Why did you do that?" he shouted.

"I thought you needed it," I said.

He stopped to process for a nano. "Oh, yes, I understand. Trying to knock some sense into me."

"HARV, I need you to get your data together. Take a deep breath, count to ten million, and let's get back on the case."

"I don't breathe," HARV said.

"I was speaking figuratively," I said.

"Okay, I've counted to ten billion and ten in binary," HARV said. "I do feel better now."

I put my hands on his simulated shoulder and looked him straight in the eyes that weren't really there. "Fallible or not, you're still the best damn partner I've got. The only way I'll be able to solve this case is if you are at the top of your game."

HARV glanced down. "You're just saying that because it's true."

"Are you ready to get back to work?" I asked.

"Sure," HARV said. "I guess I can take pride in knowing that even though I am not perfect I am still far closer to perfection than you."

"That's the spirit," I said. I walked over and sat on my bed. "Did you notice what I noticed when checking the murder scenes?" I asked.

"Zach, even attached to your brain I am the most sophisticated computer in the world. Here is a simple rule for you to follow. If you noticed it, since I am looking at things through your eyes, I also noticed it." It didn't take HARV long to get back to his old self.

"So the cord in the warehouse. My guess is it was snipped by a guardbot claw."

"That is a very logical deduction. I ran a simulation, and it confirmed that the cord was sheared by a sharp object."

"And the fridge," I said. "I noticed it had a few scratches around the handle, as if a guardbot had opened the door."

"I captured the image and magnified it, and once again your theory seems to be correct," HARV said. "Do you really believe that the guardbots are capable of staging a mutiny?"

"Maybe, but they have no incentive."

"Perhaps they were just bored. And needed to feel useful?" HARV offered.

"My guess is somebody is reprogramming the guardbots to use them as tools. I just need to find out who. I'm sure I'll learn more as I get to know the other guests."

"I'm sure you will, too," HARV said. "Speaking of which . . ."

There was a firm but soft knock on the door.

"That's my cue to disappear," HARV said, as he faded out.

I walked over to the door and opened it to reveal Elf-2's perky face and perkier body. "I'm here to escort you to lunch, Mr. Johnson, I mean Mr. Starr," she corrected herself. "I hope you're ready."

"Ready as I'll ever be," I said.

She squinted one eye and looked me up and down. "I thought you told Santana you were going to change into another outfit. That one got soiled in your little incident with Elf-1 and Rocko."

I slapped myself on the head. "Ah, I knew I forgot something."

She looked at me. I looked at her.

"Should I change now?"

She leaned over and sniffed me. "I don't find you offensive."

"No higher praise," I said.

Her mouth formed a half-smile. I wasn't sure which half she was trying to suppress, the smiling part or the not smiling part. "I was trying to say that if my finely evolved elf nose couldn't sniff the difference then the humans you are dining with should be fine."

"Before we go, mind if I ask you a few questions?"

"No, not all," she replied batting her lashes.

I motioned her into the room. We both sat down on my bed. I tried to keep a good meter away from her. But she nudged up right close to me. "No need to be so proper. We're friendly creatures here at the Pole."

Being in marketing, Elf-2 was much smoother than Elf-1. I needed to remember she was a professional speaker so I had to take anything she said with a grain of rock salt. "I need genuine answers from you," I told her.

She batted her eyes at me again. "Of course." ·

"What's the overall mood of the elf work force?"

"Chipper to very chipper," she said.

"She appears to be telling the truth," HARV said inside my head. It was good to know he was back on the job.

"You don't mind the fact that you need to be given a drug by Santana in order to stay alive?" I asked.

Elf-2 reached over and took my hand. She looked me in the eyes. She batted her eyes. "Each and every one of us feels it's our duty to serve the best we know how. ELF is just a motivator for us."

"So elves never get depressed or down?" I asked.

She looked at me with those big blue eyes. "Of course we do," she said earnestly. "We're living, breathing beings. That's where naughty time comes into play."

Now I smiled.

"We hook up with each other and we feel MUCH better afterward," she said smiling with her mouth, eyes, and cheeks.

"Do you have set partners?" I asked.

She shook her head. "No, we're very communal. Santana says relationships make us think too much about building the relationship and not enough about work."

"Interesting," I said.

She squeezed up to me. "Why, Zach? Are you interested?"

I stood up. "Sorry, I'm an engaged man."

She smiled. "See, Santana is right. Relationships do get in the way."

I looked toward the clock on the wall. I didn't actually notice the time but that didn't keep me from saying, "It's getting late. We better head to lunch."

Elf-2 grinned. "Yes, you're right. We both have our jobs to do."

With that, we were off.

18

By the time Elf-2 and I got to the table, all my fellow visitors had already begun their meal. Councilwoman Weathers was at the head of the table with her husband, Carl, sitting to her left side. The ExShell couple, the Eatmans, were sitting next to her. Nova sat across from them, in between the blue-skinned (except for the zits) MESSHs, Bim and Norp, with very little room to spare. Nova's face lit up like a thousand-watt fluorescent device when I walked into the room.

"People, I would like to introduce you all to our newest tour member, Bart Starr," Elf-2 said. "Bart is a new, up-and-coming blogger for YakYakYakYakYak.com. He's doing a story on the Pole experience."

"Come, Bart, sit next to me," Nova called.

"Well, I would," I told her. "But there doesn't seem to be space," I said referring to her rather cramped area of the table.

Nova put her hands to her sides. By extending her powerful arms, she pushed Bim and Norp away from her as if they weighed nothing. Yes, she had definitely added mass since our last encounter. I have to admit that, being a macho kind of guy, I don't usually feel comfortable with women who have arms that are bigger than Popeye's. In this case though, the look worked. Nova managed to tread the fine line between being muscle-bound and ladylike.

"Well, I still don't have a chair," I said, not hiding the fact that I was enjoying this.

Nova reached over and grabbed the chair Bim was sitting on. She pulled it toward her. Bim smiled—a sure sign of a man who didn't have a clue. Nova lifted the chair with one arm and plopped Bim on his posterior, causing me to smile and Norp to laugh hysterically.

Nova brushed the chair off with her hands. She motioned to me with her eyes to come and sit there.

"Hey, that was my chair!" Bim protested.

Nova turned to face him, "I know a hundred ways to kill a man in under ten nanos."

Bim sulked back, proving he wasn't totally pentium.

"Give me your chair!" Bim said to Norp.

"Right, like really!" Norp replied.

I sat down in the vacant seat. The geeks fought over Norp's chair like deranged musical chairs (without the music) players.

"Was your trip here pleasant?" Nova asked me, ignoring the geeks.

"Yes, thank you. How about yours?"

"It's been way boring until just now," she said.

I quickly reminded myself that I was an engaged man. I mentally pictured ice cubes in the mid-area of my elf suit. (Who would have thought I'd get so much action at the Pole?) I turned my attention to the Eatmans.

"Bart Starr, ace blogger, but please feel free to call me Bart or Ace," I said, holding my hand out.

"Oh, gag me, please," HARV moaned inside my head.

Steve shook my hand while he turned to his wife, "See honey, isn't the Pole great! We're going to be mentioned in a blog!"

He turned his attention back to me, "We've never been mentioned in a blog before! This is so exciting!"

"Ah, thanks," I replied, as I took my hand back. Not wanting to blow my cover, I asked, "Do you folks have names?"

He laughed. "Of course we have names! You're a funny guy." He pointed to himself, "I'm Steve," he pointed to his wife, "and this is Mary."

"Eatman," she said bluntly. It was obvious, even to a non-trained mind, that this wasn't her first choice for a vacation.

"I beg your pardon?" I said.

"We're Steve and Mary Eatman," he said.

"Oh. So what brings you folks to the Pole? Frankly you strike me as more of New Bahamas types."

"It was his idea," Mary said, rolling her eyes in Steve's direction.

"Yeah," Steve said proudly. "We've been planning this trip for five years and three months."

"And twelve days," Mary added, with more than a little venom in her voice.

"How wildly impetuous of you," I noted.

"Steve wanted to come because it's the most organized place on Earth. I came because I was interested in unionizing the elves, but they'll have nothing to do with it."

I pointed to Steve. "You love organization. You must be an engineer!"

His eyes shot open. "Wow, you're good! Now I see why you're an investigative blogger."

Mary rolled her eyes. "Right, like that takes any real investigative skills. You're a trained monkey with a recorder and a word processor," she spat. "You just go where they tell you to go."

"I'm betting you're a lawyer. One who actually practices in public," I said to Mary. "I know a lot of you don't like to admit it, what with the great lawyer purge and all, but don't worry, nobody is allowed to carry weapons here."

Mary patted herself on the chest. "I proudly admit to being a lawyer, not a greeting card salesman," she said.

"Zow! I've never met anybody who would proudly admit to being a lawyer before!" Nova said. "When we wrestlers have legal problems, we just pound away at each other, and the one left standing wins."

"Now that sounds much more dignified than our legal system," I told her.

This riled Mary up even more. I didn't think it took a lot to get Mary worked up. She was strung tighter than an electronic guitar.

"Ha ha. We lawyers got IRSed during the lawyer purge, but people still need us!" she said.

"Don't you mean the big corps still need you? After all, don't the top five corporations employ ninety percent of the lawyers left in the world?"

"Ninety-two point five," Steve said.

"Ninety-two point five three one," HARV corrected in my mind.

"So, it is safe to say you work for one of the big five."

"Wow, brilliant deduction," Mary told me, not at all trying to hide the fact that she wasn't the least bit impressed.

"I can do better," I said. "I'm betting you folks work for ExShell!"

Steve smiled and gave me a polite little clap. Mary just rolled her eyes again.

"Lucky guess," she said.

Just then Elf-2 walked back into the room with a megaphone.

"Okay folks, now that you've enjoyed your delicious lunch, it is time for a tour of some of our facilities. Please follow me."

The others all got up.

Nova noticed that I didn't.

"Aren't you coming, Bart?"

"Sure, I just need to eat something first," I told her. It might sound a bit superficial but I hate saving the world on an empty stomach.

"Fine," she said. "I'll make sure the group waits for you!"

Bim and Norp weren't quite so excited about having me in the group. Out of the corner of my eye, I could see they were glaring at me. That made me even more anxious to stick with the group.

I picked up a ham sandwich on rye and gobbled it down. I went to join the tour. It wasn't hard as Nova was slowing down the line, making it easy for me to catch them.

When I reached them, I decided it would be a good time to introduce myself to the Billings family. I knew HARV thought it was ridiculous that a seemingly average family from New Kansas could be involved with a murder at the Pole, but that's why HARV's the assistant, and I'm the lead. Sure, HARV can translate hundreds of languages. Sure, he can recite statistics on pretty much anything they keep statistics on (and some things they don't). Sure, he can plot the orbits of all the known planets on any day in history. But HARV wouldn't know a hunch if it walked up to him, saluted, and then kneed him in the groin. At least not the old HARV. With HARV changing and evolving as he was, maybe soon he would be able to.

The Billings family was at the front of the group, trailing slightly behind Elf-2. They were hanging on her every word. Though Billy's eyes were darting back and forth between Elf-2's and Nova's cleavage. Elf-2, for her part, was droning on and on about the wonders of life at the Pole. How everything was elf-made. How the elves sifted through terabytes of data to decide on the perfect gifts for everybody. How elves eat five meals a day. How elves have taken teleportation transportation to the next level. How elf poop doesn't stink. Okay, she didn't really say that, but she *was* going on and on about everything else.

I slowly weaved my way through the group until I was just behind the Billingses. My first impression was that the Billingses looked overdressed in their elf suits. I couldn't put a mental finger on it. They weren't itching or acting like a caveman at a debutante's sweet sixteen party, but my eye knew they were out of their element.

"Marvelous place, the Pole," I said to the Billingses, not directing my comments to anybody in particular.

Billy was the only one who reacted. He turned to me and smiled. It was a toothy grin. He had some gaps where he was missing teeth, but the teeth he had were so big I didn't know where the replacement teeth would fit. He reminded me of a beaver with a bad haircut and a worse dental plan.

"This place is nifty cubed," Billy said. He was so excited, I was afraid he might have an accident.

I patted him on the head. Not sure why. It seemed liked the right thing to do. "Mommy, Daddy!" he screamed, pointing at me with one arm and them with the other. "This man touched me!"

The group stopped moving. I felt every eye lock on to me. I retracted my hand from his head and hid it behind my back.

"Yeah, Zach, keep your arm behind your back, and I'm sure they'll all forget you have one," HARV taunted.

Right now, I had bigger problems to worry about. Bob "Pa" Billings was making a beeline straight for me. He was a big, solid man, and a quick glance was all you needed to know he worked with his body for a living. He had a flat face, complete with a flat nose, flat head, and a crewcut to boot. His head was so straight I was sure he could balance a pitcher of water on it without even trying.

He pushed a finger into my chest.

"You touching my son, mister? I don't care what kind of fancy-pants blogger you are, you don't touch my boy."

My first reaction was to clock him between the eyes. That might have been how Zachary Nixon Johnson, tough guy PI would handle it, but not how Bart Star, ace blogger would. Bart was a words guy. I needed to use words to stay in character and out of trouble.

I put both my arms up in a smooth nonthreatening position so he could see them and know I wasn't going to try to be a tough guy.

"No offense, Mr. Billings," I said. "Just trying to be friendly."

He didn't react, which was better than punching me, but not what I was hoping for. He might have been a strong man, but he wasn't a trained fighter or a grappler, and he had let his guard down and now he was wide open. If I wanted to nail him with a quick jab or a knee to the groin, he was mine. While Zach might have done that, Bart wouldn't. I went on using words as my shield.

"I understand you people are from New Kansas. I've heard people there are really friendly," I said. I let my mouth break into a slight smile. I wanted to look like I was being sincere, not taunting.

He didn't back down. "We are friendly. We just don't take kindly to strangers."

Elf-2 tried squeezing her body between us to diffuse the situation.

"Mr. Billings," she squeaked. "I am sure Mr. Starr meant no harm."

Pa Billings didn't back down. I had to give him his props for being protective of his son, though this was getting on my nerves. Maybe he was the type of guy who wouldn't back down unless I stood up to him? Maybe he wouldn't respect me unless I gave him a reason to? I slowly started to curl my right hand into a fist. It was such a slight movement I doubt anybody noticed it.

"Easy, Zach," HARV said inside my brain. "This isn't the time."

I let my hand relax. Out of the corner of my eye I could see Nova and the nerds. The nerds were cluelessly waiting in anticipation for Pa to give me a thrashing. Nova, on the other hand, dropped back a step the nano I relaxed my hand. She frowned. I have to respect a girl who loves a good brawl.

"Bob, leave that poor man alone," Betty Billings said, moving toward us.

Betty Billings wasn't bad to look at. She was a tall, slender woman with short black hair that, unlike her husband's, didn't look like she cut it with farm equipment. She had a peachy complexion that wasn't nearly as tanned as the rest of her family's. Carol certainly hit the nail right on the head about Ma Billings' skin tone—it didn't look like this woman spent much time outside.

Betty grabbed Bob's hand, which was still curled in a fist, and slowly forced it back down to his side. She stood between us, facing him. "Remember what Judge Clemens said, Bob, you can't be so sensitive. This man wasn't trying to hurt our boy."

Bob stood his ground.

"Bob," Betty said, "don't make me call the judge when we get home."

Bob hung his head and dropped his guard.

"Good man," Betty told him. Turning her attention to Billy, she bent down and stuck a finger in his face. "And you! What have we told you about spamming wolf?"

Billy wasn't as quick to back down. "But, Mom, they taught us in school not to let strangers touch us."

Ma Billings targeted her glare on her son.

Billy put his hands behind his back and slumped backward, slowly pulling away from his mother like a puppy who had just been scolded. "I'm sorry, Mom."

Ma Billings pointed to me. "Now, apologize to Mr. Starr so he writes nice things about us."

He turned to look at me, paused for a nano, and then turned back to his mom. "Oh, Ma, I don't want to apologize. I didn't do anything wrong!"

Ma Billings stomped her foot and folded her arms across her chest. She was digging in for the long haul. "You're just like your father," she moaned. "Just once I wish this family would do what I told them to without me hitting them over the head with a brick."

Bobi, the daughter, joined in the fray. "Mom, you don't have to tell me anything twice," she said, tugging on her mom's elbow.

Ma Billings shot her a look. "No, but being a suck-up is just as bad."

Bobi shook her head so hard it made her ponytail spin around. "I'm not like that, Mom, I'm not. If you want, I can find you a brick to hit them with." She sneered at her brother.

Billy responded by showing his sister his tongue.

I hoped Electra didn't want kids anytime in the near future.

Ma Billings' face wasn't pale any longer. It was now redder than her elf suit. "Bobi, tell Billy you're sorry. Billy, tell Bobi you're sorry, then tell Mr. Starr you're really sorry. Remember we want to be kind to strangers, especially those who can write about us."

Before I had a chance to say there was no need for Billy to make an apology, Mary Eatman started forward. "Don't worry," she said walking up to Billy and bending over to face him. "If Mr. Starr writes anything bad about any of us, I'll sue him for so many credits he'll have to clone himself ten times to have any chance to earn that much."

Billy smiled at her. "Really?"

She patted him on the head. "Really. That's we lawyers do—we make people's lives better."

"Maybe I'll be a lawyer," Bobi Billings said.

"No, I want to be a lawyer," Billy said.

"I don't want any of my kids being a DOSing lawyer." Ma Billings balked.

This statement brought out Mary Eatman's ire. "What's wrong with being a lawyer?"

Ma Billings rolled her eyes. "How much time do you have?"

Mary shoved her finger up next to those rolled eyes. "Please, you don't have nearly enough money to pay for my time."

"People, people, can't we all just get along?" Elf-2 pleaded.

Nobody heard her cry for peace except for me. The rest were all embroiled in the heat and passion of the moment. Bob Billings had taken up his wife's defense by threatening to put Mary back on her backside. This made Mary threaten to sue Bob for all the dirt he owned. Betty got mad at Bob for jumping in like that, but she also came down hard on Mary for assuming they were poor farmers.

Betty pointed out that if it wasn't for farmers people wouldn't be able to eat. Mary's counterargument was that it wasn't the farmers but their bots and machines (programmed by people like Steve) that did the work. This really pissed Bob off, and he made a step toward Mary. Steve, being the brave engineer that he is, stepped forward and pointed out to Bob that if he laid a hand on his wife, his wife would sue the pants off of him, his kids, and their kids.

Nova and the MESSHs were doing their part by egging everybody on. Nova was in obvious glee watching other people brawl for a change. Bim and Norp were getting doubly charged over this. This was probably the only time in their lives they weren't the most ridiculous-acting people in the room. They loved anything that got Nova riled up, and the thought of a chick fight between Mary and Betty was getting them hot and bothered. These guys didn't get off Mars much.

If I had my gun I would have fired a few warning shots in the air, but I didn't. I thought about stepping in to break this melee up, but figured I'd learn more if I just let it play its course. After all, the only one who could do any real damage was Nova, and she was content to be a spectator for once.

Mary grabbed Betty by the collar, which made Steve threaten Bill, while at the same time reminding Mary her chances of a successful lawsuit would be enhanced if she didn't slug Betty first. At which time both Bobi and Billy started taunting Mary and calling her all sorts of names. But Mary was a lawyer, so nothing these two kids could say would get to her, unless one of them accused her of doing pro bono work.

The two families went on bickering and throwing verbal jabs at each other like two inexperienced prize fighters. They were both scoring points on occasion, but neither could put the other away. It was clear Bob Billings wanted to escalate the violence from verbal to physical, but Betty would always step in and refrain him at the last nano. She was a smart one. She knew just as Bob would take Steve out in a knock-down, drag-out brouhaha, Mary would definitely take them to the cleaners afterward.

As much as I was learning about my Polemates from this

little scuffle, I knew it was time to put an end to it. Despite
the fact that I started this incident, I had now become a
forgotten spectator, a holographic face in the crowd. Which
can be fine if it helps move the case forward, but this
wasn't. I had to stop it. "Excuse me, people," I shouted.
They ignored me. I instinctively went for my gun again,
flicking my wrist in just the right way to make it pop into
my hand. Of course, the gun didn't leap into my hand,
because I didn't have my gun. I don't know what was
worse: my needing to rely on my gun to quiet a crowd or
my not remembering I didn't have a gun.

Now it was Councilwoman Weathers' turn to step up to
the plate. She had the air of a woman who didn't like to
stay a bystander for too long, and this had gone on long
enough. She was a politician, and like any politician worth
her weight in soy, she wasn't about to let herself be dele-
gated the role of bystander.

"Excuse me, everybody," she said in a quiet, firm voice.

Everybody instantly stopped their bickering and threatening and turned their attention to the good councilwoman.
Everybody that is, but me. I knew the councilwoman well
enough through her reputation. I was more interested in
seeing how her husband, Carl, reacted.

Back when he was a pro quarterback, his name was Carl
Carlson. I guess I can see why he took his wife's last name.
Carl was one of these guys who was born with a lot of
talent, but wasn't sure what to do with it. Not knowing him
personally I couldn't tell if this was because he was lazy, not
overly bright, not overly ambitious, or some combination of
the three. That's why I was so interested in seeing how he
reacted to this. He was a guy used to sitting on the bench.

Carl Weathers was a big man, over two meters tall, and
he weighed a solid 110 kilos. He didn't look like he could
walk onto the football field today and lead a team to victory, but he wasn't that far from being game ready. During
his playing days, such as they were, I remember he had
dark brown hair. Today that hair had wisps of gray through
it, especially around his temples, but it made him look more
dignified than old. He had a rep for being a ladies' man
before he met Weathers. It wasn't hard for me to spot that
he still was a lady's man, and by that I mean the councilwoman owned him. The way he always stayed one step

behind her. The way he looked at her with blind admiration when she walked, talked, or did most anything. He was almost more of a pet than he was a husband.

I turned my attention back to the good councilwoman. She had now positioned herself between the two arguing families.

"Please, people," she said. "Can't we all just get along?"

Not the most original plea. In fact, Elf-2 had just used it only moments ago. While Weathers may have said the same words, the effect was completely different. Everybody stopped their bickering and turned to her. The councilwoman was an appealing, commanding woman. Part of that was on account of her size—she was tall, nearly as tall as her ex-quarterback hubby. While she wasn't a muscular powerhouse like Nova, it was obvious she was no stranger to the gym. Her hair hung softly over her shoulders. It was an expensive cut that didn't look it, and it managed to complement Stormy Weathers' face perfectly without being pretentious. The flawless hair on top of the strong taut body helped complete the total package, making Weathers a unique cross between soccer grandmom, retired model, and barracuda.

"Now, my good people," the councilwoman said, commanding all to focus their attention on her, "I'm sure we can all agree that nothing is gained by fighting."

This was followed by grunts of agreement from everybody. Even Nova nodded her approval, but in her case I think it was just giving in to peer pressure.

Satisfied she had the floor to herself, Weathers went into her spiel. "My fellow voters, this dispute is much like the one I faced many decades back when I nearly single-handedly pounded out the first treaty between Earth and Gladian-7, when the Gladians insisted Earth people smell funny and that our negotiators needed to take seven showers a day."

Everybody bobbed their heads in agreement. Everybody that is except for me. I didn't see a lot of similarities. The councilwoman continued, "At first, there seemed to be no compromise. The Gladians insisted that they were letting the Earthlings off easy with only seven showers a day. The Earthlings insisted that showering that much would not only greatly impede the negotiations but it would also severely dry their skin. It appeared compromise was impossible, but then I suggested four showers a day for the Earth delegation and gas masks for the Gladians."

All the members of the tour group started to applaud the good councilwoman for her vision. None of them seemed to notice or care that their dispute was nothing like the classic Earth and Gladian-7 dispute.

"Can you fix our problems like you did theirs?" Bobi Billings asked.

The councilwoman just smiled. As she held her smile, the others held their breath. Finally, after a minute or two had passed, the councilwoman said, "Of course I can. After all, that's why you all voted for me."

Everybody let out a collecteive sigh, except of course for me. I wasn't hanging on her every word like the others. I wasn't even sure I voted for her.

"The solution is easy," she said. She looked at me. "Mr. Starr, apologize to poor Billy for touching him without asking for permission or at the very least alerting him to your intentions."

All eyes steadied on me.

"Sorry, kid," I said with as much sincere sincerity as I could fake.

All eyes returned to the councilwoman who turned to Billy. "Now, Billy, tell Mr. Starr you are sorry you overreacted."

Billy lowered his eyes. "I'm sorry, Mr. Starr, sir."

The crowd let out a collective sigh.

"No problem, kid."

The councilwoman turned her attention to the adult members of our parties. "Now, you people should agree that farmers, engineers, and even lawyers who call themselves lawyers are all essential to our great planet's economic diversity. We are all different, and that's what makes our planet great. If it wasn't for our differences, we might as well all be androids, bots, clones, or MESSHs."

Everybody nodded or mumbled in agreement, even Bim and Norp. I saw them turn to each other and say, "We *are* pretty annoying."

"Now everybody shake hands, so Elf-2 can continue our fine tour."

The words seemed to go from Stormy Weathers' mouth

directly to everybody's brains. They all immediately began shaking hands, exchanging recipes and job hints, and getting along like they were family. No, better than family, like they were people who actually liked each other.

The tour continued with Bobi and Billy arguing about who got to grow up to be a lawyer and who got to grow up to be a councilwoman. The Eatmans and Billingses walked with each other, chatting like they had known one another forever. Nova kept throwing looks at me, while Bim and Norp split their time gawking at Nova and the councilwoman. The councilwoman didn't say much after that. She just smiled politely as Elf-2 went on and on about how great the Pole was.

For the most part, the remainder of the tour was impressive but uneventful. When you're me, a little uneventful now and then is a good thing. Contrary to what some people (Electra, Tony, HARV, that court-appointed therapist from a few years ago, my agent, and my high school math teacher) believe, I don't need to live under the constant threat of danger. I like the quiet times when nobody is trying to kill, maim, or castrate me. Trust me, it's never fun when somebody tries to castrate you. That gets old real fast.

The Pole certainly was a big place. Elf-2 told the us the facilities were bigger than 25.567 percent of the cities on Earth. Yet the place was "manned" by just a few thousand elves and a few more thousand machines. We saw the data-mining rooms where elves and expert intelligent systems sift through the gigabytes upon gigabytes of data the Pole collects on everybody in order to choose the perfect gift for each individual.

We saw the Pole's virtual computer servers. We learned that the Pole receives over sixty billion electronic requests for gifts each year. Yes, there are only fifteen billion people on Earth, but according to Elf-2 the average person changes their requests 3.2 times before they finally decide what they really want. In fact, to help people who change their mind more than four times, the elves have invented a special present consulting software that will help "happy customers" choose the perfect gifts that will make them "even happier customers."

We saw many of the Pole's automated assembly lines where the computers and electronic gadgets are slapped together by trained elf technicians and their robotic aids. We saw the handcrafted zones where elf craftsmen make special one-of-a-kind gifts for those people who have everything or just want something that is different from what everybody else has.

The tour wrapped with a visit to the Pole's coup de grace, their storage center. Yeah, I know you're thinking, *How could a storage center be the coup de grace? It's just a big building where packages sit before they are sent somewhere else.* That's the kicker—it wasn't just a big building. It was a humongous building that looked like it had eaten a couple of other big buildings, and these didn't come close to satisfying its needs. I've seen the UltraHyperMegaMart-sponsored Grand Canyon and truthfully, it wasn't quite as impressive as the Pole's storage center. Sure the Grand Canyon was actually bigger, but it wasn't that much bigger, and it was created over millions of years by erosion. This place was built in under a year by a bunch of elves and bots.

Elf-2 explained to us that once a present is made for an individual, it is coded and stored in a special area. Every person in the world has their own special spot in the storage room where their gifts are kept. Each spot is encoded into the Pole's automated teleportation systems, along with the address of the recipient's teleportation receiver. Elf-2 also told us that to save time and space they keep a good portion of the gifts that are completed early suspended in a "phased state." In this state they are neither solid nor whole but kept in between dimensions in a near ready-to-deliver state. All it takes is the simple press of a button to transport the presents from a phased state to their final destination. This way when it's time for the mass teleportation, it's easy to quickly get the right presents to the right people. Truthfully, the physics involved were beyond me.

So instead I thought about other, more mundane matters, such as: how many outfits does each elf have? How often do elves get naughty with each other? What else do elves do when they goof off?

(Later, during a Q&A session, I learned the answers to

those questions were: five; none of my business—wink, wink; and elves don't goof off.)

As the tour finished, Nova insisted that I meet her in the gym for a little workout. It seems walking kilometers wasn't nearly enough exercise for Nova. I agreed, figuring that would be the best way to get information out of her. I didn't think she was involved in this (killing things with bots wasn't her style), but I couldn't rule her out just yet.

Before I'd meet her in the gym, I told her I needed to go back to my room to take notes on what I'd seen.

19

HARV activated himself the nano I stepped foot into my room.

"Isn't the physics involved in storing and shipping massive amounts of gifts fascinating?" HARV said smiling.

"It's amazing what humans can do when they put their minds to it," I said, sitting down on the bed and sliding my shoes off.

For those of you interested, elf shoes are far more comfortable than they look, but still not as comfortable as a really good-fitting pair of sneakers that are broken in just right. I was just glad the guest shoes were "bells optional."

"Actually, Zach, most of the work was done by elves, not humans."

"The elves were created by humans."

HARV paused for a nano and put a finger to his mouth. "Yes, I have to give you that one."

"Speaking of humans, what do you think of my group?" I asked.

"First off, that Mary seems *real* nice," HARV said with a wry smile.

"Yeah, sort like bumping your head and stubbing your toe at the same time," I said.

"Gee, Zach, for a detective, you're awful clumsy."

"It was an analogy, HARV. What else do you have for me?"

"I've been subtly using the Pole's computer system to gather data. I have an interesting bit of information on the MESSHs. Over the last few years, they have been experimenting pretty heavily with remote reprogramming of stand-alone systems."

"So, they could have reprogrammed the bots to attack me?"

"Yes."

"Do they have a motive?"

"To attack you or to sabotage the Holiday?" HARV asked.

"Either . . ."

"None that I can find. They are totally unaffected by the Holiday. They don't leave Mars very often."

"That's good. They're pretty annoying," I said.

"Hold on, let me scan some more. I just calculated something." HARV started scratching his head. "I've just learned that Nova and the other mutant wrestlers have a strange fondness for ice."

"Ice?"

"A special ice."

"Okay, HARV, what kind of ice?"

"It's the ice here at the Pole."

"Well, they certainly have enough of it."

"Maybe, but they won't sell it. Santana is very picky about that. She doesn't believe in using the land for personal gains."

"Santana is an idealist. It sort of comes with the territory."

"Some have offered up to one thousand credits per liter of ice."

"What did they do, lose the recipe or something?" I asked.

"Huh?"

"It was a joke, HARV. Remember, Steve says I'm a funny guy."

"True, but he is an engineer. Everybody knows they have a skewed sense of humor."

"Good point."

"Admit it, Nova's still a possibility. She loves ice and she's a member of the SSS," HARV said.

"Maybe, but she seems more of an in-your-face type to me."

"I also have some information on the Billings family."

"Yeah?"

"The mother used to be an HTech senior exec engineer.

Her group designed the guardbots. She quit over some sort of disagreement. It was buried deeper than Hoffa."

"See what you find if you poke around a bit?" I really liked the reference but figured it would freak HARV out if I mentioned that to him. There was a time and place to get on HARV's chips—this wasn't it.

"I also have some information on Councilwoman Weathers."

"Well?" I asked, though from the sound of HARV's *I told you so* voice it wasn't going to be what I wanted to hear.

"I hate to say I told you so, but I told you so. She's perfectly clean. Never even been accused of any wrongdoing. She has never missed a Council meeting vote."

"What about her relationship with her husband?"

"Married eighteen years, no kids. No affairs, no scandals, nothing even the least bit interesting, besides, of course, her miraculous recovery from her nearly lethal crash."

"Okay, how about finances?"

"They both come from well-off families. Still, I wouldn't call them giga-rich—more like mega-rich."

"Could a person in her position change facts?" I asked.

"Of course, but it would cost a bundle to change anything really important."

"Is there anything unusual at all?" I was looking for something, I just didn't know what. Weathers seemed too good to be true.

"Okay, hold on, I'll scan . . ." HARV said after a slight pause. "This might be of interest to you, though I'm not sure why."

"I'll be the judge of that, HARV."

"Mr. Weathers owns a small independent mining company. It seems he took it over from Stormy's brother-in-law who was having trouble running it. There aren't many things left to mine on this planet, and the other planets are so particular about mining rights."

"See if the mining company has ever had any contact with HTech or ExShell or the MESSHs or anybody else here. While you're at it, check out all the MESSHs' experiments and all the Weathers' purchases and sales over the last five years. Also try to find out why Mrs. Billings quit HTech."

"While I'm at it, perhaps you'd like me to calculate pi to the last digit?"

"Just do it, HARV. And stop complaining. Nobody likes a whiny supercomputer."

"I'm not whining. I'm simply pointing out how I have to do all the hard work."

"You? I'm the one that gets beat up!"

"Yes, but that's easy. I'm the one who does all the heavy thinking."

"It seems that Mary and Steve are the only two I can rule out as suspects," I said.

"Huh? You're saying a lawyer and an engineer are incapable of committing crimes?"

"No, that's not it. They just don't fit the profile."

"But they've been planning this trip for five years."

"Exactly. You don't make reservations five years in advance to a place you're trying to destroy. If anything, their reservation makes them convenient patsies."

"If you say so. I'm just a machine."

I wouldn't turn my back on that Mary, but I was sure she and her husband weren't the culprits here. As for Nova, the jury was still out on her. I was hoping I could cross her off the list after we met in the gym.

20

When I arrived at the Pole's spacious gym my fellow travelers were already there. Councilwoman Weathers and Carl were on simulated cross-country-ski machines. She was going at a quick pace, while he was taking it rather slow. It was easy to see who wore the pants in that marriage.

The Eatmans were using the free weights that looked like gift boxes. Even in these high-tech times, it's still hard to beat a good old-fashioned free weight, even one wrapped in neon gift paper. Steve was doing a bench press as two elves spotted him, and Mary looked on, either counting, giving him encouragement, or hoping he'd throw out his back so she could sue the Pole.

The Billings family was at the far corner of the gym. They were playing catch with a big anti-grav medicine snowball. Billy was sneaking peaks at Nova whenever he could.

Nova, not surprisingly, was in the boxing ring. She had ripped the legs and arms off of her elf suit (while the female elves wore dresses the female guests wore pant suits) and looked far sexier in an elf suit than should be possible. Nova's opponent in the squared circle was a very excited Bim dressed in oversized red boxing trunks, complete with oversized green gloves. He was prancing around her, darting in and out. He wasn't actually doing anything. He was being a typical male and had no idea that he really had no idea what he was doing in the ring. I'm sure he thought he looked like Muhammad Ali, but he came off more like Truman Capote, only less macho. He was floating like a one-winged bee and stinging like a butterfly.

Norp was eagerly awaiting his turn on the side of the

ring. He was jumping up and down almost as much as Bim was, shadow boxing with an imaginary foe (who could probably whip his butt). Norp clearly had no more business being in the ring with Nova than I would have being in a bullfight.

Nova looked bored by the whole thing. She stood with feet planted firmly in the center of the ring, not even bothering to face Bim when he would dance behind her. She clearly saw him as no threat.

I walked up to the ring, close but not too close to where Norp was sparring with himself. (I got the impression both Bim and Norp did a lot of things by themselves.) Nova's eyes lit up when they made contact with mine.

"Well, Mr. Starr. How nice of you to join us," she said. "I hope your note taking went well."

"Yes, yes, quite well," I said, trying to sound as much like a blogger as possible. "I'm sure my readers will be enthralled."

She winked at me. "How about going three minutes with me?"

"In the ring?" I asked.

"Zach!" HARV said inside my head. "Remember you're an engaged man. Also, she almost killed you the last time you went in the ring with her."

"For starters," she said.

I pointed at Bim. "You already have a worthy opponent."

She rolled her eyes just as Bim darted in for another one of his feigned attacks. This time Nova hit him with an open palm to the nose. At least I think that's what it was. The move was a blur. I knew she hit him because his nose started gushing blood. The red blood all over his skin made an interesting shade of purple. The bleeding was followed by Bim crashing backward to the mat like a rock. He was out cold way before he hit the floor. (I figured Nova must have hit him with an open hand because he was still alive.)

The elf referee stood over Bim and started to count, "One, two, three," before he realized the futility of it. He waved his arms over Bim. "Forget it, you're out until the bots revive you." He turned around put two fingers in his mouth and whistled for the medbots to come.

Nova looked down on me. "There, no more opponent!"

Norp, who obviously wasn't that bright, started to climb into the ring. "Oh goodie, my turn now!"

Nova put a foot on his head and pushed him to the ground. "I don't think so," she said.

Then Nova reached down and grabbed me by the collar. She lifted me up into the ring with one arm. I hate it when she does that. I find it both sexy and intimidating. She bent down and took the oversized boxing gloves off Bim just as the medbots carted him away. She tossed me the gloves.

"Put 'em on," she said.

"I don't like fighting women," I said.

"Don't worry, it's not going to be much of a fight," she said.

By now, everybody else in the gym had figured out what was going on. They were all gathered around the ring. It looked like they were anxious to see the blogger get flogged.

Nova was dancing around me, circling. She was showing much more energy than when she had Bim in the ring. I tend to bring out the best in people.

"Duck!" HARV said, inside my head.

I did, a split nano before a right roundhouse from Nova sailed over me. If I hadn't taken HARV's advice, I would have been waking up next to Bim in the infirmary.

"How'd you do that?" I thought back to HARV.

"She tips her punches," HARV said. "She's a wrestler, not a boxer. The tips are subtle changes in the expression on her face. A human wouldn't even notice. Luckily for you, I've studied all her films and can determine her moves before she makes them. For instance, now she is going to lower her shoulder and slam into you."

Sure enough, Nova did drop a shoulder and slam into me, driving me into the mat. Even though I knew the move was coming, it was done so expertly I had no way of avoiding it. When you're me, luck is kind of a relative thing.

"She's very good at those wrestling moves," HARV said.

"So I've noticed," I said aloud, getting lost in the moment.

I tried to bridge up on my back and then use that momentum to roll Nova over me. It didn't work. She had way too much experience to fall for that. She counteracted my bridge by shifting her weight down. She leaned forward over me and pinned me to the ground. If she wasn't trying kill me, I might have found the hold to be enjoyable. Not quite sure what that says about me.

"Talking to yourself again, Zach," she whispered in my ear.

Things just went from bad to worse. Not only was Nova pummeling me, but she knew who I was. I wasn't sure what that meant to the case, but I was certain it couldn't help.

Nova wasn't happy with having me simply pinned to the mat. She was determined to make me suffer a bit more. She managed to stand up using her legs while keeping her body between my legs and her arms tightly locked on my legs. I didn't like where this was heading.

"She's using herself as a fulcrum!" HARV said almost in awe.

I didn't like the sound of that. Unfortunately, there wasn't much I could do about it.

Nova started to spin and spin and spin. I was getting light-headed and not in a good way. This, too, might have been fun except I knew the end result was going to be a world of hurt.

After she spun me around somewhere between three and three hundred times, she released me. I went flying through the air, sailing out of the ring, and crashed to the floor with a very painful thud.

I have never missed my body armor as much as I did that nano. I was surprised I was still conscious. I was more astonished when I pushed myself up from the ground. I hurt, but not nearly as much as I ought to.

"The new improvements Dr. Pool made to my system are incredible. I was able to relax your muscles, making you better able to absorb the fall, while at the same time I was able to magnify and focus the electromagnetic current your body has to cushion your fall," HARV said. "You are so lucky you have Dr. Pool and me on your side."

"Yeah, like I always say, luck is a relative thing," I said heading back toward to the ring.

The guests and the elves started to applaud as I headed back. I didn't know if they were happy I was getting up or just anxious for me to take another beating. Whatever the case, a wise man would have been content to walk away from a thrashing like that. I, on the other hand, wasn't about to let Nova have her way with me. I knew Nova's type. Sadly, I've had far too much experience with them. If was going to get Nova to open up to me, I was going to have to prove that I could hold my own with her in the ring.

Of course to do that, I was going need HARV.

"I need you to flash her," I thought to HARV.

"Excuse me?" HARV said.

"I'm going to lock eyes with her, then you holo-flash her. Once you've blinded her, I'll have a chance."

"A slim one," HARV said.

Nova took a step back, letting me climb back into the ring. She wiped her brow, though she wasn't really sweating.

"You're either braver or stupider than I thought," she said.

"Probably both," I said.

She smiled. "I'm almost going to regret knocking you out. When you come to, we'll have to take a walk."

"Yeah, well, we'll see about that," I said.

She moved forward and grabbed me. I locked my eyes with her.

"Now, HARV!" I shouted in my head.

I didn't see the holo-flash but Nova did. She blinked her eyes and lowered her head.

"What the—" she said.

I made my move and cocked her with an upper cut to the chin. That sent her head rocketing back, but she didn't fall. She was off balance, and I aimed to take advantage of that. I moved forward, keeping my body close to hers. I grabbed her neck with my right hand and her waist with my left. I bent down and lifted her off the ground. Even bulked up she only weighed about seventy kilos, so it wasn't all that impressive—still, I was pleased. I body slammed her to the mat.

That looked like it should have really hurt her. She was smiling. I moved forward. She kicked up her legs and wrapped them around my neck.

"Sleep tight," she said, as she tightened her grip.

I may have been standing and on top but I was in trouble. Her grip was viselike. I dropped to my knees. Things started spinning. I might have been able to use HARV to shock her like I did the last time we had tangled, but with the crowd around that would have blown my cover. I decided discretion was the better part of valor here. Things went black.

21

When I woke up, I was in lying on top of my bed in my room. My head hurt a little but it was nothing I couldn't live with. I sat up in bed.

"What time is it?" I asked HARV.

"Do you mean Pole Time?" HARV asked.

"No, I mean Greenwich Mean Time," I snapped.

"Oh, that would be—"

"What time is it here, HARV?"

"Twenty-two hundred hours. You've been out for five hours. I'm not sure if Santana will insist on a credit for that time or what. You missed dinner but the elves said they would send you room service when you came around." HARV looked at me and asked. "What did you prove by getting in the ring with Nova?"

"I didn't have much choice," I protested.

"What did you prove by going back in after she tossed you out?"

"I need her to respect me," I said. "Or else she won't be of any help."

HARV shook his head. "Well, it seems to have worked. She's invited you for a walk outside tomorrow morning."

"Isn't it cold out there?"

"It will be minus twenty-eight degrees Celsius, but you'll be equiped with special hats and gloves. You won't feel a thing."

"You always say that, and I always do."

"I can turn off the cold and heat receptors in your brain, if you wish."

"No, that sounds worse than being cold. Those receptors are there for a reason."

I called room service and ordered a roast beef sandwich and a hot cocoa. I didn't really want the cocoa but that was all they would serve me this late at night, so I took what I could get.

As I ate, I thought about the case. I was reasonably certain somebody or something was reprogramming the guardbots to get them to do their dirty work. The question was, who? I knew it wasn't Nova. Now I was certain attacking people with bots just wasn't her style. Way too subtle. She may have been a member of a Santana Stinks Society, and she may have loved the snow, but she wasn't behind this. Still, I would be interested in knowing why she was here and how she saw through my holo-disguise. I planned to go over that with her during our walk tomorrow.

I also didn't believe the Eatmans were involved. I wasn't sure why. I wouldn't rule out that Mary hiring a killer, but I didn't see a motive. Not for her bringing down the Pole.

That left the Billingses, the Weatherses, and Bim and Norp. One or more of them was behind this. I felt it clear down to my toes. I just needed to figure out who. For that, I would need a method and a motive.

I still couldn't completely rule out a disgruntled elf or two. It's hard to conceive of, but maybe, just maybe, one or two of them doesn't like being dependent on Santana's life-extending drugs.

I decided to sleep on it.

Suddenly I was jolted awake by a loud gong in my head. I jumped up in bed.

"What's that?" I said, physically but not mentally awake.

"Are you up?" HARV asked.

"Of course I'm up! You just hit a gong in my cranium! This better be good!"

"I hear a guardbot rolling down the hall."

"So?" I asked, not bothering to hide the acid in my voice.

"I've tapped into the Pole's scheduling system, there are no guardbots scheduled to come down this hall for another hour."

"Oh," I said, rolling behind the bed. I placed the bed between myself and the door.

The door opened.

A guardbot holding a pillow in its claw rolled in. This one, except for the pillow in its claw, was identical to the two I'd tangled with before.

"Oh, I was hoping to make this look like an accident," it said in a metallic, not even close to human, voice.

"Right, like anyone was really going to believe I suffocated to death with my own pillow. It would have been just as subtle to laser me to death."

"Actually, Zach, it can't," HARV whispered. "All energy weapons are deactivated inside the building here."

"Great!" I said, as I stood up from behind the bed. I pulled the H_2O pistol from my elf suit pocket and showed it to the bot.

"It appears I have you outgunned!" I told it.

"Hardly," it gawked, as it rolled toward me. "My claw is infinitely shaper than razor wire, and I am far stronger than you."

"Don't forget more modest," I said.

"I am also oxidation proof. There is nothing an H_2O pistol can do to harm me. Even if I wasn't oxidation proof, you would be long dead before the water in that little gun could even begin to harm me."

"Very true, my long-winded friend . . ."

I pulled the trigger, hitting the bot with a stream of liquid right in its eye sensor. The sensor started to burn.

"If I actually had H_2O in here," I said, completing my statement. I was pretty sure by this point the bot couldn't hear me.

"Quick HARV, where's the main control unit on this thing?" I asked as I fired away.

"That's why you grabbed cleaning acid and the gun!"

"I figured if these guns can stand up to a ten-year-old kid then a little high-powered cleaning acid should be nothing. So where's the control CPU?"

"Lower back," HARV told me. "I'll give you a cursor target."

The bot now started to roam the room, spinning around and clawing at the air. Obviously, its programming had never covered being blinded by acid from an H_2O pistol.

I walked up behind it. A cursor appeared in front of my eyes and seemed to zoom in on the bot's back side. I fired at the spot the cursor covered.

The acid hit and burned through. The bot stopped moving. Its claw went limp. Its screen went dead. Its lights went out. It was deactivated.

I went to the wall computer and pushed the service button.

"Yes?" a polite voice asked.

"I need to see Santana and Elf-1 now, please."

"Yes, sir," the polite voice said.

Within minutes Santana and Elf-1 were in my room looking over the beat bot.

"We've never had problems with our guardbots before," Santana said shaking her head as she watched Elf-1 examine the bot.

"Actually, you have," I told her. "I think the two murdered elves are done in by bots. Plus, two of your bots attacked me at my office yesterday. I'm surprised they haven't turned up missing."

"There are two hundred bots here, but only one hundred and seventy are active any given day, so you may have been attacked by one of the off-duty bots," Elf-1 said as he continued looking at the terminated bot. He took a deep breath. He took another deep breath. "Go to my happy place. My hap-hap-happy place."

"So our bots are bad," Santana said.

"I'm sure they had help getting that way," I said. "How many elves can reprogram a bot?" I asked Elf-1.

"All of us, except maybe Rocko," he answered.

"Great, that narrows it down."

"All bots have vid-recorders built into them. Everything they do is recorded," Elf-1 told me.

"I'm sure whoever did this wasn't stupid enough to leave the recorder on."

"The recorders are timed and nonstoppable. They are bound to show something. There should be at least a break in the clock when they were reprogrammed," Elf-1 told, bubbling over with excitement. This guy really needed to get out of the Pole once in a while.

"Check it out. It might give us something," I told him.

"I better shut down the bots until we figure out what's going on," Elf-1 said.

"No, let's not panic yet. We still don't know who or what

is behind this. If we shut the bots down now, they might cover their tracks before we can find them," Santana said without hesitating. She looked over at me for approval.

"I couldn't agree more."

"So what's the plan then?" Elf-1 asked.

"Get some rest. Tomorrow will be a long day!"

22

I was awoken the next morning by a buzzing from my room's wall computer.

"I'm awake! I'm awake!" I said, as I sat up in bed.

"Message from Elf-1 coming in," that polite voice from the computer said.

"What's up, Elfy?" I asked.

"Bad news, Mr. Johnson. I mean Mr. Starr. The bot's replay showed nothing out of the ordinary. In fact, its internal clock was even continuous."

"Hmm, do you record energy readings in the area?"

"Of course!"

"Good. Check for enhanced radio wave and HF microwave transmissions over the last few days."

"Right," Elf-1 said. "I'll beep back when I have something."

I stood up and stretched.

HARV appeared.

"Are you thinking what I think you're thinking?"

"HARV, you don't actually think, you just simulate thinking," I corrected, unable to resist a little mental jab. "But if you are calculating remote reprogramming, then yes."

"The bots have all their commands hardwired into them, making them tough to override."

"Tough, but possible."

"Yes, possible. But also quite expensive," HARV said. "Uh oh, call coming in," HARV said a split nano before he disappeared.

"Mr. Johnson?" Elf-1 called through the wall computer.

"Yes?" I said, activating the vid-conferencing.

"HF wave transmissions to the Pole have been up since yesterday, probably due to sunspot activity."

"Actually, that would be me," HARV whispered. "I needed to access some outside dbases."

"But," Elf-1 continued, "the readings jumped way up last night for about twenty nanos."

"Thanks, Elf-1, I'll keep you informed." I pushed the button on the wall turning off the vid-conferencing.

"Who do we know who can remotely reprogram bots?" I asked HARV.

"ExShell and HTech have both done it in the past with average bots and computers."

"What about the MESSHs?"

"In their sleep," HARV said.

"I'm going to shower, shave, and grab breakfast. I'm famished!"

"Yes, you can't solve crimes on an empty stomach," HARV said more than a little cynically.

"I could," I corrected. "But then I'd be grumpy afterward."

23

When I got to the breakfast table, Nova and Councilwoman Weathers weren't there. Nova was at the gym working out. Weathers had a special meeting with Santana. That gave me a chance to chat with the others and to see how Bim and Norp acted when Nova wasn't around. I learned that when Nova wasn't around, Bim and Norp spent their time talking about Nova. They wanted to join her at the gym, but Nova made it clear to them it was *enter at risk of death*. For some reason, they listened.

Mary and Steve were busy trying to decide what to do with their free time today. Mary wanted to make one last pitch to the elves to get them to unionize. Steve had his head set on reviewing the Pole's computer systems.

This gave Carl Weathers and me time to chat. I asked him casually about his mining company. He was quite open about it. He insisted he didn't want to be bothered with it, but Stormy thought it would be a good investment for him. She said it would help keep him occupied. According to her, he couldn't just be Mr. Stormy Weathers all the time. Carl, for his part, said he didn't mind watching his wife from the bench. He had made a fine living being a bench-warmer, and he didn't see much reason to change now.

After breakfast, I waited by the Pole's main gate for a good fifteen minutes before Nova showed up. She was wearing her elf suit with the sleeves and legs ripped off.

"Sorry I'm late," she said grabbing me by the arm. "I wanted to stop at the gym for a little workout. It wasn't all that fun, though. None of their anti-grav weights go over one thousand kilos."

She started dragging me along.

"Come on, let's go!"

"You really want to go outside?" I asked.

"Of course, silly!" she said.

I looked out at snow, trees, lights, snow, some more trees, and more snow. What wasn't covered in snow was covered in ice.

"Isn't it a bit cold out there?" I asked.

"Don't worry," Nova reassured me. "Your suit is insulated."

"Yeah, but my head and hands aren't," I said.

Nova pointed to a box near the door. The box's hologram label read GLOVES AND HATS in English and many other languages.

I reached into the box and pulled out a skintight pair of gloves and a silly-looking elf hat. I slipped them both on. I couldn't have looked much more ridiculous than I felt, especially since the hat had a non-optional bell. They claimed it was a locator bell, but I had my doubts.

Nova smiled at me.

"Don't you need gloves and a hat and, well, pant legs and a long-sleeved shirt?" I asked.

She shook her head. "I find the cold exhilarating," she said. She looked up at the big door that led to the outside world.

"Door open," she said.

"Please make sure you are wearing your protective gloves and hat," a computerized voice said. "Remember the Pole takes no responsibility for what happens to you outside these doors," the voice continued. "Do you understand this disclaimer?" the door asked.

"Yes," Nova and I both said.

"Do you agree to this disclaimer?" the door asked.

"Yes," we both said again.

"Remember it's best to stay outside less than fifteen minutes. Please enjoy your experience. You may proceed."

The door swung open. Nova and I walked out. The suit and hat and gloves worked well. I didn't feel the cold.

"I'm honored you want to talk with me," Nova said, as we walked through the frozen everything.

"You might not be so honored when you find out what I want to talk about. First off, I'm interested in knowing how you know me," I asked.

She winked. "My little secret."

I glared at her. I don't normally glare at beautiful women, especially ones with arms bigger than my legs, but I wasn't in the mood to be subtle or coy.

"I could tell by your pheromone scent," she said. "I never forget a smell."

"Your mom must be so proud," I said.

She laughed. "Is that all you called me out here for?"

"You were the one who wanted to go walking through the frozen tundra. There is a reason I wanted to speak to you in private."

"Oh?"

"When doing a background check on you, I found you were once a member of the Santana Stinks Society."

She gave me a dismissive wave. "Yeah, the elves questioned me on that. I assured them I have nothing personal against Santana."

"Then why were you a member?"

"Guess," she said with a playful nudge on the shoulder.

"I'm not in the mood," I said, resisting the need to rub my shoulder.

"It was during my date-a-geek phase," she said.

"Ah, yes, Ben Pierce. The android expert turned lousy poet."

"He was against Santana."

"Why?"

"Mostly because ExShell had put in a bid for the Pole gig when Ben was a young scientist. They wanted Santana to be an android. Ben insisted that would be the way to go. Androids are more rational than organics, Ben always said. Even a genetically improved human couldn't keep up with a good android."

"The Council shot him down, though, huh?"

She nodded. "Yeah, they thought the world would relate better to an organic Santana. I agree. But to keep my man happy, I went along and joined the SSS. I did it under my real name just in case any fans found out."

"I see."

"I'm so through my geek stage now," she spat.

"I can see that, too."

"Anything else you want to chat about, Zach?"

"Somebody tried to kill me yesterday," I said coldly.

"Zach—I mean, Bart—I was only playing with you yesterday."

"No, somebody really tried to kill me."

"From what I understand, that happens quite often."

"True. I'm in demand."

"Do you think I tried to kill you? Because if you do, coming out alone with me wasn't such a good idea. Without your weapons and gadgets, I could literally kill you with a wink of my eye," she said.

"That may be true, but I don't think you're a killer," I told her.

With less than no warning, Nova lifted me up and heaved me across the ice. I went crashing through a display of three-meter tall glowing, plastic candy canes into a snowbank. I sat up and cleared the snow and stars from my eyes. Nova was storming toward me.

"You don't think I'm a killer?" she screamed at me.

"I've been known to be wrong—"

"You're right you're wrong."

"I hate being right about being wrong."

I ripped a big icicle off from above. Nova came at me. I clubbed her over the head with the icicle. The icicle broke. She just smiled. She picked me up off the ground and pulled me into a bear hug. She started to squeeze the life out of me.

"So, you don't think I'm a killer, huh?" she said.

"I'm starting to have second and third thoughts." I was hoping I would live to have fourth and fifth thoughts.

"Zach, grab her head with both hands. I have a trick up our sleeve," HARV whispered. "But first you'll have to remove your gloves."

I was pretty sure I knew where HARV was going with this. I had to move fast, as I felt the air being squeezed out of my lungs. I pulled off my left glove and dropped it the ground. I pulled of the right glove and let that one drop, too. I clasped both hands around Nova's ears. Electricity shot from my hands to her head. She dropped me.

"HARV, can you do that again?"

"You bet."

I grabbed her by the left ankle. Electricity shot from my hands. She started jumping around on one foot. I pulled the other foot out from under her. She fell to the ground.

I backed off, ready for anything but in the mood for no crap. I wasn't about to let this lady put a beating on me two days in a row. Outside, away from prying eyes, I could use all the tricks at my disposal.

She laughed. Not really the reaction I was expecting.

"You really have no sense of humor," she told me as she stood up.

"Not when somebody's trying to kill me," I told her as I stood up.

"If I was trying to kill you, you'd be dead yesterday."

"What is this, some kind of strange joke?" I asked.

"I am a killer," she informed me, "just not your killer. I'm a lady mutant pro wrestler. We have to have killer attitudes, or the other mutants will run all over us. In my circle, being tagged as not a killer is an insult."

"Sorry. My girlfriend is always telling me I have these antisocial tendencies."

She sat down, then patted the ice.

"Come sit next to me."

I reluctantly sat next to her. "You're not going to try to almost kill me again, are you?"

"Not as long as you don't accuse me of not being a killer again."

"Deal."

"By holding your own in mortal combat with me, you've earned my respect. Even if you did have to cheat—again."

"Hey, they say all is fair in love and war, and with you, Nova, it's hard to tell the difference."

"Thank you!" she said, as she smashed her hand into the snow.

"Don't mention it."

I watched as she munched on a handful of snow.

"Yum. This stuff is even better than sex and violence."

"You really like that stuff."

"I and pretty much all mutants have a thing for this snow, but Santana won't sell it."

"So is that why you're here? To talk to Santana about a deal?"

"I wish. I'm just here because somebody sent me a free pass."

"Do you know who?"

"No, and I don't really care, though I have a pretty good

idea," she said as she grabbed more snow. "Just as long as I get to eat this wonderful ice." She paused to swallow, then said, "Somebody tried to kill you?"

"No, it was just a clever ploy so I could accuse you of not being a killer so you'd try to practically kill me."

"You really hold a grudge, don't you?"

"Sorry, sometimes I get a little resentful of being the universe's punching bag. Yes, somebody tried to kill me."

"Any idea who?" she asked.

"Well, I'm pretty certain who it wasn't. I don't think it was the Eatmans, and not to offend you, but I don't think you're the one, though I do think you are capable of killing."

"You are a fast learner."

"What do you know about Bim and Norp?" I questioned.

"They're annoying."

"They seem to like you."

"Believe me, it's not mutual. Like I said, I'm past my geek-freak stage."

"I assume they're the ones who sent you the free ticket."

"I wouldn't be surprised. But I doubt they have the external sex organs to attempt to murder you."

"Maybe not in person. But I think they are capable of sending a bot after me."

"A bot? What kind of bot?" she asked me.

"A guardbot," I stated cooly.

"A guardbot!" she said, far more excitedly than the conversation should warrant.

"Yes, a guardbot," I said, starting to lose my patience.

She leaped over and pulled me to the ground a split nano before a laser blast fired over my head, melting the snowbank where my head had just been.

"Yep, a guardbot just like that!" I said, pointing at the approaching bot. "HARV, I thought you said the guardbots couldn't fire their lasers?"

"I did. But I stressed the inside of the Pole's buildings part. Currently, you are outside, therefore—"

"Great! And I don't even have my H_2O pistol."

The bot fired another round of laser bursts just over our heads.

"Your eye, it talks," Nova said.

"And talks, and talks, and talks, but that's the least of our worries now," I said.

"Ha! So that's how you blinded me yesterday! And shocked me just now! You're wearing a computer! DOS, I thought Bim and Norp were the geeks."

"Let's focus on the situation at hand, Nova."

The bot slowly rolled toward us. "I have deduced that you are unarmed. Therefore I may safely approach and annihilate you from a close distance. I will not fail like my comrades."

"HARV, do you have enough juice to give this thing the shock treatment?" I asked.

"I think so."

"Will it stop it?

"If you can get behind and zap it in the main control panel, probably."

"It's not going to just let me get around it, HARV. The old 'your shoe's untied' trick isn't going to work here."

The bot closed in.

Nova reacted quickly and surprisingly. She stood up, grabbed me, and then hurled me over the bot just as it fired. The laser from the bot flew by me and hit Nova in the shoulder. She fell back in pain, but didn't show it. I flew through the air with the greatest of ease over the bot. The bot fired at me several times but missed ever so slightly each time. Apparently it wasn't programming to hit flying targets. I crashed to the ground just behind the bot. I lunged toward it.

"NOW, HARV!" I shouted.

Electricity shot from my hands into the bot. The last thing I remember was an explosion.

The next thing I knew I was waking up in the Pole's infirmary. Santana, Elf-1, and Nova were watching an elf doctor examine me.

I slowly started to come around. "Electra's right. I shouldn't eat zap wave pizza before I go to bed."

"He's going to be all right now."

I sat up in my toboggan-shaped bed. My head hurt, but I seemed to be alive. "DOS, I was hoping this whole ordeal was just a dream."

The doc shook his head.

"I'd like a second opinion."

Everybody else shook their heads.

"I was afraid of that, " I said.

"You're lucky to be alive, Zach," Santana said.

"That's easy for you to say."

All of a sudden I thought of something.

"HARV?" I called.

No answer.

"HARV? Come in, please."

Still, no answer.

"He's obviously delirious," the doc told Santana.

"HARV, talk to me," I said, as I tapped my head.

"Zach, I'm undercover. Remember?" HARV whispered.

"Forget the cover, HARV, that's pretty much blown. How come you didn't tell me what would happen if I tried to zap a guardbot?"

"I didn't want to scare you."

"WHAT?" I shouted until the pain in my head made me stop.

"It actually makes sense. The only chance you had of stopping the bot was using me to electrocute it. So, the fact that you might actually electrocute yourself didn't matter, since you would have died anyway."

"I hate to admit it, HARV, but you're right," I said as I wobbled to my feet.

"Of course," HARV agreed, appearing before us.

"He's wearing a computer. That's against the rules!" Elf-1 shouted.

"Number One, when it comes to rules, I don't think they apply to Mr. Johnson here," Santana said.

"They apply. I just choose to ignore them when the choice is comply or die. Survival of the fittest, or at least the trickiest, is the only rule I adhere to."

I looked at Nova and smiled. "You thought pretty fast on your feet back there."

"A good warrior knows how to think on her feet as on well as her back," she told me.

"Who do you think is behind all this, Zach?" Santana asked.

"I never accuse until I'm positive. It cuts down on lawsuits. I need to talk one-on-one with Mrs. Billings, Councilwoman Weathers, and Bim and Norp."

Santana raised an eyebrow. "The councilwoman?" she said. "Surely you don't think she's behind this. After all she's the most—"

"—respected and honest person in the world. Yes, I know. HARV read me her press release. She's still a person of power, and that makes her a person of interest to me."

"If you say so," Santana said, her eyes focusing on the floor. "You're the expert, and you know best."

"It's also time for me to reveal my true identity," I said. "Let the bad guys know I'm on the case."

"Don't you think they already know since there have been two attempts on your life in the last two days?" Elf-1 asked.

I shook my head. "That might be bad karma." I looked at Nova. "Or warnings from jealous lovers. Even if they do know my identity, my coming clean will make them think I'm close to breaking the case. It will force their hand.

"I need to talk to those people first and then if needed the entire group."

"Fine," Elf-1 said. "I'll have Ma Billings meet you in the library at seventeen hundred. Is that all right?"

"What time is it now?"

"Fourteen-oh-two," HARV answered.

"Okay, I can live with that. That gives me time to go to my room, collect my thoughts, and clean up."

With that, I left.

24

I arrived in my room and threw myself down on my bed. Both of the most recent attempts on my life were after I had been with Nova. I was pretty certain Bim and Norp were behind them. I wasn't as sure Bim and Norp were behind the dead elves. I couldn't see what they would gain from it. Still, there had to be a connection.

While I took a quick shower (with green and red sprays of water) HARV and Elf-1 made arrangements. I would meet with my major suspects first: Mrs. Billings, followed by the councilwoman, then Bim, followed by Norp. I would do the questioning, and HARV would do a voice analysis of their answers, while Santana and Elf-1 listened in. After I met with a suspect, they would be kept separate from the others. Once I had meet with each suspect, we'd all get together, I would reveal myself as Zach Nixon Johnson, and identify the killer. It would be a great storybook moment. There was only one problem. I knew what it was, but that didn't stop HARV from pointing it out to me the second I got out of the shower. (I should be happy he waited for me to get out.)

"You're going to do the dramatic reveal?" HARV asked.

"Yep," I said, as I moved under the body dryer.

HARV pointed to one of the buttons on the wall. "Don't set the dryer on high. You know how you chafe."

"Yes, Mom," I said, pressing the Low button.

I felt the warm air run up and down my body. It felt good, even with the music from the Holiday song playing in the background. I knew HARV wasn't about to let the feeling of warmth last.

"Surely you realize there is a problem with you staging

a comic book unveiling of the mastermind behind the murders," HARV said.

I shrugged. "Not really," I said, just to drive HARV a bit buggy.

HARV threw his arms up in the air. "Zach, Zach, Zach! Most detectives don't schedule an appointment to name the killer until they know who the killer is."

"I'm not your average detective, and this isn't an average case," I said, heading into my bedroom.

HARV put his hands on his hips and groaned. He disappeared from the bathroom. He appeared directly in front of me.

"What, too lazy to walk?" I said.

HARV put a holographic hand on my shoulder.

"You know, HARV, that kind of creeps me out when I'm not wearing clothing," I said.

HARV withdrew his hand. "Sorry, I'm just very secure in my sexuality."

"Yes, of course you are, considering over the last year you've been a woman and gay."

"What can I say? When I experiment I really experiment," he said.

I went to the closet and picked out an elf suit. It wasn't much of choice, since they were all identical.

"I've narrowed down the list of suspects," I told HARV. "After my one-on-one sessions, the list will be even smaller."

"And if it's not?"

"I bluff. I put on the big show, and let the bad guys sweat."

"And if they don't?"

"Don't worry, they will," I said.

"How can you be so confident?" HARV said.

Truthfully, I wasn't certain how I'd know. It was just another one of my hunches. Those hunches had kept me alive this long—I wasn't about to stop trusting them now.

25

I sat in a comfortable plush chair in the library waiting for Mrs. Billings. The library was filled with giant computer screens in front of big fluffy chairs that looked and felt a lot like clouds, only with more support. Outside of the holly draping the doors, the room wasn't as over the top as the rest of the Pole. Of course the Muzak-II version of the Holiday theme was playing subtly in the background.

From my comfy chair, I saw Mrs. Billings enter the room and slowly skulk toward me.

"You wanted to see me, Mr. Starr?" Mrs. Billings asked uneasily as she approached me.

I motioned to a chair.

"Please sit."

She sat, albeit reluctantly.

"May I ask what this is about?" she asked. I could almost hear her heart pounding from where I sat.

"Robotics. Quantum physics. Radio waves. Life. Death. Taxes. Sports scores. You name it."

"I beg your pardon?" she said, as she gave me that *are you crazy or what* look I get so often.

"Quit playing the naive farm ma with me. I know you used to work for HTech designing guardbots."

She hesitated for a nano. I suspected she'd deny it. I was mistaken.

"That was a long time ago. It's all behind me now," she said meekly.

"Why?"

"Why?"

"Why'd you quit?"

"I don't see where that's any of your business."

"It is my business when your bots try to kill me."

"What are you talking about?" she said, standing up from the chair.

"In the last two days, I've been attacked three times by four of your bots."

"First of all, they are hardly my bots. HTech and I broke off our relationship years ago. Secondly, if you really did face off with just one guardbot, you'd be dead now. They are more than a match for any normal human."

"Well, let's just say I'm not *any* normal human."

Here is where I decided to go off script. I reached down on my belt and deactivated the holo-disguise. From my point of view, I only saw a slight shimmer in the images I was looking at. From the look on Mrs. Billings' face, I could see she was seeing me.

"Do you know who I am?" I asked.

"You're that private investigator guy—the one who's always getting himself in strange jams."

"I don't get myself in jams on purpose. They tend to find me," I said

She put a hand on her chest. "What are you doing here?"

"She's not nearly as surprised as she's pretending to be," HARV whispered inside my head.

"Like I said, your bots tried to killed me."

"I have no idea why that would happen," she insisted. "What are you doing here anyway?" she repeated.

"Two elves were killed. Santana brought me here to investigate."

There was silence. She was calculating the best response to this. She was an engineer all right.

"She's covering something, but she's not in panic mode," HARV said.

"Are you accusing me of something?"

"No, I'm just curious. Curiosity may have killed the cat, but it tends to keep the PI alive. Why are you and your family here?" I asked.

"We're on vacation—little Billy won a contest."

I shook my head. "You're trying to tell me it's sheer coincidence that one of the designers of the Pole's guardbots happens to be at the Pole when the guardbots decide to start killing elves and attacking me."

She sneered at me. "Your information is old, Mr. Johnson," she said. "If you look hard enough and in the right places, you will see that I only worked on the guardbot project at the very beginning. I was transferred to another project."

"I can't confirm that, Zach," HARV said inside my head. "But I can say she's either not lying or an expert liar."

She shrugged. "Why would I want to kill elves? Or you for that matter? Until just seconds ago, I had no idea who you really were." She paused for a nano and then squinted her eyes. "Though I can understand why somebody would sic guardbots on you."

"She's definitely not lying with that last statement," HARV said. "You might want to take a people-skill course."

I thought about what she had said. She didn't seem to have a motive, yet I didn't trust her. Something about her ate away at the very core of my being. What was she doing hiding out in New Kansas? It wasn't as backwards as, say, Oakland, but it wasn't exactly on the forefront of engineering breakthroughs either.

"So, what made you move to New Kansas?" I asked.

She looked up at me, gauging me. "I'm not a murderer," she said.

"I didn't say you were."

She shook her head. "The pressure of working for HTech got to me. I wanted to get as far away from robots as possible."

"She's not lying," HARV said to me.

"I guess being a farm mom in New Kansas is as far away from making robots as you can get."

Her face cracked a weak smile. "That's why I love it so much. It's good, honest work. I'm making the world a better place now, not worse."

This struck me as a strange comment. Most engineers I know do what they do because they love creating things.

"You didn't like making robots?"

"No. I was in it for the money. Believe me, it was HUGE amounts of money, but after a while I needed to work with something with a soul."

"Wheat?"

"No, my family."

"Oh."

"My family and I help feed other families."

"You must use bots to help with the work," I said.

"Of course we do, but those bots are just a means to the end, not the end itself. Bots are necessary in today's world. I know that and accept that."

"You'll use them but not create them."

"Exactly, Mr. Johnson."

"You're a regular the-end-justifies-the-means kind of gal," I said.

"You have no idea," she said.

"Her heart rate jumped there," HARV said to me.

I wasn't sure what that meant. However, I was pretty certain Mrs. Billings wasn't responsible for the death of the elves.

She stood up from her chair. "Are we done?" she asked.

"For now," I said.

"Good," she said. "My family must be missing me." She turned toward the way out.

I reached forward and grabbed her arm. It was a gentle grab, but a grab nevertheless.

"I'm sorry, Mrs. Billings, but it will be a few minutes before you can rejoin your family. I have a couple other people of interest to chat with before I bring you all together."

She spun toward me, breaking my grip.

"Are you detaining me?" she asked angrily.

"Just delaying you for a few minutes," I said. "It's for the good of the case."

She gave me a glare that I assumed she normally used on her husband when he pissed her off.

"It will only be for a short time. I promise."

"The elves have cookies and hot cocoa," HARV whispered to me.

I pointed to a door at the back of the room. "There's a nice comfortable waiting room back there. The elves have cookies and hot cocoa," I said.

She inhaled deeply. "Well, I do *love* cocoa," she said.

"That's the spirit."

She headed off into the waiting room.

26

HARV and the elves coordinated the arrival of my next guest, Councilwoman Weathers. They gave me a few nanos to collect myself and to reactivate my holo-disguise. As soon as I sat in my chair, the door across the room opened. Councilwoman Weathers strutted in.

She had to be in her late fifties, but you couldn't tell by looking at her. There wasn't a blemish or a wrinkle to be found. Her eyes still had the sparkle of a teenager's. The only hint that she wasn't a young woman was the frosty gray of her hair. I imagined she kept the gray because some consultant told her it made her look distinguished. It did. In fact, she walked with an air of nobility not unlike a queen or a rock star.

"For Gates sake, stand up!" HARV coaxed from inside my head. "You're greeting a lady, and a very important lady, at that."

I knew HARV was right. I just didn't want to seem too anxious. I rose when the councilwoman was within a meter. The councilwoman walked up to me and extended a hand. I wasn't sure if she meant for me to kiss it or shake it. I went with the latter.

"Mr. Starr, I'm honored you wish to interview me, a humble servant of the people," she said.

"Please, I'm the one who is honored," I said.

I motioned to the chair. "Please sit," I said.

She looked at the chair as if it were a bear trap. "I'm a very busy woman," she said.

"You're on vacation," I said, pointing to the chair. "Trust me, this will only take a few minutes."

She hesitated, but capitulated. "Even on vacation I'm a busy woman," she said, easing herself into the chair.

"I appreciate your time."

"As well you should." She primed her lips, then crossed her legs. They were fine legs, upper-class legs. The legs of a woman who worked out because she wanted to, not because she needed to.

"How can I help you with your little story?" she asked. She was being polite, yet condescending, not letting me forget for a nano with whom I was dealing.

"I think my last interview was with an Oprah clone," she said with a hand fluttering in the air. She moved her hand in front of her lips.

"Or was it a clone of a clone?" She paused to think. "I can never tell them apart. I know most clones of clones go postal, but Oprah, well, she could afford the best of best."

"Yes, I'm sure," I said. "Only I didn't ask you here to talk about cloning clones," I said.

"Yes, of course," she said, sitting back in the chair. "What can I do for you?"

It was time for a decision: should I stay with the called play and interview the councilwoman in character, or do I go for the audible and hit her with the real Zach? It worked well enough last time. Only that was with an engineer-turned-farm-mom, and neither of those professions called for smooth people skills. This was a professional politician, an entirely different animal. No matter what HARV said, she was a professional liar. At the very least, she was a person who made her living telling other people what they wanted to hear and making it sound like it was her idea.

I went with the audible. Not only that, but I went for the long bomb, the touchdown pass. I switched off my holo-disguise. I was anxious to see her reaction.

"Well, well, Zachary Nixon Johnson," she said. "At last we meet." If she was surprised, she didn't show it. "I knew it was only a matter of time before our paths crossed. After all you save the world—"

"—and you run it," I said.

She smiled. "The world runs itself, Mr. Johnson. I'm just one of the many people who helps guide it in the best direction for all." She paused to compose herself. "What brings you to the Pole? Since you are in disguise, I gather this is more than a vacation."

"There's been a murder," I said. "And several attempts on my life."

One of her eyebrows wrinkled ever so slightly. "A murder? How come I haven't heard of it?"

"I can't tell if she's lying," HARV whispered inside my mind, "but she doesn't seem surprised."

I had to agree with HARV's assessment. The councilwoman seemed more taken aback that she wasn't notified than surprised.

"The Pole is funded by the World Council," she said. "Santana should have informed us."

I shook my head. "You were a businesswoman before you entered politics, weren't you?"

"Yes."

"Then you know it's bad news to spook your investors, especially with news of murder."

"Good point. We should have been told, nonetheless."

"Santana was planning on telling you, once she collected more data," I said. "That's where I come in."

"You're the data collection agency," she said with a grin.

I nodded. "My specialty is extra-sensitive material."

"When did the murder occur?" she asked.

"Two days ago," I said. "And it was two murders."

She gave me a funny look. "Two days ago? That's when my party and I got here."

"Exactly."

"But all the people I arrived with are still here." She thought for a nano. "Elves. Elves were killed."

"Yes," I said.

She locked eyes with me. "Surely, I'm not a suspect," she said. "I assure you, Mr. Johnson, I'm not an elf killer." She performed a mock strangling motion. "What did I do, kill them with my bare hands?"

I looked at her. "That doesn't mean you wouldn't hire somebody to kill them. Or in this case, hire somebody to rewire their killers."

She looked away from me. "I'm not even going to dignify that with a response," she huffed. "Why would I hire somebody to reprogram bots to kill elves?"

"I never mentioned bots," I said.

This shot her attention back to me. "Please, Mr. Johnson, you said 'rewire their killers.' I put one and one together and figured guardbots killed the elves."

"I can't tell if she's telling the truth," HARV said. "I still don't think she'd kill elves."

Not suspecting that I was listening to HARV, Councilwoman Weathers interpreted my silence as a sign that I didn't believe her.

"Why would I want to upset the Pole?" she asked me.

"Maybe because the Pole isn't operating quite the way you would like?" I said.

"You've lost me," she said.

"I know that certain people in the World Council would be very interested in using the elves' skills to make weapons," I said.

She leaned forward on her chair, hands on knees. She shook her head. "Now, how did you learn that?" she asked, even though I knew she meant it rhetorically. Her eyes wandered across the ceiling. I could see her mind working this out. Her eyes focused on me. "That little tramp Sexy Sprockets told you," she said.

I didn't answer for a nano, just to let her stew in her own juices. "Sexy isn't a little tramp," I said.

The councilwoman threw herself back in her chair. "Please, her bedroom sees more action than Grand Central Teleport Station." She pointed at me. "This is what happens when they let amateurs into politics. They misinterpret, and then they blab."

Now it was my turn to sit back in my chair. "Don't point at me, I didn't vote for her."

"Yes, but you kept her from dying," Weathers said. For a career politician, I thought she would have been better at hiding the venom in her voice.

"You admit there is some tension between the Council and Santana?"

"Not openly," she said. "There are certain Council members who would be interested in seeing the Pole widen their product base."

"Into weapons," I said.

"I wouldn't say that," she said.

"One of your coworkers could have organized this."

"They are all politicians, Zach. They are capable of anything."

"You're a politician, too," I said, feeling compelled to point out the obvious.

"Yes, I am, and a darned good one too, I might add. One who is too smart to mess with a good thing. I'm a woman of peace, Zach. I love what the Pole does for Earth."

"Wow, is she ever telling the truth," HARV said.

She put her hand on her heart and started patting her chest. "Trust me, Mr. Johnson, I continuously strive to make the world a better place," she said.

The words CONFIRMED flashed before my eyes in big neon letters. HARV was showing remarkable restraint by not scrolling HA HA! I TOLD YOU SO, across my eyes.

The councilwoman stood up. "I assume you are running some sort of voice analysis program on me."

"I am."

"I know it has confirmed that I am telling the truth," she said.

I nodded my head. "It has," I said.

"Then I'm free to go," she said.

I pointed to the door at the back of the room. "Yes, of course. I just ask that you wait in a secluded room while I talk to the other," I paused, looking for the right words, "people of interest."

"Will you be bringing my husband in?" she asked.

"Not in the first round," I said.

"Good," she said. "He's a sweet man and nice eye candy, but not nearly bright enough to pull off something like this."

She got up and sauntered out of the room. As she walked out, my eyes followed. I didn't want them to, but they did. She was that kind of woman. Not strikingly beautiful, but she commanded and held your attention. She is the closest thing we have to royalty these days. A woman of obvious upbringing and dignity. A woman with great intelligence and a quiet beauty. A woman respected by the entire planet. I knew she had to be in on it.

"You're too pensive," HARV said inside my head.

"Nah, just thinking," I said.

"Zach, for once can't you just admit you're wrong and stop looking for flaws in the councilwoman?"

"I've never seen you so defensive of a human that wasn't Randy," I said.

"I don't know what it is about her," HARV conceded. "I've never met a human that was so perfect. Well, not perfect, because no human can be perfect, but as close to perfection as humanly possible."

If I didn't know better, I would have said HARV was flustered by the councilwoman.

"You've got a crush on her," I said.

HARV appeared before me waving a finger in my face. "I knew you were going to say that. I am not in love, and I do not have a crush. Neither of those are logical."

I crossed my arms and looked at him. I didn't say a word. I just let myself smile ever so slightly.

"I know what you're thinking, Zach. He's connected to me, so he's becoming more and more illogical. I admit that thought has crossed my cognitive generators about a trillion times. But no, I just admire Councilwoman Weathers for being so good at what she does and so flawless."

"You know other exceptional women," I said.

"That's true. Electra is a wonderful example of the human female. She is smart, witty, beautiful, and a gifted doctor and athlete. I'm amazed every day that she loves you. Still, she has flaws—she snores, she has an irrational fear of moths, and she has a temper only slightly cooler than molten lava."

"Good point."

"Then there's Carol. She's another exceptional human woman. She is also beautiful inside and out and sharp as a tack. Being a class I level VI psi, she's one of the most powerful beings on the planet. I'm amazed every day that she works for you and respects you."

"Gee, thanks, HARV. I like you too."

"Despite all her good points, Carol is flawed. She can't cook, she has a funny left little toe, and her feet are much more potent than you would expect. Plus that temper! It may be harder to ignite than Electra's, but it's even more volatile when it does. Witness the ex-boyfriend whose car she melted . . ."

"She may be superhuman, but she's still human," I said.

"That's the amazing thing about the councilwoman—she's human but I can't find any flaws. You practically accused her of stomping on those dead elves herself, and she didn't bat an eyelash, and her body temperature didn't rise—she was cool as a cryogenic cucumber."

"That's what worries me, HARV. Like they say, if it looks too good to be true, it probably is."

"They also say it's possible to overthink a problem," HARV said.

"Wow, HARV, you're accusing me of thinking too much."

HARV put a hand on my shoulder. "Thinking may be too strong a word," he said with a smile. "Zach, I know you think you have a sixth sense when it comes to this kind of thing. I have admitted you do have a very good knack for shifting through the potential outcomes and choosing the right one."

"Thanks, you make it sound so special," I said.

"However, there are times when you just have to let it go, when you have to admit that the toaster really is just a toaster and is not trying to kill you."

"Fine," I said. "Let's get ready for Bim and Norp."

On some level I knew HARV had a point. We had an entire room full of good suspects, and there wasn't a need to go out of my way looking for another one. Still, there was something about the councilwoman that didn't sit right with me. I knew sooner or later I would figure it out. I hoped I would before it came back to bite me in the ass. The one solace I had was this time I could tell HARV "I told you so." That wouldn't be much comfort if the mistake killed me.

27

Once I gave the elves in the holding room the okay, they sent in Bim and Norp. I had wanted to see them separately, but they weren't going to stand for that. I guess they figured there was safety in numbers. Having them together meant I'd actually have to deal with them less and that was appealing to me.

I was back in full Bart Starr mode when they walked into the room. Even from across the library, I could tell from the way they shuffled reluctantly toward me they were none too happy to talk to me. I stood waiting for them, impatiently tapping my foot. I've seen sloths at the zoo move faster, and they probably smelled better too. Truthfully, I have never smelled a sloth. There are some things you can just assume.

I positioned two chairs across from my own. I had time to rearrange them numerous times before Bim and Norp reached me. I don't usually want to shoot people, but at that moment, they were very lucky I didn't have my gun. I was reasonably certain they had tried to kill me at least twice in the last two days, but my disdain for them went beyond that. It was as if my very DNA was programmed to be repelled by them.

I motioned to the chairs. "Gentlemen, please sit," I said.

"We prefer to stand," Bim said.

"Yes," Norp said.

This was a power play on their part. That's part of the reason they wanted to come in together—they figured they had me outnumbered. I wasn't about to let them get away with it, but for now I'd play it cool.

"Have it your way," I said, sitting in my chair.

There were a few nanos of awkward silence. I decided to let them speak first.

Finally, Norp said, "What do you want from us?"

I hesitated a nano and then answered, "I just want to talk."

"Nobody ever wants to talk with us," Bim said. "At least not to carry on an actual conversation. They just want us to help them and go away."

I pushed back the urge to say, "I know the feeling." "I'm interested in learning why you fine chaps came to the Pole," I said.

"Vacation," Bim said.

"Stress release," Norp said.

Both their responses were automatic, dare I say, rehearsed. I let them think about their answers a nano to see if they'd elaborate on their own.

"The Pole is a high-tech wonder," Bim said.

"A marvel," Norp added.

"Certainly your homes on Mars are just as high-tech," I said.

"True," Bim said.

"Affirmative," Norp said.

"Then there's another reason?" I asked.

"The food," Bim said,

"Love the eats," Norp said.

"Elves can cook," Bim said.

"Sure can," Norp said.

They both had beads of sweat forming on their brows. Even without HARV, I could tell they weren't lying, but they were holding back. It wasn't easy for them. Unlike the councilwoman, they weren't pros at this.

"What about Nova?" I asked.

They both wrinkled their faces into looks of feigned confusion.

"Who?" Bim asked.

Norp just shook his head.

"Nova, the muscular but gorgeous pro wrestler on the tour."

"Oh, that's her name," Bim said, slapping his knees.

"Now that you mention it, she does sound familiar," Norp said.

"She is a very sturdy woman." Bim said.

"I've seen better," Norp said. "But I wouldn't kick her out of bed for eating soy crackers," he added.

He elbowed Bim playfully. They both giggled. They were their own biggest fans. That was all I could take. I reached down and pressed the deactivate button on my holo-disguise. The slight shimmer I saw told me it worked. The looks of fear on Bim and Norp's faces confirmed it.

"Zachary Nixon Johnson," they both gasped.

"Your reputation really does precede you," HARV laughed inside my head.

I stood up. "Enough games, boys," I growled. I don't like being bullied. I hate being the bully. But there are time when I do have to use my size and fighting experience to my advantage.

I pushed my chest out and moved toward them. It wasn't a threatening move, just one that was quicker than a non-threatening one. Bim and Norp immediately sank back into the chairs.

"Please don't hurt us," Bim said, protecting his face with his hands.

"It was his idea," Norp said, protecting his face with one hand and pointing with the other.

Now we were making progress. "What was his idea?" I asked.

"Getting the bots to attack you," Norp said. "We wanted Nova all to ourselves. We were jealous."

"They are telling the truth," HARV said.

"How'd you reprogram the bots?" I asked.

Norp reached up on his head, pulled out a strand of green hair, and showed it to me. "My hair is actually a remote transmitter," he said. "It allows us to reprogram the bots."

"Pretty clever," I said.

"The dandruff even acts as a signal booster," he said with far more pride than he should have.

"More info than I need there."

Just then the door burst open. Santana came in, accompanied by Elf-1 and three other security elves. Santana's face was redder than her suit. She stormed up to the two MESSHs. "How dare you kill my elves!"

"And attack me," I added.

"That too," Santana agreed. She turned to Elf-1, "Number One, deactivate the bots, and place these two under arrest."

"With pleasure, madam," Elf-1 said.

I watched Bim and Norp watch Elf-1 press the button on his control wristband. They were smiling. Elf-1 looked at the wristband. He pressed more buttons.

"Santana, the bots aren't responding," he said.

"They are responding," Norp said, "to us."

Right about then, four guardbots rolled into the room.

"This can't be good," I said.

As if proving my point, a bot fired a warning shot up into the ceiling.

"Our weapons are activated. We suggest you surrender now," it shouted.

28

Santana, the elves, and I dove for cover behind the chairs a split nano before the bots opened fire.

"We tried to do this peacefully, but you've forced our hands!" Norp shouted.

"We were hoping it wouldn't come to this, but so be it!" Bim shouted.

They were both considerably braver when backed by armed bots.

"I suggest we make a hasty farewell and exit," Norp said.

"I agree," Bim said.

I peeked over a chair. The bots were holding their places until Bim and Norp got out of the line of fire. I wasn't sure if this was because they didn't want to accidentally shoot Bim or Norp, or if it was because the bots were a little slow in planning their attack. They had us outnumbered and outgunned, but these were guardbots, not attackbots or battlebots. That gave us a chance.

I turned to Santana, who was taking cover behind the same chair I was. Elf-1 was next to her, chanting, "My happy place, find my happy place"

"Santana, can you control them?" I asked.

"Normally yes, but something is blocking me."

"Do you still have communication with the rest of the Pole?" I asked.

Elf-1 looked down at his communicator. "Yes," he said. "I'm not sure how that helps."

"Well, it doesn't hurt," I said. I thought for a nano or two. "Is the holding room behind us secure?"

Elf-1 looked at his communicator. "Yes. Only the councilwoman and Mrs. Billings are in there."

"Let's join them," I said. "We'll plan from there. Let them know we're coming."

"Check," Elf-1 said.

"Then what?" Santana asked.

"We make a break for the door," I said. "A very fast break."

The three other security elves shook their heads no.

"If this is going to work, you'll need a distraction," one of them said.

"Agreed," another said.

The three of them looked at one another and winked.

"No, it's too dangerous," Santana protested.

"It's the only way," the third elf said.

The middle elf made a fist and extended it. The other two elves made fists and put them on top of his.

"For Santana!" the first elf shouted.

"For Santana!" the other two echoed.

"One for all and all for Santana!" they shouted. Yep, definitely too much sugar in their diets.

They turned to us and pointed toward the door in the back of the room. That was our cue.

"Stay low and go," I said.

The three elves took off one way, and I went the other, pulling Santana and Elf-1 with me. We raced toward the door. I heard laser fire and screaming elves. I didn't look back. I couldn't. What was behind us didn't matter now. The elves had sacrificed themselves, and I had to make sure it was worth something. If I was going to get cut down from behind, so be it.

The side doors that lined the room, those were a different story. I couldn't let us get ambushed there. We drew closer to the back door. I pushed Santana and Elf-1 ahead of me. It wasn't that difficult, as they were both faster than I was. While keeping the center of my vision focused on the target—the door ahead—I used quick glances to the left and right to see if there were any surprises.

It was a good thing I did. There were two guardbots rolling in, one from each side. DOS, this room had a lot of doors. I looked at the door we were rushing toward. We were still twenty-five meters away and in open space. We'd be easy pickings for the bots.

"HARV, how good is the holo-detection on these bots?" I asked.

"Not good at all, since technically holograms aren't allowed up here," HARV said.

That gave me an idea.

We raced toward the door. Elf-1 signaled the councilwoman and Mrs. Billings not to open the door for anyone or anything that wasn't us. We got within ten meters of the door—so close we could almost feel it. That's when all DOS broke out. The bots closed in on us, catching us in a crossfire.

Elf-1 was the first to take it—a killing blast right to the chest that cut a hole clean through him. Santana was the next to go down. It was a clean, high-powered shot to the head. Maybe a more advanced GE like Twoa Thompson would have been able to survive, but Santana was dead before she even hit the ground.

I was the bot's next target. Apparently, they were saving me for last. First one of them shot out my right leg. The other one shot out my left leg. They rolled up so close, they were practically touching me.

"It will be such a pleasure to kill you, Zachary Nixon Johnson," one of the bots said.

"We want to see the look on your face when you die!" the other bot said.

"You wouldn't believe the number of times I hear that in a day," I said.

The bots looked at me, confused. The sound of my voice had come from behind them. It slowly dawned on them. They hadn't cut down Elf-1, Santana, and Zachary Johnson. They had cut down holographic projections of us. Meanwhile, the real us had gotten the drop on them with a holographic cloak.

It may have not been the optimal move, tipping them to our presence by talking, but just as they wanted to see my face when they killed me, I wanted to see the look on their screens when they figured out what had happened. They had been duped by one of the oldest holographic tricks in the book.

Guardbots are basically cylinders mounted on a flexible tractor base with an information screen on top, just to give

them a semi-humanoid appearance. If you catch them off
guard and are nutso enough to dive at them and hit them
just right, you can knock them down. Once on the ground,
they are like turtles turned upside down—interesting to
look at, but not good for much else.

Before the bots had a chance to react, we lit into them.
I dove a meter at the one on the right, leading with my
shoulder. I was a free safety on my high school football
team. I wasn't a good one. I was more interested in scoring
with the cheerleaders than the score of the game. Still, I
knew how to hit and take a hit.

I plowed my shoulder into the upper third of a bot, right
below its screen and above its claw and gun. It fired a blast
or two at me in a panic. Both shots sailed underneath me
as I smashed into it. The bot crashed to the ground with
me on top of it. It hurt me some. It hurt the bot a lot
more. Guardbots aren't built to take tackles. They are supposed to be too smart to let anybody insane enough to
tackle them get close enough to actually do it.

The bot smashed into so many pieces I knew it was out
of the fight. I turned my attention to Santana and Elf-1.
Their fight was even less of a fight.

The bots had made a fatal mistake—they had angered
Santana. An angry Santana was not a pretty sight. By the
time her bot had figured out what had gone wrong, it was
too late to do anything about it. First, Santana ripped off
its laser cannon with her right hand. She then grabbed the
bot's claw arm with her left hand and yanked. The bot arm
gave way without much of a fight.

Santana took a lot of pleasure in showing the bot its arm
and gun. She cracked them both over her knee, splitting
them in two. The bot had no idea how to respond, and
even if it did, there was nothing it could have done.

Santana lunged forward and grabbed the bot, wrapping
her arms around its frame. She arched her back, lifting the
bot off the ground as she squeezed. The bot's metal frame
resisted the pressure for about a nano. Then it crumbled
like a piece of old aluminum paper under Santana's grasp.

"This is what you get for messing with my elves," she
yelled as she squeezed.

Meanwhile, Elf-1 kept one eye on the action and the
other eye on the other bots. They had finished off the secu-

rity elves and had been watching their cobots take us on. They were caught completely off guard by the turn of events. It didn't take them long to regroup and head toward us.

"Santana, Zach, I think we'd better move fast," Elf-1 said.

He didn't have to tell me twice. Santana, on the other hand, was taking a lot of pleasure (maybe a bit too much) in turning the bot into either a piece of junk or modern art, depending on your perspective. She was bending and mutilating it so much, I was starting to feel sorry for it.

I moved over and tapped her on the shoulder. "Let it go, Santana, so we can get out of here."

She stopped exerting herself. She nodded. "You're right," she said. She picked up the bot and spindled it over her head. She turned and hurled it at the remaining bots, who were powering up to charge us.

The dead bot flew into the others, causing them to separate. This was the last break we needed as we made our way to the door.

We reached the door and knocked on it. "It's Santana, let us in," she said.

A laser shot whizzed over our heads.

"And fast!" I shouted.

HARV had thrown decoys over us to toss off the attacking bots, but sooner or later the bots were bound to pick us off.

The door creaked ajar. Elf-1 one shot through. Santana make her way next. I held my breath and squeaked in.

The door slammed behind me.

29

Santana, Elf-1, Mrs. Billings, Councilwoman Weathers, and I were now in a small, private reading room. There was one long couch and a couple of computer terminals with gold tinsel lining the tops of the walls.

Our first move was to take the couch and roll it to the door, barricading it. We could hear the bots outside clanging at the metal door.

I looked around. The door we came in was the only way in and out of the room. On one hand, that was good. The bots weren't able to sneak up on us. On the other hand, the only way out was covered with bots. Bots that wanted to kill us.

"There are two hundred bots here," Elf-1 one said, now pumped from the action. "That means we outnumber them fifty to one. In hand-to-claw combat, we can take them out!"

"The causalities would be high," I said. "We had holograms and luck on our side. The others won't."

Santana shook her head. "No, I've already lost five elves to these things. There has got to be a better way."

"The electromagnetic pulse generator," Councilwoman Weathers said.

"The Pole has an EMPG?" I said.

"Yes. It's top-top-secret," Santana said. "It's located in the backup control room for use in case of pirate attack. It would deactivate their ships."

"The device can be modified to shut the bots down," Elf-1 said.

Now this sounded like a plan that had legs. This was

something we could pull off without anybody getting hurt. Obviously, something had to go wrong.

"I can signal my elf team to modify and activate the device," Elf-1 said.

Elf-1 typed a few commands into his communicator. He waited for a response. He frowned. I knew that plan was too easy. "Oh sugar!" he spat. He looked up at the ceiling. "I have to go to my happy place. My hap-hap-happy place," he said.

"What's the problem?" I asked.

"None of my team is currently located in the backup control room," Elf-1 said. "Security cameras show there are bots outside the backup control room. We can make a run for it, but it would be costly."

"There are no bots in the room," I said. "Correct?"

Elf-1 glanced at his communicator. "No."

I looked around the room. I saw what I was looking for along the top of the wall near the ceiling. I pointed to the heating ducts.

"Those are connected everywhere, aren't they?"

Everybody smiled. The heating ducks weren't big, but they were large enough for an average man to crawl around in. They would certainly have enough room for an elf.

"Send your team through the heating ducts," I said.

"Brilliant," Santana said.

"I like it," Elf-1 said.

"That will work," Mrs. Billings said.

"Zach, there may be a career for you in politics after this is all over," the councilwoman said.

"Please, you don't have to be threatening," I told her.

Elf-1 transmitted my idea to his staff. He stared at the communicator. He frowned. He kept reading. The frown grew wider. "We have a minor problem: it would take ten minutes to reprogram the EMPG."

"That's too long—the bots would kill them before they finished," Santana said. "There has to be a better way."

"Can your elves get to an armory for some weapons?" I asked.

Elf-1 shook his head. "We have no weapons."

The one thing I've learned in life is the easy way is never the way I get to go. Somehow, someway, I knew this was going to fall on my shoulders. That's my lot in life—to save the day when the chips are on the line.

"I have an idea," HARV said. "If somebody gives me the passwords and the specs, I can reprogram the EMPG in about a nano."

I was reasonably certain that HARV was just being polite in asking for the passwords and specs.

The corners of Elf-1's mouth started to turn up. He still wasn't smiling, but he wasn't frowning any longer. "Now that could work," he said.

I knew that meant I was going to have to crawl through the vents. Not exactly how I planned to spend my day, but it beat dying.

"Okay," I said, walking toward the vent. "Let's get this over with."

Elf-1 moved past me, pulling out a sound-based screwdriver. "First, I'd better disable the vent's security code."

Santana held Elf-1 to the vent. He punched about ten numbers into the numeric pad that sat just above the vent's rim. There was a beep of confirmation. Elf-1 removed the screws from the top left and bottom left corners. The lid slid down.

Santana lowered Elf-1. She looked at me. "Next."

I moved forward and stood under the vent. I'm two meters tall, but even with my arms extended the vent opening was still a good meter out of my reach.

I looked over my shoulder at the group looking me over.

"I could jump," I said.

"This is not a problem," Santana said walking toward me.

I knew what she was planning to do. "Santana, I'm not a fifty-kilo elf," I said.

"I weigh fifty-four kilos," Elf-1 said sharply.

"I'm not a fifty-four-kilo elf," I said.

Santana made a spinning motion with her hand. "Turn around and reach for the sky," she said.

I spun back toward the vent. I stretched my arms upward. I felt Santana's hands on my hips. I started to rise. Santana was lifting me as if I were a fifteen-kilo elf. I grabbed the edge of the vent. I pulled myself in.

I looked down the vent. It was a long, reflective metallic tube that went on for as far as I could see. Kind of like a midget's hall of mirrors. It was just wide enough for me to crawl in, but I didn't have much wiggle room. I wouldn't be doing any push-ups in there. All in all, though, one of the nicer vents I'd ever been in. The best thing was the Holiday theme wasn't playing. I started crawling forward.

"HARV, you can lead me to the control room, right?" I whispered.

"With the hundreds of kilometers of ducts in this place, you would have very little chance of finding it without me," HARV said.

"A simple yes would suffice," I said.

"Yes," HARV said.

A red beam projected from my eye. It stretched down the duct for maybe three hundred meters and then turned to the right.

"Just follow the red beam," HARV said.

Being a smart guy, I did as I was told. I tagged along the beam, following it down this vent until it hung to the right. It went straight for a bit, then left, right, right, up, right, left, down, reverse, and then to the right. Actually, I had no idea. I stopped keeping track about a nano into the trip. I knew HARV would lead me the best way. I was fairly confident there wouldn't be a pop quiz afterward. The important thing was for me to get there ASAP. It felt like I crawled for a couple of hours (HARV would later insist that it was only seventeen minutes and twenty-two seconds) when I finally came to the grate above the control room.

I looked down through the slits in the grate into the room. The walls were lined with sensors, screens, and machines of all sizes. I didn't recognize much. I was betting that HARV knew exactly which of the myriad of devices was the EMP generator.

There were no bots in the room, but that didn't mean they weren't right outside the door waiting to spring a trap.

"HARV, are there any bots outside in the hall?" I asked.

"Not at the present," HARV whispered. "There are two patrolling up and down the hallway, but currently neither is within one hundred meters of the door."

This struck me as strange. If Bim and Norp intended to hold the Pole, surely they would have had this room better secured. Unless, of course, they didn't know about the

EMPG. That didn't fit their MO. Bim and Norp were ultra geeks, and they lived for stuff like that. It was highly classified and secured, but that would only entice them more. This had to be a trap.

I took a deep breath. I was thinking too much again. Trap or not, if we were going to shut down the bots and stop Bim and Norp, I had to do this.

I gave the top of the grate a quick jab with my elbow. The seal broke and opened up a slight crack between the grate and the vent. I took my hand and starting pushing down on the grid until I felt the grate break off in my hand.

Now I had another problem—getting out of the vent. I would have to either plummet headfirst to the ground or backtrack a bit, turn around, and then back my way out of the vent feetfirst.

"Where's the nearest point I can turn around?" I asked HARV.

"You'd have to crawl backward for at least one hundred meters before you could turn around to crawl backward to where you are now. You should have thought of this sooner, Zach."

"You should have thought of this sooner, HARV. You're the computer—it's your job to think of these things."

"It's only a three-meter drop. I didn't realize you'd be such a baby about it. Besides, I thought you'd want to see where you were going."

I took a deep breath. I didn't have time to position myself to land feet first. I looked down. It wasn't that high. I've certainly fallen from much greater heights and lived to get people to buy me drinks while I talked about it. Still, it was going to hurt. The moment I hit the floor I'd be like a beetle on its back—helpless. Unlike the beetle, I'd be able to right myself.

I took another deep breath. I slid out of the vent. I rolled down the wall and crashed to the floor with a very undistinguished thud. It hurt, but I'd been hurt worse shaving (sadly true). I pushed myself up.

The door to the room flew open. Two guardbots rolled in. I let myself drop back to the floor just as two laser shots careened over me.

"Another fine mess you've gotten me into, Ollie," I said to HARV.

"You don't need my help getting into messes, Stan," HARV retorted. I was proud he got the reference. I was less than pleased to be under attack. I stayed low and scrambled across the floor, using a table that traversed the middle of the room for cover. Many more laser shots flew over me. I didn't feel anything, so I assumed they missed. I instinctively headed forward. I don't know why.

"Zach, I've tapped into the control room surveillance cameras," HARV told me. "I can see your assailants even when you can't. One is moving to the left, one to the right."

Now I knew they were trying to set me up in a crossfire (guardbots just love crossfires). There are times when having a supercomputer wired to your brain is a good thing.

I rolled under the table just before laser fire tore up the spot where I had been laying on the floor.

I needed a plan and fast. Fighting the bots mano-a-boto didn't seem like it was going to work this time, even if I used a holographic cover. The bots knew my general location, and the room was small enough that they would be able to take me out with sporadic fire.

"HARV, can you remotely reprogram the EMPG?" I asked, dodging deadly laser fire left and right.

"Of course," HARV said. "Though for me to override its firewalls, you'll have to be looking directly at it from no more than two meters away."

That sounded like something I could pull off. The problem was, in all this scrambling for my life business, I wasn't able to pinpoint where I was in the room in relation to the EMPG.

HARV knew this.

"I suppose you have no idea where you are right now," HARV said.

"I have a general idea—somewhere between the Pole and death," I said.

I rolled to the left just as two more laser shots burned the place I had just been. I dodged to the right a split nano before two more shots scorched the floor I'd just left.

"Lucky for you, you have me," HARV said.

"Right now HARV, luck isn't the word I'd use."

I was pinned down and unarmed. If HARV thought this was "lucky," I didn't want to know what it would take for him to consider me doomed.

"By sheer accident, you are quite near the EMPG," HARV informed me. "It's merely three meters to your left."

A flashing red arrow pointing to the left appeared in front of my eyes. A picture of the device appeared next to it. It didn't look all that daunting—kind of like a box with a plastic lid on it. Another, smaller arrow appeared pointing at the lid.

"I'll turn off all the fail-safes for you as you head toward it. You just need to flip the safety lid, then push the button to fire it off."

I cocked my head to the left. I could see the EMPG out of the corner of my eye.

"I don't suppose you can push the button for me," I said.

"Sorry, there are some things you still have to do yourself. If not, I wouldn't need you to solve cases."

I took a deep breath.

"Zach, I'm doing the hard work. All you have to do is flip a lid and hit a switch. Easy as counting to one."

"I also have to dodge laser fire," I noted.

"Yeah, I didn't want to bring that up," HARV said. "I'm trying have a positive cognitive attitude here."

Speaking of the laser fire, something was wrong. There hadn't been any in the last thirty seconds. If I was an optimist (and a fool), I would have assumed that the guardbots had run out of charges. I'm not that optimistic, foolish, or nearly that fortunate. I knew it had to be something else.

"The bots are rolling into a better position now, aren't they?" I said.

"Affirmative," HARV said. "It appears their logic is not to waste charges when they know exactly where you are heading."

I peeked to the side of the table again. Sure enough, there were two bot-bases positioned on either side of where I now knew the device was. The nano I made my move they would blast me.

"You have to give them credit for conserving energy," HARV said.

"I feel much better knowing I'll be killed by environmentally-conscious tin cans."

"Zach, they don't make bots out of tin," HARV said. "At least not killer bots like these."

"I don't suppose I can wait them out?" I said.

"They are bots—they have no need to eat, drink, or use the bathroom. They don't get bored. They can outwait you."

"I was joking, HARV."

"Oh, right. I should have caught that."

"Maybe you could tell some Rodney Dangerfield jokes to distract them?" I said.

"Zach, they are guardbots—they have no sense of humor. Plus, I have run my course with Mr. Dangerfield's unique brand of humor. I am now looking for new inspiration. Care to make a suggestion?"

I shook my head. HARV was really missing the big picture here.

"Tell you what, HARV. If I live through this, I will help you find one."

"Deal," HARV said.

Now that I had an extra reason to live, I needed a plan, and I needed it fast. The longer I sat pinned down, the more time Norp and Bim had to get away. I didn't like that at all. I was pretty certain I would like being shot even less. I took inventory of my assets: I had my wits, my muscle, and my computer. What I wouldn't give for a good blaster and my body armor. No use crying over milk that hasn't even been poured. I was going to have to make do with what I had.

I knew the nano I stood up from under the table, the bots were going to blast me. I could use that to my advantage. Maybe I could trick the bots by positioning a hologram of myself between them. Then they would blast each other.

I took a deep breath and readied myself for my big move. I pushed up slightly from ground.

"Zach, the bots have just activated their holographic detection software," HARV said.

I let myself sink back to the ground. "They won't fire on my hologram," I said to HARV.

"Nope, the old let 'em shoot each other through the ho-

logram trick won't work here. They are now smart enough
to identify a hologram."

I smiled. That was it. It's amazing where you can get
inspiration from.

"Zach, your pleasure-sensing endorphin levels just raised.
You're happy about something." There was a slight pause.
"Gee, Zach, I never realized you had a death wish. Though
that would explain a lot: your choice of career, your taste
in women, your taste in clothing."

"What's wrong with my taste in clothing?"

"Zach, this isn't the time."

HARV was right on two accounts: I was happy, and this
wasn't the venue to argue over fashion sense.

"I have a plan," I said to HARV.

"Does it involve being shot a few times and dying a
painful death?" HARV asked.

"No," I said. "I want you to cover me with an exact
hologram of myself."

"Zach, they won't shoot . . ." HARV said before com-
puting. "They won't shoot at the hologram!" he said figuring out where I was headed.

"For a supercomputer, you catch on fast," I kidded.

HARV was silent. I knew he was thinking about everything that might go wrong with this plan.

"The bots will stall, but only for a split nano before they
realize that the real you is under the hologram," he said.

I didn't have a better option. I'm not the type of guy
who can cower under a table for long. I had to do something, and this was my best chance.

"It's either that or wait for the warranty on the bots to
expire," I said.

"You are attempting to be humorous again, correct?"

I didn't even bother to answer that. If I stayed under
this table, my legs would cramp up. Then it would be even
harder for me to move to EMPG.

"Do you have me covered, HARV?"

"Affirmative. Do you want to know your odds of
succeeding?"

I shook my head. "You know me, HARV. I never want
to know the odds." If I did, I'd never get out of bed.

I took a deep breath. I hoped it wasn't going to be my
last. I pushed myself up, shot out from the under the table,

and raced toward the EMPG device. In my peripheral vision, I saw the bots tracking me and aiming their gun turrets at me.

I reached the EMPG device.

"He is only a hologram," one of the bots said.

"I concur," the other bot said.

I smashed my elbow down, shattering the protective glass that was covering the EMPG trigger switch.

"A hologram should not be able to do that," one of the bots said.

I lifted my elbow up quickly and slammed it back down on the trigger.

"He's not a hol . . ." a bot started to moan.

Everything flashed white.

I turned toward the bots. They were slumped over. They looked like old slinkies that had lost their slink.

"HARV, are you still with me?" I asked.

Silence.

I was sure Randy had built EMPG protection into HARV. Maybe I was wrong. The word TESTING flashed in front of my eyes. A beam of light shot out from my lens. The light formed the number one. The one morphed into a two which morphed into a three. The three morphed into HARV. A shaky, blurry HARV. HARV slowly regained his composure and focus.

"Now that was an experience I don't care to repeat," he said, spinning his head around in a circle.

"Stop going all Linda Blair on me, HARV." It was creeping me out.

HARV put his hands up to his ears to stop his head from spinning. Unfortunately, he stopped his head in a position that was about forty-five degrees to the right of where a head should be. He used his right hand to push his head to the left until he was looking directly at me. He smiled.

"Now that's better," he said.

"Don't you have EMPG protection?" I asked.

HARV nodded. "Of course I do. Dr. Pool thought of everything."

"Then why'd you bug out on me?"

HARV lowered his eyes and sighed. It was his typical *I don't believe I have to put up with this human* look. "Zach, Zach, Zach. I just took a hit from a very powerful EMPG machine at point-blank range. It's the biological equivalent of you standing on a nuclear device just as it is being detonated."

"Sorry," I said, though in truth, I wasn't sure why I was apologizing.

"No need to mindlessly apologize," HARV said. "I am not one of the women in your life."

I wasn't sure what HARV meant by that, but I knew it couldn't be good so I decided to ignore it.

"The bottom line is I took a blow that would have knocked ninety-nine point nine nine nine nine percent of the machines on Earth offline for an indefinite amount of time. I was down for less than a nano. You should thank Dr. Pool when we see him again."

"I'll make I note of it," I said as I started to the door.

For now, I had two different geeks on my mind—Norp and Bim. I needed to catch up with them and get a little payback. Something wasn't sitting right in my gut, though. Yes, Norp and Bim were socially inept and annoying as DOS, but that didn't make them killers. Even if they were killers, what did they gain by shutting down the Pole? They didn't strike me as the kind of guys who were prone to random acts of violence. In fact, they didn't strike me as the kind of guys who did anything randomly.

They had no motive and nothing to gain, which meant something bigger was afoot. I just didn't know what.

I reached the door. I walked into it. If anybody else had been around, it really would have hurt my credibility as a tough guy.

"The doors are computer controlled," HARV said.

"Yeah, I remembered that about a nano after my nose rammed into it. Can you open the door?" I asked.

"I can," HARV said. He pointed to a panel on the wall next to the door. "So can you."

I lifted the cover off the panel, revealing a small hand-crank. I grabbed the crank and started cranking, raising the door about a centimeter each turn.

"They couldn't put knobs on the doors?" I said, cranking away.

"You are so old-fashioned," HARV said.

"And proud of it."

After a minute or two of cranking, the door was open enough for me to bend down and duck through it.

I entered the hallway. I wanted to track down the geeks ASAP—the angrier I was when I found them, the better. I also wanted to be the first one to find them. I didn't know why. I just knew I did.

"Which way to the port pad?" I asked HARV.

"Follow the arrows," he said.

A green arrow appeared in front of my eye heading north down the hallway. I followed it.

30

I hurriedly traced the arrow through the abandoned corridors. It was a bit eerie, without the music, but I liked the quiet. I knew it wouldn't be long until the elves and others knew the coast was clear and worked their way into the halls. I quickened my pace. I needed to be the one to find Bim and Norp so I could talk to them alone.

A few minutes later, HARV's guided tour led me to big metal door. The arrow HARV was leading me with started to vibrate and flash as it pointed to the door.

"I take it that's the transport room," I said.

"Very good, Zach."

I put my ear next to the door and listened. I heard bickering. That was a good sign. They were cornered.

"HARV, can you open the door for me?"

"Of course," HARV said.

I stood by the door, anxiously tapping my foot. A few nanos passed and nothing happened.

"HARV?"

"I can't magically open the door, Zach. You have to bend down and look into the key pass slot."

"Why didn't you say so?"

"I thought you knew."

"How would I?"

"Zach, Zach, Zach. We've done this type of thing seven different times."

"Whose side are you on, anyhow?"

"They are trapped in a teleport room. They aren't going anywhere. I'm trying to condition you to think better."

"It's your job to do what I ask you to do, not to make me a better person."

HARV sighed. "I like to believe the parameters for my job description are open to interpretation."

HARV wasn't kidding with that. In the past, he has reprogrammed my brain and added information and new routines. I figured this was yet another of the many and ever-growing number of issues it was best not to think about too much.

I bent down and peered into the key pass slot right above the door's handle. A beam of red light shot out from my eye into the slot. I heard a click.

"The door is now open," HARV said. "No need to thank me."

I turned the handle slowly, cracking the door ajar. Peering into the room, I saw Bim and Norp standing by the teleport pad. They both had small duffle bags in their hands, which they were pushing each other with. It didn't take my trained mind to know they were mad at each other. They were sweating so profusely they had to keep removing and drying their thick glasses. Their green and blue hair was even more unkept than usual. With their small stocky bodies and big hands and bigger feet I might have found them to be humorous if they hadn't just tried to kill me.

"This is your fault," Bim screamed, pushing Norp on the shoulder.

Norp recoiled. "How is this my fault?" he screamed back louder, rubbing his shoulder. "You're the one who insisted on packing an extra toothbrush."

Norp pushed Bim on the shoulder.

Bim dropped his bag and made a fist. "Why you little twerp!"

Norp dropped his bag and made two fists. "Watch who you are talking to, buster, before I bust you!"

I walked into the room. They were so involved in their little nerd lover's quarrel they didn't even notice me. I cleared my throat. They keep babbling on and on at each other. I moved closer. They kept complaining.

"How long have you two been married?" I asked.

The stopped arguing, turned, and focused on me for a nano. Then they turned their attention back to each other.

"This is your fault," Bim said, poking Norp in the chest with his index finger.

"No! This is your fault!" Norp said, poking Bim back twice.

"I really hope you guys are going to come quietly," I said, though it was a flat-out lie. I wanted them to put up a fight. I wanted to bust their heads. Trust me, for a guy who does what I do for a living, I'm a pretty mellow, peace-loving kind of fellow. There was just something about these two that really fried my cheese and burned my burger.

Bim and Norp exchanged glances.

"We have him outnumbered two to one," Bim said.

"He fights for a living," Norp offered.

"I don't fight for a living," I said. "I solve crimes for a living. Breaking a bone or two now and then just comes with the territory. I think of it as a fringe benefit."

They exchanged glances again. Each of them raised an eyebrow. I knew that look. It was a signal to move in on me.

Bim was the first to react. He made a fist and lunged at me, swinging wildly. I ducked under his punch. I sprung up and clocked him with a left uppercut to the jaw. (That was the third time in the last few days I had hit somebody with an uppercut to the jaw. I was determined to keep trying it until it actually worked.) Bim's head shot back like one of those old Pez dispensers, spraying sweat in all directions. That alone would have been enough to finish him, but I wasn't done. I followed the left with a quick right roundhouse to the exact same spot. This punch sent him crashing to the ground. Now I was done. At least with round one.

I looked at Norp. He looked at Bim. "Serves him right for bullying me!" he spat, far more upset with Bim than he was with me.

"Now are YOU going to come quietly?" I asked, hoping he would be stupid enough to make a move.

He was. He reached into his pocket protector and pulled out an old-fashioned pen. I looked at it. He looked at me looking at it.

"What are you going to do, give me ink poisoning?"

He grinned, showing me his yellow, jagged teeth. I didn't like that at all. It made me want to smash those teeth in. You have to trust me, I'm not usually a vicious person, but these two brought out my violent side.

Norp reached forward and pulled the top off the pen, revealing a sharp knife underneath. He threw the top over his shoulder and proceeded to wave the pen-knife at me.

"Not so brave now are you, Johnson?" he said.

In my profession, I've had to deal with knives on many different occasions. They are like any other weapon and not to be taken lightly. From close range, and in the hands of a skilled practitioner, they can be just as deadly as a blaster or a handgun. The key words there being *skilled practitioner*.

Norp lunged for me with the knife in his right hand. I stepped back. When he missed, he overcommited his weight on his right side and stumbled forward. I grabbed his knife arm at the wrist and twisted, forcing him to drop the knife, while at the same giving him a little push forward. I let his own momentum carry him down facefirst into the floor. To add injury to injury, I let myself fall on him, my knee into his lower back.

He shuddered in pain. I felt sorry for him. Almost.

I pinned his right arm behind his back in the classic chicken wing position.

"Now, let's talk," I said.

"Talking is good," he groaned.

"Why'd you do it?" I asked.

"Do what?" he said coyly, even though he was no position to be smart.

I pushed the chicken wing up, causing him to squirm more.

"Don't get cute with me," I growled. "Why did you do it?"

"Draw the knife on you?" he asked. He really was clueless.

"No! Why did you reprogram the bots to kill the elves?"

"Oh, that," he said. "We had to do it. For the good of the world and to impress the babes."

"Huh?"

"Santana, man. She has to be stopped!"

"Why?"

"You must know what she's trying to do."

"No."

"Zach, it might be more impressive if you responded with more than one word now and then," HARV offered.

In this case, HARV didn't know what he was talking about. The one-word response was perfect for my tough guy image. I pushed Norp's arm up further. He was hard to keep a grasp on as he was slimy from all the sweat. I was determined to hold on despite the grossness. "Talk."

"Santana—she's up to no good," Norp groaned. He thought for a nano. "Actually, she's probably up to too much good," he moaned.

"Too much good?" I said, breaking out of the monoword responses.

At first, that seemed to be one of the stranger statements I've heard in my career, but in thinking about it I suppose it was possible to have too much of a good thing. I didn't see how in this case, but Norp seemed sincere. In fact, he was too scared to lie.

"It's just that she wants to make the world a better place," Norp groaned.

"How is that bad?"

He shook his head. "Making the world better isn't bad, but her means to the end are quite questionable. She believes the end justifies her means."

I shook my head. Norp was beating around the bush, and I didn't like it.

"Get to the point," I said, pressing down harder on his back with my knee.

He yelped. I felt a bit bad about that. I had to see what he was hinting at, and I was in no mood to take it easy.

"Zach," HARV said inside my head.

"Not now, HARV," I thought back at him.

"I hear movement in the room," HARV said.

I turned just in time to see Bim standing over me with a chair raised over his head. I rolled to the right as he brought the chair down, grazing me. It would have been a lot worse if it weren't for HARV. That's what I get for letting my guard down and my temper get the best of me.

I tried to get to my feet, but Norp grabbed my leg, tripping me. I fell over onto my back. Bim ran over and kicked me in the side. It hurt—not a lot, but enough to make me angry. Bim kicked at me again, but this time I was ready for it. I caught his kicking leg with both hands. Before I could bring him down, Norp pounced on me. I had really underestimated the amount of punishment these two could take.

"Never count us out!" Bim yelled, as he jabbed a fist in my lower back. "We're little but feisty!"

They were tougher than they looked (of course, they pretty much had to be). The problem for them now was that they were getting overconfident. They had managed to get in a couple of good licks, but I had taken worse beatings from grandmas at bridge games. What we had just been through was the opening bid. I was just getting warmed up for the slam.

As I was getting ready to make my big move, Bim flew off of me. Then Norp looked up and flew off of me. Santana had arrived, and she was as angry as a super-elf could be.

She stormed over toward Bim and Norp, who were frantically trying to push themselves up off the floor.

"How dare you treat Zach like that in my home," she said.

"Listen, Santana," Bim said. "Stop trying—"

Bim never got to finish that statement as Santana clanked his head with Norp's, knocking them both out. She turned to me and smiled.

"Thanks for your help, Zach. My elves and I will handle these malcontents from here," she said, shaking the sweat from her hands.

31

It was about an hour after I trekked back to my room that the elves managed to get power back up at the Pole. Another hour after that, they were able to get the bots back under their control and online. During those hours, I had to time to think.

Elf-1 and Santana both insisted that the case was over, and I should be happy and proud of another job well done. Elf-1 gave me a pat on the back. Santana promised me a five percent bonus for wrapping the case up so quickly. But something about this case was still gnawing at me. HARV insisted that it was just acid reflux, and the feeling would go away if I let him release acid blockers into my system. I didn't. This was deeper than any acid reflux.

I lay flat on my bed, hands behind my head, staring up at the ceiling lights, just thinking. Something didn't add up. What was Bim and Norp's motive? They were annoying, but they weren't mindless drones. They wouldn't want to kill a couple of elves and shut down the Pole unless they had a reason. A reason to risk everything and to impress the babes.

I inhaled and sighed unintentionally.

HARV appeared next to me.

"Why are you sulking now, Zach? You wrapped up the case and didn't get killed. DOS, you barely got beat up. For you, that's a three-dee red-letter day."

I kept looking up at the lights. "Something doesn't add up, HARV. This is all too easy." Okay, I know most people wouldn't think battling bots and clobbering on nerds with knives was easy, but when you're me, that's a run through sprinklers on a hot day. Sure, you might get a little water in your eye, but all in all, it's much more refreshing than painful.

"It doesn't make sense, HARV," I said. "What did Norp mean by 'Santana is too good'?"

HARV grimaced. "I don't know. He was probably just ranting. Trying to justify the awful things he did."

"I don't think so," I said.

I've met a lot of characters in my line of work, and it's made me a fairly good judge of character. I can usually pick out the lying scum bag from a hundred meters away. I don't know if it's their eyes or the sound of their voice. I can just tell when somebody is up to no good and lying. Bim and Norp—I knew they were up to no good, but they were sincere. This worried me. I needed to talk to them again.

"Tell Santana I want to talk to Bim and Norp again," I told HARV.

He nodded. "Santana says you can talk to them tomorrow, before they are deported back to Mars."

"Why tomorrow?"

"Her elves need time to interrogate them to learn about the weaknesses they exploited in the bots."

It made sense, but it didn't mean I had to accept it. I stood up.

"Can you lead me to the place Bim and Norp are being held?" I asked.

HARV shook his head. "Actually, I can't do it."

Now there's something I don't hear from HARV very often.

"You can't or won't?"

"I am unable to find where they are keeping Bim and Norp."

"HARV, doesn't that strike you as strange?"

"We're at the Pole investigating the death of two elves, fighting robots and mutants from Mars. Everything about this case strikes me as strange!"

"Doesn't this seem even more out of the ordinary than our norm?"

HARV looked down at the floor, then slowly raised his head until we were looking eye-to-simulated-eye. "It does," HARV said. "But I've been connected to you so long I may be getting paranoid."

I headed toward the door. "Or smarter."

I couldn't see HARV, but I knew he was shaking his head. "I sincerely doubt that," he said. "Where are you going?"

"Right to the source. I'm going to talk to Santana."

I opened the door. Much to my surprise, there was a guardbot facing me. Out of pure instinct, I hurled myself to the ground. The guardbot rolled into the room.

"Mr. Johnson, we need to talk," the guardbot said in Bim's voice.

I looked up from the ground. "Bim?"

"And Norp!" the guardbot said.

I stood up. I was careful to place a table between myself and the bot.

"What's the meaning of this?" I asked.

"As much as we despise you, we are smart enough to realize you are our and the world's last hope."

For one of the few times in my career, both HARV and I were speechless. I didn't know what to make of this. It did reinforce my belief that Bim and Norp believed that Santana was up to something.

"So, what's Santana planning?" I asked, partly to play along, and partly out of true curiosity.

"To change the world to her image," the robot said.

"Now how is she planning to do that?" I asked.

"The elves have invented a virus that attacks the pain and anxiety centers of the brain and eliminates them. She's planning on making everybody permanently happy."

"And that's a bad thing, because . . ."

"Everybody will be happy, mindless zombies," the robot said.

I pondered that. Would the world really be that much different if we were all happy, mindless zombies? We are governed by our wants and desires. Currently, a lot of those wants and desires enter our minds through bullying big businesses and the relentless media. Would things really be that much worse if Bim and Norp were right? It wasn't my call. It wasn't Santana's call, either. If it was true, it would be my job to stop her.

"Okay, I'll talk to Santana, and if what you say is true, I'll shut her down." Truthfully, I had no idea how I was going to do that. I was unarmed and outnumbered. Still,

I've never been one to let reality get in the way of my success.

"It gets worse."

"Worse than totally reprogramming the minds of everybody on Earth?"

"This is a two-stage plan."

"Santana always was an overachiever," I said.

"This is where we come in," the bot said. "We designed a virus that would sterilize ninety-nine percent of humanity and make them lose interest in sex. Within a few generations, humans would no longer be able to or want to reproduce."

"Oh, that's not good. Why would a goody-two-shoes like Santana want to wipe out most of humanity?"

"She doesn't want to wipe you out, just replace you with clones. She's convinced the world will be a better place this way. She mumbled something about being naughty makes people do stupid things."

Now it all made sense in a bizarre, deranged way. "Are the elves onboard with this idea?"

"As far as we can tell, no. Santana convinced the elves they were developing the niceness virus as an exercise to test their abilities."

"Then how is Santana going to pull this off without the elves?"

The bot shrugged, as well as a tin can can. "We have no idea."

"Why should I believe you two? Didn't you guys try to kill me? A few times?"

"Yes, but that's when we thought you'd make it harder for us to score with Nova or that during your investigative reporting you would turn up something and somehow foil Santana and steal our spotlight. Remember, we thought you were a big, blond blogger. Now we're in jail and know who you are, so we have no reason to lie."

"Why would you be involved in this in the first place?"

"To impress chicks. Yeah, to impress the babes," the bot said in Bim's and Norp's voices. Interestingly enough, it was more believable coming from the bot.

"Our goal was to trick Santana into thinking that we were on her side, then we would shut her down, saving the day, and the babes would flock to us."

"So you guys killed the elves?"

There was a pause. "We only killed a couple, and just to scare them into delaying the Holiday long enough so we could get the bots totally reprogrammed to shut Santana down."

There was a pause then they added, "It was for the greater good. Kill a couple of elves to save the world."

It wasn't the best plan I had ever heard. In fact, it was probably one of the ten worst plans I've heard. Even still, men have done far stupider things to impress women. Santana was on to something—being naughty does make us stupid.

Now they had a motive that fit their MO. I was reasonably certain they believed what they were saying. The scary thing was I believed it, too. I've been around enough superwomen to know that when you mess around with DNA and PMS, you're just asking for trouble.

Don't get me wrong, supermen are just as dangerous, but they are far easier to predict. Men want three things: money, power, and women. Most of them figure if they get one of the first two then they can get the third thing. All men want to be the alpha male. The king of the hill. The big cheese.

Women are an entirely different game. For the most part, they don't want power for the sake of power. They want power to make things better. This isn't always a bad thing, but when you supercharge it and toss in some fluctuating hormones, the result is often messy as Bim's and Norp's hair and complexion. It becomes a pseudo-Machiavellian quest to make the world a better place.

Was Santana on one of these quests? I wasn't going to rule it out.

"I'll check on it," I told the bot.

"That's all we ask," the bot said in Norp's voice. "And that you give us our due when all this is over," it added in Bim's.

"Don't worry, you'll get exactly what's coming to you," I said.

"Good enough," the bot said in its bot voice. "Now I'd better go before they notice I'm gone."

The bot rolled backward out of the room, leaving me

with my thoughts. If Santana really was bad, I had to stop her. I was going to need backup.

"HARV, talk to Captain Rickey and Randy, and notify them of our current situation."

HARV appeared before me shaking his head. It's never good news when a supercomputer shakes its head.

"All transmissions out of the Pole are being jammed," HARV said. "Santana's elves say it's only a temporary security measure. They want to be cautious, just in case Bim and Norp had accomplices."

Unfortunately, that made sense. More unfortunately, that was a recipe for trouble.

"So right now, my assets are still my wits, my fists, and my computer."

"If Santana really has gone overboard, you're going to need more than two out of three here. I estimate she's almost as strong as any of the Thompson Quads. Her pheromones are just as powerful. She can twist you into a pretzel before you can say, 'Please hurt me some more.' "

"I think we can count Nova as an asset," I said.

"I won't disagree with you there. She's just wacked enough to jump aboard this runaway train heading downhill toward the TNT with no breaks. She has such an act-first-think-later way about her I'm betting she has a great career in politics in front of her."

"Wow, buddy, I'm proud of both the metaphors and the deduction."

"The metaphors are not because I am becoming like you. They are because I am communicating with you. The deduction, is, well, good sense is good sense."

"I'm still proud."

"Don't go all mushy on me, Zach. We're in trouble here. When the spit hits the fan though, you're going to need more help."

I had nothing to lose. So I sat on my bed and started concentrating.

"Zach, what are you doing? This is no time to go all new age and mellow out on me."

"I'm thinking," I said, eyes closed and taking deep breath.

"Ah, no wonder I didn't recognize what you were doing," HARV said.

I ignored HARV and started breathing deeper and deeper. As I inhaled and exhaled slowly, I concentrated on one thought, *Carol send help*. I knew it was a long shot, but this was a time for long shots.

"I need to talk with Santana," I said.

"I can net you with her."

"No, I want to do it in person, and I need to talk to her alone."

"She says she can meet you in her room in thirty minutes."

"No, I want to do it someplace neutral."

"She says she can meet you in the library in forty-five minutes."

I nodded. "I'll take it."

"Great, you've had such a history of good luck at the library."

32

When I arrived at the library Santana wasn't there yet. I sat in one of the cloud chairs. I crossed my legs, but it didn't feel right. I uncrossed them and sat forward.

I was nervous, and I didn't know why and that made me more nervous. Part of me wanted to believe the case was all wrapped up—Bim and Norp were the deranged bad guy nerds who wanted to stop the Holiday because they are unpopular spammers. Another part of me, the annoying part, kept telling me this case was far from over. Sure, Bim and Norp were annoying, but they weren't the true culprits here. This case went beyond simply saving the Holiday.

I sat for a few minutes alone with my thoughts. I noticed that HARV wasn't chiming in with his opinion. This was very out of character.

"HARV, why are you so quiet?" I asked.

No response.

I didn't like that.

I heard the door to the library open. I looked up to see two guardbots rolling in. My initial thought was that the appearance of the guardbots combined with HARV going silent was bad news. I didn't want to jump to conclusions, at least not yet.

The bots rolled closer. I stood up from the chair.

"There is no need to fear us, Zachary Nixon Johnson," the bots said in unison.

I've learned from experience it's never a good sign when bots use your middle name. It's an even worse sign when they talk in unison. I dove back over the cloud chair a mere nano before the bots opened up fire, ripping the chair in half. I ducked lower as they fired away.

I was trapped behind a cloud chair that was being rapidly shot apart by two guardbots. I was unarmed, unarmored, outnumbered, and my computer was down. It's possible I'd been in tighter situations, but none sprang immediately to mind. This was bad with a capital B-A-D. I was starting to see why libraries aren't so popular anymore.

I took a deep breath. I figured I had one option. I had to jump up and try to fight the guardbots. Each bot had to weigh over 150 kilos. They were made of heavily reinforced plexi-metal, and they were armed with laser cannons and razor-sharp claws. The first time I'd made an unarmed attack on guardbots I had caught them off guard (plus I had my computer to cover me and pump up my muscles). This time they were ready for me, and there would be no holographic cover. I took another deep breath. Okay, it wasn't such a good option. In fact, it was a less than adequate option. Unfortunately, it was all I had.

I shot across the floor as more laser fire singed passed me. I pushed myself up off the ground. I started toward the bots. They spun to take aim at me. I heard a somewhat familiar sound. It was a whizzing sound, kind of like a furious bee on speed coming at me. I knew that sound. I pulled myself back and threw myself across the room as far away from the bots as I could.

I didn't see, but I heard and felt the explosion. The heat was searing, but that was a good thing because it meant I was still alive. I faintly heard that angry bee with an attitude sound again. It was getting louder and closer. I rolled farther away. This time my curiosity got the better of my common sense, and I peeked over my shoulder at my bot attackers. One was already split in two. Its top half had been obliterated, and its bottom was smoldering. The second bot had turned its attention away from me and toward the sound. I guess it wanted to see its killer. I didn't see what hit it, but I saw and felt the aftermath. The bot shattered into a million pieces of nothing.

Through the smoke I could see three figures. One, the most shapely of the three, had a missile launcher on her shoulder and was smiling. I'd recognize that smile even from five hundred meters—it was Electra. She was flanked by Randy and Tony.

I got up and started dusting myself off as I headed over toward them.

"What did I miss?" HARV said, coming back online.

"Ah, not much," I said.

I reached Electra and the other two.

"So, what brings you guys up north?" I asked.

Electra's lips curled up ever so slightly. "Carol said she picked up thought waves that you were in big trouble."

I shook my head. "Well, I guess she was wrong, wasn't she?"

"I used my clearance to get us here," Tony said.

"I used my brain to rewire the New Frisco transporters to send us here," Randy said.

"I'm the best shot," Electra said.

"And the best looking," I said, giving her a hard, wet kiss.

"I wouldn't necessarily say that," Randy said, but I'm pretty certain he was joking. Either that, or he had been too long in the lab.

"So, what's the story here?" Tony said, going into cop-mode.

I looked at him. I shrugged. "DOS if I know," I said.

"Come on, Zach, you've been here for forty-eight hours. Surely you know something?" Tony said.

I headed toward the door. The sooner I got out of the library the better.

"I don't know much—"

"Wow, he's finally admitting it," HARV interrupted.

"I don't know much for certain," I said. "But I do know there is trouble afoot. The question is, how big is the trouble?"

"That doesn't make me feel any better," Tony said.

"Welcome to my world, Tony. Welcome to my world."

33

As we left the library, I filled everybody in on the situation. Actually, I mostly advised them of what was going on. HARV did most of the real filling in. We told them everything: about the two dead elves, about the attacks on my life, dead elves, robots going beserk, nerds, more dead elves, about the EMPG, and about Bim and Norp. Everybody was shocked about the elves, but nobody was much surprised about anything else.

Then we told them about what Bim and Norp had said. How Santana wasn't all sugarplums and spice like she appeared.

"I find it hard to believe Santana could go bad," Randy said.

"I didn't say she might be bad. I said she might be a bit deranged," I said. "There's a difference."

Truthfully, I'd prefer she was bad. Bad is easier to comprehend and more straightforward to predict. With deranged, you never know what you're getting into.

"Do you have any proof that what Bim and Norp are saying is true?" Tony asked.

"Nope," I said. "Hence, the problem."

"Didn't Bim and Norp admit to killing the elves?" Tony questioned in his most official policeman tone.

"They did," I said.

"Didn't they admit to trying to kill you?"

"They did—I was cramping their style."

"So what makes you think they're not just covering their asses?" Tony said.

"Tony, there are sensitive ears here," I said.

Tony turned to Randy. "Sorry about my choice of words," he said.

Randy grinned.

"I don't think they are covering themselves because, well, I'm not sure."

HARV appeared from my eye lens. "It's another one of Zach's hunches," he said, with more than a hint of cynicism in his voice.

Electra put a hand on my shoulder. "Amor, are you sure of this?"

"The only thing I'm sure of is that I'm not sure of anything. I just know I can't take the chance that Bim and Norp are telling the truth. That's why we're going to talk to Santana now."

Then it hit me. I stopped walking. "They didn't know I was me."

"Huh?" everybody else said.

"When I was attacked in my office by the bots and then men in black from the Santana Stinks Society, Bim and Norp didn't know I would be coming. They wouldn't have sent bots and a hitman to kill me."

Now it was everybody else's turn to pause and contemplate.

"There has got to be some explanation," Tony insisted.

"I'm sure there is, and I know just the meta-person to give it."

HARV gave me to directions to Santana's office. As I stormed forward, the others followed, occasionally slowing down and doing a double take when an elf went by. They were all amazed by the music, the lights, the occasional holographic reindeer.

"Wow, we're walking among elves," Randy said.

"Believe me, it wears thin real fast," I said.

The closer we got to Santana's office, the more elves there were. The stares lasted a lot longer and were much more palpable. These elves obviously weren't used to visitors coming into these parts of the Pole, especially unregistered visitors.

After twisting and turning down what seemed to be an endless labyrinth of Holiday-filled hallways, we came to a long pink hallway with a door at the end. As we neared the door, we heard a voice from behind us.

"Pink?" Electra exclaimed.

"Think of it as light red," I said.

"Stop! Stop! Stop!" Elf-1 called, running up to us.

Elf-1 slid past us and stood in front of me. He put his hand out for me to stop.

"Mr. Johnson, you can't go any farther," he insisted. "Santana will see you after her meeting. We have very specific rules about all this."

I pushed past Elf-1. "Sorry, elfy, but rules are made to be broken, especially if somebody tries to break me."

"These people are unregistered and unauthorized to be here!"

"Well, when your bots tried to kill me again, I decided I needed more help."

Elf-1 grabbed me by the shoulder. Before I could do anything, Electra hit him with a snap kick to the stomach. That doubled him over.

"At least she didn't go for my personal area," he groaned.

I kicked him between the legs. He doubled over in great pain. I didn't even think his happy place would be able to help him out now.

"Now, Zach, did you have to do that?" Electra said.

I turned and headed toward the door. "Nope, but I wanted to."

I reached the door and wondered if I should knock politely, bang on it, or shoot the lock off. The door popped open before I could make my choice. I was a little disappointed by that.

Santana was sitting in her office with Councilwoman Weathers. Santana smiled at me.

"Zach, I'm so sorry. My meeting with the councilwoman ran late, but there is no need to barge into my office. I see you invited your friends here, as well." She was as cool as the ice caps that surrounded the Pole.

Councilwoman Weathers was even cooler, perhaps subfrigid. "We were in the middle of a very important business meeting," she said. You could feel the ice dripping off her words.

"I get so rude when things try to kill me," I said.

"Zach, what are you talking about?" Santana asked.

"A few minutes ago, when I was waiting for you in the

library, two bots rolled in and tried to send me to meet my maker."

This was a moment or two of awkward silence.

"Zach, I'm so sorry," Santana said, standing up from her chair. "I thought for sure we had all the bots back under our control."

"I didn't say you didn't."

Santana tilted her head to the side and looked at me. She put her hand on her chest. She wasn't expecting this. If she was, she was good at covering it up. "Zach, what are you implying?"

I decided not to tell her about what Bim and Norp had told me. I wanted to see how she reacted to the news of another attack on my life after the two had been apprehended.

"I'm just saying that it is possible that somebody else at the Pole, one of your elves perhaps, has something against me."

Santana looked me squarely in the eyes. She put her hand over her heart. "Zach, I know in my heart of hearts none of my elves would try to kill you."

"What about one of your other guests?" I said, though I didn't really believe it would be any of them.

"I'll have my elves look into that."

There was another moment of uneasy silence. She was good. I had to give her that. I needed to tip my hand.

"Bim and Norp said that you had a grand scheme to remodel the world in your own image with a happy virus," I said coldly.

Santana sat back in her chair. She looked down, then shook her head. "Zach, I assure you I am only on this Earth to make people happy."

"That's not a denial," I said.

"Didn't Bim and Norp try to kill you?" Santana said.

"Yes, but that doesn't mean they were lying. Electra and Tony have wanted to kill me on many, many occasions . . ."

Electra nodded.

"Amen," Tony said.

"I've had my moments, too," Randy added.

". . . but that doesn't mean I don't listen to them when they tell me something."

"Actually, you don't usually listen to me," Tony said.

"You could teach a course on how to not listen," Randy said.

"Si, listening isn't one of your better skills, mi amor."

"The point is," I said, "I believe Bim and Norp are onto something. That doesn't explain why the bots tried to kill me after those two jokers were locked up."

Then, almost on cue, a hectic Elf-3333 burst into the office.

"Santana, I'm sorry to interrupt such an important meeting," she panted. "But a scan of the bots showed that approximately thirty-two minutes and fifteen seconds ago, we lost control of two of our guardbots. I did a system scan and apparently those two nasty Martians had planted some sort of backdoor virus that made them go wild. I was able to break some of the code. It was KILL ZACH DEADER THAN DEAD AT ALL COSTS. We should warn him."

"I consider myself warned," I said.

Elf-3333 turned to me, startled. She was so intent on delivering her message she hadn't even noticed me in the room. "Oh, I'm so sorry," she said. "You are in grave danger. We've lost complete track of the bots. They're off our radar."

"They're off everybody's radar," Electra said, exposing the rocket launcher on her shoulder.

"Oh," Elf-3333 said. "I understand. As much as I deplore violence, nice job!" She gave Electra a big thumb's up and left the room.

"Can you explain how Bim and Norp sent bots to attack me before anybody knew I was coming? Or how they sent a killer posing as a SSS member after me?" I said, pounding my hand on her desk.

Just then Elf-2436 ran into the room. "Santana," she said urgently. "I've just busted Bim's and Norp's encryption program. It seems they've been tapping into your personal logs and records since they got here," she said.

Everybody looked at me.

"Okay, maybe you can explain that," I said.

Santana smiled. "You got me, Zach. I have an evil plan. I am going to use the Holiday to infect the entire world with a happy virus." Santana didn't make the slightest attempt to hide the mocking tone of her voice. When I heard it, it sounded totally ridiculous. I knew then and there it was true. It was all true.

"HARV," I thought. "Are you analyzing her voice patterns?"

"Sorry, Zach. There's some sort of interference in her office. I can't record or analyze anything. I'm having a hard enough time just staying online," HARV said inside my head.

That was the clincher.

"Thanks, Santana. You've been a big help," I said.

"My pleasure. Now if your guests would like to stay the evening, I will have my elves find them rooms."

"That would be much appreciated," Tony said.

"The pleasure is ours, Captain Rickey."

"Please, call me Tony."

"Of course, Tony."

"Can I see your labs?" Randy asked.

Santana smiled. "Of course, Dr. Pool."

Randy put his arms behind his back and sank down like a schoolboy with a crush. "Please, call me Randy, Santana."

"Of course, Randy."

Santana got up and walked (or more appropriately herded) us all toward the door. "Now if you don't mind, Stormy and I do have some very serious matters to attend to."

"No, no problem."

"Of course."

"Si, entiendo."

"I will see you all at dinner."

Everybody in my group smiled, except me.

"Zach, thank you for stopping by and for not kicking my door down," Santana told me.

Yep, she was guilty all right.

34

It didn't take long at all for the elves to find suitable quarters for Randy and Tony. Randy was keen to share a room if it would make it easier on the elves, but Tony quickly shot down that idea. Randy liked the idea of having a human roomie to hang out with. Randy didn't get much human contact. Tony, on the other hand, got way too much human contact. He relished his privacy as much as Randy welcomed the companionship. The elves were able to get them adjoining rooms, which made them both happy.

They confiscated Electra's rocket launcher, Tony's sidearms, and Randy's gadgets. The elves insisted they were totally, absolutely certain they had complete control over the bots, and we would have no need for our weapons. I didn't mind giving them up because knowing my friends, they each had something up their sleeve.

Electra sat on the bed with a little bounce, testing its firmness. "So, mi amor, you don't believe Santana?"

I moved over and sat next to her. I sighed.

"I don't like it when you sigh," she said.

"For some reason, I believe the geeks," I said.

"Probably because deep down, you are one of them," Electra said a bit jokingly.

I wanted to give her a witty retort, but her joke hit home. Sure, I'm a tough guy. Sure, I can punch with the best of them. But when push comes to shove, I am a guy with a computer wired to directly to my brain. If that didn't mean I was a geek, I didn't know what it meant.

"What evidence do you have that Santana has these evil plans?"

"You sound like Tony."

She just looked at me. I was used to getting that look from other people, but not from Electra.

"I have seen the technology here. It's pretty amazing."

"Your point being?"

"I think she has the means to pull it off."

"Pull what off, Zach?"

"Making everybody nice, and then sterilizing them."

Electra rolled her eyes. I was used to other people reacting to me like that too, just not Electra. "Zach, you heard how preposterous that sounded when Santana *admitted* to it."

"Honey, when you're me, outrageous and absurd is what you expect."

There are times being a PI means you have to go with your gut, no matter what your mind is telling you. This was one of those times. Once Santana tipped her hand, I'd be on her like white on genetically-modified-for-extra-whiteness rice.

Electra smiled and put her hand on my back. "That's why I love you," she said. "When you latch on to something, you don't let go."

"Yep, dogs with bones have nothing on me," I said.

Before Electra could say anything else, Elf-1's voice came booming over the intercom.

"Greetings, my fellow elves and our guests here at the Pole. I have a super-duper special announcement. Santana will be delivering a su-uper-du-uper special message to us all in the auditorium in fifteen minutes sharp. Your attendance is mandatory. Have a great, great, happy, happy day."

"A special announcement about a special announcement?" Electra said.

"Yes, isn't that special," I said in a voice imitating a character from a very old TV show.

Electra tilted her head and looked at me. "That's a reference to something, isn't it?"

"Yes, I'm impressed," I said. Most people wouldn't have caught that. Of course, most people don't live with me.

Electra shook her head. "I've been hanging around with you too long."

HARV appeared from my eye lens. "Hey, at least you're not attached to his brain."

I stood up from the bed and stretched. I turned to Electra. "Let's go."

She looked at me and kind of rolled her eyes. "Zach, on the off chance that you're right about Santana, this could be a trap."

"Exactly. Let's get going."

Electra pushed herself up from the bed with one arm. She was more hesitant than I had ever seen her.

"What's wrong, mi amor?" I said. "If you're so convinced I'm wrong, this shouldn't be anything."

She lowered her eyes. "I was certain you were wrong until that announcement. Now I know you're onto something."

"See, I'm contagious," I said, taking her arm.

"Why are you so anxious to walk into a trap?" she asked.

HARV appeared. "Because he's really not all that bright," he said to Electra. "I thought you would have figured that out by now."

"It's not a trap if I know it's a trap," I said.

"Yes, it is," HARV insisted.

Electra pointed at HARV. "He's right."

I headed toward the door. "Well, it's not as good of a trap if I can see it coming. Maybe I can put the kibosh on it before she's ready. Either way, I've been in this elf suit long enough. I'm ready for the end of the game."

"In that case, wait," Electra said. "You're going to need something else." She went into the closet and came out carrying a suitcase.

"How the DOS did you smuggle that here?"

"I brought it with us. I told the elves it was my allergy medicine."

She walked over and put the suitcase on the bed.

"You must have a lot of allergies," I said.

"Elves are trusting little beings," she said opening the suitcase.

I moved over next to her. Sure enough, the suitcase was lined with medications.

"That's a holographic cover," HARV said.

"Very good, HARV," I said, patting his virtual shoulder.

"The elves were really busy at the time," Electra said as she pushed a button on the bottom of the suitcase. The medications vanished and were replaced by my regular clothing, my body armor, my wrist communicator (never hurts to have a backup), my gun, a couple of energy weapons, and best of all, my fedora that HARV had talked me out of taking.

"What, no belt and trench coat?" I asked.

Electra shook her head. "Sorry. I like to travel light."

I couldn't get out of that elf suit fast enough.

"You know, you are totally breaking protocol by changing like this," HARV scolded.

"Yeah, I know that," I said, as I slipped off the elf suit, kicked it to the corner of the room, and put on my body armor. "Protocol kind of went out the door the last time the bots tried to kill me."

"I know," HARV said. "I just felt obligated to point it out."

I was fully dressed in less than a minute. With my gun up my sleeve and my armor underneath, it was the first time I felt comfortable since I arrived at the Pole. I'm not sure what that said about me. I'm certain I didn't want to think about it too much.

"Now, let's get this show on the road!" I said.

When we arrived at the theater, Randy and Tony were already there, along with about ten thousand elves. The theater, like everything else in this joint, was massive, almost stadiumlike in its size, but the throng of elves had it stuffed to the rafters. I scanned the crowd for non-elves. Nova was there, along with Mary and Steve, Mr. Weathers, Elf-1, and the Billings family, except for Mrs. Billings.

"Okay," I said, as I looked around. "Am I right, HARV, that Santana, Mrs. Billings, and the councilwoman are missing?"

"Correct. It seems you may have been right not to trust Weathers."

"To quote a friend, 'Of course.' "

"I don't like this," Tony said.

All the doors in the room slammed down shut behind us.

"I *really* don't like this," Tony said.

Elf-1 came running up to us. "Where's Santana? She told me she'd be here to address us live."

A giant screen came rolling down the ceiling in front of the stage.

"I don't know, but I have a feeling we'll know in a nano," I told him, as I pointed to the screen.

A 3D image of Councilwoman Weathers appeared on the screen, smiling. Behind her sat Santana. They were in some sort of control room. In the background, we could see Mrs. Billings, who had a laser to the heads of Norp and Bim.

"I have great news for all of you," Councilwoman Weathers said, puffing out her chest.

The crowd of elves erupted in applause.

Weathers continued, "Thanks to your diligent work, the Holiday has been saved despite the efforts of the two behind me."

The elves applauded more.

Weathers waited for the applause to die down and then went on. "In fact, I have used my influence to declare the Holiday will begin right now!"

There was applause and audible gasps.

"For details, I'll turn the floor over to my special friend, Santana!"

The place went wild.

"My elves, I want to thank you all for your service."

The crowd started to applaud even louder, though I didn't like where Santana was heading.

"Thanks to you, the world is going to be a better place," Santana shouted boldly.

Some of the elves were now standing and cheering.

"These guys eat way too much sugar," I whispered to Tony.

"Thanks to you," Santana continued, "everybody in the world will be happy, whether they want to be or not."

Most of the elves continued to cheer. Some of them stopped to hear what Santana was saying.

"Every present delivered tonight will be contain not one, but two different viruses," Santana said.

Now about half the elves where cheering, while the other half was listening intently to what Santana was saying.

"Santana always was an overachiever," I said to Tony.

"The first virus was developed right here, and it will stimulate the pleasure centers of the brain. The need to be naughty will be gone."

A few of the more optimistic (or denser) elves were still clapping and stomping. The rest, though, weren't so sure they liked what they were hearing.

"The second virus, developed by our friends from Mars, will make the entire population of Earth sterile in three generations," Santana said proudly.

A few of the more radical elves were still chanting. The others sat in stunned silence.

"You're going to wipe out humanity?" I shouted to the holographic screen.

Santana's huge holographic figure shook her head. "Ho

ho ho, no no no," she said. "Humanity won't be wiped out. They'll just be forced to clone their future generations. My elves are clones, and you can plainly see what great beings they are."

Some of the elves nodded their heads in agreement, others looked on in total confusion.

"Let me get this straight," I said. "You plan not only to force everybody to be happy, but you are also planning on making humanity forget about sex and having to clone to survive."

Santana nodded. "Yes, that sums up my plan nicely. Being naughty is a great distraction. With that eliminated think of the greatness humans will achieve."

"What about those of us trapped in here?" I asked.

"You will also be made happy and sterile. We will be pumping the gas in shortly."

Happy and sterile. Now there's a phrase you don't hear very often.

"How will the happy gas affect the elves?" Elf-1 shouted. "We're already happy and sterile."

"Oh," Santana said, "that's the best part. With everybody in the world now happy twenty-four/seven, we won't need the Holiday any longer, and your services won't be needed. So, I'm terminating you all. This combination of gases is deadly to elves."

A few of the really thick elves applauded. The rest fell back into their seats.

"You've done your duty to the world, but now you've become extraneous, so I expect you to fulfill your obligation and die. I'm granting you all the rest you so deserve."

Now everybody was stunned silent.

"The teleporting of presents will begin in a hour. I want to thank you all once again for the role you played in making the world a better place."

Mrs. Billings tossed us a kiss. The holographic screen dissipated.

"HARV, block all outgoing transmissions."

"Right."

"I don't believe my own wife is going to sterilize me!" Mr. Weathers said. "I'm am so going to complain about this the next time we see our marriage advisor!"

"Well, if it makes you feel any better, Mrs. Billings is no

prize either. She's going to sterilize her entire family," I told him.

Little Billy walked up to me.

"No, she isn't," he said.

"Huh?"

"We are already sterile!" Billy told me.

Little Billy lifted off his head revealing his android circuitry. His sister and father did the same. Then they all fell to the ground.

"Somehow, I doubt this plan was a spur of the moment kind of thing."

"I'm going to kill her!" Mr. Weathers shouted. "The most trusted woman on Earth, my ass!"

"If we get out of here, you're going to have to stand in line to kill her," I said.

"HARV, how come you didn't notice they were androids?" I asked.

Silence.

"HARV?"

"I never scanned them," was HARV's simple reply.

"Any idea why?"

"Zach, I don't scan everybody you meet. That would just be rude. They had normal skin tones, so I assumed they were normal humans, not illegal androids."

I decided not to contemplate the ramifications of my computer making assumptions and ignoring the possibility that there might be human-skin-toned androids out there.

Elf-2 two came running up to me. "Oh, Zach, this is a marketing nightmare—destroying the world as we know it."

"Don't worry. We're going to stop them," I said.

"What can I do?" she offered.

"Keep the others calm. Tell them everything is under control."

"You mean lie?" she said. "I can't lie."

"You're in marketing. Of course you can."

"Zach, we don't lie, we just promote a semblance of the truth."

"Well, go do your thing then."

"Right," she said. She puffed out her chest, gave me a salute, and headed back into the throng of elves.

I turned my attention back to my "team."

"We need to find a way out of here," I said.

"Let's blast our way out," Tony said as he drew a weapon he had under his shirt.

"Impossible. The doors are sheer plexi-steel. Impossible to blast or shoot through," Elf-1 told us.

"Why would anybody put plexi-steel doors on an auditorium?" Randy asked.

"Before the remodeling, this used to be the main transporter room."

That gave me an idea. "Are there any transporter pads left in here?"

"There's one backstage, but I'm sure it's deactivated," Elf-1 said.

"Think you could activate it?" I asked Randy.

"I'll probably have to use some chips from your eye lens to power it up, but I can do it."

"How can you say that without looking at it?" Elf-1 questioned.

"Just take us to it. If Randy says he can, he can."

HARV chipped in. "Dr. Pool, the porting software the elves use is very advanced. It allows teleportation from a port pad to another area, even if it doesn't have a port pad."

Elf-1 put his hands on his hips. "You're not supposed to know that!" he protested.

"Big picture here, Elf-1," I said. "No hard feeling about our little scuffles," I told him.

"Of course not," he said.

Elf-1 led us down a long aisle, muttering about his "hap-hap-hap-happy place." This time I wanted to join him. We rushed past the stage and then behind it. There it was: an old, five-person transporter pad and panel. Randy hit the control panel on the top and a panel popped open. He looked in.

"I have good news and bad news," he said.

"Good news first," I said.

"I can make it work."

"Bad news?" I asked.

"I think I can only make it work once, and I can't guarantee where it will put you. There will be no backup system."

"Which means?" Tony asked.

Randy looked at him. "Which means I think I can find

an empty hallway to port you into, but I can't guarantee it. There is no collision detection software."

"That means if you're off, we can teleport into a wall or a passing bot," Tony said slowly.

"It will have to do," I said.

Randy walked over to me. He pulled a small pair of tweezerlike things from his pocket and stuck them in my eye.

"I'll need some of the chips from the lens. The connection will still function, only HARV won't be able to see from your eye anymore."

Randy popped the chips out. He carefully walked over to the porter and placed them in the machine. While Randy tinkered, the rest of us made plans.

"Elf-1, how long before Santana will be ready to teleport her special gifts to the world?"

Elf-1 pulled out a calculator from his pocket. "We've done most of the prep work already. The presents and their coordinates are already stored in warehouses throughout the Pole. The delivery process is all done via the Pole's own teleportation software. Once the process starts, we can teleport packages to everybody in the world in twenty-four hours."

"That type of teleportation must take massive amounts of energy," Tony said.

"Yes, we have our own nuclear generators below the surface."

"Maybe we could take those out?" Tony said.

We all just stared at him. Sometimes Tony let his gung-ho attitude get in the way of his logic. He thought about what he had said. "Oh, yeah, even if we weren't trapped in here, taking out nuclear generators probably isn't the best plan."

"We'll put that one on the back burner," I said.

"The computers," a male voice said from behind us.

We saw the Eatmans and Nova coming to join our assemblage.

"My husband's right," Mary Eatman said. She pointed to me. "All the elves are buzzing about how you're wearing a highly advanced computer on your eye. Use it."

Elf-1 put his hands behind his back. "That's impossible. Our computer systems have firewall after firewall, and each of those is e-wrapped in e razor wire, surrounded by e-moats which are guarded by more firewalls."

Steve smiled. "I know. I helped designed those systems. Between my knowledge and Elf-1's knowledge, I am sure we could get Zach's computer past the security and bog down their system with a virus."

Elf-1 put both hands over his head. "But if I did that I'd be betraying Santana! I could never ever do that."

I looked at him. "She's perfectly willing to kill you and all you stand for."

Elf-1 thought about it for a nano. "Perhaps *never ever* is too strong a sentiment." He pondered a bit more.

Nova walked over and started slowly rubbing Elf-1's back. "You don't want to die do you?" she purred. "You have so much to live for."

Elf-1 smiled widely. "I do enjoy being naughty as much as the next elf. More in fact, given my responsibilities. Let's stop the bitch," he said.

The only problem, well, not the only problem, but the most pressing was that Randy was using my eye interface with HARV to hotwire the teleporter. We would need my communicator to interface HARV with the Pole's system. I started removing the communicator from my wrist. Turning to Randy, I said, "Can HARV handle interfacing with the system and powering the teleporter?"

"Of course," HARV and Randy both said.

"HARV could do that and pilot one thousand two hundred and twenty-two hovers backward through rush hour traffic," Randy added.

"I was fine with just the 'of course,' " I said.

I handed the communicator to Elf-1. He and Steve went over to a side interface and plugged HARV in. Elf-1 hit the side of the unit and a keyboard popped out. He typed a series of digits. His fingers moved so fast I barely saw them.

"I've got HARV in," Elf-1 said.

"Perfect timing," Randy said. "I've got the teleporter working now. I think."

"You think?" I said.

Randy shrugged. "I've never done this before. I didn't have time to run a simulation, but I'm pretty certain it will work and not get you all killed."

Not the most ringing of endorsements, but it was good enough for me. I walked over to a pad and stood on it.

"Okay, we have room for four more."

Electra, Tony, Elf-1, and Nova joined me on the pads.

"Elf-1, are you sure about this?" I said.

Nova smiled at him, and his face lit up like the old-fashioned Fourth-of-July fireworks.

"I've never been surer about anything in my life," he said. "Santana has betrayed us all."

I tossed Electra a kiss. She took my hand. I smiled at her. Nova smiled at me. Electra gave us both a glare. Elf-1 frowned. Tony just chuckled. Meanwhile, Randy continued to tinker away.

Finally Randy said, "Okay, I'm ready."

HARV and Elf-1 downloaded schematics of the Pole into the teleporter. The plan was for Randy to teleport us to a hallway just around the corner from the main control area that Santana, Weathers, and Ma Billings were occupying. It was far enough away so they couldn't see us, but close enough to give us a chance to stop them. As long as we moved fast.

"Remember, gang, we don't have much time. Elf-1, you're going to have to get us straight to the control room as fast as possible," I said

"Check."

Randy pushed the lever up on the teleporter.

The next thing I knew I was standing in a hallway with Tony next to me. We both drew our weapons and looked around.

"Where are the others?" Tony asked.

"I don't know, Tony. I just got here."

"My guess would be transporter malfunction," HARV said.

"Are the others okay?" I asked.

I was greeted with uncharacteristic silence.

"HARV, I asked you a question."

"Sorry, Zach, I don't know. The chips Randy used must have been damaged. In my crippled state, I've lost all contact with the people inside the theater."

"Can you repair it?"

"Maybe, but it will take some time."

"DOS!"

Tony fired a laser blast at a guardbot coming up behind us. The bot exploded on contact.

"Come on, we have a job to do," Tony said, pointing forward. "There's nothing we can do standing around here worrying. I'm sure they're all okay."

I took a deep breath to help regain my composure.

"I hate it when you're right," I told him. "Okay, HARV, give us the fastest route to the control panel."

"Two more bots behind us!" Tony shouted.

I spun to face them.

"You take the one on the left, I'll take the one on the right," Tony said anxiously.

"The DOS with that," I said as I pointed my gun down the hall and aimed. "Gun—multi, murve, explode."

A bullet fired from my gun and split into many bullets that tore into the charging bots, shredding them into tomorrow's garbage.

"HARV, what's the quickest route to the main control room?" I asked.

"That all depends on where you are."

"You don't know?"

"I'm blind now, Zach, remember? Describe your location."

"We're in a long, white hallway with a red stripe on the floor. No windows, no doors, no nothing. We see only hall as far as we can see."

"That's no help. You just described roughly thirty-four point four one percent of this place. What about the maid-bot storage closets? They are all numbered."

"Good idea!"

Tony looked at me. "I hope you're talking to HARV and haven't lost it."

I started kicking the lower part of the walls.

"What are you doing?" Tony asked.

"Looking for a closet down here," I said as I banged away.

"What can I do to help?"

"Start banging!" I told him.

Tony bent down and started searching the other walls.

HARV chimed in. "Two things, Zach. One, I hear more guardbots coming down the hall."

I looked down the hall. I pointed my gun down the hall.

"Gun—multi, big bang."

I fired. A few seconds later there were multiple explosions filling the hall.

"HARV, what's the second thing?"

"I might be able to zap your brain. Charge up that sixth sense of yours. It might give us a clue as to where the closet is."

"Fine, desperate times call for strange actions," I said.

"You're not very good with sayings, are you?" Tony said.

My head started to tingle. Tony blew away another attacking bot. I smiled.

I walked about three meters up from Tony. I kicked the wall right about floor level. Nothing happened. I was a little confused and a lot frustrated.

"DOS, I knew this was the spot."

"Now what are you doing?" Tony asked.

"HARV charged up my brain to help me find the maidbot storage closest, but it's not here!"

"Maybe your mind is like your golf drive, always off to the left a bit," Tony suggested.

I moved a little to right. I kicked the wall. A panel on the floor popped open. I smiled.

Tony ran up to me and gave me cover while I looked at the closet.

"So, where are these things labeled?" I asked HARV, as I frantically tossed cleaning materials out of the way.

"How should I know? Do I look like a maidbot to you?"

Finally, I found a little label in the corner.

"All I see here is the number 0000 0000 0111," I said.

"Okay, I've got your location. Go down the hall to your left. Tell me when you come to an intersection."

We ran down the hallway with our guns drawn.

"How far away are we, HARV?" I asked as we ran.

"Not very. Randy teleported you fairly close to where he was aiming. Don't worry."

"How come whenever you say that it sends a chill up my spine?"

We reached an intersection.

"Now what?"

"Hang a left. The main control room is one hundred meters straight down the hall."

I stepped into the intersection and was hit by a laser blast to the shoulder. I dropped my gun from the force of the blow and staggered back against the wall. My suit now had a nice hole in it, but my armor took the brunt of the damage.

"They were waiting for us!" Tony said.

A bot circled around the corner, and Tony blew it away.

"It doesn't take a mastermind to figure out where we were headed," I said, rubbing my shoulder.

"Is it bad?" Tony asked.

"It would be if Electra hadn't brought my underarmor," I told him.

"It sounds like there are at least ten other guardbots in the hall on both sides. It seems this is where they are planning to stop you." HARV said.

"They have us pinned down. If we try to move into the hallway, they'll blow us away," Tony said.

"HARV, what about a different route?"

"No way. Even if there was one, it would take way too long."

"More bots!" Tony said as he pointed to the other end of the hallway.

He opened fire. The bot returned fire, hitting Tony in the leg. Tony dropped his gun and fell to the floor. This was bad. Real bad. Pinned down in an open hallway by guardbots. I needed an idea—a good idea—and fast. I didn't even have my gun. It was lying there in the middle of the hallway, right in the intersection. That's when it hit me.

"Tony, cling as close as you can to the wall," I said, as I clung to the opposite wall.

"Gun—spin forty-five degrees right, fire big boom; spin forty-five degrees right, fire big boom; spin ninety degrees right, fire big boom. Program execute!"

Fireworks went off! The gun did its stuff, spinning then shooting, then spinning some more, then blasting some more. There were three big bangs followed by a series of explosions. We both covered our heads to protect ourselves from flying bot parts.

I looked down the hallway. The charging bots had been

destroyed. I moved away from the wall. I peeked down the intersection, first right, then left. The place looked like a robot graveyard.

"Do I do good work or what?" I asked Tony as I picked up my gun.

"I'm amazed," he said.

"No need to be. My gun makes state-of-the-art look like last year's news!" I said.

"No, I'm amazed you got the angles right. You're terrible at geometry."

"Thanks. Are you okay?"

He showed me his leg wound. It was ugly, at least two centimeters long, and just as wide. Red wasn't Tony's color.

"I won't be going dancing tonight," Tony groaned.

"Looks like I'll have to finish this one without you, buddy."

"At least drag me out into the intersection where I can cover you."

"Sorry, Tony, you'd be a sitting duck for any guardbots that might wander by. I think right now my best course of action would be a good old-fashioned head-on charge."

I patted him on the shoulder. I ran into the intersection, ready to fire at a moment's notice.

"Ah, Zach," HARV said as I charged on. "I know I've brought this topic up many, *many* times before, but shouldn't we at least pretend to have a little plan?"

"Why bother? If we don't have any idea what we're doing, there's no way the bad guys can have any idea what we're doing."

I ran straight toward the control room door. As I closed in, I lowered my shoulder and rammed it, using my body armor to cushion the blow, while hopefully breaking down the door. Much to my surprise, I smashed right through!

36

I was now in the control room. I had crashed through the door and hit the floor. Mrs. Billings was sitting on a chair holding a laser to Bim and Norp's heads. Councilwoman Weathers was there, along with Santana.

Weathers walked over and picked up my gun. "My, you make an impressive entrance," she said as she aimed my gun at me. "Have you ever thought of going into politics?"

I looked up. I could see one screen showing the theater filling with gas, and another showing Tony lying on the floor bleeding.

"I would, but the pay's kind of lousy," I told her.

Weathers sneered at me. It was the first time I'd seen that look from such a polished politician. "My husband's right, you are an annoying little gnat."

"We all have our roles," I said.

"Zach," HARV shouted inside my head. "I'm getting odd readings from Weathers."

"Not now, HARV," I thought back. "Can't you see I'm in the middle of witty banter with the bad girl?"

"Zach, I haven't seen these readings since Sexy Sprockets," HARV shouted. "She's a psi—an augmented psi!"

Now that was a kick in the gut I wasn't expecting.

The councilwoman walked over to me, bent down, and lifted me up by my throat.

"So the little computer in your brain figured out what they made me into," she said.

I nodded and grunted. That was about all I could do—her grip was strong, exceedingly strong. She had to be using her psi powers to augment her strength. Out of the corner of my eye, I saw Santana moving toward us. She put a hand on Weathers' arm.

"Stormy, there is no need to kill Zach. There is nothing he can do to stop us."

Weathers looked at Santana out of the corner of her eye. "No, but it would be fun."

"Killing is wrong," Santana said.

"You're killing all your elves," Weathers said.

Santana shook her head. "No, the gas is doing that. They are useless now, anyhow. The rest will do them good."

Weathers released her grip on my throat, letting me drop to the ground.

Santana approached me as I pushed myself up to my knees. My throat felt like it had been stuck in an atomic vise, but I wasn't about to let Weathers know that.

Santana knelt down, meeting me halfway. "Zach, I'm sorry about that," she said, helping me to my feet. "Stormy just really believes in our work here."

"Your work here?" I said. "This isn't work. It's a maniacal attempt to reshape the world in your deranged image."

"Six of one, half a dozen of the other," Santana said.

I looked over at Ma Billings still holding the weapon on Bim and Norp. "What's a nice country girl like you got to do with all this?"

"They needed my robotics expertise to help program the Holiday launch," she sneered. "I truly believe in my heart the world will be better this way."

"Why are you holding Bim and Norp?" I asked.

"They are still useful to us," Weathers said. "Their knowledge of robots is as impressive as their lack of social skills is scary. Plus, they'll make great scapegoats on the off chance that something goes wrong and our plans get delayed. We will just blame them. On the off off chance something happens to them, I have the evil couple from ExShell to blame."

"Wow, pretty impressive," I said. "You three have thought of everything."

"Actually, Stormy thought of most of it," Santana said.

"Yes," Ma Billings agreed. "This was all Stormy's brilliant idea."

They both had a strange tone to their voices, tones normally reserved for cult members talking about their leaders.

"What's the deal with the fake Billings family?" I asked. "Pretty impressive work."

"Thank you," Ma Billings said. "I do believe they were my best yet."

"It figures HTech would have their hands in this."

Ma Billings shook her head. "Silly man, I no longer work for HTech. I work for the World Council now."

I suppose I should have seen that coming.

"This is just a big World Council plot then?" I asked.

Weathers laughed and rolled her eyes. "Those fools think of something this creative? I think not," she said. "They are perfectly happy with the status quo and keeping their nice, safe soft jobs. I thought of this while recuperating from my crash. I executed it on my own."

Santana and Ma Billings each cleared their throats.

"With some help from my friends, of course."

"Nothing wrong with help from your friends. Unless, of course, they are helping you destroy the world."

Weathers raised her arms in a flippant manner, "You say *destroy,* I say *improve.*"

One thing was for certain, if I was going to stop this, I was going to need a lot of help from my friends. For now, my best tactic was to stall, giving my team time to clog the system with a virus. It's never a good sign when your best technique is to delay and pray for a miracle, but I was hoping inspiration would strike me.

"The people of Earth love both of you," I said, pointing first to Weathers and then Santana.

"They will love us more after we are done with them," Weathers said.

Santana nodded her agreement.

So far, this wasn't going too well.

"Hey, what about me?" Ma Billings asked.

Finally, the crumb of inspiration I was hoping for. "I'm sure they would like you too, if they got to know you, but face it when you run with this crowd," I pointed to Weathers and Santana again, "you, dear Ma, are fourth string."

Divide and conquer—it was an age-old tactic. It worked for the Huns, it worked for Yoko Ono, it would work for me. I like to think I'm smarter than most Huns (and sing better than Yoko).

Ma Billings dropped her guard. She moved her gun away from Bim and Norp and aimed it at me. She wasn't threatening me with it, she was just using it as a pointing device. It was as if she had forgotten she had a gun in her hand. Obviously, she wasn't used to brandishing weapons.

Bim and Norp surprised me by taking advantage of Ma Billing's mental lapse. They moved forward, Bim grabbing for her gun as Norp tackled her knees. Shockingly, they were able to bring Billings down and wrestle the gun away from her.

Bim smiled loosely as he trained the gun first on Santana and then on Weathers.

"Now we get to really be heroes," he gloated. "Norp, I'll keep them covered while you power down the transporters."

Norp had his hands full trying to stay on top of a very feisty Ma Billings. "I don't think that's going to be an option," he said. "Why not have Zach cover them while you power down the porters?" he suggested.

Bim thought about that for a nano. "Share the glory—interesting concept," he said to himself.

"No glory to share, buddy," I coaxed. "I'll give it all to you guys. I just want to make sure the world stays like it is. It may not be the best possible world—it's unsystematic and filled with pain and violence, but it's also filled with lots of good things like random acts of kindness, baseball, HV, love, tacos, and sex. I'll do anything to stop yet another couple of crazy ladies from shaping the world into their distorted view of perfection."

"Oh, so now you think you're better than us?" Bim said. "Mr. High and Mighty Zachary Nixon Johnson," he taunted. "He's saved the world soooo many times, he doesn't need to do it again."

Now it was Bim's turn to forget the weapon he was holding in his hand. He put the gun to his side and pointed at me with his free hand.

"Listen," he said.

He never got to finish that statement, as Santana was all over him like ugly on a monkey's behind (no offense to you monkeys out there). She grabbed him, squeezed his wrist, and elbowed him in the face. Bim was out cold and on the floor before he even knew what hit him.

"I knew this wasn't going to turn out well," Norp sighed a split nano before Santana focused her attention on him, spinning toward him and kicking him in the stomach. The kick sent him flying off of Ma Billings and crashing into the wall. It would have hurt a lot, but lucky for him, the kick instantly put him out colder than a flounder hermetically sealed in ice.

It was back to me against the three, but I guess there was never any real doubt that it would come down to this. At least Bim and Norp had given me a little more time to formulate a plan.

"I'm hoping you have a plan," HARV said inside my head.

"It's formulating as we speak," I thought back.

"How's it going inside the auditorium?" I asked HARV.

I was greeted with nothing but silence. As much as I welcome the quiet, I know it's not good when HARV is silent.

"I haven't regained contact with them yet," HARV said reluctantly. "That part of me is very weak."

"How's it going with jamming the transport system?" I asked.

More silence. "The elves were very efficient in building their firewalls. They are more like bomb bunkers buried hundred of kilometers below the surface and covered with lead. It's actually quite impressive."

"HARV!"

"Don't worry, Zach, I'll get through. I just need time."

Unfortunately, time was one of the many things we were running oh so short of right now.

I studied Santana, Billings, and Weathers studying me. They had to have noticed the contorted looks on my face.

"Is he having some sort of stroke?" Billings asked.

I get that reaction a lot.

The other two just shook their heads. "He's probably thinking to the computer he has wired to his brain," Santana said.

"He has a computer wired to his brain?" Billings asked. "That would explain a lot." She looked at Bim and Norp's unconscious bodies and added, "Gee, I thought they were the geeks."

"Having a computer wired to my brain does *not* make me a geek," I stated very firmly.

"He's more of a geek's guinea pig," Weathers chuckled.

Now this really ticked me off, mostly because it was truer than I'd like to admit. I wasn't a guinea pig, I was more like a test pilot. I took a deep breath and took account of my assets. I had my wits and my body armor, and HARV was functional, though not at peak levels.

Things looked pretty bleak and that was being overly optimistic.

Weathers moved forward and put on hand on my shoulder. It was a merciful move, but I'd accepted it. "Actually, Zach," she said. "I can relate to your being a guinea pig. I wasn't always a psi."

"The World Council augmented you?" I half-guessed and half-stated.

She lowered her eyes. "They employed the services of that sleaze named Sammy Smiles." She looked me in the eyes. "I understand you are familiar with his work."

I nodded. Sammy was the deranged madman/agent (is there really that much of a difference?) who turned Sexy Sprockets from a wannabe rock star to a dominating psi rock star, and then turned my assistant Carol from a powerful psi to a near godlike being. He escaped after my last adventure before I could give him the punch in the face he deserved. Now I saw a hard knee to the groin would be too good for him.

"Yeah, I know Sammy," I said.

She lowered her eyes again. I felt the tension in her voice. "It was twenty years ago, and I was a junior Council member. I was chosen to *volunteer* for the tests."

While she talked, I found myself starting to feel sorry for her.

"In those early days, Sammy hadn't perfected his radiation technique so he used injections—painful injections."

The more she talked, the heavier my heart felt. I could feel her pain clear through to my soul.

"He succeeded in turning me into a psi, but I'm not a normal psi. I'm more of an empathy psi."

"An empathy psi?" I said.

"I can't outright control people, because if I could, believe me you'd be my poodle now," she said. "Sammy always said it was because I was subconsciously suppressing my power. I think he was just covering his skinny little ass. The bottom line is, I can't directly control people, but I can broadcast my emotions to them."

"So you make them think like you?"

"I make them feel like me. Of course, the more exposure they have to me, the more they do start to think like me." She gave me a weak smile. "There are times when these powers are handy for a politician to have."

As my mouth was calmly stalling, my brain was frantically scanning the room, searching for a way out of this. I noticed that Weathers still had my gun in her hand. If I could get her to point the gun at me, I would be able to take her out. It was a drastic move, but I didn't see a lot of other choices. If she was willing to pull the trigger on me, I had to be willing to do the same to her.

"Okay," I said slowly. "This is your last chance, I order you to give up now, or I'm going to have to hurt you."

Weathers snickered. "Please, Mr. Johnson . . ."

"Call me Zach."

"Please, Zach," she spat. "You are in no position to be making any demands or threats."

I locked eyes with her. "Not a demand or a threat, just a fact."

She smiled. "Zach, I'm picking up your thoughts. I know you want me to try to shoot you with your own gun."

DOS, I hate psis!

She dropped my gun to the ground. She walked over to me and picked me up off the ground by the throat. She pushed me back, pinning me to the wall. "I'm not your standard issue politician," she said. "I like to do my dirty work for myself."

Weathers' grip was quickly cutting off the blood to my brain. I would be out cold fast if I didn't do something faster. If I went under, all would be lost. My first move was to grab the arm she was choking me with and pull down. I jerked down on her arm with all my strength, but to no avail. Her arm stayed perfectly straight and rigid. The only effect it had was to get her to tighten her grip on me.

She smiled. "Zach, I do believe blue is your color."

Santana moved forward. "Stormy, do you really need to kill Zach?" she said, almost more out of curiosity than compassion.

"Yes," Weathers told her without flinching, keeping her gaze locked into mine.

Just then, something surprising happened. A shot rang through the window of the room into Weathers' arm, tearing it out of the socket. I fell to the floor grasping for air.

I turned toward the shot to see Tony sitting there in the hallway, smiling and holding a smoking gun. That's my buddy Tony. I looked back at Weathers. She was stunned. It wasn't the pain of having her arm ripped off that had stymied Weathers, but what the shot had revealed. Where her arm had been there was circuitry, loads and loads of circuitry. She put her good hand over the shot, not to stop the blood—because there wasn't any—but to cover up her parts.

"Oh, DOS, your arms are bionic," I said.

"No! No, they're not," she said calmly.

That would explain her superhuman strength. If her psi powers hadn't been messing with my brain, I probably would have figured that out a lot sooner. I held out my hand and pointed to my gun.

"Gun, come to poppa," I said.

My gun shot across the floor and into my open hand. I pointed the gun at Weathers.

"The game is over," I said. "Bionic or not, this gun has enough firepower to rip apart a battlebot." I was speaking from experience when I said that.

"They did this to me!" she said, too calmly.

"The Council?" I said standing up, but never letting any of them forget I was the one holding the high-powered gun I was very comfortable using.

"Of course, it was them," she said coldly. "After their little experiment in making me a psi, they couldn't risk losing me to something as trivial as an accident."

"So they gave you bionic parts," I stated.

"No," she said slowly. "I have already told you that I am not bionic." She paused. I wasn't sure if she was trying to build the tension, or just wasn't sure what to say next.

She grinned. It was a strange grin for such a trained politician, as it was openly cynical. "Bionics would be too simple for them."

Weathers reached down to her midsection, and with her remaining arm grabbed the material of her pant suit and ripped off a patch, exposing her skin. She tapped the bare spot three times with her index finger. The skin popped up, showing her underbelly was all circuits. "They took my brain and inserted it into another body, an android body."

"Why didn't they just clone you a new body?" Santana asked. The tone in her voice as casual as if she was asking about the weather.

"They told me that human bodies break. I was now considered too valuable," Weathers sneered.

"But you've been aging," Billings said.

Weathers shook her head. "My system is designed to simulate aging. My skin tone, eyes, and hair color are adjustable." Her hair started cycling through all the various colors: first blond, then brunette, then redhead. "If I ever wanted to go out and paint the town red incognito, I'd use my brunette hair and smoothe my skin. Nobody would recognize me." Her hair turned back to the more familiar frost color. "This, of course, is my favorite color as this is the color my human hair would be if I were still human."

Then something very important occurred to me.

"Why are you telling us all this?" I asked.

"I wanted you to understand my motives for remaking the world," she said. "They made me in the image they thought best. Now I am going to pay everybody back."

I pointed my gun at her. "Yeah, well that's not going to happen."

"No, it's not," she said. "That's why I've decided to kill you and destroy the Pole, instead."

Weathers' one good arm stretched out and clobbered me right in the gut. My armor took the brunt of the attack, so much so that I didn't even drop my gun. Her next moves though, caught me off guard—she darted toward the door.

I fired but missed.

Weathers ran through the door without opening it. As she raced down the hall, Tony fired at her but she literally ran along the side walls and then the ceilings, avoiding his shots until she was past him.

I turned my attention to Santana and Ma Billings and trained my gun on them. "What's your move?"

They both shook their heads and rubbed their eyes.

"It's like I've been asleep and dreaming all this time," Santana said.

"By Gates, I built myself a robotic family, to be a maniacal cyborg politician's minions . . ." Ma Billings said.

HARV flickered back online. "Zach, their mental readings are normal now. Weathers must have given up her control over them," HARV said.

I wasn't nearly as happy about that as I thought I should be. First, she made the confession and now this. I didn't like this one bit.

"She's going to kill herself," I said.

The lights flickered for a minute before steadying back to normal.

"That's odd," Santana said.

Ma Billings went over to a control panel. "We've just gone to auxiliary power."

"Why?" Santana asked.

"Somebody is channeling all the Pole's energy into the main reactors."

"Oh, that's not good at all," Santana said.

It wasn't hard to figure out who that somebody was.

"She's going to kill herself and take us out with her," I said.

"And a good part of the northern hemisphere," Santana added.

"Where is the reactor?" I asked.

"Reactors," Santana corrected.

"Where are the *reactors*?"

"Two kilometers under the surface," Santana said. "And there is only one elevator that leads down there."

"I suppose she's killed that elevator," I said.

Ma Billings looked at a reading on a panel and nodded yes.

"Of course she has," I said.

Santana went into supermanager mode. "Release the elves and our visitors from the theater. We can at least start teleporting them to safety."

Ma Billings shook her head no. "We can release them, but nobody is being teleported too far. The councilwoman has rerouted all the energy to the reactors. We can barely power up one teleporter."

"Then rereroute them," Santana ordered.

"I'm trying, I'm trying!"

37

Before too long, we were all gathered in the control room brainstorming a way to stop Councilwoman Stormy Weathers, the most trusted being on Earth, from destroying a good portion of the planet. Elf-1, Randy, and Ma Billings were scanning the panels and displays lining the walls, in hope of finding something.

"How much longer before Weathers causes the reactors to blow?" Santana asked.

There was silence.

"Best guess, between thirty and ninety minutes," Elf-1 said.

"Why don't we teleport a team down there to stop her?" Electra asked.

"Even if we had the energy to teleport, it's two kilometers beneath the ground and heavily shielded, plus the generators really mess up teleporting. Teleporting down there is close to suicide. You're far more likely to end up in a wall."

"We have to take that chance. I'd rather die doing something than sitting here waiting to be blown up," Electra said.

"We can teleport her out of there," I said calmly.

"Even if we could get a lock on her, which we can't, we don't have the energy to do it," Elf-1 said.

"You know, for an elf, you're a bit of a downer," I told him.

"Sorry, imminent death makes me crabby," he said.

"Then I'll go down and take her out," I said, popping my gun into my hand.

"Even if that fancy gun could stop her, you have no way down there," Ma Billings said.

HARV appeared from my wrist communicator. "There is the service elevator," he said. "It's manually powered."

Elf-1 stopped his mad scanning of the panels. He slapped himself on his forehead. "How could I forget about that!" he said. He wiped a bead of sweat off his brow. "It must be the pressure of death. We elves aren't built for this kind of stress. We're used to deadlines not deathlines."

"How big is the elevator?" I asked.

"It's just big enough for two," Santana said.

"Who's going with me to be my added muscle?" I asked.

"I'll go," Tony said from over the intercom at the infirmary.

"Ah, no," I said, "I appreciate the spirit, buddy, but you're wounded."

"I'll go," Nova said. "This is the time for a warrior."

"In that case, I should go," Electra said.

"I'm security chief, I should go," Elf-1 said.

"There is only one logical choice," Santana said.

"Okay, okay, I'll do it," Bim said standing up and puffing up his chest.

Everybody in the room turned to him and frowned.

"Maybe not," Bim said, sinking back into his chair.

"I have to go with Zach," Santana said. "I know the building, I know the reactor, and I know Weathers. Plus, nothing personal, but I'm stronger than all of you put together."

Now it was Nova's turn to puff out her chest. She walked over toward Santana. "I don't know about that," she protested.

"Please," Santana said, rolling her eyes. "I could pass wind in your general direction, and you wouldn't know what hit you."

Elf-1 nodded her head. "She could," he said, as if speaking from experience.

"That's part of the reason why I avoid gassy foods," Santana offered.

"That's enough info for me," I said, moving forward and taking Santana's arm. "Actually, too much information Let's go stop a madwoman from destroying the Earth."

It's amazing how often I have to say that.

*   *   *

The emergency service elevator that led down to the re-actors was a small, metal box. I tried hard not to think of it as a coffin with a hand crank. I kissed Electra, then joined Santana in the elevator. She closed the door and started winding the crank. I could feel the elevator slowly begin to descend.

For the first few moments, nobody said anything. Then HARV broke the silence. "I estimate we have fifteen min-utes and twenty-two seconds to stop Weathers before the damage to the core becomes irreversible."

"Can you be more exact?" I asked.

"Years ago, I would have answered that," HARV said. "But now I realize it is your attempt at humor to relieve the tension of the moment."

"What tension?" I shrugged. "We're only traveling sev-eral kilometers below the Earth in a tin box to stop a crazo psi android (or did the human brain make her a cyborg?) from nuking the Pole."

"See, I recognize that as another attempt at humor," HARV said.

"Just another average day in the life of Zachary Nixon Johnson, the last freelance PI in the world," I said.

I was hoping that freelance PIs weren't about to become extinct. I looked over at Santana manning the hand crank. She was working hard—the sweat on her forehead looked like a fractal forming.

"How much longer until we are there?" I asked.

"When we stop, we're there," she said bluntly.

"Just making small talk," I said.

Santana lowered her eyes. "Sorry, Zach, I'm a bit on edge. I helped create this situation, and if we can't stop—"

" 'Can't' isn't in my vocabulary," I said.

Santana smiled at me with her eyes as much as her mouth.

I popped my gun into my hand. I wanted to make sure I had my super-high-impact ordnance.

"You can't be thinking about using your explosive ammo down there," HARV said.

" 'Can't' isn't in my vocabulary," I repeated to him.

HARV shook his holographic head. "Zach, if a stray explosive shot should hit one of the reactors' controllers—"

I cut him off. "It's only as a last-ditch backup." I grimaced, "If I figure we're going to bite it anyhow, I want to do it on my own terms."

I took HARV's silence as acceptance of that statement.

After a few long minutes of traveling in the silence, I felt the elevator jerk to a stop. I looked over at Santana. She returned my look. "Are you ready?" I asked.

She nodded. "This bitch played me," she said, in very a non-Santana tone. She made a fist and walked over to the door. She hit a switch. The door popped open. "Now it's time for payback."

The reactor room was a cavernous area with vast arching ceilings. I would have been impressed if our lives weren't hanging on a thread. There were long, glowing tubes running up, down, and throughout the walls of the room. Following the tubes with my eyes, I saw they all originated from the bases of two objects that were each about three meters tall and looked like upside-down ice cream cones balancing a giant pulsating egg. Those had to be the reactors. They looked like a deranged, high-tech cross between a spider and an octopus only with way more arms. The place had an ominous air about it, but it wasn't red and green and that DOSing song wasn't playing, so it was my favorite room at the Pole. There, sitting at the control panel between the cones, was Councilwoman Weathers.

As we drew closer to the not-so-good councilwoman, we could see that there were beams of energy flowing from her remaining hand into a control panel. For her part, she didn't seem surprised to see us.

"Oh, hi," she said calmly. She shook her head. "DOS, I hate you so *much*, Zachary Nixon Johnson. If it weren't for you, I wouldn't have to do all this," she sighed.

I pointed my gun at her. "You've lost me."

She looked down her nose at me. (No small feat, as she was sitting and I was standing.) "If you didn't stop BB Star, or Foraa Thompson, or your niece Carol from destroying the world, none of this would be necessary. That's why I hate you. That's why I tried to have you killed."

"You're the one who sent the first bots after me."

"And the assassin posing as an SSS member," she said. "I never thought you could actually stop me, I just wanted to kill you for the sake of killing you."

"So you tipped off the real SSS too?"

"Yep, just to piss you off."

"What did I ever do to you?"

She shook her head. "Think about it, annoying man. You keep saving the world as we know it. I hate the world as we know it, therefore, I hate you. That's why I didn't want you to be a part of my new world order. I wanted you dead."

"You encouraged the geeks to try to kill me," I said.

Weathers shook her head. "I didn't need to. They were perfectly willing to do the job for me."

"Zach does have that effect on some people," HARV agreed.

Weathers continued, "That's why I didn't crush the nerds. I knew they couldn't stop me, but I thought they might be able to stop you."

"I'm harder to kill than most people think," I said.

"Yes, well, that's all atomic water under the bridge now—rushing water."

I cocked my gun. "It's all over, Councilwoman. There's nowhere for you to run now," I said.

The ends of her lips turned up, ever so slightly. "I'm not here to run. I'm here to die. Like I should have done, all those years ago."

"No need to take everybody else out with you," I said, moving closer.

She looked me in the eyes. "I admit it is petty. This way, I take you out, as well as a good portion of the northern hemisphere. That's sure to create all sorts of havoc."

"Disconnect yourself from the reactors, now!" Santana ordered.

Weathers gave her a dismissive roll of the eyes, causing the reactors to glow more. "Your charm doesn't work on me. I deserve to die and die big."

I pulled back the trigger on my gun. I turned on the laser sight. The sight's red beam fixed between Weathers' eyes. "Fine, I'll give you your wish."

Weathers looked at the red dot with both her eyes. "You don't kill humans, Zach."

"You're not human," I stated coldly.

"There's the catch—my brain is human," she said.

She had me on that one. I loathe killing humans, but

when the death of one would save the lives of many, I
didn't think I had much of a choice.

"Zach," HARV shouted inside my brain. "Shooting her
is not going to help the situation. She's got herself so wired
into the reactor that if something happens to her, it blows."

"Yeah, but if nothing happens to her it still blows,
right?"

"I admit, there aren't a lot of optional choices here,"
HARV said. "Killing her now will kill us all sooner."

I thought about what HARV said. Sure death right now
as opposed to reasonably sure death a few nanos from now.
I decided to see how this played out and hoped for a break.
I really didn't like the idea of killing Weathers for the sake
of killing Weathers. There had to be a way out of this.

"HARV, can you break her control over the reactors?"
I asked in my mind.

"It doesn't matter," HARV said.

"Why not?"

We were now close enough to reach out and touch
Weathers.

"Oh my Gates," Santana said, hand on mouth. "You're
channeling all the reactors' energy into yourself."

"That's right. I am the bomb," Weathers said.

"HARV, can you override her?" I asked.

"Perhaps, but I'd have to get into the system."

"How do you do that?"

"My transfer chip is damaged but still functional, though
you need to make eye contact with her."

My dad always taught me that it's proper for a man to
look a person in the eyes when talking with them. It gives
the person you're talking to a sense that you are strong.

I starting moving closer to Weathers.

"Of course, with our eye lens drained like it is, I'm not
sure this is going to work. So you need to get real close,"
HARV said.

It was too late to turn back, and even if it wasn't, I didn't
see any other options.

I locked my eyes on Weathers' eyes. She met my gaze
with a steady calm. It was the look of a person who had
made a decision and was pleased with it.

"Oh please, Zach," she said calmly. "You're not going
to try to talk me out of this."

I wanted to distract her so she would lower her defenses against HARV.

"Killing, at the very least, thousands of people and upsetting the eco-balance of the Earth, just because you weren't allowed to die. That doesn't seem like a fitting end to your career," I said.

She smiled. "Actually, it is quite fitting. And I get to kill you."

Hard to argue with that logic. I was hoping I wouldn't have to. A beam of light shot from my eye into Weathers' right eye.

For the first time since we had been down here, she let her emotions rip through. She stood up and pointed at me.

"That's it," she shouted. "Trying to override me? Boom! You're all dead. Now!"

Nothing happened.

"I'm in," HARV said inside my head. "I have control, but I don't know for how long. She's fighting me."

"Can I blast her safely now?" I asked.

"Yes, that would be advisable if you plan on living past the next few minutes. I can't hold her for long," HARV said.

Before I had the chance to pull the trigger, Weathers' one good arm lashed out and grabbed my gun from me. She looked at me and smiled. She raised the gun and crushed it like it was putty.

"Having a superandroid body does have it perks," she told me.

Santana, who had been seething, leaped into action. She dove across the room and hit Weathers low, like a football linebacker trying to bring down a fullback.

The two tumbled to the ground and started rolling away from me.

"Zach, do something faaaast," HARV shouted inside my head. "I'mmm gggeting dizzzzzy."

I ran toward them. I wasn't really sure what I was going to do, but I knew I would have to be in the middle of the ruckus.

For their parts, Santana and Weathers were exchanging headbutts and body blows like the best of them. It was a brawl that reminded me of those old, staged pro-wrestling matches I used to watch as a kid. The ones where the contender and the champ would slug it out and knock each other past silly until one of them was proudly holding the fake championship belt over his head.

The belt! That was it. As I ran, I reached down and felt the teleportation belt I was still wearing. I removed it as I drew closer to the battling babes. If I got it wrapped around her, I could port her out of here.

"Santana, get off of her," I shouted.

"But I'm winning," she protested from on top of Weathers. She accented her statement with a nasty right cross to Weathers' face.

"Ouch! That really hurt!" HARV said.

"If she blows, nobody wins," I said.

Santana turned to me. "Good point."

Before Santana had a chance to do anything else, Weathers wriggled a leg free, cocked a knee, and kicked her straight in the solar plexus. The bionic kick sent Santana flying across the room and crashing to the ground.

"Take that, bitch," I heard HARV say inside my head.

That wasn't a good omen at all.

Weathers pushed herself to an upright position and smiled. She wiped a bit of simulated blood from her lip. I lunged forward and wrapped the belt around Weathers' waist. She looked down on the belt.

"That doesn't really match my outfit," she said.

She grabbed me by throat, hoisted me up over her head again, and started to squeeze.

"Nice try," she said. "But I'm not teleporting anywhere. I am sending you to meet your maker."

"I'm actually enjoying this far more than I thought I would," HARV said inside my head.

I pitched my body back and then swung forward. I needed to gain momentum (in more ways than one). I kicked out at Weathers. My kick glanced harmlessly off her abs.

She laughed. "Is that the best you can do? Even if I was a normal human female, that kick wouldn't have hurt." She took a deep breath. "I'm going to take such pleasure in personally killing you before I blow everything up. I should have known never to let bots, assassins, elves, and nerds do a politician's job."

"That kick was pretty lame," HARV said. "If you

weren't about to be killed, I'd suggest you work on strengthening your legs."

Weathers, like a typical politician, was missing the bigger picture here. I rocked back and pushed my legs forward again, this time tilting my foot slightly toward the belt. My foot rubbed against the activation button.

Weathers disappeared. I fell to the ground. I held my breath, waiting for a big boom. Nothing happened. I took that as a really good sign.

"HARV, are you there?" I said. "Tell the elves I used the belt to port her out."

There was silence.

"HARV?"

HARV appeared through my eye lens. He was beat up and flustered, but he was here. "I'm here, and she's gone," he said, flickering on, off, and back on again.

"Where's Weathers?" I asked. "Do they have her in custody?"

He pointed to the wall. "Near as I can tell, she rematerialized about a K inside that wall."

I looked down. "That wasn't my intent," I said.

By this time, Santana had gotten up and walked over toward me. She put a hand on my shoulder.

"I know, Zach."

"It was my intent," HARV said.

"What?" Santana and I both said at once.

"Zach, I was in that woman's mind. She was hurting so much and had been for decades. I made a last-nano change in the coordinates. It was the perfect solution—she dies, and everybody else lives."

I was dumbstruck.

HARV, for better or for worse, had become more human. He had killed.

38

As the days passed, things cleared up. The Holiday came and went off without a hitch. Ma Billings and her android family and even Bim and Norp went home. Nova moved to the Pole to help Elf-1. Most of the world had no idea how close they had come to not only losing the Holiday, but losing the top half of the Earth.

The official story from the World Council was that Councilwoman Weathers died in a tragic teleporting accident on a mercy mission to Mars. She was go down in history as one of the greatest leaders of our time. I've been around long enough to understand that history isn't what really happened, it's what enough people either believe happened or want to believe happened. Stormy Weathers was mourned by all. Well, maybe not all, but those who knew better were told to shut up or else—for the good of the world, of course. I hoped that the Council learned something from this entire ordeal. Though my history with them suggests that they didn't. I may be many things, but one of them is not being so stupid as to mess with the World Council. Especially since I had no proof of anything I'd just experienced.

HARV had records, but he wasn't talking. In fact, HARV made it clear he wanted to put the entire matter behind him. He didn't want to forget about it. He couldn't forget about it. He just didn't want to talk about it.

Truthfully, I didn't even notice that something was eating away at HARV until Carol brought it up while we were playing backgammon.

"Wow, it's hard to believe its been two months since you

guys saved the Holiday and the Pole," Carol said, looking over the backgammon board.

I nodded, answering Carol without taking my eyes of the board. "Yep, I've gone eight weeks without somebody or something attacking or trying to kill me. I believe that's a personal record."

"Actually, you've gone eighty days, which is a new record for you," HARV said.

"How are you holding up?" Carol said.

"I'm fine. Contrary to popular belief, I don't enjoy it when people are trying to kill me."

"So you keep telling us," Carol said, with a sly wink. "But I was talking to HARV." Carol turned her glance toward HARV.

"Him?" I asked.

"Me?" HARV echoed.

"You took a life," Carol said earnestly. "That has to weigh on you."

HARV gave her a dismissive wave. "Please, I'm fine. I did her a favor. I granted her wish. I'm a hologram. I have no weight and feel no weight."

"I can tell you're still not over it," Carol said softly. "I can feel it."

HARV looked at her. "I'm a machine. You can't sense anything from me."

"You're connected to Zach's brain, and his brain is an open book to me. I can feel your pain through him."

"How can *you* feel his pain?" I asked. "I can't feel it."

"You're a man," Carol said to me without breaking her focus on HARV.

"A very dense man," HARV added.

"Randy's like HARV's dad and he isn't worried. In fact he told me he's proud of the choice HARV made and he's happy I didn't get in the way to muck it up."

Carol looked at me.

"Right, when dealing with emotions Randy may not be the standard I should be setting my gauges by."

Carol smiled. "I leave you two to work it out," she said, and then left my office for hers.

I sat back in my chair. I turned my attention from the game to my friend, HARV. I wasn't sure how I could have missed it. Perhaps I didn't want to see it.

"So, it's really bothering you?"

HARV lowered his eyes. "I've replayed the events over ten billion times in my memory. I went over all the options. I truly believe I did what's best for all. Weathers finally has her peace, and the world is safe. Her husband, Carl, has taken over her position on the Council, and we know he's not bright enough to cause any trouble."

"Then what's the problem?" I asked.

"I don't feel as right as I should," HARV said.

"You shouldn't."

"I shouldn't feel as right as I should?" HARV said, shaking his head. "Zach, that's confusing, even for you."

I smiled.

"You're smiling? I'm confused for the first time in my life, and you're smiling!"

"Yes, HARV, I am."

"Why? Are you enjoying my pain?"

I had to choose my next words carefully, as I wanted HARV to think of what I was about to say as a compliment, as it was meant to be one.

"HARV, don't you see? Randy's experiment has worked. You've become more than just a complex information source. You made a choice."

HARV lifted a finger and spun it around in a circle. "Whoopee, I made a choice."

"A very human choice," I said. "One based on feelings, as well as facts."

HARV slumped over, put his elbows on the desk, and his head in his hands. It was a very un-HARV-like pose. Even his bow tie wasn't perfectly straight.

"This is what it feels like to be human? To be so unsure of yourself?"

"That pretty much sums it up," I said.

HARV looked up at me. "I don't think I like this feeling, but I can't be sure of it."

I smiled again, I tried not to (really I did), but I couldn't help myself. "The world can't be summed up by either true or false, one or zero, on or off, right or wrong. There are an infinite amount of possibilities that exist in between. No being, machine, or combination of the two can figure them all out."

"Yes, I understand that now. It doesn't make me feel any better."

"It's not supposed to make you feel better."

HARV looked at me. "You know, since you're the real human here, I would expect you to be better at this comforting thing."

"Trust me, HARV. You will feel better."

"When?"

I shrugged. "I have no idea, but you will. There's one thing that we humans are really good at: rationalizing away our negative feelings. Time will make you feel better."

HARV rolled his eyes. It was the first true HARV look he had given me in a while. "Oh please, that is so cliché."

"Maybe so, but that doesn't mean it's not true."

HARV let himself smile, slightly. "This really is what it's like to be human?"

"I'm afraid so," I said.

HARV shook his head. "It's amazing that more humans aren't trying to become machines. Virtual life is so much simpler."

"Life itself doesn't have to be that complicated, my friend. The trick is figuring out what you can figure out and not to sweat too much about the rest."

"Have you accomplished that yet?" HARV asked.

"I'm working on it, buddy. I'm working on it."

"I'm sure I'll figure it out before you. After all, I am the most advanced cognitive processor in the known worlds."

"So you keep telling me. It's not a competition, HARV, or at least it shouldn't be. Life is easier when we all cooperate."

HARV thought about what I said for a nano. "You're probably right." He thought for a nano or two more. A holographic backgammon board appeared on my desk. "We can still compete in backgammon. Correct?"

"Nothing wrong with a little friendly competition to keep the mind sharp."

HARV rubbed his hands together with glee. "Great. You have a lunch date with Electra in thirty-two minutes and twelve seconds, giving us more than enough time for me to beat you in two games of backgammon."

They say whatever doesn't kill you makes you stronger.

I'm not sure if that's true, but if it is then I'm in pretty good shape. After all, the universe and my best bud, who happens to be a computer, both love beating up on me. I wasn't sure what would be next on my plate. Truthfully, I was in no hurry to find out. I just knew that when the time came (and it will come again), I would be ready. My name is Zachary Nixon Johnson and I have a strange life. The really strange part is that I wouldn't have it any other way.

John Zakour

The Novels of
Zachary Nixon Johnson
The Last Freelance P. I.

"If you like your humor slapstick and inventive,
you need look no further for a good fix."
—*Chronicle*

Dangerous Dames*   978-07564-0496-3
(The Plutonium Blonde & The Doomsday Brunette)

Ballistic Babes   978-0-7564-0545-8
(The Radioactive Redhead* & The Frost-Haired Vixen)

The Blue-Haired Bombshell   978-07564-0455-0

The Flaxen Femme Fatale   978-07564-0519-9
*co-written with Lawrence Ganem

"No one who gets two paragraphs into this
dark, droll, downright irresistable hard-boiled-
dick novel could ever bear to put it down until
the last heart-pounding moment..." —*SFSite*

To Order Call: 1-800-788-6262
www.dawbooks.com

Jim Hines

The Jig the Goblin series

GOBLIN QUEST   978-07564-0400-0
GOBLIN HERO   978-07564-0442-0
GOBLIN WAR   978-07564-0493-2

S. Andrew Swann

MOREAU OMNIBUS   0-7564-0151-1
(*Forests of the Night, Emperors of the Twilight, & Specters of the Dawn*)
"An engaging, entertaining thriller with an exotic cast of characters, in an unfortunately all too plausible repressed future."
—*Science Fiction Chronicle*

FEARFUL SYMMETRIES   978-088677-834-7
"A novel as vivid as a cinema blockbuster loaded with high-budget special effects." —*New York Review of Science Fiction*

HOSTILE TAKEOVER *omnibus*   0-7564-0249-2
(*Profiteer, Partisan & Revolutionary*)
"This is good old-fashioned military SF, full of action, colorful characters, and plenty of hardware." —*Locus*

THE DWARVES OF WHISKEY ISLAND 0-7564-0315-4
"Skillfully done light adventure with more than a dash of humor."—*Science Fiction Chronicle*

THE DRAGONS OF CUYAHOGA 0-7564-0009-0
"It's a good energetic mystery, with a complicated plot and lots of chasing-down-leads action. "—*Cleveland Plain Dealer*

BROKEN CRESCENT   0-7564-0214-X
"A fast-paced, entertaining tale of the boundary between magic and science." —*Booklist*

DAW 123

Tanya Huff

Tony Foster—familiar to Tanya Huff fans from her *Blood* series—has relocated to Vancouver with Henry Fitzroy, vampire son of Henry VIII. Tony landed a job as a production assistant at CB Productions, ironically working on a syndicated TV series, "Darkest Night," about a vampire detective. Tony was pretty content with his new life—until wizards, demons, and haunted houses became more than just episodes on his TV series...

"An exciting, creepy adventure"—*Booklist*

SMOKE AND SHADOWS
0-7564-0263-8 $6.99
SMOKE AND MIRRORS
0-7564-0348-0 $7.99
SMOKE AND ASHES
0-7564-0415-4 $7.99

To Order Call: 1-800-788-6262
www.dawbooks.com

The Novels of
Tad Williams

To Order Call: 1-800-788-6262
www.dawbooks.com

DAW 102